PINCH HITTING

MORRIS HOFFMAN

Black Rose Writing | Texas

This is a work of fiction. Names, characters, businesses, places, events, and incidents are either the products of the author's imagination or used in a fictitious manner. Any resemblance to actual persons, living or dead, or actual events is purely coincidental.

ISBN: 978-1-68513-438-9
PUBLISHED BY BLACK ROSE WRITING
www.blackrosewriting.com

Printed in the United States of America
Suggested Retail Price (SRP) $24.95

Pinch Hitting is printed in Minion Pro

*As a planet-friendly publisher, Black Rose Writing does its best to eliminate unnecessary waste to reduce paper usage and energy costs, while never compromising the reading experience. As a result, the final word count vs. page count may not meet common expectations.

For Tuffy and Bob

Early Praise for
Pinch Hitting

"There is magic here, of a curious kind. Morris Hoffman's *Pinch Hitting* is a sweet and tuneful ode to the rich wonders of our national pastime, as it is sometimes played in our hearts and minds. Hoffman's wonderfully unlikely tale of Harold Fungo, 'The Joltin' Janitor,' takes its place in the dugout alongside Bernard Malamud's *The Natural* and Robert Coover's *The Universal Baseball Association, Inc., J. Henry Waugh, Prop.* as a timeless baseball fable, shot through with wonder – a seeing-eye single of a novel that finds a hole in the infield and comes to rest safely and surely in the soft grass just beyond the second base bag."
–Daniel Paisner, author of *A Single Happened Thing* and co-author of Ron Darling's *The Complete Game*

"Over the past several days, I read *Pinch Hitting*, the new novel by Morris Hoffman. What a magical journey from mid-century America to the here and now! Like one of those bizarre acts on the old Ed Sullivan show, *Pinch Hitting* manages to get a lot of plates and hats and canes into the air from atop a unicycle. It is so audacious that you dare not look away.

That's where the magic sets in: the novel will keep those beautiful and crazy items in the air all the way to the last page. And the laws of gravity be damned.

At its heart, *Pinch Hitting* is a baseball story. And yet it's not. Rather it's a story that uses baseball's fundamental quirkiness—quite lovingly I must add—to discuss where we find our heroes in life, where we find our loves, and our heartaches … and where we find the pluck to insist that, yes, the odds may be mortally against us, but we can still give a joyful finger to outrageous fortune.

Deion Sanders and Michael Jordan both said without hesitation that hitting a baseball was the most difficult athletic challenge they'd ever faced. Inside the first chapter of Mr. Hoffman's wonderful novel, Sanders and Jordan are brought low in this regard by the unlikeliest of heroes. It's at this point that, like filings to a magnet, other unlikely heroes begin to gather themselves into the story.

The tale is an impossible one, and yet, weirdly, it is very believable. Indeed, the overused concept of 'magical realism' popped into my mind, as I began to write this review; and, I found myself tutt-tutting it aside. 'After all,' I thought, 'hadn't Mr. Hoffman provided a satisfying explanation for each and every one of those hats and plates and canes in the air?' Yes he had. And hadn't I pulled mightily for every one of *Pinch Hitting's* delightfully-crafted central characters, even as the gods of fate—if occasionally bittersweet fate—were coming for them? Yes, I had.

It is one of those books where you come to dread looking at the page odometer. And of saying goodbye."
–Dennis Wanebo, singer–songwriter, and two–time winner of the John Lennon International Songwriting Award

"*Pinch Hitting* is an ode to baseball, set in a world where ordinary decency prevails and written in prose as spare and poetic as the game. Thank you, Morris Hoffman, for making me see why baseball is the enduring American pastime: it brings out the best in us."
–Stephanie Kane, award winning novelist and author of *True Crime Redux, Object Lessons, A Perfect Eye, Extreme Indifference, Seeds of Doubt, Quiet Time,* and *Blind Spot*

"Life, love, and baseball, the holy trinity of many a fine novel, work their magic once again in *Pinch Hitting*, a novel by Morris Hoffman. Set in Colorado, an assemblage of colorful characters tells the remarkable and romantic story of Joe Skelton, who mysteriously starts telling a story in his sleep about the life and times of Harold Fungo, a shy ballpark janitor–turned–minor league baseball hero. Skelton's wife, Katherine, stays awake nights in their small home to take down the story of Harold's remarkable transformation, and eventual rise, to the major league Cincinnati Reds. Completion of the book takes on urgency as Joe's untreatable tumor signals that death approaches. Morris Hoffman's novel takes the reader deep into the lives of ordinary people as they confront life's most unpredictable challenges and deepest disappointments, while attempting to hold onto their hopes and dreams."
–Bob Rothman, author of *A Terrible Guilt*

"A goodhearted fable and minor league baseball belong together, like a ball nestled in a well–oiled glove. Morris Hoffman's ode to Harold Fungo is clever, preposterous, and ultimately loving. Get ready to cheer (and weep). A charmed and magical journey indeed!"
–Brian Kaufman, author of *The Fat Lady's Low, Sad Song*

"A book written with heart and a keen passion for the game, *Pinch Hitting* is continuing proof that baseball provides a perfect canvas for storytelling in a wide variety of styles. Morris Hoffman has devised an intriguing structure and two intertwining tales that will keep baseball fans captivated."
–Mark Stevens, author of *The Fireballer*

PINCH HITTING

CHAPTER 1
IMPOSSIBLE

Baseball was in its heyday, and no one knew it. That's how heydays work. More than two hundred teams at all professional levels were sprinkled across America in dozens of leagues, scattering down into our daily lives and fertilizing the roots of our connections. We didn't just watch baseball together, we played it together. We marveled at Bob Feller and Willie Mays not just because they could do things we couldn't do, but also because we were still trying to do them. We played and watched, then played again. Professional, semi-professional, and recreational leagues shared happy porous boundaries. In a decade it would all be gone, its far-flung filaments pulled into tight bands on organizational charts with a single relentless goal: feeding insatiable big-league teams in insatiable big-league cities, playing before insatiable television cameras. Most of us stopped playing baseball, sat on the couch, and watched.

–Roger Angell, *Harold Fungo: The Poetry of Pattern*

It was still April, but the cool morning sheets of spring fog were already giving way to summer's warm and sticky bug-laced blanket, getting warmer, stickier, and buggier by the day. The cicadas had arrived, and by noon their electric hum sounded like a short in the ballpark's PA system. Two nights ago, when they began emerging from their 17-year buildup, squadrons of them strafed the infield, and the game had to be called. Now, there was no evidence of the invasion, save the sounds of the survivors' afternoon drone and the evening crunching of shoes on a million of their dead comrades strewn across the concourse and parking lot.

The grounds crew was playing with the new pitching machine, rewarding themselves for the extra work they had to do to get the dead bugs off the infield. The coaching staff and players didn't mind, as long as the crew's work was done, and as long as they were off the field before the players arrived for batting practice.

Municipal Field's crippled janitor, Harold, watched them from the top of the first base stands, near the plywood snack bar. He was tired. Cleaning up took twice as long with all these dead cicadas everywhere. They were hard to sweep up completely, so he regularly had to bend down and grab the carcasses that resisted his broom. And it wasn't easy for Harold to bend down.

He wondered why so many of them died, and hoped they'd gotten to sing before they crashed to earth and were crunched by shoes. He concentrated in the area near the snack bar. Nobody would want to buy a hot dog if they were standing in black bug parts and smashed green guts.

Mrs. Tejada ran the snack bar, and after some early mutual suspicion she and Harold came to a détente. Harold took extra care cleaning in and around the snack bar before every game, and Mrs. Tejada insisted on treating Harold to a coke and a hot dog.

"You are too skinny, Harold," she would say. "One of these days I'll bring in some of my homemade burritos. They'll stick to your ribs."

Harold was a little surprised that this phrase actually made sense for a change. Mrs. Tejada tried to fit "stick to your ribs" into virtually every conversation, whether apt or not. Harold had not come across the phrase before hearing it from Mrs. Tejada, but was pretty sure it was not applicable to any of the non-culinary situations in which she used it.

This afternoon was, finally, to be the day of the burritos. Mrs. Tejada invited Harold to come up to the snack bar a little later than usual, after she had a chance to set up, ostensibly for burritos but actually to introduce Harold to her shy 25-year-old daughter Demetria. Harold was finishing up a rib-sticking burrito and pretending to concentrate on watching the grounds crew hitting off the pitching machine, an activity he usually missed since he was almost always finished cleaning up and long gone by the time the grounds crew started.

After a while, Nick shouted up to him, "Hey, Harold, want to take a swing?" Nick was the newest member of the grounds crew, and Harold's roommate. Nick also served as Harold's unofficial translator on those rare occasions when anyone needed to understand what Harold was saying. His speech was thick and marbly, but if you were around him enough, like Nick was, it could be decoded.

Harold was surprised by the invitation. Nick, who was really asking just to be nice, was even more surprised that Harold accepted. Harold would have done anything to get away from Demetria. His big smile bloomed across his face as he swallowed the rest of the burrito and loped awkwardly down the steps, wide colorful tie swaying.

Nick ratcheted down the machine's speed to its lowest level, equivalent to a soft toss, and Harold picked up a bat. He didn't stand at the plate like any other batter would. His twitching feet were both facing front, like he was getting ready to throw a bowling ball instead of swing a bat. And they straddled the plate in a wide stance, one foot barely in the left-hand hitter's box and the other barely in the right.

Nick had second thoughts about the whole thing, and especially the suicidal stance. But he didn't want to embarrass Harold in front of everyone, and figured it was unlikely he would get hurt by such a slowly tossed ball even if it hit him right on the noggin. The other crew members were cheering Harold on with sarcastic patter.

The pitching machine wasn't entirely automatic as they are nowadays. After setting the speed, which moved a metal catch that changed how far back the spring-loaded arm went before cocking into place, the arm had to be pulled back manually. A lever moved a plate that could put a small amount of spin on the ball.

"OK, here it comes," warned Nick as he pulled the arm back, no spin, and readied the release.

Harold's mouth, which was still in a tight wide smile, switched into slack-jawed almost toothless as soon as Nick cocked the machine. Holding the bat in his right hand like a flyswatter, but moving to the side at the last second, like a tennis player, Harold somehow managed to backhand a slow grounder right up the middle, hitting the machine.

"Beginner's luck," yelled a crew member.

"That'll stick to your ribs," yelled Mrs. Tejada from the snack bar.

"Way to go," yelled Nick, relieved. "But turn sideways to start, put both feet on one side of the plate, and swing with both hands on the bat."

Harold obeyed, missed three times in this new stance, then smashed the next pitch for a line drive right into the pitching machine, this time knocking it over.

"Faster," yelled Harold, ear-to-ear smile back on.

The crew members didn't know what he said, but Nick did. He lifted the heavy machine back up, placed it on its markings, and cranked it up to the next setting, which was a batting practice fastball. Harold knocked the machine over again with another line drive. The same thing happened three more times, even though Nick was increasing the speed and even putting spin on the balls. Harold's legs jiggled, anchored by his heavy black shoes, the smile dropped to the open mouth, his orange/red/blue tie swung, and bang, his line drives knocked over the machine. Every single time. Nick and the grounds crew went silent. Nick was about to try the highest setting, but discovered the main spring on the machine was sprung.

"OK, Harold, I guess you're done, because the machine's broken," Nick said.

Harold felt terrible about breaking it, walked back to Mrs. Tejada's snack shack with his head down, and then felt even worse when he remembered Demetria was there. He picked up his broom and started sweeping again, slowly. The crew furiously tried to repair the machine before the team arrived. They couldn't.

The players and a few coaches started to file in. The chief of the grounds crew, Bob Hayford, knew he'd have to come clean. He confessed to the hitting coach, Fred Christianson, that they'd broken the pitching machine while doing their own batting practice, when one of the guys hit several line drives right back into it. Hayford often thought back to that day and wondered what made him say that somebody hit *several* line drives into the machine. Had he just said that someone broke it by hitting a line drive into it, the incident would have been attributed to chance and Harold would still be a janitor.

"Oh, well, these things happen," Christianson responded. "Live pitching's better anyway. Hey, Greg, would you mind throwing batting practice? The machine's broke."

When the manager, Wally Berens, walked onto the field and saw his pitching coach throwing batting practice he got steamed. He'd paid for that machine out of his own pocket, and this bullshit from Fred about how batters need live pitching was bullshit. It's a ball, flying in the air. It doesn't matter whether it came out of a rocket or outta your ass, he'd told Fred a hundred times, it's the same if it has the same speed and spin, which this machine can deliver, at least as for speed.

"What the fuck, Fred?"

"The machine's busted, Wally."

"How'd that happen?"

Here, Fred had a complicated decision. He could tell the truth, though blaming those poor guys on the grounds crew seemed a little chickenshit, or he could lie, say he didn't know. But if he said he didn't know, Wally would get suspicious, Fred would get more and more nervous like he always did when he lied to Wally, and then Wally would think for sure he busted it on purpose.

"I guess one of the guys on the grounds crew busted it."

"How?"

"I guess he hit a bunch of line drives into it."

"Bullshit," said Wally.

Wally Berens had been around baseball for 40 years. With a dismal lifetime batting average of .223 over a few sporadic stints in the major leagues, Wally knew that hitting a baseball was the hardest thing in sports, maybe the hardest physical task humans had ever conjured. He also knew Fred would do anything to go back to live batting practice.

"Which one? I'd like to meet the Tris Speaker on our grounds crew who could hit a ball hard enough and regular enough to break this machine. Maybe we should sign him up."

Fred said he didn't know who broke the machine. So Wally asked Bob Hayford, who was standing next to the visitor's dugout, leaning against the tarp and fidgeting.

Hayford would also have had a complicated decision if he was as devious as Fred. But Bob's default was to tell the truth. He worried a bit about getting poor Harold in trouble, but he knew Wally Berens was a kind soul underneath everything, and that he'd never get Harold fired or even embarrass him over this. Heck, Mr. Berens had given Harold one of his treasured World Series balls when he heard Harold was asking some of the guys if they would sign a ball for him.

"It was Harold who hit the line drive. Mr. Berens."

Wally didn't believe it. He was certain Fred broke the machine on purpose, and had somehow roped Hayford into the plot. He was furious.

"Oh, is that so?" Berens looked up to the concourse and roared, "Harold, get down here."

Harold had heard and seen everything, and he was delighted to get further away from Demetria. He ran, in his fashion, down the steps and onto the field, smile fully in place.

Everyone knew Harold. You couldn't help but recognize his clomping ballroom dancing with the push broom, loud wide tie, and the almost toothless smile. Besides, putting on a baseball game in the minors in those days was a collective effort that often blurred the lines between player and non-player. There were seldom enough members of the grounds crew just to pull out the tarps, so the players helped, usually the rookies. In the instructional leagues the players had to retrieve all the foul balls. And although they drew the line at sweeping up, in small operations everyone got to know everyone. Every player knew Harold.

"Harold, did you hit a baseball into the pitching machine a bunch of times?" Wally asked sarcastically, turning and glaring at Fred, one arm around Harold for comfort. Wally was not yet conversant with Harold's way of speaking, so he got the head nod. Yes yes yes.

"What?" Yes yes yes. Christianson had drawn Harold into the conspiracy. Wally figured that even a scumbag like Christianson would come clean before he'd let Wally embarrass Harold in front of the whole team. So Wally grabbed a bat and handed it to Harold.

"Show me. Greg, throw him a few slow ones." To this day, Wally can't believe that he came so close to embarrassing poor Harold.

Greg D'Antoni was their pitching coach. He had a solid career as a starter in the Phillies organization, and spent his entire time in the majors—seven years—in Philadelphia. He was known mostly for his big tailing fastball. When he lost speed as he grew older, he turned into a serviceable middle inning man. He was just starting his coaching career, so he could still put some mustard on the ball.

Before Wally could call the whole thing off, his bluff called by that goddam Fred Christianson, D'Antoni, who had already warmed up for batting practice, tossed Harold a slow looper that Harold hit right back to him so hard that D'Antoni had to drop to the deck to avoid getting beaned. Harold flashed one his big smiles. That did it.

D'Antoni was in a rage, fueled by decades of pitcher versus batter tribalism. Forgetting this was Harold, the gentle slow-witted janitor everyone loved, forgetting this was not even batting practice let alone a game, D'Antoni grabbed another ball from the bag, reared back, and launched a fastball as hard as he could throw it, right at Harold's cheek.

Harold leaned back, got the inner part of his bat on the ball, and knocked another line drive right back to the mound. This one hit D'Antoni in the leg. He went down, then jumped up, dropped his glove, and ran toward Harold, who dropped his bat and opened his arms for a hug. Wally jumped between them.

"Greg, Greg, it was Harold. Easy, it's Harold."

D'Antoni came to his senses. He looked over at Harold, who was still offering a hug, then D'Antoni took him in his arms like they were battery mates who just won the World Series.

"How'd you do that, Harold?"

Harold mumbled something only Nick understood.

"He says he doesn't know, but are you alright?" Nick translated.

"Yeah, yeah, I'm fine. Let me throw you some more." Greg threw a few more, each a little harder than the one before, some off speed, and Harold hit every one back at him.

After witnessing this unlikely scene, Wally signaled for Greg to stop, and said, "Get Buzzy warmed up and out here and have him throw the kid some real heat. And pull out the L-screen so Buzzy doesn't get his head knocked off.

Buzzy Bernardi, a finalist for last year's double-A player of the year and Wally's top pitching prospect, threw Harold everything he had. Harold hit every pitch into the top of the L-shaped screen used to protect the batting practice pitcher. Buzzy threw inside, outside, curves, change-ups.

Wally explained to Harold that he didn't have to swing at a ball if it was too far away. Harold seemed to understand, but it didn't matter because Harold swung at everything and hit everything. Buzzy even lost his grip on one pitch that came in a foot outside, and Harold reached out and hit it, to the same spot at the top of the L-screen. It was impossible.

CHAPTER 2
ORANGE CONES

I finally met Harold Fungo at a doughnut shop in Trinidad, Colorado, to interview him for a New Yorker essay I'd been commissioned to write about him. After meeting him I tore up my working draft, which was about Harold the Hammerer, his unparalleled wizardry at the plate. But we didn't talk about baseball at all. He asked most of the questions, about The New Yorker, writing, poetry, editors, falling in love. The closest we came to baseball was when he asked me whether I believed the God of Fate was in a mortal battle with the God of Chance. That was the best description of baseball I'd ever heard.

–Roger Angell, *Harold Fungo: The Poetry of Pattern*

That night after the game Wally invited Greg and Harold, and Nick as interpreter, to have a late dinner with them at a downtown steak joint, a few blocks from the ballpark. By all rights Fred Christianson, his hitting coach, should have been at this historic meeting, not Greg, his pitching coach. But Wally couldn't stand Christianson.

Harold had never been to a steak restaurant, or any restaurant for that matter, given his lack of experience, lack of money, and lack of teeth. Wally was so curious about Harold's hitting that he didn't even think of the food. When Nick told the waiter Harold just wanted mashed potatoes and gravy, Wally realized how inconsiderate he'd been to take the almost toothless kid to Steak World.

"How old are you, kid?" Wally began the serious interrogation after the shrimp cocktail, which Harold politely tried to gum down.

"He says he's 35," interpreted Nick.

"Shit. OK, well I damn well better stop calling you kid." Harold made some more noises.

"He says he's pretty sure he's 35, but he might be older."

"Shit. OK, OK. Can you run? I don't want to embarrass you, Harold, but I didn't think you'd be able to hit, but dammit you really can hit. I ain't seen nothing like that my whole life. But can you run? Can you run fast, Harold?" Harold shook his head slowly. No, no.

By the time the cigars and brandy came around they had a plan. They needed to get Harold to spray the hits around. If he could hit the pitcher every damn time, he should be able to hit the holes every damn time. Greg had the idea of putting up big markers, maybe some of those orange cones, near the pitcher, get Harold to knock those down, then slowly move the cones to line up with the holes. That was the plan.

They also needed to time Harold to first base. He didn't need to be a rocket. If he could get there before the outfielder could throw the ball back in, then they could pinch run for him. Otherwise, he'd be just a long out. Unless they could teach him to hit extra base hits or even homers. That was Plan B.

It took a full week, but Greg's cone idea eventually worked. He began that first morning by telling Harold, "If you can hit the ball between the bases instead of right back at the pitcher, we might be able let you play in a real game. So, the idea here is for you to hit balls being thrown to you by the pitcher, but don't hit them back at the pitcher. Hit the orange cone, and we'll slowly move it out to where you are hitting the ball where we need you to hit it, where the fielders can't catch it."

Harold understood, and was flabbergasted. He had no idea last night's dinner talk was anything but Wally and Greg overcompensating for being mad about Harold breaking the pitching machine. Play in a real game!

He didn't really know anything about baseball, never having read about it. He tried to figure it out when he watched a few games with Nick and Mrs. Tejada, but he didn't want to bother either of them with questions. He didn't understand the game, but he understood what Greg wanted him to do with the cones.

Nick put up an orange cone just off to the first-base side of the mound. "OK Harold try to hit the cone," Greg yelled as he let a batting practice fastball go. Harold whiffed on it. He whiffed on a dozen others, and hit a few right back to the L-screen protecting Greg.

This was hard for Harold. For as long as he could remember, 30 years at least, he had trained and trained to hit things back to where they came from. Boys throwing things at him when he ran to the store, the tennis ball he'd hit up against his bedroom wall with his open palms. Good thing Ma was deaf. Every once in a while, if he hit it too hard, she'd feel the vibration and she'd yell, "Not so hard."

But she never told him to stop. She encouraged him. She explained that the tennis ball game might help with his troubles from being born. Help him walk better and maybe even talk better. Harold knew he didn't run or walk like the other people he saw when he ran to the store. Ma said he probably also wasn't talking right, though she couldn't be sure. He didn't realize until she died and he moved out into the world how much trouble other people were having understanding him.

Once, he asked her how she was able to learn to talk if she couldn't hear. "Some special teachers at school, and God." Harold was aching to ask her about school—that magical place he'd only read about—but he knew from experience that she'd just talk about God if he probed too much into her childhood.

She found an old tennis racket in an alley, two strings broken. "Here, use this to hit the ball, but not inside. In the backyard, hit it against the wall of the house."

When the tennis racket broke completely, she found him a two-by-four, then a proper bat, which she said she bought at the Goodwill Store. The bat was engraved in cursive, which he could not read but which Ma told him said "E. Collins" at the top and "Hillerich Bradsby" in the middle, Ma skipping over the ampersand between Hillerich and Bradsby. She read the words to him, but she didn't know what they meant. Harold made up a story. Hillerich Bradsby was his father, who was killed in the Great War when Harold was just a baby. E. Collins was his father's best friend, who survived the war and went on to build a bat factory, dedicating his very first bat, this one, to the memory of his friend Hillerich.

Harold spent 30 years hitting tennis balls against the back wall of the house with that Hillerich & Bradsby bat. Four, five hours every day. Even though he was using a baseball bat, Harold stood like a tennis player, facing forward to be prepared to go either to his backhand or forehand, holding the bat with only his right hand. His mind was usually on a kind of concentrated hold, though it sometimes wandered to thoughts of the happy couple Hillerich and Ma once were.

The house was clapboard, so he had to concentrate on hitting the ball right into the center of a plank. If he was too high or too low or off center it would hit the edge of a plank or the seam between planks, and fly up, down, or sideways instead of coming back.

Once when he was very young and still working on avoiding the edges and seams, he hit a badly bulged seam and the ball flew across their high and unkempt hedges into the neighbor's yard behind. He fell to his knees and sobbed, sure he'd never be able to play again, because Ma's most important rule then was to never leave the yard. Ever. When she finally noticed him sitting and crying, she came out and hugged him, and told him she'd find more balls, which she did.

Every two weeks or so Harold would have to move ever so slightly to avoid the dents he'd made in the siding after thousands of strikes in the same spot. When one row of siding was all dented, he'd move up or down to a new row. Good thing the back of the small house was so wide. In all those years he didn't dent more than five or six rows. The paint came off those rows, and every spring Harold would repaint them.

Now, being asked to hit the ball somewhere other than exactly where it was coming from required Harold to unlearn three decades of practice. After a week he could consistently hit the cone on the first base side of the mound. The team then left for a long road trip, but Greg and Wally instructed Nick on what they wanted him to do.

Every morning Harold and Nick would take out the pitching machine and practice hitting the cone, working up from medium to high speed, and mixing in curves. Even though most of the grounds crew was off because of the road trip, every one of them came in to watch Harold's workouts, helping shag the balls and cheering him on. Not a sarcastic cheer in the group.

After a couple days Nick moved the cone a few feet further out toward the first base line. This time it only took Harold a half dozen swings to be able to hit it. And Nick made sure, as instructed, to move it back to the first position every once in a while, so that Harold wouldn't forget how to hit that one.

When the team got back, Greg telephoned Nick and asked how it went. "You just watch," was Nick's reply. They agreed to meet up early the next morning before anyone else arrived.

Nick set out cones on which he'd stuck cards with big numbers written on them. Three between third and second, three between second and first. "No way," Greg said as he arrived and saw the set-up. Harold came bounding down the stairs, carrying the Hillerich & Bradsby. Greg took it from him, hefted it in his hands, and swung a few times. "This is a fine bat, Harold. Where'd you get it?"

"Ma," and with a big smile Harold stepped up to the plate.

"One," shouted Nick just as the machine let loose a fastball at maximum speed, and Harold slammed a worm burner knocking over the cone numbered one, just inside the third base line. And so on, with Nick mixing in off speed pitches, until all six cones were dead.

"Jesus Christ. That's impossible!" said Greg.

"Wait, watch this," Nick said as he grabbed four new cones numbered seven through ten and placed them in the outfield.

No way, Greg said to himself, his mouth open just like Harold's. Nick had taught Harold to put a little bit of loft into the ball, which wasn't that remarkable given that Harold had to go up on a couple rows of siding when one row was all dented, but what was remarkable was that Harold was almost as accurate with his outfield hits as with his infield ones. No ball landed further than five feet from any outfield cone. And he actually knocked one over.

"Let me throw to him," Greg said.

He and Nick moved the machine off the field and set all the cones back up. Greg grabbed a bag of balls, warmed up for a few minutes, then started firing at Harold. Greg gave it his best stuff, changing speeds and locations. Nothing mattered. All the infield cones went down, and a few in the outfield.

"You're shittin' me," Wally said when Greg explained the drill to him. "I gotta see this, but in private. Tonight after the game. We'll see if he can do it under the lights." Wally knew this might be big. The next step was to time Harold to first base. Maybe later they could work on power, but Wally wanted to wait and see. He didn't want to jinx anything.

They timed Harold to first, and it wasn't good. "Billy, get Harold a pair of cleats. We can cut a half-second off just by dumping those clodhoppers. And Harold, take off that damn tie."

Harold loved his new shoes. He wore them all the time, until Greg told him the cleats wouldn't be good for him all the time, and got him a pair of regular sneakers.

Harold couldn't believe how comfortable the sneakers were. He'd worn the same kind of shoes—heavy black rubber-soled ones—for as long as he could remember. He didn't know where Ma got them, but she'd come home with a new pair every year or so when he was younger. These current ones must be four years old. The thick rubber soles had worn down to almost normal size. But the sneakers were heaven. They made Harold's feet feel like they were floating in a bowl of chilled Jell-O.

Harold could perform his magic from either side of the plate. Wally told him to always bat as a left-hander, to save a few feet running to first. But neither the cleats nor the southpaw stance did much for Harold's speed. He just couldn't coordinate his arms and legs into a run. So he defaulted to the way he ran to the store—a super-fast walk with arms and legs straight as boards, like Frankenstein. It became a little less important now that he could reliably hit the ball to left, where the left fielder would have the longest throw to first. But Harold was so slow there were occasions during drills when even some of the left fielders could throw him out at first, maybe one out of ten times.

"Hell," Wally said to Greg, "that means Harold can still bat at a .900 clip, and even if he's thrown out, he can move runners over with less than two outs. Besides, our outfielders are getting a jump because they know the ball will land near the cones."

They spent another week trying to get Harold to hit the ball harder, so his drives in the outfield gaps would go all the way to the wall instead of being cut off. But that didn't work. Even more fruitless were their efforts to get him to loft the ball a little higher, maybe even for home runs where there were short porches. When he started to miss the ball consistently, Wally called a halt.

Wally and Greg realized early in this whole process, Greg a little sooner than Wally, that Harold wasn't stupid or retarded. He just had a problem forming words. Hell, once they could understand him half the words Harold used they didn't even know.

This relieved Nick, who they insisted stick around as interpreter even as they came to understand Harold better and better. Nick was a college boy and knew most of Harold's big words. He usually translated the big words into simpler more ordinary ones. It also occurred to Wally, always looking for an edge, that they didn't need to worry about anyone from the opposing club overhearing Harold or reading his lips. They wouldn't understand his highfalutin words even if they could make them out.

The final tune-up was to get rid of the cones.

"OK, Harold," Wally explained, "we are going to take the cones away. All they really stood for was that area between the players and the foul lines, or between the players themselves, where a ball could get through. But remember where the cones with numbers were, because sometimes in a game we might have to tell you which gap you should hit, OK?"

"Understood," said Harold.

Wally was right about the outfielders getting a jump because of the cones. Without them they almost never could throw Harold out at first, despite his geologic speed. Even the right fielder. Wally now knew for sure he had stumbled on something really big. Bigger than he ever had. Maybe bigger than any baseball man ever had.

CHAPTER 3
THE CONTRACT

Owner hopeful. Robert "Big Bob" Cooper told reporters today that he was optimistic about his local double-A professional baseball team this year, whose season begins in just one week. "We have a good roster, terrific coaches, and there's no reason we can't compete for the crown again." The team finished first in the Midwest League last year, but was knocked out in the second round of the playoffs. Its new season begins on the road with a three-game series in Garden City followed by two games in Manhattan. The team returns for its home opener at Municipal Field on April 13 at 7:00 p.m. against the Sioux City Sioux. Tickets for all home games may be purchased at the Municipal Field ticket office, at Cooper Farm Equipment on Elm, and at Cooper Realty on Adams.

Wally called in one of the big club's minor league scouts. Muttering a bunch of No Fuckin' Ways and Jesus H. Christs during and after the workout, the scout immediately called the big club bigshots, and they flew in for Harold's official tryout a few days later.

Before the workout in front of the scout, Wally needed to find Harold a uniform. This was double-A, not the big leagues, so he couldn't just call someone with measurements and have a uniform delivered overnight. They scoured the roster to find someone built like Harold.

Max Downey was the closest. They called him Stick because he was so skinny. But he wasn't quite as tall as Harold. Clevon Sumford was Harold's height, but 100 pounds heavier. Clevon's huge shoulders must have been 50% wider than Harold's. They tried both uniforms, forced to pick between Harold swimming in Sumford's tent but perfect at the cuffs, or the Stick's perfect fit on the torso with Harold's legs jutting out.

They decided to go with Stick's, because Harold preferred it. It fit him more like his everyday clothes did—showing four inches of bright white ankles. They managed to disguise them by using Stick's gray road uniform, and with an unofficial pair of gray socks that matched the road pants almost perfectly.

"What's this guy's last name, Wally?" the scout asked in the middle of the workout. Goddamn it. That was one thing they forgot to cover. Wally knew Harold had no last name, at least that Harold knew.

"Fungo," Wally extemporized.

"You're kidding right?"

"No. It's Italian."

"Christ, a 1,000 hitter, an Itie, and named Fungo? This is something from fuckin' PR heaven. How old is he?"

"Thirty," Wally rounded down.

"No kidding? Well, it's nice to hear that everything about him ain't perfect. Where's he been all this time?"

"He played a lot of local ball, but never organized."

"Where'd you find him?"

"Right here. Home grown."

"You're scouting local playgrounds for 30-year-olds now, Wally?"

"For anyone who can play."

The scout's enthusiasm waned considerably when he timed Harold running to first. "Christ, Wally, what's wrong with his arms and legs? He's slower than my grandma."

"We're working on it, Donnie, but do you really care how fast he is when he can hit 1,000?"

"Where would you put him in the field? He's probably too slow even for right field, but I should still see him shag a few. Could he catch, or maybe play first?"

"He's tired, and he's done for the day. You just saw a guy who can hit 1,000, and place the ball anywhere he feels like it, and you want to see him shag a few balls? Come on, Donnie, we have a gold mine here and you know it. Even if all he ever does is pinch hit, he's a gold mine."

When the bigshots came, it was more of the same. Hit after hit, hole after hole, gap after gap, expletive after expletive. At first, Wally left Harold free to hit a few balls wherever he wanted, but then he told the bigshots Harold could pick which holes to hit.

"OK, Harold hit this to 1," he yelled, then turning to the bigshots, "That would be down the third base line, gentlemen," and Harold knocked one that looked like it was running in a channel dug just inside the line. "Now you guys pick."

"Center-rightfield gap," one of them said, Wally yelled "Ten," and boom. "And he can decide at the last second, in case they steal our signs. Tell me where you want the next one."

"Down the right field line," one of them said, still shaking his head in disbelief. Buzzy wound up again and just when his arm started to come forward Wally yelled, "Six." Painted down the right field line. They ran through the full complement of Buzzy's pitches, all with the same results.

"Who's got the best arm down here?" one of them asked.

"Buzzy. He's got the best stuff across the board, probably one of the best pitchers in double-A. I'm starting to worry he's losing a little confidence pitching to Harold."

"Let's see him hit a lefty."

"Doesn't matter," Wally said. "It's the same deal. And, not that it matters, he can do the same from the right side of the plate." But the bigshots insisted, so Wally brought in his best lefty, Stick, and had Harold hit from both the left and right sides, all with the same results.

Just like the minor league scout's, the bigshots' expletives came with gleams about what Harold could mean for the big-league team, and for their careers. But unlike the scout, they managed to hide their gleams with professional reserve. Even their expletives exploded out of clenched teeth trying to hold them back. These were guys who had negotiated hundreds of contracts between them, and their job was to lowball.

They tried to sign Harold on the spot. But Harold insisted, Nick explained as interpreter, that some guy named Jack read the contract. Although Harold's reading was improving, these ten stapled pages of single-spaced words were just too much for him, and he said so. Nick didn't translate that last part, he just said Harold needed to have Jack look the contract over. The bigshots assumed Jack was Harold's agent, or worse, his lawyer. Jack was actually the fireman who took Harold under his wing the night Harold's mother died in a house fire.

"OK," said the head bigshot, we'll bump up the salary to $10,000 for two years, with $1,000 of that as a signing bonus, but that's it." He scratched out the lines of the contract that had the two numbers in them and put in the replacements, initialing the changes.

"Harold says he needs to let Jack read the contract."

"Goddammit. He's a public relations nightmare. And he can't run for shit. $15,000 with $2,000 up front is our final offer."

Harold was getting a little angry so he grabbed the contract, and said as clearly as he could "NO," and shook his head for emphasis.

"Fine, but this 15/2 offer will be our final one, and it expires tomorrow at noon. We have planes to catch."

Nick and Harold took the contract to Jack at the firehouse. Jack read the whole thing, every word, looking up every few minutes at Harold, smiling and shaking his head. He didn't understand the lion's share—it was mostly legalese—but he understood Harold was being offered three times the amount of money Jack earned in a year as a fireman, to play baseball for two summers. And he understood Harold would be starting in an instructional league in Texas. He described the contract to Harold, who also couldn't believe it. Neither of them liked the Texas part, but Jack said he'd talk to the bigshots about it later that evening.

They met in the hotel conference room. It was the fanciest room Harold had ever seen. He couldn't take his eyes off the bookshelves, which seemed to have dozens and dozens of the same book, beautifully leather bound. The three bigshots and Wally sat on one side of the table, Harold, Jack, and Nick on the other. The head bigshot started talking once everyone sat down and introduced themselves.

"Look, he has no track record, he never played high school ball, he's slow as molasses, no offense son, he's 30 years old, and apparently can play no position. I have been given final authority to go to $20,000 with $5,000 up front, but that's it."

"That salary and bonus are fine, but Harold wants to play for the team here," Jack announced. All six of the bigshots' shoulders simultaneously dropped a couple inches in relief.

"Can't be done. This guy hasn't even played little league. The instructional league is where he needs to go."

"To learn what?" Wally piped in, to the bigshots' surprise. "Harold hits 1,000. Let's call it 900 just to be safe. You want a 900 hitter to sit in Shithole, Texas to learn about when to tag up? Hell, he should probably be up with the big club right now. But he and Jack are showing good faith here. They realize we need to figure out how best to use him. And we all realize there could be some PR issues. Let us work all that out down here. Let him stay here for two-and-a-half months. If you still want him in the Texas instructional league on August 1, I'm sure he'll agree to go, right Harold?"

Jack started to answer but Harold interrupted him, shaking his head yes and booming out a clear "Yes," followed by other stuff not so clear, which Nick translated. "Harold says yes, if you let him play here for Wally until August 1, then he will go to Shithole, Texas."

Everyone laughed and shook hands. Harold signed the contract. That contract was bigger than any non-pitcher's in the history of the Cincinnati Reds farm system. It was also the strangest. It expressly provided that Harold would remain in double-A with Wally Berens as his manager at least through August 1. Nick was to be his interpreter, paid handsomely by the club, to accompany him to all games, home and away.

Harold almost backed out of the whole deal when they told him half the games were played in other towns—he thought "road" games meant that for some reason they played out in the streets somewhere nearby. There were no baseball books in Ma's library.

One other clause of Harold's contract, added a few weeks later, was the strangest of all. Harold agreed to wear his newly fitted false teeth in public, but he didn't have to wear them while batting. This was the compromise between the marketing people and the baseball people. Harold liked the way the false teeth made him look normal, and after a few days he didn't even notice them. They even helped him speak more clearly, though he continued to exaggerate his impediment because he wanted to keep Nick around. But he couldn't hit a lick with the false teeth in. Nobody knew why. The marketing people went along with the compromise because they had to, and also because this was before the days of the live TV closeup in baseball, and heck, this was double-A for now, where there was hardly any radio let alone TV.

The marketing people also decided on a strategy of trickling out information. They had their PR department write a terse press release the day after Harold signed, to be issued locally only, mentioning just that he was a "late blooming utility player," local to the double-A town, who would probably break in as a pinch hitter. Despite being issued just locally, the Cincinnati paper somehow got hold of it and splashed the story with the headline "Reds Sign Mystery Sub." Papers in archrival St. Louis were less charitable, with small stories near the back of their sports sections with headlines like "Cincy Signs Unknown Geezer to Pinch-Hit" and "Grandpa Signs with Desperate Reds." All this coverage made Harold a bit of a celebrity before he ever played his first game of baseball, which only magnified the legend.

CHAPTER 4
TALES OF HAROLD

Team loses season opener. Last year's pitching phenom Buzzy Bernardi gave up six hits, two of them one-run homers, as our local boys lost their season opener on the road 6-3 to arch rival Garden City. The team plays two more games against the Bluebells, then two in Manhattan before returning for the home opener on April 13 at 7:00.

His muse was a brain tumor. Before, Joe Skelton never wrote anything longer than a shopping list. After, the words marauded through him, though he never wrote them down. He told them to Katherine at night, sleep-talking. It was strange, lying there next to him in the dark, listening to his words like they were bedtime stories and she a child fighting off sleep. But she didn't go to sleep. She furrowed with worry. And she wrote the words down.

They eventually realized the words were a story, an implausible story about a crippled janitor named Harold who became a professional baseball player. Though he struggled walking and talking, Harold could hit a baseball like no one before or since.

Tales of Harold, as they came to call the story, unfolded in mutual mystery. Before the diagnosis, Joe had no idea where the story was coming from or, really, whether it was actually coming from him. Katherine had no idea where the words were coming from. Joe was a wonderful husband and a complicated introvert, but she was the voracious reader, the English lit major. Joe never even went to college. Each time an exotic new character or fertile turn of phrase appeared, Katherine would ask him "Where did *that* come from?" and Joe's answer was always the same. "I don't know."

She wasn't jealous about his writing, just confused and worried. And a little adrift. Joe probably hadn't said 500 words to her in a single day in all of their married life, and now hundreds of words poured out of him almost every night, sometimes more than a thousand. He hadn't read a book since high school, and was now writing one. Except for his time in the Navy, Joe never traveled, but was now describing truck stops on country roads, the laden farmlands of the Midwest, and big city skylines. It was all impossible.

Katherine clung to the small life preservers in the story that seemed to come from the Joe she thought she knew. She couldn't remember any crippled people in either of their lives, but there was that blind Fuller Brush man they befriended when they first got married. His name was Daryl, which is awfully close to Harold. Like Harold, Joe and Katherine had an unusual dog, though Harold's was considerably stranger. Joe was shy by nature and circumstance; Harold should have been shy by both, but wasn't. Maybe he was what Joe always wished he could be, except for the handicapped part.

Then there was the baseball, the biggest life preserver of all. Joe loved baseball. He read the box scores every summer morning. He listened to the Denver Bears broadcasts almost every night through the season, and on clear nights he could sometimes get the St. Louis Cardinals games on KMOX. Still, Katherine wondered who this man next to her really was, sleep-talking strange tales she did not recognize, tales that went beyond baseball.

"I like the sportswriter stories that begin every chapter. You've really managed to capture how they write those. I suppose that's from reading the sports pages."

"I suppose."

"They create a nice architecture that helps organize Harold's baseball adventures. The only thing that stuck out for me is that the sports stories never mention the team's name, or the town where they play. Local papers, even as small as the one in Tales of Harold, surely would mention the name of the team and town. They wouldn't just say 'the local team' or 'our team.' That seemed a little strained. But I suppose it was intentional, a way to make the story universal and timeless."

Joe didn't exactly understand what Katherine was saying. He didn't like the sports stories. They seemed confusing and complicating. He just wanted to get on with the Harold story, and didn't need sportswriters to interrupt.

What Katherine wanted most to ask Joe was what she wanted to ask all writers—how they chose the words, how often they changed them, how they performed this magic skin-grafting of words becoming phrases, phrases sentences, and sentences stories. It was the awe she felt whenever she read, starting way back with her first McGuffey Reader.

Like most English lit majors, Katherine had taken stabs at writing. She just couldn't do it, not really. When she read writing that moved her, she felt legless, marveling at sprinters. So writing remained a deep mystery to her, but at least it was a comfortable mystery that enriched her love of reading.

But now the mystery was not so comfortable. Joe was writing, writing really well, but he couldn't answer any of her questions. He didn't choose the words or change them. The story just rolled out, in ready-to-read barrels of paragraphs. This is not the writing she'd learned about, the one born of relentless struggle. She realized later that Joe was just the tumor's crier, and she the crier's scribe.

She asked him one night whether he ever thought about editing, changing the words after she wrote them down. He looked at her like she was speaking Martian.

"What do you mean, change the words?"

"I mean, for most writers this is a long process that involves lots of changing things around."

"Why?"

"It just does. Writers think of better ways to say things, to sharpen things, make them clearer or prettier or stronger."

"But I couldn't change anything. I wouldn't know how. I'm just enjoying the story."

"But you're writing it."

"I suppose."

In the tumor's telling, the story's protagonist, Harold, became an international celebrity, his journey from sweeping up to sports stardom to respected poet chronicled by dozens of magazines and newspapers, including three appearances in Life magazine. Katherine's favorite piece of fictitious journalism was when the tumor imagined what Roger Angell would say about Harold.

"Have you ever actually read anything by Roger Angell?"

"I don't think so."

"He writes a lot about baseball, mostly in The New Yorker. You've never read that magazine, but some of his baseball articles must have made it into your sports pages."

"Maybe."

"Otherwise, how would you even know Angell's name?"

"I don't know."

Here's what Joe's tumor had Roger Angell writing about the first time he met Harold:

The remarkable light from his copper eyes gets scattered by all the ridiculous things about his bearing. He is a cherub stretched skinny across a 6'4" frame, though he never reaches that height because of the curve of his spine, stoop of his shoulders, and downward and outward protrusion of his bird-like neck. He is all thin elongated ovals, which saves him from being a simple stick figure, but just. Take a flattened disk of silly putty, transfer a comic strip image of Charlie Brown onto it, stretch to three times its original height, then bend ten degrees off the vertical. That's Harold.

His oval face is flat, except for a Bob Hope nose. His head, out of which prominent ears jut like outriggers, is drizzled with hints of light brown hair. His mouth is almost always closed in a wan smile, the way mothers smile at sick children, which hides the fact that he only has four teeth—two canines above and their stalagmites below. When he talks, even without any exaggerated movements of his mouth, his missing teeth amplify the distance between his lips, making even the calmest declarations look like screams. His voice is deep and rich, but the words are round and unformed, tongueless.

When he smiles—really smiles—it is atomic, erupting closed-mouth from the bottom of his face so high and wide its corners almost touch his earlobes. His eyes shut in little versions of the same smile. A crippled Stan Laurel.

His toothpick arms and legs are neural strangers to one another, moving to separate syncopated drummers. The disconnection isn't so noticeable when he just stands or walks slowly, though even then the percussion occasionally erupts into spasms. It is when he tries to run, which for him is just a very fast walk, that the cacophony reaches its most frightening Frankenstein extremes.

But then there are those eyes, light refracting through an unlikely alloy of contentment and wonder. Reminders that something triumphant lives in this broken body.

CHAPTER 5
SNEEZING

Crazy. The team was dazed last night in Garden City when it lost 4-3 on a balk by veteran reliever Sam Fresne. He was called for the offending move in the bottom of the ninth, scoring the winning run from third. Neither Fresne nor manager Wally Berens disputed the call. Scouring this newspaper's morgue, this reporter could not find a single instance in all the team's history when a winning run, by or against it, was scored on a balk. Poor Sam Fresne is now in the record book! The team will try to avoid a sweep in tonight's finale against the Bells.

The hurricane that would become Harold Fungo, and would carry Big Bob Cooper's team into minor league history, was still swelling just below the horizon of the tumor's imagination. Now, he was just plain Harold, a light spray, living with his deaf mother, the two of them alone in the small bungalow.

She lived a life of profound worry, trying to prepare him for a world she did not know. After she died and he conquered that world, he often thought about how terribly sad it was that she worried so much, for so long, for no reason. But then he always came to his senses. It was her worry that floated him over the horizon.

The sneezing that started it all began on the Friday morning after Thanksgiving, a cold bright porcelain day rustled with a soft westerly wind. Only a few leaves were still up, stubborn twitching holdouts. A couple patches of dirty snow hidden in shadows interrupted the dry brown landscape.

Joe was in the backyard sawing up a big plastic trash can with an old rusted handsaw, not his good dovetail saw. He'd been trying to get rid of the trash can for weeks, ever since he noticed gaping holes between its bottom and sides, leaking snail trails of garbage whenever he dragged it out front. The bottom looked like a flat gunmetal starfish, only a few points tenuously still attached.

How do you throw away a trash can? Joe put it out front with the other trash, but of course the garbagemen didn't take it. It was a trash can. Then he put a big sign on it that said "Trash." Someone put their own trash in it, which the garbagemen duly emptied. A second more explicit sign—"This trash can is broken—please take away"—was apparently too wordy, the letters too small to be noticed.

Admittedly, the whole idea of trash collection was rather new in Greeley. It wasn't that long ago that everyone burned their trash in brick ash pits. Joe and Katherine still had an ash pit out by the garden, which they'd turned into a flower box. Joe had vivid memories, often triggered when he was tending the flowers in the ash pit, of his mother in the kitchen suddenly sniffing the air like a bear in a stream, then running outside, panicked that the wash she'd hung out on the clothesline was being smoked by some inconsiderate neighbor firing up trash on a non-ash-pit day. Or, worse still, ruined beyond re-washing by a shifted wind bringing the stink from the packing plants.

Joe finally decided he had to cut up the worn-out trash can and put the pieces inside the remaining good one. Every time the dull saw snagged, the plastic sides of the trash can flopped like freshly caught fish.

"Goddammit," he bellowed when the rusty teeth jumped the channel and bit his left hand, between thumb and forefinger.

"Use scissors," Kathrine called out from the house, lifting then shutting the kitchen window against the November cold.

Scissors? Ha! No scissors will cut this thick plastic. Then Joe remembered his tin snips. They worked like a charm. When Katherine came out to check on his progress, the old trash can, now reduced to small geometric shapes plus one dissected starfish, was safely stowed inside the newer one. Joe was quite pleased with his dismembered Russian doll solution to the problem.

"I see you finally listened and switched to scissors. What did you do to your hand?"

Then Joe started sneezing. Not continuously but regularly, every 20 seconds or so.

Joe's best friend, Lester Buckley, was a solar sneezer. He sneezed every single time he went outside into the sun. And it was always three times. Three times and done. All conversation between them stopped after that first sneeze because they both knew two more were coming in quick succession. Never at night, or even on those night-like northern Colorado summer afternoons when the black thunderclouds blotted out almost every trace of sun.

Once when they were sophomores in high school Joe bet Lester a quarter that he would sneeze at least once if he walked outside during what was supposed to be an 80% eclipse of the sun. Unfortunately, their teachers made all the students go outside to begin watching the eclipse long before it began. Teachers and students gathered in the playground abutting the ball field, Lester sneezing three times as usual as soon as he went outside. They quickly changed the bet. Lester would give Joe a quarter if Lester sneezed once the eclipse was over, and Joe would give Lester a quarter if Lester didn't sneeze.

They watched Druid-like as the moon's black disc nibbled away at the cheddar sun, whose light was rendered a greenish purple by most everyone's sunglasses. Within minutes, only a Turkish crescent of sun remained, and everything darkened to dusk. The two celestial bodies danced their minuet, and the bright slice began to precess to the top of the descending moon. Before or after it was over, depending on which boy's version of events you believed, everyone was ordered back into class. Lester had not sneezed. He demanded his money.

"No, the eclipse isn't completely over." Joe insisted they wait for it to get lighter. They straggled across the playground under the suspicious eye of their home room teacher Mr. Gechter, who twice had to say "Inside, gentlemen," the last one punctuated by a no nonsense "now." Gechter was Joe's baseball coach and science teacher, and Joe fleetingly considered telling him about the experiment and begging him to let them stay outside until the sun was entirely free. But the tone of that "now" made Joe relent, and both boys returned inside.

"Twenty-five cents, please," Lester whispered with outstretched hand as soon as they were inside and walking back to class. They then began what would become a lifelong debate about how dark it got during that eclipse, and how dark it still was when Gechter the Specter made them go in. The sacred debt was never paid.

Unlike Lester, Joe was a traditional, situational sneezer. He only sneezed when he had a cold or something got up his nose.

"Something got up your nose?" Katherine asked as she started back inside. "Probably from that dirty old trash can. And you'd better put a band aid on that cut." Joe didn't answer because he sneezed again. And again.

Katherine called Doc Kasten, who told her to keep Joe away from their black lab Soot as much as possible, change the furnace filter, and not fix Joe any spicy foods. He said the sneezing should calm down after a few hours and if it didn't to call him back.

The sneezing didn't calm down, and Katherine called Kasten's office that afternoon. His nurse said he was out of the office but that she would page him.

He got the page while he was enjoying a closely fought high school basketball game in the Greeley Central gym. He was not happy. It was the third time this week he'd been interrupted at a sporting event.

"Geeze Louise," he grumbled, crab-legging out of the packed third row to call the office. He never cussed, at least that anyone in town could remember. After talking again with Katherine, he told her he'd swing by their place after picking up some medications at his office.

Russ Kasten was one of only three family doctors in Greeley, and the only native son, if you counted Fort Lupton as being part of Greeley, which Fort Luptoners seemed more willing to do than Greeley-ites. Lucky for Kasten, Greeley's two other family doctors were from Chicago and California. If he was an outsider then they were visitors from other planets.

So his practice was always a little busier than he wanted it to be, especially now, in what everyone was telling him were supposed to be the twilight years of his working life. He reluctantly hired a second nurse in 1950. But he never caved-in to suggestions that he take on a partner. He believed, with a faith immune to all evidence, that there just wasn't room in Greeley even for three doctors, let alone four. Never would be either.

The Kasten family had deep roots in Fort Lupton. Rumor was that one of Doc's grandmothers was a second cousin to Lancaster Lupton, the young Army lieutenant who founded the town. Lancaster was a member of General Henry Dodge's Regiment of Dragoons. Dodge's 1837 mission, which he undertook without an ounce of irony, was to persuade the plains Indians to respect the rights of the Indians being relocated from the East.

Lancaster was leading a patrol through the Platte Valley one day when he came across a beautiful spot on the banks of Adobe Creek, full of Indians and traders. He was convulsed with such a powerful entrepreneurial spirit that he resigned his commission the next year and returned to that very spot, or as close to it as he could remember, to build a small trading post. He exaggeratingly dubbed it "Fort Lancaster." When the trading post got big enough to warrant a real fort, more formal authorities built it and called it Fort Lupton.

These deep roots may have had something to do with Doc Kasten's odd tendency to think Greeley *was* Fort Lupton. For example, he was sure Greeley had just one stoplight, because Fort Lupton had only one stoplight when he left there for medical school. He was often surprised when he encountered the other stoplights, regularly slamming on his brakes. He was just as sure Greeley could not support more than one doctor, probably because Fort Lupton couldn't, and was just as surprised when the other two moved in and didn't go broke.

Kasten had a wiry frame, but with arms much thicker and stronger than you'd imagine could sprout from it. He was 5'7" on his tip toes, 125 pounds in the shower, and had a generous and caring round face that always made Joe think of a balloon. His eyes were piercing blue, but inquiring, not aggressive. He was always clean shaven and smelled of rosewood, disavowing the more popular Old Spice. He wore small round wire-framed Teddy Roosevelt glasses, with loops hooking so far back around his ears that they couldn't be taken off or put on from the front in a casual one-handed move, but had to be deliberately coaxed off and on first from one side and then the other. His light brown hair was wispy thin. It seems he'd been going bald since he was a teenager. He had a booming voice, which to those who didn't know him was as surprising as his grip.

Driving to Joe's, and remembering this time to stop at the light on 8th street, Kasten went through his differential diagnosis with the ease and clarity earned by 40 years of practice. The list appeared in his mind's eye as a kind of bar chart: Cold, Flu, Allergy, Sinusitis, all in big tall blocks of thick three-dimensional letters, shortening and thinning slightly as they went left to right from Cold to Sinusitis. Corticosteroids further to the right, even shorter and thinner. Kasten couldn't remember prescribing any nose sprays for Joe, but some over-the-counters could cause non-allergic rhinitis. Drug Withdrawal in tiny script; heck, Joe was a teetotaler. And at the far-right end, really just a haze hovering near zero probability, was Idiopathic Neurological Source. Kasten never had such a case, but he vaguely remembered some discussion in the literature about neurologically caused sneezing, so he included it as a blurry possibility. And, a blur within the blur lay a tiny formless red speck of a monster. Harold's author was stirring.

CHAPTER 6
EXAMINATION

Dinged by Bells. Our local baseball team continued its losing ways, falling last night 6-2 to the Garden City Bluebells. They will now move on to Manhattan for two games against the Muskrats before returning for the home opener on April 13 at 7:00, against Sioux City. Tickets for all home games may be purchased at the Municipal Field ticket office, at Cooper Farm Equipment on Elm, and at Cooper Realty on Adams.

The three of them sat at the light green kitchen table while Kasten asked Joe about all the circumstances surrounding the sneezing. Then he asked Joe to join him in the living room for the physical examination, and grabbed one of the green metal kitchen chairs. Katherine stayed in the kitchen, washing the already washed dishes and listening. It wasn't a strain because the house was so small.

Kasten put the kitchen chair right in front of the orange herculon sofa and pointed for Joe to sit in the chair. Kasten sat less than an arm's length away, more than half his rump off the sofa, like a hopeful shoe salesman.

The physical examination, as always, proceeded on two parallel tracks, driven by two different motors. The reliable, smooth motor drove the examination through the comfortable routine Kasten must have done 50,000 times, the settled order, the rational moving through the body systems, all accompanied by the friendly patter between a patient and doctor who'd known each other for decades. The other motor, which drove the diagnosis, sputtered like a chain saw running out of gas. It lurched and leaped ahead beyond the evidence, then forced itself back to the task at hand.

Today, as it often did, the jumpy motor made Kasten marvel at the complexities of the human body, and the way those complexities sometimes seemed rigged. He thought of the high school science fair experiment he saw years back, when they invited him to be a judge. The student—he couldn't remember her name—called the experiment by some fancy name Doc also couldn't remember, no doubt authored by the math teacher, who was flush with pride to have any math problem be part of a science fair.

What caught Kasten's eye was the contrast between the fancy title, which appeared in large attractive dark blue lettering at the top of a carefully prepared poster board, full of equations below in different bright colors, and the embarrassingly dull set-up of the "experiment" itself, which comprised a single sheet of plywood porcupined with a triangular grid of hundreds of finishing nails one inch apart. The plywood was held slightly off the vertical by a rough two-by-four frame.

The young mathematician placed marbles one at a time in a tube fastened above the apex of the porcupine, and as a marble dropped to the first nail it sometimes deflected right and sometimes left. Then it rolled down to the next row, encountering yet another nail, and so on. The whole setup reminded Doc of a pinball machine, and he found himself silently urging the student to hit the flippers before the marbles fell completely to the bottom, where they stacked up in a neat normal distribution, many more huddled around the center than at the sides. There was one marble in the extreme left column, meaning that every single time it hit a nail it bumped left. Every single time.

"What are the chances of that?" Kasten thought he said to himself.

"Well, as you can see from the equations on this poster board," the excited student responded, holding her hands and arms out like she was inviting Kasten to go through a door, "it all depends on the number of nail rows and the number of marbles we drop. No matter the number of rows, if you drop enough marbles, you are almost certain to get these outliers."

Kasten occasionally thought of the nails and marbles as he bounced his way down his own life's inclined plane. But more often he thought of them when he was doing exams and considering diagnoses. Today, at each and every diagnostic nail Joe's marble kept bouncing to the same strange side, as if pushed by vengeful gods. Kasten's well-trained poker face hid his surprise at each step, covered in the smooth purr of the fact-gathering motor.

Joe sneezed throughout the exam. Kasten had to time parts of it, like a boxer in training timing his fancy footsteps to the rope's metronome of snaps on the gym floor. When he was finished, he said to Joe, "Let's go back into the kitchen so Katherine can hear this."

Joe stood up, Kasten grabbed the metal kitchen chair with one of his Popeye arms, jerking it into the air like it was made of balsa wood, and the two men walked into the kitchen. Katherine had been sitting at the table, hearing everything, but when she heard they were coming in she jumped up, grabbed a dish towel, and started wiping down the clean and dry counter, which gave off a few protesting squeaks.

All three sat down around the table, Kasten fiddling with things in his worn black bag. He told them he wanted Joe to see an allergist in Denver because it was almost certainly some kind of new allergic reaction—either an age-onset reaction to old stimuli like dust or mold, or a reaction to something new to which Joe had recently been exposed. He gave Joe a steroid injection, which immediately reduced the frequency of the sneezes, and also gave him a prescription for a strong antihistamine. He repeated what he told Katherine on the phone about changing the furnace filter and keeping Joe away from Soot and spicy foods, at least until things calmed down, which they probably would in a few days.

When Soot heard his name, he immediately popped up from the floor and walked over to Doc then to Joe, who instinctively ruffled the lab's ears and coat, like always. Katherine frowned. Doc Kasten shook his head with a smile.

Joe was irritated at the uncertainty of the diagnosis and especially at the feeble treatment plan. After all, he was still sneezing, even if less frequently after the injection. But Joe and Doc Kasten had known each other forever, so Joe held his tongue. But Katherine didn't.

"You said 'almost certainly' allergies. What else could it be?" she asked, creasing her brow, slightly tilting her head down, and raising her eyes up, an interrogating senator glaring over reading glasses.

"It could be a mild cold or flu, though he has no symptoms other than the sneezing. Could also be a mild sinus infection. There's a remote possibility its neurological."

"You mean a brain tumor?" asked Katherine. She'd named the tiny red speck, which grew a little just in the naming.

"No, no. There are many things that could cause this sneezing neurologically, a tumor is just one possible cause."

"How possible?" Katherine was relentless when the homestead was threatened, and she didn't care who or how many might be offended by the rounds she fired from behind the circled wagons.

"Katherine, dear, please don't worry too much about this. Is there a possibility? Yes. But it's small. Now, I'm not a cancer or brain specialist, but even if it is a tumor these things are often benign, and even if they're not some can be treated. But for now I wouldn't worry any more about a tumor than about getting struck by lightning. Is it possible? Sure. But it's just not worth worrying about now. If the allergy tests are negative, then I'll send you to a neurologist. But let's not worry about the lightning until we know whether there's even a storm, OK?"

He knew his meteorological take on probability would do the trick with Katherine, who came from a long line of farmers. She visibly calmed down, and promised to call the Denver allergist immediately.

"Thanks, Doc," they said almost simultaneously. Kasten grabbed his bag and patted Soot's head as he left, looking down at his watch wondering if he could make it back for the end of the basketball game.

Katherine called the allergist before Doc even started his car. She always made appointments for Joe because he didn't like to use the telephone. They got an appointment for next Thursday.

That night, as they did every night after dinner and before bed, the two sat in the matching red Adirondack chairs on the back porch. They couldn't see anything through the moonless and starless sky, so dark even the blanket of clouds was black. A cold front had blown in off the mountains and the forecast called for a little snow.

Katherine dubbed this nightly porch talk "The Skelton State of the World Report." Joe agreed this was a very funny name, given the Report's typically provincial scope. Unless other developments intruded—such as when they heard about the Foxley twins or if there was a World Series going on—the Skelton State of the World Report seldom went beyond the day just ended in Greeley and the one to come.

To Katherine, the Skelton State of the World Report was like that big breath you took at night right after you switched off the reading light, turned, and closed your eyes. And in fact, on the rare occasions when some other activity prevented the Report, Katherine had trouble getting to sleep.

If the weather was miserable, they'd do the Report in the living room, but it really had to be miserable. Living room Reports just didn't feel official. It was as if they weren't fully consecrated unless Joe and Katherine were outside, sitting on their wooden chairs on top of the bulging edge of the Great Plains. That night, Katherine tried hard not to let the bulging red monster become the topic of conversation.

"Doc Kasten doesn't seem to be slowing down much," ventured Joe, noticing that Katherine seemed reluctant to start the Report, which was her traditional role.

"Frankie told me he still fills way more prescriptions for Doc than for those other two combined," Katherine responded.

"How old is Doc?" asked Joe.

"I always thought he was 15 years older than you."

"He sure don't look that old."

"Oh, I don't know. But you sure don't look your age. I would have guessed Doc was at least 20 years older than you."

"Why'd he never get married?"

"Same reason you almost never did."

Joe mulled a bit. "Nah, Doc's a handsome, sociable guy, and he must have a fair amount of money. And he's smart. Girls should've been all over him."

"*You're* handsome, Joe," and Katherine reached out and placed the heel of her hand on the wide arm of his chair, her fingers lightly resting on the back of his hand. Her touch still gave him a jolt.

"Yeah sure."

"You *are*."

"OK, sure. But Doc ain't shy like me. He loves to be around people. You can't go anywhere in this town but there's Doc in the middle of a bunch of people, talkin' and laughin'."

"That's true. Maybe that's why Doc never needed to get married. He's married to the whole town." They both thought about that for a while. Joe thought about sex and Katherine about loneliness.

Joe knew Doc had had a few girlfriends over the years, but he couldn't remember seeing him with anyone for a long time. *Did Doc still have the urge? Would I still have the urge when I'm his age? Not at this rate, given the drop off so far.*

Katherine wondered how it would feel to wake every morning knowing that everything you did during the day would stay inside, and then you'd just go to bed again, alone, everything still inside. Who did Doc talk to about books, about life, about what happened today and what will happen tomorrow? Sure, he had the whole town, but the really important things couldn't be shared so casually. She remembered Doc had a brother who lived in Santa Fe, but she'd only seen him a couple times over the years.

The angle of the chair backs left them looking at the black sky. A low glow in the east announced the moon would rise soon.

"Hatchoo."

"Hey, that's the first one in a long while. You shouldn't have any trouble getting to sleep."

"You mean *we* won't have trouble getting to sleep," Joe said smiling and turning his head so Katherine could see the smile. Katherine, turning her head, repaid the smile with a quick raise of her eyebrows, squint of her eyes, and purse of her lips, all acknowledging that yes, she was also a little worried about whether Joe's sneezing would keep her up.

They returned their heads to the default Adirondack position, looking about a quarter of the way up from the eastern horizon, most of which was blocked by the rooflines of the Collins' house and shed. Off to the right was the big white house where Katherine's sister Mary lived with her family. On clear evenings, the big house reflected the setting sun like a searchlight.

On clear nights moon and stars were the usual objects of their gaze, and often of their discussions. Sounds and smells were also part of the conversations, though usually wordless.

On cloudy nights, like tonight, the outside sounds seemed closer, louder. The crickets were done for the year, but Joe and Katherine heard other wild noises in the neighborhood, the eastern edge of which was less than a mile from where the Platte captures the Cache la Poudre. They heard lots of twigs snapping, succumbing to secret heavy things. The distinctive whap whap of a single bat late for fall hibernation. The easterly wind swishing through bushes and stirring the Hutchinson's barbeque tools into a dull wind chime.

Joe thought about how the wind almost never smelled to him anymore, even when it came directly from the meatpacking plants to the northeast. Greeley was famous for its meatpacking stink. Most visitors could hardly stand it when the air carried the strange reek of life and death. With the right, or wrong, conditions it was an unholy vapor of sweet grass, living cows and their manure, and the sharp, ferrous smell of blood.

Natives like Joe seldom noticed it anymore, except occasionally on early spring evenings, especially if it had rained during the day, the drops forcing the stink to ground until it was picked up again by a drying late afternoon breeze. Joe thought about how people could get used to just about anything after enough time, and then thought about Lester in Philadelphia so long ago.

Katherine wondered whether the bit of air bumping up against her face had come from China, or if it had always been there and was just being bumped by other pieces of stationary air in a world-wide rush of air dominoes. She concluded it was probably a combination—little bits of air moving a little bit, slowly traveling around the globe but at a speed much slower than the wind itself. Then she thought of how little things could cause big things, and then of Joe and the red monster.

She quickly shut her mind, and began her nightly struggle to get out of the darn chair, a clumsy dance that announced the official end of the Report. Katherine was in charge of adjourning in this fashion. As always, after her battle with gravity and the Adirondack's colluding angle of repose, not to mention having to step over Soot, who always lay down between the chairs, she went inside to dress for bed. Joe stayed out. He always rose when Katherine did, but stayed outside to do his nightly property inspection.

Hands in his jeans (he never wore shorts, even in the hottest, muggiest summers), he and Soot would first walk around the edge of the backyard fence, checking for any gaps Soot might have dug between the ground and the chain link in his never ending and never successful attempts to escape. Joe often wondered, when he came upon these abandoned tunnels, what Soot would actually do if he ever managed to excavate enough dirt to scoot under the fence. He guessed that Soot, unlike some of their more adventurous dogs, might do nothing at all. That the holes were just for digging, not for escaping.

After circumnavigating the fence line, Joe would then open the door to the detached garage to check that the light was off and the garage door closed, while Soot did his business in the yard. In the summer Joe would then inspect the garden and try to count the fireflies.

Joe was proud that their garden regularly attracted fireflies. They were rare at this dry altitude, this close to the Rockies. He attributed his luck to being so far east and near the rivers, which made things a bit warmer and less dry. But he also kept his back lawn and garden well-watered. The fireflies were a common item on the agendas of the Skelton State of the World Report.

In the winter, he'd think of the garden and the fireflies to come. Winter inspections started with shoveling any snow from the backyard sidewalk between porch and garage. He would have already cleared any snow from the porch and chairs before the Report. He followed any shoveling with a boundary inspection if the snow wasn't too deep, or a visual one if it was. He'd then stop by the hoses to make sure he'd disconnected them, even though he would disconnect them faithfully every year on All Saints Day, November 1, unless an early hard freeze required it sooner. And of course even though he had just checked them the night before.

He finished, summer and winter, by calling Soot inside, closing the back door, making sure it was locked, checking that the oven and stove were off, and then turning all the inside lights off as he and Soot padded back into bed.

When she heard the back door close, Katherine would always look up from her book and out the bedroom window across the back porch to the other leg of the small L-shaped house. It looked like a slow-moving power failure, the rooms going dark one by one. Before Joe quit his night job and moved to days, the nightly power failure went in the other direction, the light leaving as Joe left. Then he did his inspections on his way out to work. But now the darkness followed Joe into the bedroom.

This night, as he and Soot approached, Joe could hear Katherine crying softly. He paused in the hallway but Soot, apparently unaware of the delicacy of the situation, trotted through and jumped up on the bed, settling into his usual place on the foot of the bed right up against Katherine's legs, to make room for Joe. When Joe came in Katherine hid her crying and Joe hid his discovery of it. But he did tell her, right before his big breath and sleep, "I'll be OK. It's just allergies." She squeezed his hand and took her big breath.

CHAPTER 7
NIGHT POEMS

Home opener! Our local hardball heroes swept two road games from the Manhattan Muskrats, to raise their season record to 2-3. Their home opener is tonight at 7:00 against Sioux City, the first of four against the visiting Sioux before the team heads back out on the road. To celebrate the home opener, all fans will be given a coupon at the gate entitling them to one free hot dog, while supplies last. Play ball!

The words started that night. At first they seemed random, and then they seemed like poetry. Hurricane Harold was beginning to turn at the horizon, a rotation of meaning at the line separating the black water and black air. Suddenly, some force rocketed a capful of salt water into atomized gas and ejected it at high speed.

Katherine woke when Joe sneezed—she looked at the clock and it was a little past 3:30 —and then Joe said twelve words:

Thick purple smoke, glops of cotton candy, stuck to the bare trees.

Katherine remembered the words and wrote them down the next morning on a scrap of paper, inserting the punctuation herself. When she joined Joe in the kitchen for their coffee, she asked him if he remembered what he'd said, sure that he must have been talking in his sleep and would not remember.

"Course I remember, but what the hell does it mean—purple smoke and cotton candy stuck to trees?"

"You're the one who said it, Joe, not me."

Their calm silence settled in as they sucked their scalding coffee through short invisible straws, turning it into a cooler but less satisfying aerosol. For Katherine, the kitchen silence wasn't quite as calm as usual. The red monster was bigger now and taking a tiny tentacled shape.

They were halfway through their French toast, now drinking their cooled coffee directly, when Joe asked, drumming his fingers on the flecked Formica tabletop, "Why did I say it? And don't give me that 'I don't know, you're the one who said it' crap."

"I don't know. Seems like whatever's making you sneeze is making these words come out."

"Hatchooo," Joe replied, his inaugural sneeze for that morning. They both waited for more words, but none came. So they finished their French toast and had another cup of coffee. Joe read the sports and Katherine the rest of the paper, after starting, as she always did, with the obituaries. The rising sun, visible through the kitchen window, painted the cloudy piebald sky into a globe of jellybeans. "Well, the shot Doc gave me yesterday sure helped calm down these sneezes."

"Sure did. I was really worried you would never be able to get to sleep. *Yes*, and that *I* wouldn't either. Let's get over to the store right now and pick up the pills. Frankie said they would be ready first thing."

Joe cleared then washed the breakfast dishes, as he did ever since he changed to his day job, and Katherine went to get dressed. Joe always showered then dressed as soon as his feet hit the floor. Katherine said it was a Navy habit, but Joe had been like that for as long as he could remember. He wanted to want to luxuriate in a robe and comfy slippers like Katherine sometimes did on the weekends, but he just never wanted to.

While the clean dishes dripped on the yellow plastic drainer, Joe said to himself, as he often did after finishing the dishes, *We've got to see about one of those automatic dishwashing machines like Paul and Mary have.* He let Soot out the backdoor and followed him out to survey the need to rake any stragglers. A few had fallen in last night's winds, but not enough to bother with. The promised snow didn't come.

He watched the lightening jellybean sky melt into wide horizontal bands of orange and blue. The rising sun and shrinking shadows played like kids on an almost frozen teeter totter. About forty minutes after sunrise the light bounced along the Collins gutters in a way that made it look as though the sun was melting right on top of the buildings. It spread along the rooflines, but mysteriously never dripped down the sides.

"Hatchoo." Soot looked up to see if Joe was OK.

Soot was Joe's favorite dog. He and Katherine had many dogs during their marriage, almost always two at a time. But Soot was one of a kind. He was a black Labrador retriever, one of three black ones in a litter of seven, but the only black one to get the tawny greenish eyes of his yellow siblings. This gave him a strange look that Katherine called "dirty headlights in a tunnel." Their vet said he'd never seen these eyes, which he called "dead grass," on a black lab.

They almost took one of his yellow sisters, too, but at the last minute decided it might be good for a change to concentrate on just one dog. They had to put down both of Soot's immediate predecessors on the same sad day—two German Shepherds—one for old age and the younger one because of cancer. They'd gone dogless for six months, the longest period in their marriage.

All these things conspired to help make Soot special, though he was quite special enough on his own. He was the smartest dog either of them ever owned, or heard of. Joe didn't have dogs growing up, but Katherine had them continuously. She often regaled Joe with tales of Dutch—one of her childhood dogs she claimed was the smartest cattle dog in the universe.

"Did he know the difference between a baseball and a whiffle ball, like Lassie?" Joe often exaggerated Lassie's accomplishments when gently pushing back against Dutch's professed ones. But even Katherine had to admit Soot outshined them all.

He house-trained in a matter of hours, duly sitting by the back door until let out. After a few days, he learned to bark at the back door if neither Joe nor Katherine noticed him sitting there. Joe had to correct him just once from doing his business in the garden. After that it was not only on the grass but in a narrow strip of grass on the north side of the house. Soot's only chronic misbehavior was digging those tunnels near the fence line, a habit that slowed as he aged but never disappeared completely.

By the time he was one year old Soot knew more than 100 words. These included unorthodox commands like "spin" and "relax," as well as triggering words like "store," "work," and "movies." Perhaps most impressively, Soot knew the first names of their closest friends. Joe or Katherine could say, "Go see Paul," and Soot would get up from wherever he was and lie down next to Paul, even if the house was crowded with many other visitors. For the few years that Joe's mother Pat was still alive, Soot had some trouble distinguishing "Pat" from "cat," causing a couple dangerous kerfuffles. He also had a sophisticated musical palette. He preferred show tunes and classical to any other kind of music.

Soot knew right away they were going to pick up the pills from Frankie. Well, he at least knew they were going to be gone for a while because he heard "go" and "store," a sometimes-confusing signal that used to mean Joe would be gone for a long time, when Joe used to work at the store, or that Joe or Katherine would be gone for a short time to buy groceries. Yes, Soot had a primitive sense of the passage of time, unlike most dogs. Katherine was sure of it, Joe less sure. Occasionally, they let Soot join them on short trips to run errands, so after hearing "go" and "store" Soot waited, like a loaded gun, to hear his name instead of "stay."

"Let's go, Soot," Katherine said, opening the back door, and Soot shot outside to the door to the garage and waited there. When they opened that door Soot jumped through and waited by the driver's side door of the Chevy Bel Air. Joe opened the passenger door for Katherine, she got in, and he walked around to the driver's door. When he opened it, Soot jumped in and sat momentarily right behind the steering wheel, but relocated to the back as soon as Joe made movements to sit down. They were never exactly sure how this pattern developed. They tried once to teach Soot to go through the rear passenger doors but he refused. Katherine's theory was that in a prior life Soot's master owned a coupe.

The three of them drove to pick up Joe's prescription from Frankie Hurtado. Frankie was the hardest working high schooler the Greeley store ever hired. He started as a bagger, then joined Joe stocking at night, then moved to checking, all while he was finishing high school. "I'm going to college to study pharmacy," Frankie would regularly announce to anyone listening. And he did, even though it was a long journey, interrupted by a pregnant girlfriend, dying parents, too much drinking, and a few minor brushes with the law. By the time Frankie graduated with his pharmacy degree he was 31.

After graduation he found a part-time pharmacist job at an all-night drug store in North Las Vegas, Nevada, not far from the only pharmacy program that had accepted his application—the one at tiny Roseman University in Henderson, Nevada. He moved back to Greeley the instant Davey Millikin, his secret sponsor, phoned him to tell him that old man Gertner was retiring, before they even offered him the job. But they did offer it, and Frankie's long dream to succeed Gertner came true one cold morning in late October, when he unlocked the pharmacy door, pulled up the rolled and clanking metal screen, and filled his first prescription at the Greeley King Soopers Store No. 51. He'll never forget that first prescription. It was for an anti-inflammatory, for old man Gertner's gout! What were the chances? He was worried all morning about what exactly he would say to his grouchy predecessor, but Mrs. Gertner picked up the prescription instead, and was nice as could be.

His name tag proudly announced he was "Frank Hurtado, Pharmacist." He preferred Frank, especially since "Frankie" was now taken by his own Frankie, Jr. But he let the nickname slide for old friends like Joe and Katherine. "These are pretty strong, Joe. They should do the trick, but can really dry you out. You have a humidifier at home?"

"No. But I'll grab one of those little mini ones. Are they still on aisle seven?"

"I think so."

The pills really did the trick. Joe sneezed only once the rest of the day. But that night, through the low hum of the new humidifier, another sneeze and more words:

Three foul spirits like frogs.

"That really sounds familiar," Katherine said the next morning.

"Well not to me, and what's making me say this stupid stuff?" Katherine was sure she'd come across this phrase about the frog spirits before, maybe in some magazine article, though she couldn't imagine in what kind of magazine.

She was at church that afternoon, helping to put up the exterior Christmas lights, when she told Hilda Backstrom about Joe's strange night poems. That was a mistake. Hilda was a notorious gossip. Behind her back people called her "Times-Call," after a now defunct daily newspaper. Anything you said to Times-Call you said to everyone, especially if you told her it was in absolute confidence.

Sure enough, after Sunday's mass, as Joe and Katherine walked quickly behind the receiving line as usual, Father Stokely hooked them before they could escape to their car. "Very nice homily, Father," just about everyone said after just about every Sunday mass. Today's homily, titled "The Military/Industrial Complex of Your Soul," was not one of Charles Stokely's best, and he knew it. But he and his audience trundled through it. Joe and Katherine never waited in the receiving line. Joe was too shy. He preferred the way old Father Carbone did the mass, everyone flying to their cars the instant it was over. And Katherine never needed to see Father Stokely in the receiving line because in an average week she'd have already talked to him a dozen times about various church matters.

As Joe and Katherine tried to slide past, behind the Backstroms and Andersons, Father Stokely reached around Times-Call and tapped Joe gently on the shoulder, asking whether Joe and Katherine had a moment to talk in his office. Times-Call could not suppress a knowing glance, first to Father Stokely then to Katherine.

Joe thought about how priests and policeman must get used to having people do what they say, but with priests the gentler the request the more irresistible. Father Stokely's almost imperceptible touch on Joe's shoulder, his kind eyes, his barely audible entreaty, might as well have been the thunderous command of God. Or the screams of a policeman pointing his gun and directing a suspect to get on the ground.

"What does he want?" asked Joe. He was mildly perturbed, but mostly afraid of having to talk. He went to church on Sundays but was too shy to join in any of the other endless church activities that Katherine so loved, mainly because those activities involved talking.

"Well, yesterday I told Hilda Backstrom about your last, um, 'dream' is what I called it, about the frog spirits."

"Dammit, Kath, why did you do that? And God, why Times-Call? You knew she'd tell everyone. That's how Stokely found out."

"Sorry, Joe. It seemed familiar to me, and I thought Hilda might recognize it because she reads a lot. But she didn't. I'm sure Father is just being kind and just wants to ask us if there's anything he can do to help."

"Goddammit."

They wandered back through the nave, layers of Chanel No. 5 and Old Spice from the departed congregation still floating in the air, hanging on top of the smoky incense from the snuffed candles, the wax, and the stuffy cold of the old wood and stone. Joe had never been in Stokely's office, didn't even know where it was. Katherine led the way down the scuffed and dingy hall leading off the east transept.

The office had a pine door with an overdone reddish orange finish that suggested someone had mixed up the pine and redwood stains. A small dark metal sign with white lettering, slightly askew, hung by a piece of white string on two visible finishing nails: "Fr. Charles J. Stokely." A small anteroom outside the office—just a bulge in the hallway, really—contained a tiny worn-out sofa, a metal folding chair from the community room downstairs, and a small wobbly wooden table covered with dog-eared copies of the St. Thomas Quarterly Gazette. Joe and Katherine squeezed into the sofa, then Katherine thumbed through the Gazettes.

The nave and east transept formed a giant hearing trumpet, sending the sounds from the church entrance directly to the office, clear as a radio broadcast. Joe and Katherine could hear the noise from the receiving line dwindle to a few coughs and low whispered conversations. Joe was sure they were all talking about him and his crazy, sneezy night poems, all presided over by Times-Call. He could only imagine the condemning heads, shaking with a toxic mix of pity and scorn.

"Is everything OK health-wise, Joe?" Father Stokely asked even before he managed to get his athletic and perennially tanned frame around to the back of his wooden desk. "Is there anything we can do?" Then he took his vestments off and draped them over the back of his chair. He remained standing.

"Joe's sneezing a lot. Doc Kasten says it's probably just allergies. We're seeing someone in Denver this week." The priest's head nodded understandingly but his powerful, deep-set eyes, magnified by perfectly round horned rim glasses that made him look like Harold Lloyd doing a skit as a priest, told Katherine he was not satisfied with Joe's answer.

"Strangest thing, Father, the sneezing sometimes makes Joe talk in his sleep." The priest's slightly nodded head signaled to Katherine that she was now on the right track, but that he wanted more. "Last night he said, 'Three foul spirits like frogs'."

Father Stokely's face immediately screwed up, electrified into contraction by a small voltage of distant memories. Joe and Katherine both realized from this reaction that Times-Call must not have mentioned the actual phrase, no doubt too excited about Joe's impending madness. Father Stokely grabbed the Bible off his desk—the Revised Standard Version ("RSV"), Catholic Edition—and flipped through it for what seemed to Joe to be hours but was less than a minute. Then he stopped and poked the page as his face relaxed and brightened.

"Aha. I thought that sounded familiar. It's from Revelation. 'And I saw three unclean spirits like frogs come out of the mouth of the dragon, and out of the mouth of the beast, and out of the mouth of the false prophet.' Revelation 16:13. But this says 'unclean,' did you say unclean?"

"No, not unclean. Foul," Katherine responded.

Then another jolt and screwed up face and the priest was crouching and rummaging through his overstuffed bookcase. Books and magazines were lying flat in haphazard stacks in front of the books that were standing up properly, though none of the visibly standing books was remotely flush with any other. He grabbed a thick black soft cover booklet off the top of a teetering stack in front of the bottom shelf, tumbling the remnants over onto the worn wooden floor like playing cards. He stood up, flipped through the booklet, found what he was looking for with another "Aha," and then quickly squeezed it closed, as if the unclean spirits might escape.

"Some of these new protestant editions of the Bible use the word 'foul' instead of 'unclean.' This is the New Testament part of what they will be calling The New King James Bible," he held out the booklet between thumb and forefinger on a fully extended arm, as if it were a plate of food gone bad. "A Methodist acquaintance gave it to me for my birthday." He dropped it on his desk, thudding and burping up a few loose papers. "So you're not going—you're not imagining things, Joe, it's right from the Bible. You must've heard it in one of my homilies, and then it came out in your sleep."

Father Stokely sat, and proceeded to give a rushed, rather apologetic lecture about the meaning of the phrase, it's place in Revelation, what the whole verse meant, and what Revelation, the very last book of the New Testament, meant. Joe didn't pay much attention because he was still trying to figure out why these strange words flew out of his un-strange mouth.

". . . and so you see John is warning us about the Devil's omnipresence; he's everywhere."

Joe was almost positive he'd never heard Father Stokely ever say anything about dirty frogs, and he was even more sure that he would never in a million years have been paying enough attention for it to register, even accidentally, had Stokely ever uttered it.

But Katherine seemed relieved. On their way out to the car she said, "He used it in a homily, and it somehow got stuck in your brain, even though God knows you don't pay attention to Father Stokely's homilies. When you sneezed you dislodged it, like how sometimes phlegm comes out with a cough."

Joe remained skeptical, but was relieved that Katherine seemed relieved. Katherine was not as relieved as she let on. Why would the Reverend Father Charles Stokely, Pastor of the Most Catholic Saint Thomas Church, proud quoter of the Catholic Edition of the RSV, use a new-fangled protestant turn of phrase in one of his homilies?

CHAPTER 8
FIRE

Bug-out. Last night's home opener against the Sioux City Sioux was called in the fourth inning when a black cloud of cicadas descended onto Municipal Field. The grounds crew was eventually able to dislodge the buzzing ball of bugs with torches, and it was last seen heading west toward the elementary school. But it left behind piles and piles of dead and dying insects, so many that play could not resume. The game will be made up Sunday at 1:00 p.m. as part of a double header. In sad news, popular slugger Tommy Reedy was called up to triple-A Syracuse, quite a surprise so early in the season. The hard-hitting outfielder will be missed.

Thick purple smoke, glops of cotton candy, stuck to the bare trees. Three foul spirits like frogs flew from behind the burning house as soon as the distant sirens screamed.

Jack was on duty that night, shotgun on No. 1. It was cold, a little snow scattered on the hard ground. When he leaned around the last turn, a difficult habit to break from his younger days as a deckie, he saw an insect-thin man squatting on the curb in front of the burning house, head in hands, bony knees up to his shoulders. The shadows from the fire danced around the man like Kachina dolls, a dozen shifting shapes, now weeping men sitting, now laughing demons standing.

Jack jumped out of No. 1 before it came to a complete stop, ran to the man, and gently took his arm. He needed to move him across the street, where it was safer and where he wouldn't be in the way of Jack's crews and the others coming. He also needed to check him for smoke inhalation.

The man looked up at Jack without at all pulling back his arm. He had a long oval head. His face, patched with soot, was flat, except for a prominent ski-jump nose. His open mouth was almost toothless; Joe thought he saw one lower canine. The man had almost no hair, and what he did have was thin and singed. His big ears stuck way out. He had the eyes of a lost animal. They reminded Jack of the dying rabbit he'd once found in a trap, unable to reach his own leg to chew it off.

The man wailed a terrible primitive sound, and kept wailing over and over as he crossed the street with Jack, arm in arm. It had a definite timbre and rhythm. Jack had the impression the man was a deaf mute, the sounds not so much wails as pleas to be understood.

"Are you OK?" Jack asked loudly with exaggerated movements of his mouth, as he guided the man to the opposite curb. The oval shook exaggeratingly up and down, five or six times, as if to dislodge a wasp off the top. Then he grimaced and made a different sound, pointing to the burning house across the street.

"Maaaaaaa. Maaaaaaa."

"Is your mother in there?" The head shook frantically up and down, another five or six times. "Anyone else?"

"No," the head shook repeatedly, again in exaggeration, fully turning each time, chin almost touching shoulders.

"Where is your mom? In the back?" No, no, no, no no, the head shook even more violently. "Up front here?" Yes yes yes yes yes. "Left as you go in?" Jack guessed, given the configuration of the small house. Yes yes yes yes yes. "Stay here, I'll be right back."

Jack ran to his assistant crew chief, who was supervising the hoses, which had already begun the job of wetting down the roof and sides of the small bungalow so the fire would not spread to neighboring houses. The controlled movements of his team—uncoiling and placing the boa-like hoses, hooking them up to the hydrants, guiding the streams onto and into the house—all happened in seconds. It was an unworldly marriage of urgency and detail that always caught Jack's admiring attention, even though he'd seen it, and been part of it, a hundred times.

"We have a woman in there. Where's number two?" Without waiting for an answer, Jack yelled, "Mattie, there's a woman in there. Follow me in." To the men at the nozzles he said, "Keep that water coming, but only from the sides, through the two windows. Leave the roof alone while we're in there."

Mattie got to the front door first, axed it in, and then stood aside waiting for the flames he knew would strike out from the influx of new oxygen. Satiated, the flames pulled back with an audible suck. Mattie and Jack quickly surveyed what they could see of the small room, which was not much because of the thick smoke.

"She's somewhere on the left. I'll go hard left and you go a little straighter," Jack shouted and pointed as they both dove to the floor and started groping for furniture.

One thing most civilians don't know about big fires is their roar. The sound is deafening, as air explodes into flame. In those days, most fireman didn't have radio communications, so Joe and Mattie talked by shouting and pointing. Joe found what felt like an end table, and crawled on until he got to what he was sure was a couch. Kneeling, he reached up onto the surface of the couch, and found the body. She was light as a child.

The gawking choir of a crowd, gathered on the sloped lawns across the street, told Jack that none of them knew the mother's first or last name, that she seldom left the house, and that when she did it was to walk to the nearby grocery store at such a hurried pace she was almost running. Later, when the skinny boy was old enough, he would "walk" to the store in the same manner. Like they were holding their breath. Older members of the choir told Jack that mother and son had lived there as long as they could remember. They said they'd heard the mother call the son Harold, though someone thought she said Darold.

Bundled against the January cold, the rubberneckers said that almost every night, winter or summer, the old woman burned newspapers in the fireplace, which produced short columns of thick smoke. The Indian signals of the interrupted columns suggested pauses between the gathering up of more fuel, and the light purple smoke and flaky ash suggested paper, not wood. They assumed the pair scavenged for newspapers, and were burning them for heat, though the appearance of the lavender smoke in the summer was puzzling.

The few people who saw the smoke that night, against the modest light cast by the haze-covered toenail moon, thought nothing of it at first, until it was too late. Two of them told Jack they'd seen three boys running from the area shortly after the light from the flames caught their attention, but neither got a good enough look to be able to identify them.

Jack learned from the insect-man himself that his name was Harold, not Darold, that he was around 35 years old but wasn't sure exactly, that he had never gone to school, and that his dead mother had been his only other relative. In fact, she was the only other person he knew. He did not know his last name.

It was very hard for Jack to understand him. He sounded like some deaf people Jack had heard, a sing-songy imprecision to his words, all tone and no form. When Harold saw Jack was having trouble understanding him, he would slow down and try to exaggerate the differences between the sounds, which helped. After checking him for smoke inhalation, Jack walked him over to a second ambulance and helped him in. He told him he'd meet him at the hospital as soon as he was finished at the fire.

The house was not a total loss, but it had considerable smoke damage, especially in two back bedrooms. The roof and exterior walls were intact. Jack assumed Harold would clean it up, rebuild the interior, and move back in. But in the meantime, he would need a place to stay. Even just for tonight. There were two storage rooms in the firehouse, each half-full, and Mick and Tony agreed to empty one of them while Jack went to the hospital. Teddy found extra blankets and a pillow. Jack said this poor guy didn't even have any friends or relatives, or clothes, so Teddy asked everyone if they had any extra PJs.

No one did, but Teddy called his wife and she brought down an extra pair of his, and a bunch of his other clothes.

Harold was in the hospital waiting room, postured pretty much as Jack had seen him on the curb, though this time in a chair. Jack noticed his clothes for the first time. They were old man clothes. For a short fat old man, not a tall skinny young one. Loose fitting greenish-tan trousers cinched around his tiny waist with a plain black cloth belt. Cuffs six inches above his ankles, at least as he was sitting, and tan dress socks not nearly long enough to cover the gap, even had they been pulled up and not bunched lifeless at his ankles. Translucent skin showing between pants and socks. Big black shoes. His short-sleeve shirt was some kind of seersucker, a dull cider orange striped on cream, far too summery for the season, split in the front by a dangling skinny black tie. He wore no jacket. His arms were so thin that the seersucker sleeves folded back on themselves like tent flaps.

When he saw Jack he jumped up, ran awkwardly to him, and embraced him. "I'm so sorry, Harold," Jack said as he patted the taller man on the back. Harold began to emit a quiet sound, a cross between sobbing and humming. They stood there holding one another for a long time, wordless. When the sounds stopped, Jack said, still embracing him, "Come with me tonight to the firehouse. We're making up a room for you." Yes yes, Harold shook his long oval head up and down slowly. Jack pushed him away to look him in the eyes. The dying rabbit was still there.

"Do you need help making arrangements for your mother?" No no. Harold was still shaking his head no when Jack indicated with an extended arm that it was time to go. Harold followed Jack out to the car. Jack pulled a windbreaker out of the trunk and Harold put it on. Its sleeves were much too short. The men didn't say much in the car. Harold didn't know what to say, even if Jack could understand him. Jack wanted to tell him everything would be OK, but he didn't want to lie.

CHAPTER 9
SPARKY

Finally. Our local boys finally got to show off in front of the home crowd yesterday, after the scheduled home opener was called for cicadas in the fourth inning. The team split the double header with the visiting Sioux, taking its record to 3-4. It heads out on the road tomorrow for its annual three-game non-league series against the Kearney Yankees, then returns home to host visitors from Grand Island and Cedar Rapids, for two games each. The outfield spot vacated by Tommy Reedy, called up last week to triple-A Syracuse, was filled today by Lee Williams, a 19-year-old slugger who hails from East St. Louis, Illinois. Williams hit a whopping .296 in single-A Tulsa last year, and was hitting .315 there before his call-up. Manager Wally Berens announced Williams will start in center field tomorrow night in Kearney. Welcome aboard, Lee!

Harold stayed at the firehouse for 14 months. Jack and his crew, with one exception—Barry—welcomed him, at first like a crippled little brother, though by the end of his stay he was their wise uncle.

He walked slowly and haltingly, hands flailing unpredictably at his sides, flipper-like, as if he were wading in piranhas. Strangely, his oval head, presiding over the anarchy below, hardly moved at all.

They soon learned he wasn't a deaf mute, but that he had "trouble being born" as he first put it, which made talking difficult. He had become quite good at exaggeratingly forming his words, which made communication possible though tedious. He also had a remarkably large vocabulary, frequently stumping everyone at the station, and which only raised the communication barrier.

He never learned to write very well. Jack and Mattie tried to teach him, but his lack of motor control just didn't allow it. He could read, but at the "Run, cat, run" level. The crew brought him books their own kids had outgrown. As soon as he sounded out the first couple words of a book, he'd sometimes just close his eyes, stop turning the pages, and begin to recite the book from memory. When Jack asked him how he knew these books, Harold said his Ma read them to him.

So, to teach him to read, they had to find books he didn't already know. That wasn't easy. But once they screened the books with him, and used only ones he didn't know, his reading improved dramatically and quickly. By the time he left he was reading The Hardy Boys adventures, books he did not know before.

He'd occasionally ask to keep a book he knew. He would keep it closed, fondle it, shut his eyes, and read it from memory, sometimes out loud. He was thinking of his mother.

Harold bonded immediately with the firehouse dog, Sparky, a mutt who looked part miniature Doberman and part dolphin. The dog's face, lanky body, and bobbed tail all said Doberman, but his smooth bluish short hair said he could swim with the best of them. And he could.

Once a few years ago Sparky managed to sneak up onto the gripped step of No. 1 during a call, and somehow stayed put during all the turns. The call was a possible drowning at the reservoir. Sparky jumped off the truck as soon as he saw the woman's floating body, swam swiftly to her, and began dragging her back. The firemen saw him dive in and they headed straight for her. That saved them precious time trying to locate her, though it wasn't enough to save her. From then on, Sparky always rode along on drowning calls, in the cab on the lap of whoever was sitting shotgun. He hadn't saved anyone yet, but it was only a matter of time.

He clicked and whistled. The whistles were a kind of high-pitched screech that varied in pitch. Sparky made the clicks by opening and closing his mouth, like lip-smacking. The whistles seemed to be expressions of joy, the clicks something more complicated.

He refused to do any tricks, or respond to a single command. Jack was sure the communication failures were on the human side, and that Sparky spent most of his time being astonished at just how stupid people were. No one knew whose dog he was, who named him, or how old he was. They all assumed he belonged to an old station chief who moved to a downtown captaincy, but no one was entirely sure.

Sparky padded into the converted storage room, jumped up on the rickety bed Mattie had found, and curled up next to Harold. He slept there the next 14 months. That first night Harold caressed Sparky for what seemed like hours.

Harold's mind raced before sleep finally rescued him. How did he even get outside? She must have dragged him, then gone back in for some of the books. He wasn't dressed for bed, so the fire must have started shortly after dinner, while they were reading. Now he was trying to save her. The heat and smoke were impenetrable, mocking his seriousness. *You didn't love her enough.*

Harold could never get his mother's attention while her back was turned. She could hear him only if they were facing each other. He knew the truth of this, like gravity, for as long as he could remember. When she thought he was old enough to understand, she explained that her ears did not work, but that she could see the words coming from his mouth.

Ma told him that for the longest time, when he was just a baby, she wasn't sure whether he could hear. She'd make loud grunting sounds when he was asleep. She'd scream out of the blue while she was holding him. Sometimes he'd respond, sometimes not.

Then one Sunday morning she took him to a local cathedral and sat with him on the front steps. He turned toward the door, frowning and wriggling, when the big organ growled its deepest notes, but she wasn't sure if it was the sound or just the vibrations the music caused in their innards. So she cracked open the heavy studded door, catching a glimpse of the children's choir, and stood there holding him. The baby turned his head when the choir started to sing. She knew then that he could hear. He could hear it all. She laughed and cried when the organ began again, her stomach rumbling and the baby wriggling and frowning anew.

When he was a teenager and thought back to that story Ma told him of the hearing test at the church, Harold became sad and a little angry that a force could vibrate intestines at a distance but not his mother's ear drums. It was only when he read a section on sound in a physics book that he learned that the same waves that rumbled Ma's stomach must also have vibrated her ear drums. She just must not have any ear drums, or they are broken. He imagined a big bass drum with an ugly gash in its yellowed white skin.

Ma discovered her son's remarkable memory long after she discovered he could hear, and accidentally. She read books to him from the moment she bore him, and actually a few months before, until the day she died. They were reading Maugham's The Moon and Sixpence tonight, before the fire.

She managed to acquire a few children's books when Harold was very young, and like every parent she discovered that Harold knew whenever she tried to skip any parts of a book or story. But most of her books were not children's books. They were the Western Canon, the great novels, history, philosophy, poetry, science, and economics, with a smattering of art and architecture. There were thousands of books. At the beginning they filled two rooms. Harold's mother had carefully designed their storage. She left access warrens winding in and out of the rooms, wide enough just for her, if she stood sideways. Harold never knew where the books came from. When he was old enough to ask, his mother just said, "From God."

He never forgot that cold February sunset when she started to burn them. He never forgot the words she said.

"Dear, dear Harold," she began, cupping his face in her hands like she did whenever there was something very important she wanted to tell him. "We are in for a treat tonight. You feel how cold it is in the house? God has made it cold to give us a test. We won't have any electricity for a while, and electricity runs the furnace."

"That's why it's getting dark in here! That's why we burned wood last night so you could see the books and keep warm!"

"That's right. Our furnace won't work for a while and we are out of firewood and newspapers. What could we burn in the fireplace tonight to get warm and see?" Harold shook his head against Ma's cold pressing hands, mouth open, jaw slacked, worried. "What has God given us in abundance, two whole rooms of them?"

"Books!" Harold answered, grinning wide. "We can burn the books!" But then he frowned. "But please, Ma, not the new ones. Not the ones we haven't read."

"Of course not, I'll grab some of the ones we've already read. Just a row or two for tonight, just to get us warm."

"I can get them, Ma, I know what we've read!" He turned and ran to the library, returning in two trips with a dozen books he placed in the empty wood bin. His mother wasn't sure whether she really had read each of these to him, but what mattered was that he thought she had.

With tears rolling down her face, which Harold couldn't see because she was turned toward the fireplace, she started ripping pages out of the books, crinkling them up, and putting them between the andirons. Harold mimicked her, grabbed a book, pulled the pages out, crushed them into balls, and threw them in.

"OK, that's enough dear," she said as she grabbed some matches and set the fire. They both got as close as they could to the warming flames. "Keep putting balls of pages in, a few at a time, and I'll go get us a pan of milk to put on the fire so we can have some hot chocolate."

When she returned and placed the metal rack from their outside barbeque onto the andirons, then the pan of milk on the rack, Harold saw she was crying.

"What's wrong, Ma?"

"I just feel a little sad that we are burning these books and I will never get to read them to you again."

"But we've already read them."

"It might be nice someday for us to read some again, like Call of the Wild here," she said holding up the empty cover.

"But we've read that already."

"Someday I might like to read it again."

"I can read it to you, Ma." He closed his eyes and began,

Buck did not read the newspapers, or he would have known that trouble was brewing, not alone for himself, but for every tide-water dog, strong of muscle, and with warm long hair, from Puget Sound to San Diego. Because men, groping in the arctic darkness, had found a yellow metal, and because . . .

His mother interrupted, grabbed his arm. "You remember it, word for word?"

"All the books we've read, Ma. So, if you ever want to hear an old book after we burn it, just tell me and I can read it to you!" Harold said beaming. Now he was the reader. It was a big step. He was growing up. His mother hugged him, and kept saying "Thank God" over and over as the flames warmed the milk for the hot chocolate.

When it got cold, or Ma wanted to cook something bigger than on the hot plate, they burned some books. Even after the weather warmed up. "It's not a bad idea to start cleaning those library rooms out, Harold, now that you're my library," he remembered her saying once. They also started getting into the year-round habit of burning pages from new books right after Ma finished reading a chapter to Harold.

She had been trying to teach him how to read for years, but he was terribly slow and never really got any better. She assumed the problem was her own way of speaking, which, though Harold quickly learned to understand, must not have matched up with the phonetics of the words on the page. But now she thought it might have been Harold's own astonishing memory that was the real obstacle.

The spoken words became part of him when he first heard them; he didn't need to learn a cumbersome secondary path. It was as if God had made one complete person between the two of them: she could see words but not hear them, he could hear them but not see them. And then, as a kind of apology, God made him never forget the words he heard.

In addition to the books, Ma made sure there was always music in the house, though she needed Harold's help to confirm the radio was on and working, and to tune it. They would both sing along in preposterous harmony, Ma trying to mimic the shape of Harold's mouth as he formed the sounds. He had a pretty good voice, but she sounded like a frog.

When he was 12 or 13, he began singing what he later called "soetry." He had an impressive knack of making up stories and music together. He kept these to himself, until one day when he was 15 he decided to share one with her. She could see the words, and he used his arms to imitate the pitch of the music. She cried. After that he'd sing soetry to her almost every day. And now he'd never sing to her again.

Right before dropping off, he became conscious again of Sparky, now emitting a quiet clicking sound. He realized Sparky was now soothing him, that the comforted had become the comforter. He smiled that such a wonderful thing could happen in a world where it seemed not everything was so wonderful.

"Joe, do you think this dog Sparky is based on Soot?"

"I don't know."

"Have you ever had a miniature Doberman?"

"No."

"Did you know anyone with one?"

"No."

"And you really never knew any deaf people?"

"Nope."

"Then how are you able to describe some of these scenes about Harold's mother's deafness with such feeling?"

"I dunno." Katherine could hear some exasperation in this "dunno." Joe was getting tired of answering questions that should be directed to the mysterious author who had taken possession of his nighttime mind.

CHAPTER 10
LESTER

Yankees routed. Newcomer Lee Williams blasted a two-run homer last night to clinch the non-league road series against the Kearney Yankees. The team returns home tomorrow for a four-game homestand, beginning with a two-game series against the Grand Island Athletics. It will be "Hawaiian Night." Hardy fans dressed in shorts and a Hawaiian shirt will be admitted free. Temperatures at game time are expected to start at 47 degrees but then dip down into the 30s. Bring those thermoses!

Lester Buckley was Joe's best friend. Their parents moved into the same block in Greeley before either boy was born, two tiny cookie cutter houses between them.

There were only three styles in the turn-of-the-century "subdivision," if you can call two short blocks of 900-square-foot houses, originally built for workers at the feedlots east of town, a subdivision.

The "Cape Cod" had its front door in the center, two large rectangular windows on each side, a gently gabled roof, and two slapped-on dormers. Its perfect facial symmetry was broken only by the fake chimney stuck to one side. "The Georgian" was identical to the Cape Cod, but instead of dormers it had six sets of paired two-by-fours that formed sad little columns around a small covered concrete front porch. "The Mediterranean" had an arched door several feet off center, a large arched window next to it, two smaller arched windows opposite, and a flat roof.

The three styles were rigidly dispersed in a fixed order. The southernmost block started with the Cape Cod, on both the 20th and 21st avenue sides, back-to-back, then the Mediterranean, then the Georgian. So every fourth house was the same style. But—and here was just one of the many examples of the builder's marketing genius—after each run of the three styles the houses in the next run were mirror images of those in the last. That meant that one had to look seven houses down—into the next block!—before one house was truly identical to another, giving the two blocks a pleasing custom look. It also meant that Lester's and Joe's Mediterranean houses were mirrors of each other.

This gave both boys a built-in welcoming familiarity whenever they visited one another, although it could be a jarring welcome. Over the years they injured themselves more times than they could remember running around an interior corner expecting a hallway but finding a door or wall. They also regularly reached with the wrong hand to open doors, and into the wrong side of rooms to turn on lights.

Their mothers were pregnant with them at the same time, and they were born a little more than a month apart. Lester was tall to Joe's short, blond to Joe's swarthy, sociable to Joe's shy, and musically gifted to Joe's tone-deafness. Lester had perfect pitch.

Joe spent countless hours at Lester's house striking different combinations of keys on Lester's piano, sometimes using elbows, chin and feet, trying to trip Lester up. He never could.

"Two As, a B flat, two Cs, a C sharp, two Ds, two Es flat, and one G," Lester announced during one of Joe's earliest and most contorted perfect pitch challenges.

"Right again. But why do you say 'two Es flat' instead of 'two E flats'?"

"For the same reason one says mothers-in-law and not mother-in-laws."

"But we do say mother-in-laws."

"Well, you shouldn't."

Joe thought for a moment and added, "And we also say RBIs, not RsBI."

"What's that stand for?"

"Runs batted in. It's a baseball thing."

"Well, you said it yourself: it's runs batted in, not run batted ins. So it should be RsBI, not RBIs."

"Another thing. Why do you always say the notes in alphabetical order?"

"That's kind of the way I see them. Alphabetically, and starting at A not C, where you might think a pianist like me might start."

"You see them?"

"Sort of."

The boys had many discussions over the years about Lester seeing sounds. Joe found these fascinating, but for Lester they were frustrating. It was hard to explain how the musical notes he heard came with built-in information others did not detect. Calling it "seeing" wasn't exactly right, but it was more than ordinary hearing.

"OK," Lester once tried to explain when they were at an amusement park, right after reading off as from a score all the notes of the calliope playing in the background, "how would you tell a blind man what it meant to see colors?"

"I dunno."

"Well, you could say that seeing colors was a little like smelling or tasting them, or hearing music with them."

"No it's not."

"No, not exactly. But isn't that better than saying, 'I dunno. I just see colors?'"

"I suppose so. Red does remind me of strawberries. Let's go, we can ride on the Cyclone once more before we have to leave."

Lester was also a math genius. When they were in high school, he invented some math thing, something about logic and algebra and little squares, that got his teacher so excited she dubbed the thing "Buckley

Squares," and wrote to the American Mathematical Society to see if she could get Lester published. They wrote back, explaining that this method of converting logic into algebra had actually been invented by an English mathematician named George Boole in 1847.

Lester's teacher angrily accused him of plagiarism and of embarrassing her in front of the American Mathematical Society. Joe believed Lester's claim that he'd never heard of George Boole. After all, Lester didn't read any more than Joe did. He was too busy practicing the piano. Besides, the Greeley Public Library wasn't much bigger than the school's, and he doubted there was anything about this guy George Boole in all the libraries in Colorado. Furthermore, Joe had never known Lester to tell a lie. Not once.

Lester's mom and dad were not mathematical like Lester was. In fact, no one Joe had ever met was mathematical like Lester was. Sometimes it seemed like an infection. Once when they were in junior high school, Joe was trying to adjust Lester's new telescope to get a glimpse of the legendarily statuesque Miriam Nardone while she was changing for cheerleading practice, but instead of focusing on the sensual pleasures at hand Lester began to talk about geometry.

"If a person were X feet tall, and if the Earth were perfectly spherical, with no mountains or buildings interrupting the horizon, and the person had infinitely telescopic vision, how far could the person see before the Earth's curvature blocked his view?" Lester was staring down 20th Avenue instead of across at Miriam's bedroom window.

"I think she's changing! There goes something. It might have been a top. I'm sure it was a top!"

"It's a simple geometry problem. The challenge is converting all the wildly scaled units without losing accuracy in rounding."

"Oh my God, I think that was a bra."

"After all, the radius of the Earth is in many thousands of miles, let's just call it R. But a man's height, let's call it h, is in mere feet. Of course, the h we care about is not exactly the height of our man with telescopic vision, but the distance from the ground to the center of his telescopic eyes. And that will make a big difference. His maximum sight line is obviously that part of the hypotenuse of the . . . ."

"Nothin'. I see nothin' now," Joe reported despondently.

". . . which of course is given by multiplying the arctangent of the sum of . . ."

They were probably the closest childhood friends Greeley had ever seen, but the math was always a divider between them, tissue paper thin but there. The music, however, was glue.

Joe's family was not musical at all. No one played an instrument, and the only musical notes ever heard inside the Skeltons' Mediterranean home was if Joe's dad had the ball game on and the metallic sounds of the commercial jingles came jangling out of the radio. Joe could still hear in his head Singin' Sam's Barbasol jingle: "Barbasol, Barbasol, no brush no lather no rub-in, just wet your razor then begin."

But the Buckley house was always full of music, real music. Lester's mom Margaret had been an opera singer in Germany before the war, and if she wasn't singing arias while doing housework their fancy hi-fi was filling the house, and the adjacent houses, with classical music of all kinds. The neighbors didn't seem to mind. Mrs. Holby, in the Georgian to the north, was deaf. And the Seeleys, in the Cape Cod to the south, were childless artists—he a writer and she a painter—who claimed they were inspired by the music.

Even Lester's dad Carl, who played no musical instrument, regularly whistled, hummed, or sang to himself. Usually John Phillip Sousa. He was retired Army, and spent most of his time building model wooden sailing ships in the basement. On the rare occasions the house went silent, he'd find himself whistling Sousa marches without even realizing he'd started. If he was downstairs building his models, he became conscious he was whistling or humming only after realizing that his movements—picking up a tiny part with tweezers, dipping its edge in glue, placing it onto the ship—had fallen into the cadence of the march. If he was outside mowing the lawn or shoveling snow, he'd notice when his walking became marching, and his turnings about-faces.

When Lester played the piano, it sounded to Joe like God was singing. He didn't even know Lester could play the piano until that day in third grade when, walking home from school in a heavy February snowstorm, they saw a big blue truck in front of Lester's house.

"That must be the piano!" Lester uncharacteristically yelped as he started to run full speed toward his house, well, as full speed as Lester could run, pigeon-toed and arms flailing, kicking up the snow.

"What piano?" Joe yelled as he trotted to catch up.

"Mine," Lester said, out of breath.

It was a Steinway. The biggest they made, a Hamburg Concert Grand. The movers had to take it apart to fit it through the Buckleys' arched front door. It filled the living room. Mr. and Mrs. Buckley had to move all the living room furniture downstairs, replaced only by a small ottoman that Mrs. Buckley bought and pushed up against the far wall, "For your home concerts," she explained, smiling at Lester.

The living room was now out of bounds for any kind of running. The back of the piano almost touched the back and one of the side walls near their junction. And the keyboard's left side, the side away from the sounding board's dogleg, stuck out into the foyer. To get even halfway around the piano, which was a far as you could go, required turning sideways, like the sailors in submarine movies.

The room looked like a dollhouse into which some mean big brother had jammed furniture from a bigger toy. Looking through the large arched and mullioned living room window from the outside, all one could see was the black of the piano, the close-up of a giant spider waiting in a perfectly perpendicular white web.

Joe had no idea when Lester learned to play the piano. As soon as the movers put it back together and put it in place, Lester jumped onto the squat square leather seat, reached down and grabbed a knob to adjust it a little, and began to play.

"Don't just *play*, dear," his mother scolded in her faint German accent as she was paying the movers, "you need to *practice*. And no *poundink*. Coax them."

Pounding notwithstanding, Joe could not believe what he was hearing. He'd never heard anything like it, and never imagined there could be anything like it. And so much was going on! One hand doing different things than the other, and yet it all was one thing, Lester rocking slightly, eyes often closed. And it triggered *feelings* in Joe, an explosion detonated by remote control. Joe found it difficult to talk about this, even with Lester. When he tried to talk about it with Jill MacNeil, his first ever girlfriend, in fourth grade, it seemed, well, like he was talking about colors to the blind.

Joe realized years later that on that white February afternoon he had fallen in love with Lester's music. Love was the only way to explain the obsession, the endless hours Joe spent listening to Lester practice, the racing pulse in anticipation, the worry that Lester might be practicing without him, the physical pain when the music was gone.

"What was that first thing, before your mom interrupted?" Joe asked when Lester paused during that first practice session.

"A Chopin nocturne. E Major, opus 62, number 2."

"When did you learn to play the piano? I've never seen you playing, and we've known each other since we were babies."

"I'm not sure. I have always played. Whenever I could find a piano. At the music store, at Oma's. And when I couldn't find a real piano, then in my head. Now I have my own piano!" and he began something else.

"No poundink," came the command from the kitchen, and Lester lightened his touch.

Joe once asked Lester what his favorite piece was. Lester thought for a moment and then said, "Probably this," and he played a frilly little thing that couldn't have lasted more than two minutes.

"12 Little Preludes No. 6, by Johann Sebastian Bach."

"That's your favorite? It didn't sound so special to me."

"Listen again." Lester played it over and over, and Joe started to get a glimpse. By the tenth playing, notes that before had sounded trite and repetitive now sounded full, like they were hiding something. There was a shocking newness and a comfortable inevitability living side by side in this music. How could anyone have thought these notes up? And how could anyone not have thought them up? They were perfect.

CHAPTER 11
SCHOOL

Luau Laughs. Frigid fans enjoyed Hawaiian Night at Municipal Field last night, where our local boys edged the Grand Island Athletics 9-7 to split their series. More than 200 spectators braved the cold for free admission by wearing shorts and Hawaiian shirts. More sensible fans brought the total attendance to around 1,000. First baseman Clevon Sumpter blasted a two-run homer in the sixth inning, his third of the year, and starter Buzzy Bernardi notched his first win of the young season. Veteran reliever Sam Fresne got his first save. The team stands at 4-5, just two games behind first place Garden City. Next up: The Cedar Rapids Raiders tonight at 7:00 p.m.

The hurricane was spinning strands of clouds into the threads of a small fountain. But it was still far away and mostly over the horizon, only the tip visible, a distant wet mast.

Lester practiced three hours every day, bumping up to four hours when he turned thirteen. He practiced once every morning, and again in the afternoon. After school, the two of them would walk to Lester's house, have a snack, and Lester would practice. For Joe's benefit, Lester would always start by trying to play something all the way through, announcing the composer and the title at the beginning. But Lester's mother would invariably yell from somewhere in the house, "Playing is not practice," and Lester would have to return to the routine. Scales for warm-up, then a few difficult passages he'd been working on, over and over and over.

Even this monotonous playing hypnotized Joe. He'd alternate between standing behind Lester so he could watch his hands, and lolling on the floor, sometimes putting his shoeless feet up on the ottoman ("Yosef, you are welcome to put your feet up, but take the shoes off"), squirming around not from boredom but from wonder.

Lester's fingers were arched and strong, rippling with muscles and tendons Joe didn't remember seeing when he was trying to teach Lester to throw a ball, for cryin' out loud. How someone could have those fingers and hands, rushing across the keyboard with maniacal command, and never be able to learn how to throw, or catch, or bat, or dribble a basketball, or even just run, remained to Joe wholly unfathomable, and wholly accepted.

But not accepted by Mr. Weisen, their junior high gym teacher. When the Greeley schools got big enough to have more than one class in each grade, Lester and Joe got split up, Lester going with an advanced fourth grade and Joe with the regulars. They were never in the same class again, except for gym, where both classes were combined, both in elementary school and later.

Their elementary school gym teacher, Mr. Brosnan, was kind, but even the boys would admit he was rather ineffective. His directions were always in the forms of questions. "Why don't you all line up behind the backstop?" "Why don't we time you now in the 40-yard dash.?" Joe waited for years for some smartass to answer these rhetorical questions, but to his fellow-students' credit none ever did.

When they moved to junior high gym, the boys were in for a shock not unlike, and seemingly specifically designed to resemble, Marine boot camp. Mr. Weisen never gave commands in the forms of questions. He coached the basketball team, and was an assistant coach on the football team, and he made it clear to everyone on the first day of junior high gym class that he was willing to teach their miserable butts only because that was the price he had to pay to be able to coach the kids who actually knew their butts from a hole in the ground. "Butts" was Mr. Weisen's favorite semi-cuss word.

On that first day of class, drill instructor Weisen set up a card table at the front of the gym. He handed each boy a piece of paper and told them to memorize the number on it. It was their roll-call number. Numbers were stenciled along the baselines and sidelines of the gym's basketball court, and their roll-call number determined where along the outside of the court each boy would line up at the beginning of class. As his square angry jaw fired out each boy's name, the boy was to run to the card table ("Run, don't walk, you lazy butt") and Weisen, standing up, would hand the paper to the boy, then lean over, other hand on the shaky table and face just inches away from the boy's face, before letting go of the paper and screaming, with each and every boy, "Don't forget that number, butt-face." Lester wondered why Mr. Weisen didn't lose his voice after just a few minutes of these festivities.

The numbers corresponded to the boys' alphabetized last names. Poor Chris Adams. He couldn't understand why Weisen was yelling and frothing at him. After all, he was on the basketball team. When Weisen screamed "Buckley, Lester," and Lester ran up in his fashion, arms and legs thrashing all over, Weisen stared but said nothing, though everyone was waiting for it. When he handed Lester his paper and screamed "Don't forget that number, butt-face," spraying a bit onto Lester's face, Lester said, "Of course I won't forget it. Eight. A perfect cube," and girly- ran back into the crowd. Weisen was speechless.

Lester became a secret hero to the boys in fourth period gym. Weisen teased him, though to be fair he didn't tease him any more than he teased everyone else. But Lester never wilted like everyone else, mostly because he never understood the teasing. He always took Weisen literally because Lester always assumed the best of everyone.

The boys' private admiration for Lester burst abruptly into public during a gym class right after Christmas break. Weisen blew his whistle, as usual, to signal roll call. The boys scrambled to their numbers as usual, a crowd of young commuters rushing to different trains. Weisen noticed, as he paced slowly down the line, scowling at each inspected boy, that Lester had mistakenly put his right foot on his number 8, rather than the required left foot. It was because Randy Brady was home sick that day, and there was more room than usual on Lester's left side with Randy's 7 vacant.

"*Left* foot, Buckley, Jesus Christ," Weisen screamed, "Don't you know your right from your left?" Joe, so far away down at number 56, tensed helplessly.

"I do," responded Lester, and he started to explain, "it was just that Randy . . ."

Weisen interrupted, "What hand do you wipe your butt with, Buckley?"

"My right hand, Mr. Weisen."

"Jesus, Buckley, most of us use toilet paper." Joe looked around for the anticipated laughs, at least from the athletes, but Lester's response stopped them before the first guffaw could hit the air.

"I thought you meant what hand I used when I was wiping. You should have been clearer."

The jocks stayed silent, but there was a rippling of laughter from everyone else.

"Shut up!" Weisen screamed to the giggling group. "Twenty laps to the next person who makes a sound."

"But how long do you intend this order of silence to last?" Lester inquired. "Will you let us know when it's over? I mean, what if you asked one of us a question in the next few minutes? Which command would apply, the command to answer or the command of silence?"

The only sound in the gym was a collective swishing sound, like 60 tire pumps having their handles pulled up, as every student inhaled.

Lester was not trying to be a smart aleck. He was genuinely concerned about the logical implications of Weisen's order of silence. In what sounded like a whisper, but was probably just his ordinary, never-before-heard voice, Weisen ordered Lester to do the 20 laps. Lester didn't mind running them. He preferred running to the impossible physical demands of the class, and the way he ran it took him the entire class period to finish.

Everything changed on that day for Mr. Weisen's place in the firmament of Ulysses S. Grant Junior High School. It was like those dissonant moments in the summer when we see a teacher suddenly inserted into the real world outside of school—Miss Phelps the math teacher selling shoes!—but inverted by some mad scientist. The adult world had come into the school, in the unlikely and gangly form of Lester Buckley, age 11. He was the grown-up, and Weisen just a frustrated teenager.

It wasn't until many years later, when they met real drill sergeants, that Joe and most of the other boys from that seventh-grade gym class changed their views about Weisen. Like the real drill sergeants, Weisen was a talented mover of boys, who taught them invisible lessons about brotherhood and sacrifice.

This "whip wipe" incident, as they called it—by which they meant Lester whipped Weisen's butt over Weisen's butt-wipe comments—became legendary at Grant Junior High. Students would speak of it for decades. But Lester didn't give it another thought.

As they were walking home, Joe told him, "That was amazing, the way you talked to Wise-Ass. Everybody's talking about it."

"What?"

"In gym today."

"Oh, that. I forgot about the left foot business, with Randy not being there, and I was just trying to explain."

"No, you stood up to him."

"I guess. He's not so bad, really. I have a new piece for you I learned over the weekend, by Bruckner. I want to see what you think."

* * *

When Joe was in high school only a few of his classmates even thought about college, mostly rich kids and star athletes. Joe's father, Stan, unenthusiastically asked him one night at dinner whether he planned to go to college like Lester, who was the only boy they knew who was headed there. Lester got a full scholarship to the Curtis Institute of Music, in Philadelphia.

Joe knew his own parents didn't have the money to send him to college and they knew he knew, so everyone pirouetted, and all the dancing around had the effect of shrinking the whole discussion like a lasso. It was as if they were asking whether Joe was planning to go the movies this weekend.

It reminded him of the time his father had the facts of life talk with him by asking a single question, with no follow-up: "Do you have a girlfriend?" ("No, but I plan to," was Joe's brilliant response, unintentionally ending the discussion to his father's complete satisfaction.) The Skeltons were not a talkative family, which suited Joe just fine. It was probably harder on his sister Sue, but he knew that Sue and Mom regularly snuck off to do girl things, which Joe presumed included talking.

"Pat, could you give me another slice of meatloaf, please?" Joe's dad asked his wife before getting an answer to the college question, passing his plate to Joe to pass to Pat.

"No, I think I'll get a job at that new supermarket over on 9th," Joe said. He said this at the very moment his father handed him his plate, so it sounded like Joe was declining his father's request for more meatloaf. His father scowled for an instant, then lightened up when the plate passed on to his wife, and he realized not only that was he going to get a second piece of meatloaf but also that Joe was not going to be bankrupting the family by expecting them to pay for college. "They've had a big sign out all week advertising for jobs," Joe continued. "And the pay's good. Or maybe the Navy."

His father, a butcher, was triply pleased with the mention of the new supermarket. He thought these "so-called supermarkets," as he always put it, were a "flash in the pan," as he also always put it. But he approved of Joe working in one as a temporary detour on his way back to the family butcher shop, where Joe had worked every summer since he was 10. *They would have more time to train him at the supermarket*, thought Stan. The minor leagues, as it were, before the big call up. But when Joe said the word "Navy" the speedy scowl returned to Stan's broad face from wherever it had gone, twice as dark.

The Navy? The wounds of the Great War were still fresh for people of Stan's and Pat's age, and military life now felt at once utterly unnecessary and unacceptably dangerous. *You want to volunteer to get killed by Huns?*, Joe could see his father's face asking. Joe's father had survived the Second Battle of the Somme.

"You know, we're not at war anymore," Joe responded to the unspoken objection, "and the pay's even better than at the new market. And I'll get to see the world."

"But you never liked to swim, or even get your face wet," his mother pleaded, her eyes beginning to tear up.

That was the entire extent of the "What are You Going to Do with the Rest of Your Life" discussion Joe had with his parents. He didn't join the Navy, at least right away. He went to work at the new Busy Bee Supermarket the day after graduation, starting as a stocker at night.

Lester went off to Philadelphia right before Labor Day. A few days before, he telephoned Joe and invited him over for what Lester called a Farewell Concert. Joe missed Lester's playing, which he hadn't heard all summer. Lester was busy getting ready for the move to Philadelphia, and was playing a bunch of small evening concerts his mother had arranged, which Joe had to miss because he was on the night crew at the Busy Bee.

It was like old times. Joe took his shoes off, settled down on the floor and put his feet up on the ottoman. As usual, neither Mr. nor Mrs. Buckley ever appeared or made their presence known, other than Mrs. Buckley by voice, with just two "Poundink!" scolds. Lester played for 45 minutes, and Mrs. Buckley never once scolded him for playing an entire piece through. A Mozart prelude, a Beethoven sonata, and a Liszt consolation.

When Lester finished the Liszt, hands dramatically above the keyboard, he turned to Joe with a big smile. Joe's eyes were watering so much that he couldn't hide it despite his best efforts. Lester couldn't remember ever seeing Joe cry.

"What's going on?" Lester asked, shaking his hands out and cracking his fingers, his smiled vanished.

"I dunno. That last one was really sad, and I started tearing up and I couldn't stop."

"Thanks!" beamed Lester, "that's what it's supposed to do. It's Liszt's Consolation No. 4. It's like a sad prayer, isn't it?"

"Why don't you ever cry when you're playing?" Joe asked, wiping his face with the sleeves of his Busy Bee work shirt.

"I sometimes do when I first play something. But then I have to concentrate on making *you* cry."

The boys grabbed shoulders in that way young men do, more intimate than either would have liked and not nearly as intimate as the circumstances warranted. That shoulder grab was their true goodbye.

On Sunday, Joe and his whole family went to the Buckleys' for a Farewell Dinner, as Mrs. Buckley put it to Mrs. Skelton when she telephoned the invitation. Dinner was fine, despite the tension Joe could feel rising like steam from the legendary pool of Skelton silence. There was also the stiffness between Joe's father and Lester's mother. Stan couldn't help thinking of the Somme whenever he heard Margaret's accent. He knew he shouldn't, but he did. And she knew he did.

"This pork loin is delicious, Margaret," Stan tried to break the double tension in one fell swoop. Coming from the town's untalkative meat expert, this was a compliment indeed.

"Well, Stan, I bought it from our best butcher."

"I thought you bought it from Stan," Carl joked the required joke.

After dinner, Lester played a Brahms sonata that Joe had heard him working on in the spring. Everyone listened from the kitchen, sitting around the table, which was a new experience for Joe. He got to see the pride on Mr. Buckley's face and the closed-eyes concentration on Mrs. Buckley's. Joe and Mrs. Buckley were both relieved when Lester negotiated a rough spot that had consistently given him trouble. No "playing is not practicing" or "no poundinks." This was a performance for outsiders, which made Joe feel all the more an insider.

The goodbyes that followed seemed artificial and awkward. Like those times you bump into someone downtown, exchange pleasantries, say goodbye, and then discover you are both continuing in the same direction. But Joe and Lester were not headed in the same direction.

CHAPTER 12
DR. GOLDSCRATCH

Rebel Plaque. Robert "Big Bob" Cooper announced today that this year's recipient of the team's annual "Rebel Plaque" will be newcomer Lee Williams. The Rebel Plaque is awarded each year to the most valuable player in the team's non-league three-game series against the Kearney Yankees. Williams knocked in five RBIs in the Yankees series last week. Though the Yankees are no longer members of the Midwest League, the teams still play one three-game series every year to honor their old rivalry, dating back to the days when our team dropped its Yankee affiliation and it was picked up by Kearney. The plaque will be presented to Lee Williams at Tuesday night's home game against Cedar Rapids.

Joe's allergy appointment was at a medical office attached to Denver's General Rose Hospital. The hospital was named after General Maurice Rose, a Denver native and the highest-ranking Jewish officer in the United States Army during World War II. He was beloved for always leading his men rather than following them. On March 30, 1945, he led them right into being surrounded by a German Panzer division.

As the General was reaching for his sidearm, either to surrender or fight, no one seemed sure, a young German tank commander squeezed off a burst. Several rounds hit the General, one passing right through helmet and head. The helmet is on display in a plexiglass cube in the hospital's entrance area, complete with two general's stars and two bullet holes, one in one out.

The killing was big news back home, not just in Denver, and plenty of well-connected folks were demanding a congressional investigation. Then the war was over, and the investigatory fever quickly broke. But several local Jewish leaders had long been campaigning to build a hospital, and General Rose's famous death was just what they needed to reignite the campaign. Hollywood took notice, and with the help of a bevy of celebrities, including Jack Benny and Walter Winchell, the money was raised and the hospital built. Dwight Eisenhower dedicated its opening.

Because of its famous Jewish roots, Joe and Katherine, like many Gentiles, weren't quite sure they were allowed to be there. But Doc Kasten gave them this doctor's name and this doctor was at this hospital. They also assumed, like many people, that all the doctors, and maybe even the nurses, would be Jewish. They didn't know much about Jews. There weren't that many in Greeley. In fact, they only knew one Jewish family, the Millikins.

Assuming his Rose allergist would be Jewish, Joe dubbed him "Dr. Goldscratch" in advance. Joe always liked names that matched occupations. He himself had Mr. Fish for swimming in high school, and he knew that Katherine had Mr. Chord for band. When names didn't match, Joe made them match.

Driving back home, Joe and Katherine discussed the surprisingly Gentile allergist. "I liked Dr. Goldscratch a lot. He seemed to know what he was doing," Joe ventured.

"Yes," agreed Katherine, "but his name was Dr. Wilson. He didn't seem too worried about you-know-what." Katherine had settled on this undescriptive phrase, and noticed that the mere re-naming shrunk the monster a bit.

A nurse who also didn't look Jewish took a vial of blood from Joe's arm, and then Dr. Wilson asked Joe a million questions about whether he knew he was allergic to anything, how often he sneezed, when it started, what the trash can was made of, what was in the trash can before he started to saw it up, what other things he had sawed with that saw, and what he was wearing when he started sneezing. Joe didn't mention the night poems, but Katherine did.

Then Dr. Wilson gave Joe a head to toe physical, followed by a weird series of scratching and scrapings on Joe's back. Once they reconvened in his small office, Dr. Wilson said he would call Dr. Kasten with a summary of his findings in the next day or two, and follow up with a written report. He also mentioned that the injection that Dr. Kasten had given Joe, and the pills he prescribed, were just what he would have done had Joe come to see him first.

Katherine tried for a preview. "So, what's he allergic to?

"I really need to look at the blood results before I can say for sure."

"Why would an allergy cause him to talk at night?"

"I really can't say. I've not heard of that before, but if he has confirmed allergies then Dr. Kasten and I will look into all the possibilities. Allergies can be really strange in that they can affect different people very differently, and even change dramatically over time with the same person."

That last part sounded canned to Katherine, but she decided to declare a truce, and looked over at Joe to see if he concurred. Joe wasn't listening because his attention had been seized by a large poster mounted on the wall behind the doctor. It had a dark tall leering figure, with greenish skin, dressed in a black trench coat, wearing impenetrably dark glasses, and labeled "Mold." It was reaching out with long thin dark green fingers, capped with dirty nails, toward the alabaster arm of a young well-endowed blond woman labeled "Lungs." "DON'T LET MOLD ATTACK YOUR LUNGS!" read the urgent red diagonal caption.

"Could mold from the old trash can be making me talk these words?"

Dr. Wilson and Katherine exchanged exasperated glances, and Katherine said, "Joe, the doctor *just said* that if he discovers you have allergies then he and Doc Kasten will try to figure out the talking part."

"Oh, sorry."

"It's OK, Mr. Skelton, no need to apologize. I can imagine how disconcerting all this must be for you. Dr. Kasten and I will put our heads together and try to get to the bottom of this."

On the drive back home, they talked about Christmas. Paul Taavalaa, their brother-in-law, would be having his usual Not Christmas Dinner, where he'd invite a few of his Samoan relatives, the Millikins, Doc Kasten, and anyone else he could find who was alone on Christmas. The Millikins came every year, and in fact they were Paul's inspiration for calling it Not Christmas Dinner.

Everyone in town adored Davey Millikin, the tailor who always looked like he just woke up, had a rushed breakfast, and spilled half of it on his clothes, but whose tailoring could make other people look like movie stars. Davey was generous beyond his modest means. He'd tailor on credit whenever someone really needed tailoring, like for a job interview. Often, bills were never sent. He altered Maria Hurtado's wedding dress for free. Paul used to joke with a big laugh, "Davey Millikin would give you the shirt off his back, but first he'd tailor it to fit like a dream."

Unbeknownst to his wife Barb, Davey once lent Frankie Hurtado the then-astounding sum of $1,000 to help get him through pharmacy school. No one else knew about the loan because Davey swore Frankie to silence, and Frankie complied. When he graduated and was back in Greeley working at the No. 51 pharmacy, Frankie started putting $5 of every paycheck into a mason jar on which he penciled "The Davey Fund" and which he hid in his freezer.

Every six months, Frankie brought the frozen bills to Davey, who, without fail, said, "Now *dat's* cold cash," proud he could pun in his adopted tongue. Davey pretended to accept the bills, and sometimes even put them in his wallet, pretending to shiver, but he actually deposited them into a bank account called "The Frankie, Jr. Fund." This was several years before Frankie Jr. was even a gleam in Frankie's eyes.

It took Frankie over six years to pay off the loan, along with self-imposed interest, even though Davey protested about the interest as strongly as his broken English and secret savings account would allow. When Davey died, Barb discovered the Frankie Jr. Fund, which had grown to over $5,000. When she brought the check to Frankie, they both wept. Frankie, Jr. never went to college, but thanks to Davey Millikin he could have.

Davey was tall and thick, but not overweight. He was built like a tight end, a tight end with sickly white, pockmarked skin. His posture was so perfect he looked like he was tied to a board. Those who were used to him being rigidly vertical were often shocked when he actually bent down during fittings to mark hems or cuffs, expecting to hear the board snap. His dark brown hair didn't have a hint of gray. But it was always in a state of explosive electrocution, tufts pointed in all directions and no directions, which only put an exaggerating cap on his verticality.

Davey always wore long sleeves to cover up the death camp numbers tattooed on the inside of his lower left forearm. The numbers had stretched large and indistinct as Davey grew from the skeletal 14-year-old boy on whom they had been placed to the grown man who could not forget, but who lived as though he had somehow forgiven. Originally, they were an inky "2 1 0 1 3" but today they were a pale blue that looked a little like the word "cloudy" in cursive.

"Let's go over to Paul's and Mary's this Christmas," Katherine suggested. "We haven't been there for a few years."

"Why does he always invite us? We're not Jewish, or alone."

"Because if it weren't for Paul, we would be alone. Besides, he thinks we are lonely."

"But we're not."

"No," Katherine smiled, "but we are family."

Joe never sneezed again after the appointment with the allergist, except for colds or if something got up his nose. But the words kept coming, though Joe no longer remembered saying them.

The morning after their visit to Dr. Wilson, Katherine said, "Well, that was an interesting poem."

"I said words last night?"

"You sure did."

"But I don't remember saying any, and I haven't been sneezing."

"I don't know, Joe, maybe you said the words in your sleep but the sneezes woke you up and you remembered. Now, with no sneezes you don't wake up, so you don't remember. But you're still talking."

"What did I say?"

Katherine pulled out a Big Chief tablet, explaining, "I was getting worried I'd lose those first scraps of paper, so I transferred them to this."

Doc Kasten phoned the next day. "The allergist says you're not allergic to anything he can find." Joe was ostensibly on the receiving end of the call, but Kasten knew Joe would be sharing the receiver with Katherine. He could hear telltale noises of the phone being angled toward different ears, the speaker end rubbing across chins and cheeks. "So, here's the name of the neurologist I'd like you to see in Denver. Try to get in as soon as you can." Katherine wrote down the name and number, but said nothing.

"Are you still sneezing?"

"Not a lick."

"Good."

"Since the sneezing has stopped, why do I have to see another doctor in Denver?"

"Just to be on the safe side, Joe, and to make Katherine feel better." Katherine stuck out her tongue at Joe, and he smiled. She could not get an appointment with the neurologist until the next week.

That night's Report concentrated on astronomy. It was clear, the moon not yet up, and bright stars sprinkled the late November sky. Greeley was still a very small town, and there was little "light pollution," as people would later call it. You could clearly see the Milky Way's swirly splash.

"Beautiful star-filled night," Katherine began. "Look at all those constellations."

"I can never make out any of them. Even the dippers just look like dots to me."

Katherine disagreed. "The dippers really look like dippers to me, especially the big one. But I'm not sure I could even find it now. When I was a young girl, the Little Bear looked as real as a cartoon. It's part of the Little Dipper, isn't it?"

"Not sure. Not even sure where the Little Dipper is."

Katherine arched her back and rotated her head to the left, scanning the skies for the north star. "You take the two stars from far edge of the big dipper's cup and follow them up to the edge of the handle of the Little Dipper. But I don't see it. Maybe it's set already. Or isn't up yet. I wish I knew more about astronomy."

The night was completely still, and unseasonably warm. They'd catch a whiff of the garden's loamy scent now and then, but it wasn't carried by any wind. It was bubbling out of the ground in fizzing fermentation. Odd to be able to smell that this time of year.

It was also completely quiet. Katherine noticed that windless nights often made it harder, not easier, to hear the noises of the outside hiding things. Maybe prey and predator creeped more softly when they heard no other noise was covering their movements. All Katherine could hear was the low buzz of the streetlight in front of the Tanners', three houses away, Soot breathing, and the blood pumping in her ears.

Katherine never knew how many words there would be. Some nights they lasted as long as an hour, her right hand aching. Other nights, if words came at all, they might be just be a phrase or two, though there was a definite trend that the nightly words were increasing. The hurricane was a small spout now, still tearing at the line between air and water. Here she comes. For the next eight months, virtually every morning, Joe and Katherine would read the last night's words together, over coffee and breakfast, instead of the newspaper. She filled many Big Chiefs.

It didn't take long for them to see that these were not isolated poems, but seemed to make up some kind of story. A few more weeks and it got to be fairly rip-roaring, one that they both looked forward to reading every morning. "Our breakfast serial," Katherine joked, though she had to explain the pun to Joe because she made the mistake of telling it right when she handed him a bowl of Wheaties.

Whenever Katherine walked into the kitchen without the Big Chiefs, Joe could see her disappointment, and blamed himself. The rare days without a morning installment seemed dull and a little sad. "Maybe if I try to get a cold to start sneezing," Joe once suggested. "Or pepper. Black pepper. Right before bed."

Katherine laughed. "The sneezes don't shake the words out anymore, Joe, they come out on their own. God knows why." But she worried that she knew why.

They had several discussions about the impact this new routine was having on Katherine's sleep. Joe felt terrible that he was keeping her up. Without the benefit of the sneeze to wake her, Katherine had to stay up until the words started. That could be anywhere between minutes after Joe fell asleep to hours. On the weekends Katherine started to sleep in an extra hour or even two. Talking in his sleep didn't seem to make Joe tired at all.

The two of them were in the world's smallest and strangest book club. The author himself was one member, but he heard the book for the first time from the only other member, his transcriptionist. Katherine marveled at how quickly the story filled their lives. They now spent not just the mornings but also a big part of every evening Report, sometimes all of it, talking about last night's developments and what might happen next. For Katherine, it was a great relief to talk about what was happening to the characters in the story, instead of what might be happening to Joe.

CHAPTER 13
THE FIREHOUSE

Raiders Rousted. Hopeful fans donning brooms last night were not disappointed, as the team edged the Cedar Rapids Raiders 3-2 to sweep the two-game series. They won 6-2 on Wednesday. Before tonight's game, the home crowd was treated to the presentation of this year's Rebel Plaque by Owner Robert "Big Bob" Cooper. This year's RP goes to newcomer Lee Williams, who really showed his stuff as a Yankee killer, going five for nine and knocking in five RBIs in the non-league series against Kearney last week. The team is now 6-5 for the season, tied for first place in the Midwest League with Garden City. They head out for a short road trip to Cedar Rapids and Iowa City today, but will be back May 1 for Fools Night. More about that soon.

Ma's burned house was about to be owned by the bank. She'd been in arrears on the mortgage for months. The bank had foreclosed before the fire, but hadn't yet gotten the sheriff to serve the papers.

Two weeks after the fire, he served them on Harold at the firehouse. Harold could tell the sheriff felt terrible, and tried to ease his pain, though it was hard, still aching from Ma's death. Despite it all, they struck up a nice conversation, and the sheriff kept mentioning that he'd be happy to accompany Harold to the house so he could retrieve anything of sentimental value. There was nothing much left. Harold took a few things, some tennis balls and a bat, and a few smoke-damaged books. Once the foreclosure went through, all the insurance proceeds went to the bank. It sold the property to a developer, who tore the house down and put up a two-story townhome. There's a plaque there now, on a small pole set between the two parallel driveways: "Site of Harold Fungo's childhood home."

Harold insisted on helping out around the firehouse. He took care of Sparky, feeding him, walking him, petting him. He ran to the nearby grocery store whenever they needed something. He didn't know how to cook, but he volunteered to do their laundry. He begged them, but Jack insisted they'd stick to the usual rotation. Only after much loud protesting did Jack partially relent, by agreeing that he would add Harold to the regular laundry rota. When Harold discovered the firemen had one of those automatic washing machines—and a drying machine too!—and didn't do the wash in a tub like Ma did, hanging it out one a line in the backyard to dry, he wondered what all the fuss was about.

What Harold did for most of his working time at the firehouse was sweep, with a big red push broom. The handle was red, the block was red, even the bristles were red. He swept the whole firehouse, both the living areas above and the working areas below. He loved the waltz of sweeping, the regular advancing pushes—one, two, three—then the backsteps and sidesteps followed by yet another set of three pushes. He'd get so wrapped up he'd occasionally run the broom into the end wall right in the middle of a one-two-three, or side-step his elbow into a side wall. All the while his skinny black tie—which he always wore except while sleeping—swung in counterpoint.

In their leisure time, which wasn't as much as you might think, with all the daily chores required to run a firehouse quite apart from the infrequent firefighting itself, they played lots of cards and ping-pong. A predecessor had invented a game which combined the two activities, which he called Poker Pong, but it never caught on. It was not only too complicated to explain, it was even too complicated to learn by watching. Jack was reminded of cricket, which he unsuccessfully tried to understand when he was stationed in England in the service.

Harold never asked to join in the cards or ping-pong, and no one invited him. He didn't want to interfere; he still felt incredibly guilty about living there. Everyone else, including Jack but excluding Barry, was worried about hurting Harold's feelings by asking him to join in something he would be unable to do.

After a while Jack taught Harold to play simple children's card games. War, Go Fish, Crazy 8. He experimented one day with a small 10-card version of a game they called Concentration, where the cards are randomly spread face down and players turn over two cards, one at a time, trying to match them. If they match, the player keeps the cards and gets another turn. If they don't match, the player turns back the cards face down and it's the other player's turn. So players have to build up a memory of where all the unmatched cards are. The winner is the one with most matched cards.

Harold was so good at Concentration that Jack was soon using the whole deck, and Harold was soon unbeatable. He had a photographic memory of where the cards were. This irritated Barry to no end, who already begrudged Harold for being able to live at the firehouse for nothing.

"He's a deadbeat," Jack overheard Barry complaining one day.

"No, we're the deadbeats," Jack interjected, coming up from behind Barry. "Think about it. We get paid for sitting around here all day. Harold doesn't get a dime."

"But we have to pay for living somewhere else." Barry, a sour young man going through a sour divorce, could not be reasoned with. So, when he lost two games of Concentration to Harold, back-to-back, he blew. "Does the chief know we're letting a retard live here? Isn't that against regulations?"

"Retard? You mean you?" jibed Teddy, one of the oldest crew members. Jack knew the chief didn't know about Harold, and that yes, it was against regulations to have him live there. He also knew from that instant on that he better start thinking about finding a place for Harold.

That night's Report was devoted entirely to the Tales of Harold. "I know you don't like me asking questions about how you could possibly be writing this story. I'm sorry."

"Sometimes it comes out like you think I'm too stupid to be writing this."

"I don't mean that at all, Joe. I just think of it as a psychological mystery. There must be clues in your subconscious life that tie into what's happening in the story."

"I suppose so."

"But if it really bothers you, I will stop."

"No, I guess it's OK."

"Did you ever know any firemen growing up?"

"No. A great uncle on my mother's side was a policeman, but he died before I was born." She could see Joe was scouring his memory, then he asked, "You think they'll kick Harold outta the firehouse?"

"It sure seems like it. Jack is already worried Barry is going to turn them in. They call that 'foreshadowing' in literature."

"Does it always come true?"

"That's a great question, Joe. I'm not sure. It seems like it usually does."

"Ain't this the craziest thing? I'm writing this damn story but don't know how it's gonna end." While Joe wondered whether Harold would be able find a place if they made him leave the firehouse, Katherine wondered whether it would be just her eyes looking out at the fireflies next summer. Joe looked over at Mary's big house and mused that there was plenty of room there for Harold. Heck, they have rooms they don't even use.

Harold could play ping-pong, in a fashion. No one would have guessed it, with his movement issues. Mick was the one who discovered it. He was up late one night, heard noises down in the rec room, and went to investigate. Harold was hitting a ping-pong ball up against one wall and returning it, on the fly. He returned it every time, without a single miss, his almost toothless mouth slack-jawed in concentration. His skinny black tie swayed in syncopation with his spasmodic movements. He was remarkably light on his feet, considering they were housed in five-pound black rubber-soled shoes, the kind orderlies wear in mental hospitals.

They tried to teach him to play, but he could never get the knack of hitting the ball down onto the table. He reflexively just hit it back to whoever hit it to him, often hitting that player's paddle, or face, as if the ball were on a long rubber band. So, he played wall pong by himself.

The firehouse was Harold's family now, but it was a strange rotating family. Each fireman was there for three 24-hour days, then he'd be off for three days. Jack worried about Harold on his off days. He hated to leave Harold, especially if Barry was on duty. Because he was in charge of the duty rotation, Jack was eventually able to arrange for Barry not to be on duty if Jack wasn't, which eased his mind.

Jack invited Harold to his home on holidays, several times. The first was Easter dinner, despite his wife Dee's misgivings. "What will we talk about? What do we tell Sammy? For heaven's sake, Jack, why do we have to be the ones?"

But Harold was a big hit with Dee, and with eight-year-old Sammy. In the beginning, Sammy kept saying, "I can't understand him, Mommy, why does he talk like that? Where are the rest of his teeth?" But they just ignored him, and by the time the small spiral ham was down to just a few whirls Sammy was mesmerized, not by how Harold talked but by what he said. Children often learned to understand Harold sooner than adults, and Sammy spent much of the rest of the evening interpreting for his mother and father.

Harold told Sammy a bunch of children's stories, but Jack and Dee didn't recognize any of them. They took Harold eons to tell. But what he lacked in efficiency he more than made up for in emotion. When Harold told a scary part he got scared himself, and so did Sammy. When he told a sad part both got sad. And when the dark tension was released by the hero, Harold and Sammy were both jubilant.

Harold's emotions showed mostly in his eyes, since his almost toothless mouth was usually closed. But in those glorious happy moments of storytelling rescue and reunion his mouth curved ear to ear—his atomic smile—which always made Sammy giggle.

Harold began picking Sammy up from school on days Jack was on duty, and walking him back to the firehouse, ostensibly so Dee could run errands. But the real reason was that Sammy wouldn't stop talking about Harold and his stories, and wanted to be around him more than the occasional holiday or special visits so far. It was Harold's idea, and Jack and Dee immediately accepted.

Sammy's school was just a few blocks from the firehouse. Harold and Sparky left the firehouse at 2:33, arrived at the school at 2:41, and the school bell releasing the children rang at 2:45. When the three of them actually left for the firehouse depended on the vagaries of an eight-year-old's free path from inside school through playground to outside fence. Harold knew all of these times because of a brand-new watch the fellows gave him for his birthday. He never had a watch before. It had a big black band and a round white face, with large blue numbers. With Jack's help he had already learned to tell time from the station's big outside clock. He wound the watch every night, at 10:15.

Harold didn't really know when his birthday was, but agreed with Teddy's suggestion that they should share a birthday, April 29. Harold wept when he opened the small gift, wrapped beautifully by Dee, and took out the watch. "I know how to tell time," he beamed as he strapped on the watch. "It's 2:32 p.m." He fell silent, as did everyone else. "Now it's 2:33 p.m." He did this for a while, until it was time for Teddy to open his gift. Swimming trunks. "Do you know how to swim, Teddy?" Harold asked.

"Know how to swim?" Mattie ribbed, "Teddy won a silver medal at the Olympics, the first Olympics in Athens." It was an old joke, but a good one, and Teddy, who would be retiring in two years and was often its target, didn't mind.

Sammy became Harold's window into a lost childhood. Sammy taught him everything every eight-year-old boy knows—how to do thumb wars, the process and meaning of the double dare, how to cross your heart and hope to die, and when liars' pants do or don't catch on fire. Harold especially enjoyed Sammy's introduction to children's music. They sang This Old Man, 99 Bottles of Beer, She'll be Coming Round the Mountain When She Comes, B-I-N-G-O, Six Little Ducks, and a half dozen others. Harold's favorites were John Jacob Jingle Heimer Smith and When You Wish Upon a Star.

When Sammy first sang John Jacob Jingle Heimer Smith, Harold couldn't get enough. They must have sung it together a hundred times, always getting softer and softer at each verse until neither could hear the other and instead had to look at the other's mouths to see the words. Harold felt like he was singing to Ma. And he laughed his silent laugh, his atomic smile, when he finally thought he got the joke Sammy was too young to get: two people with the same crazy name, one who was famous and the other who basked in the other's fame. Harold often thought of this joke as his own fame grew.

When You Wish Upon a Star was their finale every day. They began singing it when they turned the second to last corner before the firehouse. Harold's favorite verse was the last one: *Like a bolt out of the blue, fate steps in and sees you through [super high note, like a howl, joined by Sparky with a real howl], when you wish upon a star your dreams come true.* They had many discussions about bolts, fate, and stars. Harold knew a lot more about stars and bolts than Sammy did—he'd read a few science books at home—and more about fate too.

They so religiously sang this song as they were approaching the firehouse that Sparky learned that when his howl was done and he looked back down, the firehouse would appear from around the last corner. Then he barked once. All the firemen knew that Harold,

Sammy, and Sparky were close when they heard the howl followed by the one announcing bark. "Sparky's bow" is what Teddy called it.

Jack also started reading to Harold, bringing in more than just children's books, since Harold had already read most of them. Jack, Harold, and Sammy also started going to the public library weekly.

Sammy went to a day camp in the summer. Jack and Dee arranged for the camp folks to drop Sammy off at the school in the afternoons, where he'd be met by Harold and Sparky and walked back to the firehouse as usual. So, their walking schedule continued uninterrupted through the summer, adjusted only a bit because summer camp was over one hour earlier than school was. In the fall, they returned to the old schedule.

One day in October, as Harold and Sammy were walking Sparky back to the firehouse after school, before they even started When You Wish Upon a Star, they were approached by two of the three O'Malley brothers. They were thick and squat, with bulbous noses and rubbery limbs. Their green eyes were far apart, closer to their ears than to each other, and always open wide, as if someone were pulling up on their splotched brows.

"Hey, who's the retard?" one of them asked.

"That's not a nice word, mister."

"Sammy, let's go," Harold said, pulling on Sparky's leash and Sammy's hand. Sparky wasn't quite growling yet, but he was on red alert. Both brothers howled in laughter as Harold spoke these words, which sounded to them like guttural gibberish, which they tried to imitate.

"Abbbby, behbehhhhhh, ooooo," one of them said, a thin long tongue darting in and out.

"Eeeeeee, thu thu thu, ahhhhh," the other replied, with an identical tongue.

Sparky was getting angry. He leapt, teeth bared, at the closer brother. "Keep that fuckin' dog off us," he yelled, then he kicked Sparky a glancing blow that caused a yelp, but only made the dog more determined.

Harold snapped. He never thought a person would ever hurt Sparky, at least not on purpose. There was that one time when Mick was running to the pole during an alarm and tripped on Sparky, and another time, more serious, when Sparky actually fell through the pole hole and Tony had to take him to the vet. Good thing there was that padding at the bottom.

But hurting Sparky on purpose was inconceivable. Harold let out a wild groan. To the O'Malleys it sounded like the same retarded noises from before, and they both started laughing again. But Sammy and Sparky knew this wasn't talking. Harold reared back like an old-time pitcher and punched the kicking O'Malley in the face so hard he knocked him out. Cold.

"You killed him, you fuckin' spaz," the survivor screamed as he bent down and discovered his dead brother coming to. The survivor lurched for Harold, who hadn't prepared at all for a counterattack, but Sparky intervened, sinking his teeth deep into a reptilian tasting arm. When the bitten O'Malley cocked his arm back to strike Sparky, Harold ripped off another old-time fastball and knocked him out too.

"You're gonna get yours, retard, and so is that fuckin' mutt," one of them yelled back, as he and his brother hobbled away.

Harold, Sammy, and Sparky ran back to the firehouse without any singing, howling, or barking, so they surprised everyone when they appeared unannounced. Sammy couldn't wait to tell his dad about the big fight.

"And they used bad words, Daddy. They called me a retard. That's bad, isn't it, Daddy?" Harold's and Jack's eyes met in a shared smile at the fact Sammy thought the O'Malleys were calling *him* a retard. But they also both knew this was a dangerous situation that might not be over.

But as it turned out it was over. The O'Malleys became deathly, hysterically, afraid of Harold. His unconventional appearance and manner of speaking, once the object of their scorn, now only deepened their fear. This retard was capable of anything. They crossed the street to avoid him. There was a third, younger, O'Malley brother whom Harold never had the pleasure of meeting. The other two must have warned him off. Harold had no further exchanges with any of the O'Malleys. He figured their evil sputtered and burned itself out, just too much gas in the carburetor. Or maybe they moved.

CHAPTER 14
GENETICS

Catastrophe in Cornville. The team was swept in its four-game series at Cedar Rapids and Iowa City, dropping to third place in the Midwest League. It returns tomorrow for a welcomed three-game homestand against the last place Manhattan Muskrats. Tickets for all home games may be purchased at the Municipal Field ticket office, at Cooper Farm Equipment on Elm, and at Cooper Realty on Adams.

The installment about the O'Malley brothers reminded Joe of the Foxley twins. Their evil did not sputter itself out.

They were identical twins, and their own mother couldn't tell them apart, a fact that Katherine found hard to believe but which appeared to be true. Strangely, their father could tell them apart, even though he was a train engineer and wasn't around much.

Ron was the older by 10 minutes, and by an equally small margin was the worse of the two. As they grew older, they began to play the favorite twin game of switcheroo. But with the Foxley twins it was always with a purpose, a bad one.

Once when they were in third grade—always separated into different classes—Ron agreed to switch class with Tom just so he could steal money from Tom's teacher's purse. It was locked up in her drawer, and Tom couldn't get it open. But Ron had perfected the use of a bent paper clip as skeleton key. He stole the money when the teacher and the rest of the class left for recess, as he lagged behind. He split it 50-50 with Tom. Well, he told Tom he was splitting it 50-50, but it was more like 70-30 after he pocketed a couple dollars before divvying it up.

It was an unintentional version of this same old switcheroo when Ron robbed a gas station at gunpoint, and the victim identified him from a lineup. But it was Tom in the line-up, so the police arrested Tom. Exasperated prosecutors only half-jokingly told police they could never convict either of these guys of anything unless it was one killing the other, which is exactly what happened several years later. Angry over Tom's constant complaints about using his identity, and drunk as a skunk because he'd lost yet another job due to drunkenness, Ron stabbed Tom to death. When arrested, Ron claimed to be Tom. It didn't dawn on him until he sobered up that the switcheroo was no longer a viable defense strategy.

The Foxley twins' criminality stimulated a broad debate in town about the roles of nature and nurture. That's because the twins had an older brother, Rod, who couldn't have been more different. He was obedient, kind, athletic, got good grades, and received an appointment to West Point. He died in a freak accident during an Army football practice.

"This proves it's nature," a fellow teacher asserted in the teacher's lounge a few days after Ron's trial. "These boys were raised the same." But another teacher, a biology teacher, pointed out that the twins also shared half their genes with Rod. "Well then, that's the difference right there. In the other half."

But they weren't raised the same, Katherine thought. The twins had Rod for a big brother and he had them for little brothers. Their parents were also older with them, and they had to fill the unfillable shoes of Rod the God, as they themselves sarcastically called their older brother, both before and after he died. Those are very different circumstances in which to be raised.

Joe wasn't so sure. "Plenty of kids in exactly their shoes, and much worse, don't end up being criminals," he ventured one night during a Report.

"That's true. But then what made them like this?"

"I dunno. Everything. Nothing. They chose this." It was always an unsatisfactory discussion.

Jack's fears about Barry squealing were realized, but it took over a year. Barry had actually come to a grudging acceptance of Harold, something he would never have admitted to anyone, especially himself. But this grudging acceptance unraveled when Jack insisted on throwing Harold a big party on the one-year anniversary of Harold's move to the firehouse.

Everybody was invited, and everybody came, whether they were on duty or not. The fellas pooled their money and bought Harold a nice new suit, a colorful wide tie, and a pair of brown wing tips. Jack bought him Hume's six-volume set on early English history, which he knew Harold hadn't read yet—he'd nonchalantly inquired one day—but which he also knew was still well beyond Harold's reading ability. Harold was touched, both at Jack's optimism and at what Harold recognized was Jack's desire to keep them connected through reading books Harold could not read himself.

This paean to Harold began to pick at the wounds Barry had thought were mostly scabbed over. He mulled and mulled for several weeks after the anniversary party, and then finally succumbed. He sent an anonymous letter to the chief. He wanted to ask him whether he knew Jack Baker was letting a retard stay at the firehouse for free, but worried that he might give himself away. So he said he was a concerned mother who lived in the neighborhood, and had seen a tall scary looking man hanging around kids. She followed him, and he went into the Fourth Street firehouse. She thinks he *lives* there. Is this allowed?

The chief called Jack, was sympathetic, but told him he needed to find a place for Harold by the end of the month. By February 28. Less than three weeks.

Then Barry had a change of heart. It was a sunny and unusually warm mid-winter day, and he was washing down No. 1 out on the driveway with Tony. Harold, Sammy, and Sparky were coming back from school, just finishing When You Wish Upon a Star. Several high school kids were walking behind Harold, laughing. One of them picked up some small white decorative stones that edged a lawn and started throwing them, missing at first. Then the others joined in and soon the pebbles began to find Harold. One even bounced off Sparky, who wheeled around.

"Hey, knock it off," Barry heard himself thundering at the boys.

"Who's gonna make us?" the instigator taunted, the shortest boy in the group. *Man, these kids today*, thought Barry. *I would never have mouthed off to a cop or fireman when I was that age. Teachers, sure, but not cops or firemen.*

"I'm gonna," Barry said, and he turned the hose on the instigator, soaking him completely. He only wished this was a fire hose and not a garden hose. Punk would have rocketed across the street.

"Hey, man, you can't do that," the instigator gurgled. "I'm telling your boss, grandpa."

Barry knew, having been a bit of an instigator himself when he was younger, that this threat was all for show, for the benefit of the instigator's pals.

"Well, since you're gonna turn me in anyway, I might as well kick your ass in addition to drowning it," and Barry threw down the hose and started running toward him. All the kids ran off, and Barry started laughing riotously. Harold had never seen Barry laugh.

"Thank you," Harold mouthed.

"You're welcome. Goddamn stupid kids."

Barry and Harold became friends after that, not fast friends—Barry was still a little chafed that Harold got free room and board while he was struggling with rent and alimony—but close enough that Barry felt bad about turning Harold in. One night they were playing what Barry knew was a doomed game of Concentration, when he blurted out his confession. "You know, Harold, I'm the one turned you in, and now you have to leave. I'm sorry."

"I know," said Harold as he turned over matching sixes.

"You know I'm sorry or you know I turned you in?"

"Both," Harold said with an atomic grin.

Jack managed to find Harold a janitorial job at the minor league ballpark, Municipal Field. An old high school friend of Jack's worked for the team in some kind of marketing capacity. The season started April 6, as soon as the big-league then triple-A rosters were set, but the first home game wasn't until April 13. The job didn't pay much, but Municipal Field was only a few blocks from the firehouse. Now they needed to find Harold a place to live.

Jack scoured the want ads and got so discouraged that he was considering asking Dee if Harold could live with them until he got settled in the new job and could find another place. It would be tight—Harold would have to live in the semi-finished basement—but Jack didn't know what else to do. And then Barry found a place for Harold to stay.

Barry's cousin Nick was taking a semester off from college and was going to work at Municipal Field on the grounds crew starting this spring. Jack's old friend got him that job, too. Barry found Nick a tiny one-bedroom apartment just three blocks from the ballpark, and eight blocks from the firehouse, and when he heard Harold needed a place, he asked Nick if Harold could stay with him for a while. Nick said he was fine with it if Harold was OK sleeping on a cot.

The firemen threw Harold a going away party. They gave him things he'd need to live on his own, like towels and washcloths, pillows and sheets (just in case he ever got a real bed), and a broom. A red push broom just like the one at the firehouse. No one gave him pots or pans because they knew he couldn't cook. They hoped Nick could.

"There's one final gift," Jack announced, handing Harold a small package wrapped in comic strip paper, ribbon-less. Harold recognized this as the fireman's own way of wrapping presents—colorful and not too much trouble. Harold slipped off the comic strips and opened the small box. It had a dog's leash in it. Sparky's leash. Harold didn't understand for a moment, and then jumped up and hugged Jack, tears trickling into the corners of his wide smile.

"But there's one condition. You have to keep walking Sparky to pick up Sammy every day when I'm on duty. Agreed?" Yes yes yes.

For the first month, before the season started, Nick, Harold, and Sparky spent all their time together, and became good friends. Nick introduced Harold to bowling, and once the manager of Fun Bowl finally surrendered and allowed them to bring in Sparky, they bowled almost every other day. Sparky sat in the seats behind the scoring table, clicking and whistling.

Nick loved dogs, and had never met a dog as aloofly smart as Sparky. He was a little surprised that Sparky didn't keep score when they went bowling.

Once the season started, Nick and Harold didn't see much of each other, because of their schedules. The grounds crew started up in the late afternoon to prepare the field for the night game. Harold's clean-up crew started at 7:00 a.m. the morning after the game, and they were usually done by 1:00 p.m.

Harold's schedule allowed him to keep his promise of walking Sparky and Sammy. Every school day when Jack was on duty Harold and Sparky would leave the apartment at 2:20 on the dot, walk to the firehouse, say hello to all the guys, and then walk their old trek to Sammy's school, and the three would walk back to the firehouse. The guys usually made some snack for them when they returned, then Harold and Sparky would head back to the apartment.

Because of their schedules Sparky was seldom alone in the small apartment. He slept at night on Harold's cot, cuddled up dangerously close. Good thing Harold was a sound and still sleeper. Nick felt guilty about the arrangement, and eventually bought a small couch that pulled out into a bed. Harold and especially Sparky loved it. Harold insisted on repaying Nick. At $5 every other week, it took a while.

Now that Harold had a job, he also insisted on paying Nick some small amount of rent. Nick refused. So Harold would run to the store to buy food whenever it looked like they needed something. Nick and Harold got along well, especially after Nick learned how to understand

Harold's speaking. It might have been his flair for languages, but Nick could understand Harold better than any adult could.

There wasn't much closet space in the small apartment, but neither man needed much. Nick wore team tee shirts and shorts every day on the crew. He had one suit for his occasional dates. Harold got most of his clothes as hand-me-downs from Teddy. They were just like the clothes his mother brought home for him. Old man clothes. Old, comfortable, out of style, and way too short in the arms and legs. Perfect. They took up less than half of the closet, even including the new suit, wide colorful tie, and wingtips.

All the weekday and weekend games at this double-A park were at night. Occasionally there were day/night doubleheaders, but only to make up for rainouts, or bugouts. Harold loved the double headers. He'd watch Nick and the grounds crew prep for the first game as he was cleaning up from the night before. Sometimes he'd just stay and watch the first game. Once in a while he and Nick would even watch parts of the second game together, down in the fancy seats behind home plate.

Harold loved sweeping at Municipal Field. It was much bigger than the firehouse. He waltzed for hours and hours. He had other duties, too—emptying the trash bags and cleaning the bathrooms—and he came to think of these less satisfying, stinky, jobs as the admission price to the dance.

"Did you go to many baseball games as a boy?" Katherine asked.

"Not too many. Dad took me to a few games down in Denver. Then I went to a few down there after the Navy, before I met you. I played in more games than I watched, in high school and before in little league."

"What position did you play?"

"Second base and catcher in little league, then backup catcher in high school." She remembered seeing a picture of Joe's team hanging on the wall near the entrance to the gym.

"Did you ever want to play professional baseball?"

"Nah, I wasn't near good enough."

"Did you play in the Navy?"

"No."

"Where do you think this story is going?"

"Maybe Harold joins the groundskeeping crew. I'd bet he'd be good at mowing the outfield grass in those pretty patterns. Then he'll have to meet a girl. Isn't that how all books work? Boy meets girl?"

"Ours did," Katherine said, smiling.

Harold's hurricane was churning the seas, it's baseball eye just about to be discovered by Joe's exploring tumor.

CHAPTER 15
DISABLED

Dunces Descend. Poor students were at long last rewarded at Municipal Field last night, during Fools Night. Fans who brought in a report card with at least one D or F were admitted free and given a dunce cap with the team logo on it. There were so many dunces the team ran out of caps, but late-arriving underachievers were still rewarded, with a coupon for a free hot dog. But the real dunces tonight were the team's relievers, who blew a five-run lead in the eighth inning, losing to the bottom-dwelling Manhattan Muskrats. The home team is now 7-11, and back down in third place in the Midwest League. Maybe they can set things right on the road with four games against Sioux City, followed by a welcome three days of rest. Next home game: May 10 against the Grand Island Athletics.

"Could someone like Harold really hit a baseball so well?"

"I dunno. There was Pete Gray, the one-armed outfielder who played one season for the St. Louis Browns right after the war. Do you remember him?

"No."

"Lost his right arm as a kid when a wagon rolled over him. He'd catch the ball with his left hand, and in one motion move his glove to under his stump arm and roll the ball out to his hand, to throw it. At the plate, he held the bat with his left hand, his right stump just hidden under his sleeve. He was a good outfielder, fast as lightning, but he couldn't hit the major league curve."

"That's sad."

"Not really. Lots of minor leaguers, with two arms, can't hit the curve. The real sad story is Sy Rosenthal. My father told me about him. He was a good player, but then suffered a bad leg injury. It caused a terrible limp. Played for the Red Sox for a couple years after the injury, in the twenties, but never could stick."

"Did he at least make it in the minor leagues?"

"Not for very long. He tried to join the Navy after Pearl Harbor, but they rejected him because of the limp. So he had surgery to fix it, paid for it himself. It worked, and the Navy let him join up. He was paralyzed below the waist when his ship was hit off the coast of France in 1944."

Once the team discovered Harold's baseball-hitting gifts, Joe started to really get excited about the story.

"So, he doesn't meet a girl after all. He becomes a baseball player!"

"Don't get too excited, Joe," Katherine said smiling, "he might meet a girl later on."

"I just as soon he didn't."

"Why not?"

"I'd rather read about baseball than romance."

"But there's romance in baseball."

"You know what I mean."

She did. Now she started to worry that Tales of Harold would end up being just some cheesy sports novel. Unsung hero overcomes insurmountable odds to win World Series. Then she caught herself, remembering that Cheesy's author was her own Joe, or maybe a hidden red monster.

The first time I saw him swing a bat was in a dripping double-A dungeon down in Cape Girardeau, Missouri. I didn't want to go, and once I got there I was not impressed. I'd been in St. Louis for a Cardinals game against the Reds, working on a piece for The New Yorker about

Stan Musial. The Reds' major league scout, Sonny Tibbets, told me they had just stumbled on some kind of crippled Ted Williams, and signed him to their double-A team. "He never misses, is what I heard."

Sonny pleaded with me for company on the two-hour drive down the Mississippi, a trip he had to make but I didn't. Undiscovered phenoms erupt in baseball like the chicken pox, and I had long given up the temptation to be part of the discovery of the next Babe Ruth, who always turned out to be the next Mario Mendoza, dragged down to his eponymous line by the heavy drooping chains of the major league curveball, unhittable by all but the anointed few. But when Sonny said the guy was a crippled janitor, accidentally discovered by the team's grounds crew, I figured sacrificing one day might just barely be worth it.

Then I saw the guy in the on-deck circle, after an hour of sweat-drenched double-A drudgery and the worst biting flies north of Panama. Sonny's "He's batting .525" was drowned out by the guy's ridiculous warm-up swings. I'd never seen anything like this in all of baseball, at any level. Even boys in Little League know the basics of swinging a bat. This janitor looked like he was trying to swat bugs, no difficult task on this night. Sure, he got a hit, a seeing eye single between first and second, but his live "swing"—and I am being generous with the language here—was no better than his practice ones.

These failings of form were specks of dust compared to his "running" style, again, a generous use of the word. He flailed to first like a wounded turkey, so slow that I thought the right fielder's throw might catch him.

I was about to complain to Sonny for dragging me down here when I saw the man on first smile. His gaping almost toothless smile was screaming an achievement as small as they come—a base hit in a meaningless backwater game—with a joy as big as they come. It felt like he was smiling for all of us. I think that must have been the beginning for me, though I confess that Harold left my consciousness for more than a month.

CHAPTER 16
THE TURD AND DOVETAIL JOINTS

Local signing. Owner Robert "Big Bob" Cooper announced today that his double-A team has added a local man, Harold Fungo, to its roster. Fungo will be the first home-grown ballplayer ever to don a professional baseball uniform here. Not much is known about him. He did not play high school or college ball, and must have been discovered in a local recreational league. Cooper said the new player would most likely begin pinch hitting until a spot for him in the field could be found. Good luck, Mr. Fungo. All us beer leaguers are rooting for you!

"But you must have at least *thought* about some of these things before writing about them," Katherine asked during one Report. "How a crippled man might still be a perfect hitter. How teams scout players. What are in baseball contracts. How the St. Louis Cardinals hate the Cincinnati Reds."

"I knew about the Cardinals-Reds rivalry. I think my dad told me about that when I was a kid."

"And the other stuff?"

"I dunno."

"How did you know Harold's team was part of the Cincinnati Reds?"

"I dunno. What town is Harold's team in, anyway?"

"It's your story, Joe."

Joe laughed. "You sound a little like your mother in that story you told me about The Turd."

The Turd was the first new car Katherine's father ever bought. He did not appreciate any of the increasingly important social aspects of the automobile. Cars were machines. They got you from one part of the farm to the other, and that's about it. He'd no more ask his wife about a new car than he would about a new tractor. That attitude is the only thing that could explain why he bought a brand-new Chevrolet Bel Air in two-tone brown.

It had a dark brown body accented by a God-awful sepia roof and sepia sides bounded by the iconic Bel Air rocket logo. The two chrome needles of the logo launched parallel to each other from the sides of each rear fin and met at a point just behind the sides of each eye-lidded headlight.

When he proudly drove it home that first night, Katherine's mother, once she was able to stop laughing, said it looked like a turd. She dubbed it The Turd. She refused to drive it, and every time he asked why, all she would say was, "It's your car. You bought The Turd, you drive it."

But he bought it for her. He didn't need a car. He drove his old flatbed truck anywhere he needed to go. Hell, he even drove her to Colorado Springs for their honeymoon in that flatbed. After months, during which she must have said "It's your car" a hundred times, he finally asked her if she'd ever drive it.

"Yes, I'll drive it if you paint it white."

"White?"

"You heard me."

When he found out how much it would cost to paint it white—many coats needed to cover the browns—he decided instead to buy her a new white car, a Ford Fairlane. She loved it. She died several years after that, but it was several years well spent, driving to and from town like the Queen of England in a white coach. He gave Katherine The

Turd. It was not the usual heartwarming scene of paternal largesse. He asked her one day, "You want The Turd?"

"I suppose so."

"You don't have to, you know."

"I know."

She was a junior in high school, and a car was a car after all, even if it was The Turd. The worst and best thing about The Turd was that it was indestructible. Mechanically perfect. Blessed, really. Not one thing went wrong with it in twenty years. Katherine drove The Turd through high school and college and teaching those first few years, and was even driving it that night she fell in love with Joe.

In honor of The Turd, the only two cars Joe and Katherine ever bought were both Bel Airs, dubbed Turd 2 and Turd 3, though neither was brown nor two-toned (one was dark blue and one dark green, if you must know).

The Turd also seemed to have inspired Joe's carpentry. He had walked Katherine back home after a matinee movie, before they were married. It was warm, and they were sitting on the porch swing sipping ice water, Joe's stomach too delicate even for lemonade. Joe was staring at The Turd, parked out front.

"It ain't so bad."

"What?"

"The Turd."

"Oh, God, yes it is. Two-toned brown? What marketing genius in Detroit came up with the idea that anyone in America would actually buy a two-toned brown car? A blind man?"

"Or at least color blind," Joe ventured.

"Yes, that's it. The designer was blue-green color blind. He thought the two browns were two grays."

"Is that how that works?"

"I don't know," Katherine laughed.

"The problem is that silver metal rocket thingy separating the two browns," Joe mulled almost to himself. "There should be a better border. Like joining two pieces of wood."

"I know what you mean. Like those beautiful dovetail joints."

"Well, maybe not on a car."

Joe attributed his interest in dovetail joints to that very conversation on the porch swing, sipping ice water with Katherine and staring at The Turd. A few years after they married, he bought a book on joinery and a small dovetail saw. He bought two 1x4 pine boards to practice on, then two more after those, then two every week for the rest of his life. He saved every scrap in a giant bin pushed right up against the front of the garage, leaving just enough room for The Turd.

He built every kind of dovetail joint known to man, and a few he invented himself, and became expert in them all. The through joint, the secret mitered, the half blind, the full blind, the sliding, the Kath. But in the end, he found he got most satisfaction from the simplest, traditional through joint.

Like cheese pizza, the through dovetail was at once the simplest and the most challenging. Getting the little squished diamond wedges, all of which were fully visible in the through joint, to be exactly the same size—not just on a single side but also on the side to be joined—required a mathematical precision that exceeded both Joe's early abilities and the margins of error of the best tape measure, ruler, or even measuring compass. Many a time in those first few months he wished Lester could help him with the math.

The through dovetail joint sat squat in the middle of a mystically pointy and ruthlessly unforgiving saddle. A 64th of an inch from perfection on the stencil, in either direction, was disaster. The next cut would be a 16th of an inch off, the next an eighth, and by the time you got to the edge of the board you were either out of board or out of cuts. And all these tiny mistakes, accumulated into complete loss of function, repeated themselves exactly on the board to be joined, a little like the Foxley twins.

Joe also found himself drawn to the simplest joinery—the end-to-end joint. He'd crosscut the 1x4s and then put them right back together with an end-to-end through dovetail joint. Those joints exposed everything. The tiniest variation in the size of any diamond was there for all to see. Plus, he just liked the flatness of the joint.

Katherine had a hard time understanding at first. "What are you making?"

"Nothing."

"Looks like you are making something. I see boards and saws and sawdust and sandpaper."

"I'm just fooling around."

"Let's see here."

The bin was a kind of archeological dig. Katherine noticed right away that the pieces at the bottom were mistakes. Notches that ran off the edge of a board. "Pins," as she would later learn the wedges were called, that did not remotely match up with "tails," as the notches were called. But they got better and better toward the top of the bin.

"I get it," she said, "you are practicing. Well, as far as I can tell from this," and she held up an end-to-end joint so perfect she had to hold it a few inches from her face to see the joint, "you've got it now. What are you planning to make?"

"Not sure."

"You know, all of our kitchen drawers have those kinds of joints, though at right angles. Some are in bad shape. You could fix those."

Joe ended up replacing every drawer in the house, whether it needed replacing or not. And every drawer in the house of everybody he knew. It took him more than a year to replace the 243 drawers in the big house. It still wasn't enough to satisfy his need to cut dovetail joints. So the bin filled, and another and another. He ended up having to build a second tool shed—the lumber all joined of course with unnecessary but pleasing dovetail joints—just to hold his bins of dovetail joints, because there would have been no room for Turd 2 with any more bins in the garage.

CHAPTER 17
PAIN AND PAUL

Brooms to baseballs. This reporter has learned that our local baseball club's newest member, Harold Fungo, used to be the team's janitor! That's right, folks. It seems manager Wally Berens discovered Fungo's hitting prowess serendipitously last week, when Fungo and some of the members of the team's grounds crew were hitting off the new pitching machine before the players arrived for batting practice. Apparently, Fungo can really knock the cover off the ball, though he has yet to appear in a game. There are unconfirmed rumors that the parent Cincinnati Reds inked Fungo to a very large contract. We hope the Joltin' Janitor can show his stuff tonight against the Grand Island Athletics at 7:00 p.m.

Joe had known Paul Taavalaa for 15 years, ever since Paul started working at the Greeley King Soopers Store No. 51. Paul was younger than Joe, who had already been at the store almost two decades.

Paul's real name was Puleleiite. He was Samoan, but he was born in the U.S. The Taavalaa clan moved here from their small seaside village of Tafua, population 804. The move was a kind of paternal paroxysm, after Paul's uncle, Ne'igalomeatiga, got a scholarship to play football at the University of Wisconsin. Panicked about his oldest son living in a foreign land alone, Paul's grandfather bought an old farmhouse and melon farm not far outside of Madison, sight unseen, from a friend of a friend of a friend, through a series of telegrams and escrow accounts.

It all happened quickly. Grandpa got the idea one day in February, and by May the entire Taavalaa clan, population 26, was living in America.

The only problem was that the farm Grandpa bought was in Madison, Arkansas, not Madison, Wisconsin. Errors in translation and some geographical naiveté had convulsed the whole family to a new land across an ocean, and still 700 miles away from Ne'igalomeatiga's football program.

For as long as Paul could remember, Grandpa would explain to anyone who would listen that this move to Arkansas was quite intentional, and the two city names quite coincidental, because he didn't want the family to be too close to Ne'igalomeatiga.

"He's got to be able to spread his wings a little," Grandpa would explain if anyone who expressed puzzlement at the move, all of whom would then nod their heads in knowing acceptance. Grandma Taavalaa, who knew the truth, howled with laughter every time she heard this story. After a while Grandpa forgot it was a lie and thought Grandma was laughing at his cleverness.

Ne'igalomeatiga means "unforgettable pain." Going against Samoan tradition, Grandma was the one who named him, after spending 20 hours in labor. He weighed 15 pounds.

"I will name him Fetu, God of the night," Grandpa majestically announced to the family and villagers gathered round the fire in front of the hut. With a tired but firm voice Grandma responded from inside, loud enough for everyone to hear, "His name is Ne'igalomeatiga, and Ne'igalomeatiga it is, if you ever want to have any other children with me." Ne'igalomeatiga it was. It was a great name, especially for a football player. They called him Pain at Wisconsin, and of course the name stuck, even within the family.

The Taavalaa clan became well known in east central Arkansas, and not just because 200-pound Samoan teenagers stood out in the Arkansas River Valley. Pain, who did well in college football, stuck around in the pros for two years after being signed by the Los Angeles Rams, and he used his signing bonus and salary to add to the family's Arkansas landholdings. Eventually Taavalaa Farms, run by Pain after his playing days, became St. Francis County's third largest employer (at least if you included all the Taavalaas who worked there).

Mead, Pain's sister, became a nurse, and she ended up teaching nursing at the University of Arkansas in Fayetteville. Today, a nursing classroom there is named after her. The next oldest brother became a lawyer. But most of the younger ones, including Paul's father, who was the youngest, drifted in and out of agriculture. Unwilling to work for Pain forever, they were largely unsuccessful on their own. As Grandma put it, they were in love with growing things, but the love was unrequited.

At Pain's invitation and expense, Paul visited him once in Los Angeles when Pain was playing for the Rams and Paul was still in elementary school. It was the first time Paul had ever flown in an airplane. Paul paid only for one ticket, so the eleven-year-old traveled alone.

The flight from Little Rock to Los Angeles stopped in Denver. Paul couldn't believe it when the airplane took off from Denver, and approached the giant mountains he had seen from the airport lounge. He was sure the plane would crash, cursing at his own substantial contribution to its payload. When it skipped over the first snowy peaks, and reduced the rest of them to a flattened diorama, Paul promised himself he would return to those mountains someday and thank them for not leaping up and devouring him.

A decade later he moved to Denver, after a couple uneventful spurts at university in Fayetteville. He loved Denver's blue enamel skies and sharp, cool, dry night air, so different from Arkansas. And he couldn't take his eyes off those mountains, which, even after several excursions into them, still seemed like cardboard cutouts propped up by the abutting prairie.

His favorite mountain trip was to Leadville, a remote mining town near the headwaters of the Arkansas River. He often camped at those headwaters, a rocky glen in the Mosquito Range where snowmelt collected in unambitious pools that eventually became the East Arkansas River, and then, joining Tennessee Creek, the mighty Arkansas itself. Looking at the pools he imagined flakes of melting white snow married to specks of black dirt traveling together 1,000 miles on their honeymoon to fertilize watermelons at Taavalaa Farms.

His move across those plains didn't seem to be a momentous decision at the time, just part of his general drifting. Drifting in and out of the soil, in and out of college, in and out of relationships, in and out of apartments and towns. He was still searching, but it was a happy search because Paul was a happy young man. He was a happy baby, a happy child, a happy teenager, and died a happy old man. He couldn't help himself. Visiting the headwaters reminded him both how far away and how close home was. And like most of his thoughts, these conflicting ones made him happy.

Paul was especially happy here in the produce section at the Greeley King Soopers Store No. 51. If he couldn't make a living actually growing things, at least he could have something to do with getting people to enjoy them. He knew everything there was to know about every kind of fruit and vegetable. He got the produce job by dazzling the day manager with his knowledge of broccoli Romanesco.

"Excuse me, do you have any broccoli Romanesco?"

"Right over there," the tired manager said, pointing to the broccoli, giving Paul the usual surprised once-over that most people gave the 300-pound squat man with a slight Southern lilt and a fuzzy ponytail undulating as he moved.

"I'm sorry, but that's broccoli. I'm looking for broccoli Romanesco."

The manager made the mistake of asking, "What's that?"

After a 5-minute laugh-dotted lecture, featuring heavy doses of plant reproductive biology, grafting, entomology, and the delights of the stir fry, with dashes of the mathematics of fractals, the manager offered Paul the job of produce manager on the spot, which had been vacant for a few weeks. Paul already had a good job at a tire warehouse, but he accepted the produce job offer instantly, even for a little less pay. He could already smell the soil clinging to the radish tendrils he'd be cleaning.

Besides knowing his fruits and vegetables, Paul knew everything there was to know about Broadway show tunes. At least twice a week Grandma Taavalaa would walk all the pre-school Taavalaa children, and in the summer and weekends all the children, into nearby Forrest City to watch matinees at the movie theater.

She preferred musicals, and when one was in town she would take the kids to see it over and over. They'd sing all the tunes, coming and going, but Grandma was strict about not making noise during the movies. No singing during. So all the kids, and Grandma, mouthed the words silently. From the front of the theater, they would have looked like a strange lip-synching Polynesian children's choir.

Paul was the youngest grandchild, and so he spent years going to musicals in Forrest City with Grandma. He must have seen Show Boat twenty times. When he discovered that most movie musicals were based on Broadway shows, he tried to get his hands on every book and magazine about Broadway. There weren't many. Grandma knew nothing about Broadway, but uncle Pain had been to New York several times, in college and the pros. Paul always tried to prise information from Pain whenever he was at the farm.

"Why do they call it Broadway, Uncle Pain?" he asked out of the blue at one family dinner.

"Broadway is the name of the street where most of the big theaters are."

"Are they bigger than the theater in Forrest City?" Paul asked, even though Grandpa was signaling that he'd heard enough and wanted to get back to their discussion of Pain's football career.

"Some are."

"In the Broadway theaters the people are really there, singing and dancing on the stage, not just in a movie like in Forrest City. Isn't that so, Uncle Pain? Have you seen them singing and dancing in person, for real?"

"They are there in person for real. I've never been, but I'll take you to a Broadway show some day, Paulie, and we can both see it, OK?"

Uncle Pain was good as his word, though by the time he got around to keeping it Paul was in college and had already seen several live musicals in Little Rock. Still, Pain called him one day during the summer and whisked him away to New York, where they saw a reprise of Annie Get Your Gun. Paul had seen the movie eight times. He had to force himself not to mouth the words. He didn't want Uncle Pain to think he was a sissy.

But on the way back to the hotel in the taxi, to Paul's astonishment, Pain started belting out "There's No Business Like Show Business." They finished it together, Pain even throwing in a little harmony at the end.

"You too?" Paul asked when they finished, smiling.

"Of course. It was only a few times, when I was home for the summer, but your grandma, my mother, roped all of us into it." They sang "Colonel Buffalo Bill" and finished up with "I'm an Indian Too."

When he was older and became a little bored with the lyrics he'd memorized and sung so often, Paul would sometimes rewrite them. To the title tune of "Oklahoma!," Paul wrote this ode to one of his favorite members of the produce section:

Paaaaaaaaamegranate
Where the seeds are hidden in the core
And the bitter starts turn to sweeter parts
Then your puckered mouth begins to soar!

Paaaaaaaaamegranate
Every orb is full of tiny pearls
That can stick 'tween teeth like a sword in sheath
But it's darn well worth it, boys and girls!

We know it is a kind of fruit.
And an old deciduous shrub to boot.

And when we saaaaaaaaaay
Punica granatuuuuuuuuuum
We're only sayin'
You are the best pomegranate
Pomegranate, the best.

Joe's and Paul's schedules meant they only saw each other at work for a few minutes on Monday mornings, as Joe was getting off and Paul was getting in early to sort out the big Monday morning produce deliveries. Even though Joe was considerably older, they liked each other right from the beginning. Joe loved Paul's big Taavalaa laugh. Paul noticed Joe was damaged, and Paul was a sucker for repair jobs. Paul could tell Joe was *tagata le vaaia*, which in Samoan roughly means "invisible man." He knew Joe had a shyness to him—heck everyone knew that from just meeting him—and Paul was sure it came from some injury, that Joe wasn't always like this.

"So how come you have been on the night crew for so long?" Paul asked Joe one Monday morning shortly after joining the store.

"I like it."

"Isn't it lonely?" Paul asked as he punched in, popped his timecard back in his slot, and reached for the keys to the forklift.

"I don't really like to be around people that much."

Paul began singing.

Walk on through the wind
Walk on through the rain
Though your dreams be tossed and blown.
Walk on, walk on
With hope in your heart
And you'll never walk alone,
You'll never walk alone.

And then he let out a big rumbling laugh. "Carousel, 1945. Rogers and Hammerstein. You know it? Nettie's trying to comfort Billy's widow, Julie. Billy has just died from falling on his knife trying to rob Mr. Bascombe. What a dope, that Billy! A weak incompetent criminal dope." Paul began another round of big Santa-like laughs, complete with the bowl full of jelly. "And a wife-beater, too. Ah, you didn't know that did you? They took that scene out of the movie, where stupid, weak, criminal Billy slaps Julie. Let's see, *he's* the one who gets fired and *he* slaps *her*? Even after he comes down from heaven and meets his daughter, the daughter that his own stupidity and criminality have made fatherless, what's he do? Slaps her hand! Julie and her daughter were both better off without that Billy."

Paul was about to let out another roar of laughter, but caught himself. He took a deep breath, furrowed his brow, spread his arms, and started staring out in front of him, roughly toward the area with the mop and bucket, and began singing again:

Move on from that jerk
Move on to a life
Feel your face, it is slapped and red.
Move on, move on
With relief in your heart
With the knowledge Billy's dead.

Then he let our such a roar that a passing customer pushed on one of the swinging metal doors, stuck her head in, and asked if everything was OK. That make Paul laugh even more, but Joe assured her everything was fine.

Joe was trying to punch out, but Paul's considerable frame was blocking the time clock. "You like music, Joe?

"I used to but . . ."

Paul interrupted, "You should come to my house this Saturday night. I invite a few friends over every other Saturday and we play show tunes from my record collection. I ask everybody questions about the tunes and the musicals. We have lots of fun."

"Maybe next time, this Saturday I'm going down to Denver for a baseball game."

"I thought you didn't like crowds," Paul inquired with a look of exaggerated, theatrical suspicion.

"Hardly anyone shows up at Merchant's Park these days. I can usually find a whole section with nobody in it." Another roar, and Paul was still laughing when Joe managed to circumnavigate him and punch out.

CHAPTER 18
KATHERINE

Under wraps. Our newest slugger, local man Harold Fungo, has not cracked the lineup since joining the club earlier this week. After a home loss to the Grand Island Athletics in the first of a three-game series, maybe it's time for manager Wally Berens to unleash our Joltin' Janitor for game two tonight, which starts, as usual, at 7:00. Tickets for all home games may be purchased at the Municipal Field ticket office, at Cooper Farm Equipment on Elm, and at Cooper Realty on Adams.

Joe did eventually drag himself to one of Paul's Saturday night singalongs. He was miserable, at the beginning. Paul was quite sensitive to Joe's misery, which no one would have guessed from the way Paul sang and laughed non-stop.

Paul's real name, Puleleiite, means "ruler who can tell the future." The ruler part didn't really work out, but Paul did have a knack for telling the future, of sorts. Not who was going to win a ball game, or get elected, or even win this year's Tony Awards (though Paul had highly educated guesses on that subject). He could tell which people would get along. He saw people's personalities like a jigsaw master sees puzzle pieces. Even at this relatively early stage of his adult life Paul had already foreseen three marriages and a half-dozen lifelong friendships.

He had one rule about his special power, and his special power had one rule of its own. Paul's rule was that he never did any matchmaking.

His powers were entirely passive. Some small voice—it sounded like Judy Holliday's—told him that if he ever tried to matchmake it would actually interfere with the match, and possibly even destroy his power forever. This fear was reinforced by vague memories of science fiction time travelers who just happened to step on and kill the only amphibious link between fish and air breathers—what were the chances?—and then promptly disappeared themselves, retroactively never having evolved. Paul always stuck to his rule.

The power's rule was that Paul couldn't use the power for himself—to find a girlfriend, or even to tell which people would become his own good friends. He knew lots of people, had lots of casual friends, and even had a few close friends, but he never saw the close friends coming. He'd had a few girlfriends, but could never tell whether they would last. None had.

When he saw Joe and Katherine talking that night, Paul knew instantly that they were made for each other. She was a friend of a friend, and was also at her first Saturday night singalong. Once they met, Joe and Katherine talked only to each other the rest of the night—well, Katherine talked and Joe would occasionally answer with a word or even sometimes two. They ignored the singalongs and quizzes, and were still talking to each other when the last of the other guests left.

"More music, you two?" Paul asked, though he knew the brief madness had taken them far away, and also knew it wouldn't be brief. They hadn't even heard Paul.

"Do you like music, Joe?" Katherine asked. Joe answered that he did, that he especially liked classical music, classical piano music. Paul had never heard him utter so many words at one time. But that was just the beginning.

Joe turned and asked Paul, "Do you have any Liszt?" Before Paul could answer Joe continued, "Or Bach or Mozart or Godard or Bartok or Debussy or Chopin or Dvorak or Brahms or Tchaikovsky or Grieg or Corelli or Beethoven or Shostakovich or . . . ." Joe was in some kind of trance. He was looking up, but not at anything in particular, and his body rocked back and forth a little each time he incanted a composer's name. His voice was different, mechanical. He'd started crying, and he must have named 100 different composers, many of whom even Katherine, who liked classical music, didn't recognize.

When the machine was done, Joe lowered his eyes in embarrassment, blinking his way out of the trance, drying his tears on his sleeve, and breathing hard. He was sure this beautiful and interesting woman, this Katherine, would think he was some kind of nut, which apparently he was, and that would be the end of that. But instead, he saw she was looking right at him, her own tears leaking. *OK, then, she feels sorry for me and that will also be the end of that.*

"Joe, are you alright?" he heard Paul asking. "I never realized you were such a fan of classical music. Did your grandma drag you to concerts?" Paul then began one of his shorter laughs, casting a concerned eye at his friend. "I don't think I have any classical records."

"There's a classical radio station in Chicago I can sometimes get on the radio at home," Katherine said. "Let's go there." Paul stayed back to clean up from the singalong. He knew he mustn't interfere.

Harold's team was owned by Big Bob Cooper, a local farm implements supplier and real estate developer. His daddy, Big Ed Cooper, originally sponsored it as a recreational team. Big Ed was their catcher. He bought the uniforms—"Big Ed's Tractors" blazoned on the front in square red letters, and plain red caps—but refused to buy any bats, gloves, balls, or other equipment after the first year. Those damned things were expensive. You know how much one stupid bat costs?

So before Year 2 the team's players skulked around town begging for more sponsors. Art Rickert, owner of Fun Bowl, agreed to pony up for half of the equipment but only if the team agreed to wear Fun Bowl caps, light blue adorned with a small black bowling ball in the center surrounded by the words "Fun Bowl." He agreed to supply the caps, but only as replacements. He couldn't afford half of all the other equipment and also all the new caps. The Fun Bowl caps never did entirely displace the plain red ones Big Ed supplied. It looked pretty strange those first few years, some fielders wearing Fun Bowl blue caps and some plain red ones. They got lots of ribbing from teams whose players all wore caps of the same color.

Ted's Auto Body agreed to pay for the other half of the equipment, but only if the team let them bring a big sign to every game that read "Ted's—Best Bodies in All the Midwest." That also generated lots of ribbing.

They played six other local teams, rotating between two different local school playgrounds. Every once in a while they'd play on the road in nearby towns.

Big Ed's tractor business really took off, and after just three more years the team had matching caps and carried around a professionally painted sign that said "Cooper Farm Equipment, Inc." They started playing regional semipro teams and Big Ed started paying some of his better players, the ones who didn't already work in various of the family's now far-flung businesses.

By the time professional baseball people approached him about taking his team into single-A, Big Ed had no trouble paying for the construction of a small field. Because the damn city agreed to donate the land, Big Ed had to agree to call it Municipal Field instead of Cooper Field. It had real, though rickety, bleachers on three sides, a real scoreboard operated manually by Big Ed's nephew Terrence, and a plywood cube on stilts from which the local 20-watt radio station broadcast the games. The team played officially at the single-A level, but they were unaffiliated with any major league club.

Then the New York Yankees—the goddamned New York Yankees!—called Big Ed one day about becoming one of their double-A affiliates. He nearly fainted. Of course, he'd be delighted to pay tens of thousands of dollars to upgrade Municipal Field. Of course, he'd be delighted to pay the Yankees a $10,000 "affiliation fee" and take over their $100,000 minor league payroll and $15,000 annual operating expense. They were the goddamned New York Yankees.

Big Bob ended up a lot richer than his daddy, but he was twice as cheap. He terminated the affiliation with the Yankees as soon as he took over, and the team reverted to being unaffiliated. He fired the woman Big Ed put in charge of making all the travel arrangements, and with whom Big Ed reportedly had had a 20-year love affair, and installed his own son Todd as traveling secretary. Todd was even cheaper than his father. He insisted on calling himself the "travel secretary" instead of the more traditional term "traveling secretary," because he had no intention of actually staying with the team in any of the fleabags he booked.

After a few years of being unaffiliated, Big Bob reluctantly accepted a new deal with the Cincinnati Reds, mainly because affiliated teams could save a lot of money when the big club called up players to triple-A. Although players seemed to get a little lost on unaffiliated teams, and thus get called up much less frequently, Cincinnati was bad. They called up a lot more players than the fabled New York Yankees. Plus, big league teams paid all the bonuses and some of the salary when they signed a big prospect, like Harold.

By the time Harold signed his contract, Big Bob's double-A team was notorious for being one of the worst-run shoestring operations in all of minor league baseball. That made it all the more mysterious that the club had one of the best coaching staffs in double-A.

"Now, you have to admit that all this minor league baseball minutiae must be stuff you actually once knew, seeping into your brain from years and years of listening to and reading about baseball. Then, for some reason," and here the monster flared, "there was a kind of crack in your brain and all this stuff started seeping back out."

"I suppose. You've always said I'm a little cracked."

"I'm serious, Joe. I'm getting a little afraid that you aren't Joe anymore."

"Remember, I'm hearing this stuff for the first time, too. I'm still Joe, I just don't know who's writing this story."

CHAPTER 19
DEBUT

Fungo finally? Manager Wally Berens told this reporter after last night's game that he will try to insert local newcomer Harold Fungo into the lineup at some point in tonight's game. "He'll pinch hit tonight if we need a pinch hitter." Tickets for all home games may be purchased at the Municipal Field ticket office, at Cooper Farm Equipment on Elm, and at Cooper Realty on Adams.

Harold was late for his first batting practice. "Where the hell is he?" Wally asked Nick. Nick found him up in the third base stands, sweeping. No one told him that the baseball job replaced the clean-up job. Harold was a little sad to say goodbye to his dance partner broom.

They played almost three full home games before Harold saw any action. Dee, Sammy, and every fireman from the station who was not on duty attended each of those first games, as Harold's special guests, well, Greg's actually. He made all the arrangements, though Harold paid. They all had VIP seats behind home plate. Harold also invited Mrs. Tejada, but she said she needed to man the snack bar, especially because big crowds were expected, and that she and Demetria could watch him from there.

Wally and the Reds' front office had decided on their own trickling strategy. At the beginning, they would insert Harold infrequently, let him get hits in meaningful situations, but otherwise tell him to ground out in meaningless ones. They didn't want the pressure of a minor leaguer hitting even just 500, let alone 1000. Plus, Wally wanted to unleash Harold when he could do the most good for the club, which had high hopes of reaching the minor league playoffs again, though Wally was sure Harold would be called up long before that. Shithole, Texas wouldn't be on anyone's radar in a few weeks, when Baseball World saw what Harold could do. Wally and the bigshots had extensive discussions about the arms race they expected once news got around about Harold's hitting prowess.

"Dammit, Wally, they'll just walk him."

"Every time? That'd be stupid. With no one on, a walk is as good as a hit."

"OK, then they'll walk him every time someone's on base."

"No, it will depend on the situation."

"The situation? Hell, Wally, this is double-A. Nobody gives a fuck about the situation."

"But they will when he's in the big show."

Wally was already several steps ahead of the bigshots. He knew that eventually, when Harold was called up and started hitting, other teams would start walking him whenever they could. He also realized that Harold's impact, even when he could avoid intentional walks, would always be limited by being a pinch hitter. So, Wally was mulling over four possibilities, one immediate and three distant.

The immediate possibility was that Wally would work with Harold on reaching out and trying to hit pitches thrown during intentional walks. Wally had seen Harold do just that in his first workout. This would not be a long-term strategy, but dammit, if they insisted on walking the best hitter to ever play the game Wally could at least make them throw so far outside they'd risk a wild pitch with men on.

It worked out better than Wally imagined. Harold could reach across the plate and hit intentional walks if they were anywhere within two feet. Once, he even lunged with his left foot to the other side of the plate to reach one. They all had to scramble to the rule book to see if this was kosher. As long as Harold did not step on the plate or out of either side of the batter's box, he could hit any ball any damn way he pleased. This was good. This would put even more pressure on any pitcher trying to walk him intentionally. Even if the ball was behind him, he could sometimes swing around and hit it right-handed. They discovered this when a pitch slipped out of Greg's hand during batting practice. But Harold could do this only about 50% of the time. If pitchers ever discovered this, they'd intentionally walk Harold by throwing behind him.

This gave Wally an idea.

"Try standing facing the pitcher straight on, Harold, like they tell me you did that first day with Nick, but with both hands on the bat," Wally told him during batting practice one day. "Then it won't take you so much time to reach around if the ball's thrown behind you. But remember, you can't touch the plate, with either foot. And each foot has to stay in each of the boxes until after you swing."

It worked like a charm. Now Harold could reach out and try to hit intentional walks thrown on either side of the plate, though it was harder for him to loft the ball to the outfield. But he could still tap grounders through the infield holes, even when the pitch was thrown right at his face. Wally decided to keep the new stance, which they code-named Ping Pong, under wraps until the road trip.

The three more distant possibilities lurking inside Wally's mind were: (1) seeing if there was anything medically that could be done to help Harold with his running; (2) trying again to teach Harold to loft the ball enough to hit extra-base hits, maybe even home runs; and (3) teaching Harold a position—with his lack of speed it would have to be first base or catching, probably first base. He'd still be a huge liability anywhere in the field, but it seemed to Wally that the liability would be more than outweighed by Harold's perfect batting average. Keeping a bad fielder who hits 250 out of the lineup to make room for a better fielding 230 hitter was one thing. But having a 1,000 hitter changed all the rules. Hell, the rules had flown out the window. But these were early days and Wally didn't want to rush anything. Wally Berens was nothing if not patient.

Harold had his debut in the sixth inning of the third game of the homestand. Jack was there, with Dee, Sammy, Terry, Mick, and Barry.

"Harold, I know we said we'd ease you in, but it's a scoreless tie and I'm afraid we'll never get a run off this guy. So I'm putting you in, right after Charlie."

Harold smiled, took out his teeth, and grabbed Hillerich to warm up. Harold had never warmed up when he was doing his tryouts, or in his 30 years of practice. But Wally, Greg, and all the other players told him it would help him avoid injuries if he stretched and swung the bat around before going to the plate. So that's what he did, in the small white chalk circle they called "on-deck."

Charlie Swanson walked. Wally jogged over from the third-base coach's box to the on-deck circle to talk to Harold.

"OK, Harold, you're up. Take the first pitch—remember that means do not swing—and Charlie will try to steal. But then on the second pitch, whether Charlie makes it or not, hit it to Number 5. Got it?" Yes yes yes. Wally signaled this same information to Vince Mahoney, the first base coach, who passed it on to Charlie Swanson.

Harold took the first pitch for a ball, and Charlie stole second. Harold knocked the next pitch into the infield hole on the right side, between the second and first basemen. Charlie got a terrific jump and scored easily.

It was Harold's first of what would be a double-A record 52 pinch hit RBIs in a single season—actually just a little less than half a season. He loped to first, kept turning his head to watch Charlie run, and was so excited he almost fell down. But the throw went home, allowing Harold to make it safely to first. He would have been out by a mile if the right fielder had thrown it to first. The hidden detectives of Baseball World all took note, and the invisible telegraph lines burned with Harold's lack of speed. Wally took note too.

Davey Richardson pinch ran for him. Harold came off the field to as thunderous a mid-inning ovation as anyone had ever heard at Municipal Field. It was so loud no one could hear Mrs. Tejada yelling from the snack bar, "That'll stick to their ribs!" They won 1-0.

After the final out Harold's teammates walked him around the field on their shoulders. Wally invited Harold's guests down to the field, and this time Harold waved Mrs. Tejada to join them, which she did, bringing Demetria. He gave them all autographed balls (pre-signed by Nick), carried Sammy on his shoulders, and introduced them all to Wally, Greg, and his teammates. A photographer from the local paper snapped a picture of a duly toothful Harold with Sammy on his shoulders, and that was the first picture that made it into Life magazine.

Sammy asked him to wear his baseball uniform when he and Sparky came to pick him up from school tomorrow.

"Sammy, I'm not sure Harold will be able to keep walking you home from school. He has to practice with the team," Jack explained.

"No, I can walk him. I insist." And in fact, every day when the team was at home and Jack was on duty at the firehouse Harold and Sparky would walk Sammy from school to the firehouse, Harold in uniform, unless the team was playing the first half of a double header or had a bus to catch.

At the beginning they got a few caustic hoots, but as Harold's fame grew cheers replaced hoots. Everyone recognized the tall thin baseball player walking the small kid and the blue dog. Harold was John Jacob Jingle Heimer Smith.

Sammy couldn't stop staring at Harold's uniform. The black "15" on the back. The red stripes. The funny looped socks. Sammy was especially intrigued with Harold's cleats. "Don't those pointy things hurt?" Sammy asked.

"They don't go all the way through, Sammy. Look." Harold took one shoe off and showed Sammy that the inside of the shoe was smooth just like a regular one.

"Why do you have these pointy things coming out?"

"They help me run. And I really need help because I'm not a fast runner."

"But Daddy says you hit the ball better than anyone ever."

"But I still need to try to learn to run better. They might take me to see a doctor who might be able to help."

"Daddy says now that you are a baseball player you need to go away sometimes to play games in other places."

"Yes."

"And that Sparky will sleep at the firehouse, but sometimes he can sleep at my house."

"That's right."

"How long will you be gone?"

"I think just a few days, maybe sometimes a week. But then I will always be back here."

The only change to the pre-baseball routine when it came to picking up Sammy from school was that instead of walking from the apartment to the school Harold and Sparky ran. In deference to Sammy, and to give Sparky a breather, they walked from school back to the firehouse, but when Harold and Sparky left to go back to the apartment, they again ran. Sparky dragged at first but quickly adjusted. Harold thought all the running would help him run to first a little faster, and it did, but not enough to really matter.

CHAPTER 20
PHILADELPHIA AND THE UTAH

Dashing Debut! A bigger than usual crowd of 1,500 saw our own Joltin' Janitor, Harold Fungo, make his debut last night against the Grand Island Athletics. He did not disappoint, pinch hitting in the sixth inning and knocking in the winning, and only, run. The crowd went wild, and his teammates hoisted him on their shoulders after the final out. He returned the favor by lifting his young son on his shoulders, to the delight of the crowd. The only bad news: Fungo suffered some kind of injury running to first base. Here's hoping our new hero has a quick recovery. The homestand continues with three games against the Sterling Strikers. First pitch tonight at 7:00. Tickets are going fast.

Katherine lived in a small clapboard house on what was once her parent's farm east of town. Her Father was still alive, though long retired from farming. Katherine's younger sister Mary lived with him in the big house. By the time Katherine went off to college her father had sold off almost all the farmland, including plots around and between the two houses, though both houses retained half-acre gardens and the traditional rows of tall blue spruce wind breaks. The wind breaks were on the northeast sides of the houses, rather than the traditional northwest. Despite the almost universal westerly winds on this side of the Rockies, Katherine's ancestors had noticed that winds on this farm were almost always upslope, from the northeast, especially the strongest most damaging ones.

Katherine didn't know it at the time, but her father had to sell the farmland to be able to send her to college and keep food on the table and coal in the furnace. Farm prices had collapsed everywhere. Her father had lost his implacable independence, now facing the alien prospect of not being able to take care of his family. He of course hid it all from his two daughters.

Fortunately for Katherine, he was unable to hide it from his wife, who was smart and strong enough to conclude that these terrible uncertainties made it more important than ever to arm her daughters with education. She insisted that Katherine go to college. Katherine, who got straight-As in high school and probably could have gotten into any college in the country that admitted women, enrolled at the Greeley State Teachers' College, which was cheap and allowed her to live at home. She didn't particularly want to be a teacher, but she loved books, and figured that she could major in English literature, which she did.

When she was finished with college her father encouraged her to move into the small house, which until then he had rented out. Farm prices were rebounding, and the family no longer needed the rental income. They all called the small house "Tiny" for as long as Katherine could remember. "Tiny needs some tending," is the way Father had put it, but Katherine knew what he really meant was that with a home of her own maybe his eldest daughter's marriage prospects would improve. She was happy to accommodate. She'd be close to her first teaching job in town, and it would be temporary. She dreamed of moving one day to a big city. New York, maybe. Teach in the day and spend evenings reading books she would check out from the New York Public Library.

Houses had sprouted on most of the farmlands outside of town, scattered in a ring ten miles wide. Dozens of houses appeared on the lands Father had sold off, so many that Tiny and the big house now looked just like two white clapboard houses that happened to be in the same neighborhood, though with unusually large backyards. The big house maintained its beautiful wall of blue spruces, but Tiny lost hers to the parcel to the north. The new owners cut down the lovely trees, but it did clear Tiny's view of summer sunrises. Tiny's view of the big house also survived all the new construction, aided by the two houses' large gardens. That view was blocked only if Mrs. Collins, who lived in the new house right between the two gardens, put out her laundry on her clothesline, and even then Tiny could still see the big house's second story and gabled roof.

Tiny and the big house shared many architectural details. In a reverse nod to Monticello, Tiny's faux two-story front elevation looked like a smaller version of the big house's real one. Katherine's grandfather, who built both houses, was a big Thomas Jefferson fan. He also insisted that both houses be fitted with a lacey gingerbread trim, which now seemed out of place next to the boxy plainness of the post-Victorian newcomers that surrounded them. The big house had a traditional rectangular footprint, while Tiny's smaller rectangle sprouted a leg on the east side.

On the inside, both houses had fancy fireplace mantels, on which were centered identical carvings, though they were differently scaled. They showed symmetrical lions standing on hind legs on each side of a giraffe, handing the giraffe pineapples. Unfortunately, the size difference made the carving on Tiny's fireplace look more like two cats playing with balls of string divided by a strangely uneven wall.

Father said Grandfather had carved the mantels himself, but the story of the lions, the pineapples, and the giraffe, if there was one, never made it into the family's oral history. Katherine made up her own stories. There was a terrible famine and the kindly lions offered the starving giraffe pineapples, in exchange for which the giraffe kept lookout for approaching hunters. The giraffe had been elected new king of the jungle, and the lions were paying him pineapple tribute. The giraffe had kidnapped the lions' cubs, and the pineapples were the ransom. After the war, Katherine couldn't shake the idea that the pineapples were hand grenades. When she moved into Tiny, and spent so much time reading in front of its much smaller fireplace, she imagined the two cats were really just one, standing in front of a broken and angled mirror, four shards propped up against the bottom looking vaguely like legs.

Joe and Katherine stayed up the whole night in front of the cat and broken mirror, listening to crackling classical music fading in and out from Chicago. Joe wasn't exactly sure what came over him at Paul's. He didn't remember saying all those composers' names.

When they had to turn the music off at dawn because of poor reception, Joe told Katherine about everything. About Lester and the Utah. He must have talked for an hour. She mostly just listened. When he was done, and exhausted, he realized he'd been talking about himself the whole time and that he didn't know, or couldn't remember, anything about her. He knew she was a teacher, tall and beautiful, with long auburn hair that hit the sweet spot between straight and curly. She had a gorgeous aquiline nose which years later he would discover, with astonishment, that she hated. Her hazel eyes, trending toward green, were feline, but without feline duplicity. Her teeth were so white they made her face look two shades darker whenever she smiled. As he talked to her about Lester and the war, he could feel weights on his shoulders drop away like the coats, which he also told her about.

It was a warm May afternoon. He was at the Busy Bee, where he'd gotten promoted to days after just a couple months on the night crew. He was cleaning up a spill on the pet food aisle. The Foxley twins, who were probably ten at the time and out of control as usual, were playing a game in which they threw cans of dog food at the highest shelf, the winner the first one to knock an item off. One of them connected on a 15-pound bag of Purina puppy chow, which rebounded off the steel column behind it and fell, exploding on impact. Neither twin was a bit remorseful, or even afraid. Mrs. Foxley, as usual, was clueless, or perhaps just exhausted. "Come on boys, would you like ice cream? Let's go over to the ice cream section," she said, stepping over and around the Purina ball bearings rolling on the concrete floor. The boys kicked as many of them as they could, spreading them across the length of the aisle, a few even reaching the dairy case across the aisle's north end, as they and their mother walked away from the scene of the crime.

Joe had just about finished cleaning them up, all the time thinking about whether Mrs. Foxley had made the twins or they made her, when he saw his mother approaching. She'd never come into the Busy Bee while he was working. He'd never seen her look like this. Eyes red and distant, cheeks striped from fresh and dried tears, ashen. She told him Lester was dead. Police found his body in an alley. He'd been stomped to death. Virtually every bone in his body broken. Joe imagined those beautiful hands, lying flipper-like in a puddled alley in Philadelphia.

He ran home, still in his Busy Bee apron. He was cold. He grabbed a sweater and put it on, right over the apron. Then a jacket, then his winter coat. He stayed in his room in these bulbous layers, curled up on his bed, for two days, inconsolable. He never went back to the Busy Bee. He joined the Navy. Grief was an unpredictable wolf.

For 12 years, until that night at Katherine's, Joe kept putting on coats, real and imaginary. For 12 years he had three recurring dreams about coats.

In one, he was back in Wise-Ass's seventh-grade gym class, shivering from cold. He kept putting coats on, but they didn't help. Wise-Ass was yelling at him, something about his big butt, because his coats were crowding everyone off their roll-call numbers. This version ended with an explosion when his coats got too big for the gym.

In another he was lost on a giant empty snowy plain, dressed only in jeans, tee-shirt and Busy Bee apron, shivering from the cold. He thought it might be Siberia. He walked for miles and found a small town. There was only one store in the town and it sold only two products: pianos and coats. He bought every coat in the store, and put them on one after the other until he was so big he couldn't get out. So, he sat down at one of the pianos, realized he could not reach the keyboard because of the coats, and anyway that he couldn't play, and then woke up.

The third dream had him in a small village high in the Andes where a special light gave the villagers a strange sort of x-ray vision. They saw right through each other until they hit the one anatomical thing that made a person special. Some villagers appeared as big, happy blood-squirting hearts, others as bitter lumps of bilious intestine. Joe was invisible. The special Andean light ran right through him to the alcohol-damaged liver or brilliant brain standing right behind him. When he realized he was invisible he started putting on coats, colorful village coats. But they didn't help, either with his feeling cold or his invisibility. He asked a young boy what he should do, the boy's face turned into a wolf's, and it replied, "Give up." Then he woke.

Joe didn't dream every night, but when he did it was always one of these three, and they never departed from script. The only change was that after he joined the Navy the Peruvian dream ended with the little wolf boy saying, "The smoking lamp is lit."

They called him Sam at basic training in San Diego, short for Silent Sam. Later, his nickname became Sammy Ice, or just Ice, because he was always cold. He got along with everyone, and did his assigned jobs well. But he always wanted to get away, from the cold and from other people. The Navy was an odd career choice for someone with these proclivities. Although he managed to sail away to Hawaii, without it making him much warmer, it was on a warship crammed with over 500 men.

The USS Utah was a strange vessel. She was called a "dreadnaught battleship," built at the turn of the century, but was nothing like the giants that would later displace the meaning of the word "battleship." Compared to them, she was more like a cruiser, a small, slow cruiser. She saw action in the Great War, based in Ireland and used mainly as a show of force to protect convoys from German surface ships and a handful of submarines, the deadly days of the U-boat twenty years in the future. She was demilitarized under the terms of a post-war naval treaty, and humiliatingly converted into a radio-controlled target ship.

But in 1931 she was reborn, equipped with every kind of ship-based anti-aircraft gun the Navy had, and converted into an anti-aircraft training vessel. A floating metal blowfish, guns sticking out everywhere. She was in Long Beach when Joe got his orders to join her crew for training. He trained for two months on one of the five-inch 51-caliber guns and eventually became a trainer on that gun. The Utah was then ordered to Hawaii, to begin anti-aircraft training exercises for the Pacific Fleet, stationed at Pearl Harbor.

Joe spent his days, and occasional nights, training anti-aircraft gunners as the Utah sailed between the islands doing its best to simulate the repulsing of enemy air attacks, sometimes even with live fighters playing the role of the attackers. Even less frequently, they would float weather balloons and allow the trainees to fire live rounds. But more often than not the training was about all the mundane things that needed doing before the guns were fired. Maintenance and operation. What route to take for battle stations so sailors didn't run into one another, and what to do when you arrived at your station. And the never-ending drills on cutting down the time between the battle stations call and being fire ready.

Joe spent his off-duty time on board trying to keep warm. The ship usually moored in a berth at Ford Island, at the center of the harbor. He never joined his mates for liberty, such as it was back then with Hawaii hardly developed at all, other than the one time they kidnapped him. His physical intolerance to alcohol—he would immediately throw up the smallest amounts—saved him from additional kidnappings. He wasn't exactly the life of any party. And in fact his teetotaling also saved him from tattooing.

For enlisted men, getting a tattoo was as venerated a Navy indoctrination ceremony as joining Neptune's Court, which involved being beaten and sometimes even thrown overboard on one's first trip across the international dateline. But unlike Neptune's Court, tattooing required the victim to lie still. This was accomplished by cajoling him to drink enough alcohol either to render him unconscious or to so disable his judgment that he actually wanted a tattoo.

Joe's gunnery mate, Tommy Trujillo, had the customary Sailor Jerry pinup girl on his right bicep, but a strange text tattoo on his left forearm: THINGS ARE NOT WHAT THEY SEEM. Joe once asked Tommy what that meant, but all he said was that it made sense at the time. The best tattoo Joe ever saw was on one of the Utah's chief petty officers. Devils on each side of his belly button were shoveling coal into it. On his flip side, complementary flames on each butt cheek marked the roaring fire blaring out of his ass.

Because Joe could never keep down alcohol, they couldn't get him drunk enough to get a tattoo. A few of the guys, while they were drunk, suggested knocking him unconscious or slipping him a mickey, but they never followed through. One of the reasons they were so deferential to Joe was that he once let himself be court-martialed to protect them. It all started with the Utah's captain when Joe got there, Arthur T. Reemus. Captain Reemus was reported to be a personal friend of the President, and he sure acted like it. Joe saw admirals who were less arrogant. The only reason Captain Reemus wasn't already an admiral was his well-known battle with scotch whiskey.

One day when the ship was moored at Long Beach, a squad of marines marched ten cases of Balvenie 17-year-old scotch onto the dock. One of the marines even held onto the cargo net and rode up with the load as the ship's crane hoisted up the cases, the others double-timing up the gangplank to meet the cargo when it landed on deck. The captain got on the horn. "These marines have been instructed to shoot anyone tampering with this cargo. It is intended for a special presidential reception later this month. I will not be embarrassed." Everyone suspected that a large part of the special cargo was intended for the old man's own liver, already on life support.

The marines, unfamiliar with the design of the ship, made the mistake of storing the cases in a small compartment on a lower deck that seemed most defensible—steel bulkheads two inches thick and a locked door of the same. The captain, who should have known better but didn't, approved the marine sergeant's storage decision, and ordered that a marine be stationed outside the door, 24-7. But the far bulkhead of this compartment contained a small emergency hatch, with a watertight door accessible only from the other side. From the inside, the hatch was virtually invisible—a tiny score in an oval shape, just big enough to accommodate a small sailor. It was there, right up against the oval scoring, that the marines stacked the ten cases.

A group of sailors—all gunnery trainers like Joe—decided that the captain's liver would not miss six measly bottles, and in fact that it would be good for him. They talked one of their members, Frank "Slim" Cohen, into performing the good deed. Their only mistake was that when they tasted the scotch, it was such a moving experience that they could not stop.

When their dim-witted ensign discovered them all drunk, with empty scotch bottles strewn around them, even he figured it out, though only after visiting the cache of scotch and seeing for himself that one of the cases was cleverly resealed but half-empty. Joe, who was on liberty and had taken one of his long walks around the city to try to warm up, had the misfortune of returning to his drunk companions in between the ensign's two visits. When the ensign returned and demanded to know who was responsible, Joe, who was the most senior of the gunnery trainers, said he was. He meant it as a statement about seniority, not as a confession. But once the confessional ball got rolling it just never stopped.

Everyone assumed that the lieutenant commander who presided over the summary court-martial never told the captain about it, and that the captain never missed those six bottles, otherwise Joe, and the real culprits, might have faced dishonorable discharges, or worse. Instead, Joe was summarily busted one grade, from seaman first class to seaman second class. He took a hefty $20 per month pay cut. The lieutenant commander, who had several dealings with Joe and knew he was honest and didn't drink, didn't believe he had anything to do with the theft. He shook his head, with no small amount of admiration, when he accepted Joe's plea and imposed the punishment. He in fact never did tell the captain, or any of the other senior officers.

The cut in pay didn't really matter since Joe never spent his money anyway. But what he got in return was his comrades' permanent respect. They were also always asking him if he needed anything. All he needed was to get warmer. Slim Cohen bought him a fleece-lined jacket, not easy to find in southern California.

Joe always felt cold, even in these Hawaiian tropics, and could be seen wearing windbreakers and long pants on days everyone else was in shorts and tee shirts, or no shirts at all. On occasion he'd even break out Slim's fleece. A small part of the heat of the real world must have slowly seeped into Joe's imaginary temperature, because his dreams about putting on coats slowly became less frequent, and even when he had them, he put on fewer coats.

One Sunday morning he got up early to work on a sticky turret gear on his gun. It was a clear day, a few clouds glued to the mountaintops on the big island, too stuck to be pulled away by the gentle winds. Temperatures were mild, meaning Joe was cold. Before he knew what was happening fighter planes were strafing the Utah's deck and explosions were shuddering its hull. The strafing rounds ricocheted off the deck and various structures with puzzlingly silent metal-on-metal flashes. All sound was drowned out by the overpowering roar of the explosions below.

The water caught fire, the deck began to tilt, and Joe's mates began sliding off into the flames like checkers off a checkerboard. He saw the chief with the devils tattoo slide off. Joe imagined the devils using their shovels to paddle madly against gravity. He saw Tommy Trujillo and Slim Cohen side off, and a few others he didn't know. Most of the dead were trapped inside as the ship rolled and sank, all in less than 15 minutes.

But Joe didn't know any of that. All he remembered was having his arm locked around a turret brace when he saw sailors scudder off the foredeck and into the flames. He woke up in the base hospital. Both legs were badly burned, and he had to have several skin graft surgeries on the mainland. They told him it was a good thing he was wearing long pants otherwise he might have lost his legs. They told him he'd saved six other men by pulling them out of the burning water, and gave him a bunch of medals and a medical discharge. All he wanted to do was go home and put on a coat, and then another and another.

CHAPTER 21
THE WINCHELL DONUT HOUSE AND CABARET

Fungo Famous. Our own Harold Fungo, the pinch hitting phenom discovered in the ranks of Municipal Field's clean-up crew, appeared this week in none other than Life magazine. The venerated national publication reprinted a photo, first published in this newspaper last week, of Fungo hoisting a young boy on his shoulders after his game-winning debut at Municipal Field. Fungo is not just turning around the fortunes of our local team, which is now just four games out of first place thanks to his torrid pinch hitting, he is putting this town in the national spotlight. Thank you, Harold Fungo!

Paul liked dropping the dough into the hot oil. He noticed it bobbed in a characteristic rhythm. The doughnuts and specialty items—bear claws, long johns, cinnamon rolls—bobbed much more slowly than their little brothers, the doughnut holes. Their cooking time and manner were also different. Paul had to flip over the donuts and the specialty items with his extended-handle wooden spoon, when their bottom halves were done. The holes he just tried to tap sporadically to get them to rotate so they cooked more or less evenly. Everything cooked so fast that it was important to keep their order.

Within the two main categories of doughnut holes and everything else, the first item into the oil had also to be the first item turned and then the first item taken out, otherwise some things got burned and others underdone. This forced beginners to cook in batches of only one category at a time. All doughnut holes in one batch, everything else in the next. But after those first clean runs in the early morning things could get complicated. They might need more doughnuts holes and more bear claws, now. Mixing in items in the cooker really took concentration about timing, and the ability to keep track of different items' different cooking times. Many overcooked rejects found their way into the garbage while a new cooker was learning the ropes. Working at the Winchell's Donut House was a lot more complicated than Paul would ever have imagined, had he ever imagined it.

It was his first job when he came to Greeley, and he liked it. But the owners, Mr. and Mrs. Lee, were leery about hiring him, mainly for marketing reasons. They worried what customers would think about having a 300-pound man making the doughnuts. What subliminal dietary message would that send?

There was also the risk that Paul would eat their profits. Every new employee ate some of the profits, and the Lees learned early on that the best guard against pilfering was to allow, even encourage, all new employees to eat as much as they wanted. The pattern was always the same: new employees gorged for a day, two at the most, and then never ate another thing again. The bigger threat came from employees' friends. The Lees always had to look out for serially gorging friends. But if they allowed Paul to gorge even for a day, they feared he could eliminate a quarter of their daily inventory, something they just couldn't afford on their small margins. They hired him only after he mentioned during the interview that he didn't really like sweets, that he was a fruit and vegetable man. But they were wary just the same.

Things worked out better than they dreamed. Paul never pilfered and he had no pilfering friends, and in fact didn't seem to have any friends at all, having so newly arrived in Greeley. Not only that, sales increased 10% the week after Paul began working there, then another

10% after just a few more weeks. They peaked at 30%, where they stayed for the whole time Paul was there. Paul loved the job, singing and laughing all day.

The Lees couldn't figure out why sales had jumped so dramatically. After much study, Mrs. Lee decided it was Paul's laugh. Laughter must make these people eat more doughnuts.

After Paul left for a better-paying job at a tire warehouse, Mrs. Lee told Mr. Lee to buy a tape-recording machine, and to ask Paul to make some tape recordings of his various laughs. Mr. Lee had names for them. The jelly laugh. The rolling thunder. The machine gun. The bear claw. Paul agreed, but the taped laughter didn't work. After Mr. Lee reported back that his taped laughs weren't working, Paul offered to sing some Broadway tunes into the tape machine, and even a few of his special versions—nothing off color, mind you. The Lees enthusiastically agreed. After all, Paul not only laughed when he worked there, he also sang show tunes all the time. Maybe it was the show tunes that were increasing sales.

Paul taped a few of the standards, and a couple with his patented special lyrics. Mrs. Lee unnecessarily reminded him to make sure he laughed before and after the songs. This one he sang to the tune of It's Almost Like Being in Love, from Lerner and Loewe's 1947 hit Brigadoon:

What a place this is here
With these sweets everywhere
Why it's almost like being in love.

There's a crumb on my face
From this fabulous place
Why it's almost like being in love.

All the long johns are here filled with cream
Like a treat that you'd eat in a dream.

And from pastries so filled

You'll be certainly thrilled
You will swear you were falling, swear you were falling
Why it's almost like being in love.

The Lees offered to pay him, but Paul agreed instead to take two dozen doughnuts for the fellows down at the tire warehouse.

The new musical version of the Lees' 4th Street Winchell's was a hit with everyone except the Winchell franchise representative who visited the shop several months later, on an anonymous tip believed by the Lees to have been phoned in by their archrivals, the Andersons, who ran the town's only other doughnut shop, a Dunkin' Donuts. The Lees got into the rhythm of doing four shows each day: 6:00 a.m., to open and to keep those early risers coming in; 9:00 a.m., when the morning rush usually petered out; noon, when almost no one was around; and 4:30 p.m., when the work crowd stopped by on their way home but in small numbers on every day except Saturday. Paul's tape-recorded performances changed everything.

All the early risers kept coming in, some getting up even earlier to make sure they could squeeze into the first show. The 7-8 crowd almost universally stayed for the 9:00 show, and of course ate more doughnuts while they were waiting. Productivity throughout downtown Greeley plummeted and waistlines ballooned, as dozens and dozens of customers didn't even consider going into work until the 9:00 show was over, at 9:30. The non-existent noon crowd was now the biggest of the day, people off for lunch crammed into the shop, lines snaking outside, and all the time eating doughnut after doughnut. The end-of-day lull was no longer a lull. People rushed in, taking off early, just to hear the day's final show. Sales hit the roof. They doubled the first month, quadrupled by the second, and stayed there only because the Lees had reached the tiny store's production capacity. They hired three full-time cookers, and were considering expansion when the Winchell representative came to visit.

He was thin and short, probably around 40 years old. His skin was a creamy off white, and it peeked out of a wrinkled russet shirt. He wore a narrow brindle tie, loose tan pants, and a maple jacket with arms too short and sides too long. The lenses of his dark horn-rimmed glasses angled down markedly because the temples were too short to put the tips properly behind his ears. So the tips instead rested behind the very tops of both ears, causing tufts of brown hair to fray outwards. He carried a worn coffee-colored briefcase.

It's a good thing he came after closing time, because there was no place to sit at any other times. He banged on the locked door, holding his business card up against the glass, like a policeman with a warrant. Mr. Lee let him in, and it was downhill from there.

He introduced himself as "Wayne Keller," in a high-pitched sugary voice, and handed his card/warrant to Mr. Lee. *Wayne Keller, Assistant Vice President, Franchisee Compliance, Winchell's Corporation, City of Industry, California.* At the bottom of the card, in teeny barely legible letters: *Home of the Warm and Fresh Donut®*.

"So what is it you want, Mr. Cruller?" Even though English was not his first language, and the "r" and "l" in cruller difficult for him to pronounce, Mr. Lee knew a humorous opportunity when he saw one.

"It's Keller." The man opened his briefcase, took out a stack of papers five inches thick, lifted the stack a foot above a nearby table, dropped it with an imposing thud, then sat down at the table. He said these were the "controlling documents."

He started off talking about the franchise agreement and its various provisions, and with a Winchell's Donut emery board he cut off a thick horizontal slice of the stack to indicate these were the impressively numerous pages of that very agreement, none of which of course the Lees nor or any other Winchell franchisee had ever actually read, though all had signed. The Lees recognized their eager and optimistic signatures on the last page. Keller then referred to a set of rules and regulations, slicing off a somewhat thinner layer, which he said were themselves referred to in the omniscience of the franchise agreement. These rules and regulations likewise went unread by all. Mr. Keller then deftly applied the lofty principles in these two slices of documents to the dirty facts at hand, tying each violation to a paragraph or subparagraph of the agreement or the rules and regulations.

He began with the sign Mrs. Lee had made from a bed sheet, on which she had painted "And Cabaret," and hung to the bottom of the official Winchell's sign out front. This apparently violated five separate provisions, some of which had sub-sub-sub-sub paragraphs, requiring for their citation resort to lower case Roman numerals.

Keller then mentioned the fire code, which itself was somehow incorporated somewhere into the pages by other pages. Mr. Keller had kindly gone to the trouble of making a copy of the Greeley Fire Code, and served it as the bottom slice from the stack. The Greeley Fire Code, sub-sections cited, prohibited more than 25 people in the store at any one time.

"You'd think Winchell's would want as many people in the store as we can cram in, since they take 6% off the top," Mrs. Lee whispered to Mr. Lee. The alert Mr. Keller overheard, and responded sharply.

"Not if there's a fire in here and people die trying to get out."

Mr. and Mrs. Lee, lifelong experts in survival, each came to the quick conclusion that the costs of such a tragedy, multiplied by the infinitesimal chance it would ever occur, would never even come close to eclipsing the known benefits of their 400% increase in sales. Each was puzzled by this creature from Donut Central who didn't seem to know anything about Donut Survival 101.

Keller also mentioned copyright violations, and the music industry's Mafia-like patrolling of its right to royalties. This didn't bother the Lees much; that was Paul's problem, wasn't it?

Then Keller's eyes narrowed, and his voice got a little lower, when he said he'd heard rumors of the unauthorized sale of liquor. *Well*, Mrs. Lee thought but did not even whisper this time, *we only sell booze at the 4:30 show. Who would drink before then?* Mrs. Lee had given lots of thought to the kinds of alcoholic beverages that would go well with a doughnut, and settled on vodka for the traditionalist—something to take the edge off the sweetness of your powdered sugar or cinnamon— and crème de menthe—a different direction entirely, a continuation of the glucose experience. Keller mentioned something about this being illegal, and how there could be jail time involved. This got their attention. Their margins on the liquor were good, but not good enough to risk jail.

Keller finished by handing them a sealed envelope, which he directed them to open, and which he said contained a summary of what he'd just told them they had to do, and could no longer do. Keller told them they each had to sign the bottom of the letter, where it said they had read it, understood, and agreed to comply with all the terms and conditions of the franchise agreement and the rules and regulations. Both Lees signed, without reading a word. Mr. Keller took back the signed letter and gave them an unsigned copy. He said he'd stay while they took down the "And Cabaret" sign. He also said he'd send out a member of his staff, undercover, to check up on them, which the Lees thought was probably a lie. Why go to the trouble and expense of sending in a spy all the way from City of Industry, California, when the Andersons would be doing Cruller's dirty work for free?

As soon as the sign came down and the word spread that Paul's recordings were no longer being played (and, perhaps also relevantly, that no liquor was being served), business returned to its depressing baseline. Mr. Lee, who was always looking at the sunny side of things, mentioned on several occasions to his angry wife that at least they didn't have to worry about the fire code violations anymore.

The whole experience—and those margins on alcohol!—caused Mrs. Lee to look into the liquor business. She talked Mr. Lee into selling the doughnut shop and buying a small liquor store in Eaton, where they made so much money that they bought another in Greeley then another in Ft. Collins. They eventually sold the liquor stores and bought a regional liquor distributing company. They became the Chinese Edgar Bronfmans of the Rocky Mountain West. They knew Mr. Cruller would not appreciate the irony.

CHAPTER 22
MISSOURI

Fungo 400? Our own Joltin' Janitor, Harold Fungo, is on some streak. He is pinch hitting a whopping .385 since joining the team two weeks ago. No doubt that ridiculous number will fall back to earth as he gets more at bats, The last minor league player to bat 400 over a single season was Joe Schmidt, who hit .441 for the Duluth Huskies in 1939. After sweeping three games from the Sterling Strikers, our home team is tied for first place in the Midwest League with rival Garden City. It heads out to Missouri for a two-week road trip today, then will be back home for a seven-day homestand.

It didn't take long for them to tumble into a new morning pattern. If there were words, Kathrine would come into the kitchen first thing, carrying the Big Chiefs. As the story got longer and longer, she would sometimes review, going back several nights if necessary. They both then talked about where the story had gone, why, and where it might be headed. It was all very exciting, and sometimes they talked about it the whole day, a luxury they could indulge in even on weekdays once Joe was no longer working.

In the beginning, away games were hard on Harold and everyone in his adopted family. "What about Sparky?" he asked guardedly when they first explained road games were out of town. Jack suggested they add a clause to the contract that said Howard could take Sparky with him on road trips, but after some thought Harold himself nixed the idea. "I'm alien enough. I don't want to look or act any stranger. And I don't want to seem like I'm a prima donna demanding the moon. Heck, we already have the moon." Atomic smile. "Most of all, it would be unconscionable to make Sparky sit on a bus for hours and then sleep in some strange hotel room. That'll be hard enough for me."

Jack agreed they'd make up Harold's old room at the firehouse and Sparky would stay there with Jack while Harold and Nick were on the road. He'd bring Sparky home to Dee and Sammy on his off days. Harold spent a few nights at the firehouse with Sparky before the first road trip, to get Sparky re-acclimated. Everyone made up a roster to sleep in Harold's old room with Sparky, on the creaky uncomfortable bed, so Jack didn't have to all the time.

On the road, Harold discovered that different states had different personalities. Kansas was as flat as home, but kinder and more hopeful—wetter, greener, warmer. Colorado was the schizophrenic, its eastern plains lulling visitors into Nebraskan dullness, then shocking them with blue exploding mountains. Iowa, across the Missouri and therefore not technically part of the Great Plains, was Harold's favorite, its plump and laden hills built from licorice black soil. Missouri was a mystery, hidden rivers everywhere, and segregation.

The gripping loneliness that would seize him in future trips was now just a dull ache on this first one, when everything was new. It was the longest road trip of the season—more than two weeks—during which they'd play 15 games, all of them in Missouri. They'd start their loop in the north, in Kirksville, then head south to Columbia and Jefferson City, then further south and east all the way to Cape Girardeau near the Mississippi, then back west and north for a final set of games in Springfield and St. Joseph. Not every team down here was double-A. They'd be playing exhibition games against the single-A teams in Kirksville and Springfield. The rest were non-league, but they still counted in the standings.

Harold had never been on a bus before, or in a car for that matter. He'd never been out of town. Though he read about the Great Plains, and lived on them his whole life, he never imagined their scale. He'd read they were the world's breadbasket, but he never realized their vastness, even at this sliver of their eastern edge, or the stunning beauty of acres and acres of bright spring growth. He recognized the early corn but everything else was a mystery. Nick told him he thought the little iridescent plants hugging the ground were young sugar beets, and that the taller grass was winter wheat, whatever that was. Harold actually knew what winter wheat was but didn't lord it over Nick. He drank in the scenery.

Though he read about the cities dotting the Midwest, he never imagined there were so many small towns, one every few miles along the two-lane road. He noticed a pleasing pattern. First, there was a sign lowering the speed limit. Then a sign announcing the town's name and population. He could seldom read both town name and population at once, given the speed of his reading and the speed of the bus. So he alternated. This time he read the name of the town, next time the population. In almost every town there was a white church steeple a few blocks off the main road, a water tower, some grain elevators, houses hidden by a thin light green blanket of spring trees, then another garage/gas station capping the other end of the road on the way out.

He marveled at the size of the Missouri River, which their road paralleled for 50 miles before cutting over to Kirksville. The water came upon them like some maniacal oasis, after the miles and miles of dry Nebraska.

When the bus slowed down at one of the towns then actually stopped, Nick woke up and said they must be stopping for lunch. Harold couldn't believe that he'd been riding in the bus for five hours. It seemed like five minutes. Now he was about to enter a restaurant in a town he never knew existed (Lancaster, Missouri, population unread), and eat food he probably never even heard of before.

Lancaster was a tiny town 45 minutes north of Kirksville. Todd, the team's travel secretary, liked to book meals whenever he could in roadside diners outside of their destinations. He claimed they were cheaper. He was taught by his predecessor to make reservations for off hours, because the team typically took over an entire restaurant, especially small ones.

They were scheduled at the Lancaster Riverside Diner for 1:30. Despite the promise of its name, the diner was not adjacent to, nor within any view of, any river. Heck, Lancaster was 120 miles east of the Missouri behind them and 50 miles west of the Mississippi ahead. But there were some river scenes painted on the diner's walls.

Food being only a sporadic topic in literature, Harold predicted that because of the classical emphasis of Ma's library, most of his food choices at the Lancaster Riverside Diner would be novel. He was right. There were cheeseburgers, chili dogs, split-pea soup, chicken fried steak, corn beef hash, grits, meatloaf, and turkey sandwiches. And that was just what he managed to get through on the top of the first page of the menu. The only restaurant Harold had ever been to was Steak World, and he only ate shrimp cocktail, mashed potatoes, and gravy. Now he had his false teeth and could eat anything, but he didn't know what most of it was.

There must have been 100 things on the menu, only a few of which he recognized from the firehouse, where they rotated between a dozen or so different meals. Nick and he dined exclusively on TV dinners. Ma fixed only four things. Beans and franks, Kraft macaroni and cheese, tuna casserole on Fridays, and Campbell's chicken soup with a fried boloney sandwich. She scrupulously alternated these four meals for dinner and lunch. Dessert was an apple or banana. Breakfast was Wheaties, Breakfast of Champions. Harold remembered dreaming as a young boy about having strong arms like Bob Richards, and vaulting into the air on the top of a pole. And here he was at a restaurant—a restaurant!—eating lunch with baseball players—baseball players!— and not only that, he was one of them. He!

He was thanking his Ma prayer-like when he heard the waitress say, "And for you, hon?" She was clearly in a hurry, maybe so she could go smoke the cigarette behind her ear. Harold wanted to finish reading the menu but knew he just didn't have time.

"I'll have what Clevon is having," he said to Nick, who translated, and pointed to Clevon Sumford, the biggest player on the team. Harold assumed somebody that big must know a lot about different kinds of food, and anyway Harold was famished, and figured Clevon would also order a lot of food. What Harold didn't know was that Clevon was on a diet mandated by Wally. He needed to lose five pounds on this road trip, or risk going down to single-A. So Clevon and Harold both had salads and a side of cottage cheese. Harold loved them, Clevon didn't, and both were still hungry when they were done. Nick, who saw what had happened, shared his French fries with Harold.

Clevon and Harold became inseparable. There were three other black players on the team, and Clevon was their leader, probably because of his age and size. Clevon's unprecedented friendship with this old, skinny white rookie gave Harold immediate membership in their small club, and helped build a tiny bridge between the white and black players. It was a bridge, but it wasn't nearly big enough. A half dozen of the white players, and one of the black players—Lee Williams—simply would not cross the bridge. So the recalcitrant rednecks, joined strangely by Lee Williams, ended up hardly ever talking to or having anything to do with Harold or Clevon.

Wally had seen this before. It was the rule, not the exception. Blacks and whites insulating from one another except during the game—even sitting apart in the dugout. Pitchers seemed a little better at getting along across racial lines—they were mostly crazy to start with and didn't much like any position player, black or white. But Wally had never seen a team broken in three parts—white, black, and a third group that got along with most of both but were hated by parts of both. Wally figured winning would help. It had in the past.

Clevon told Harold to expect trouble in Missouri, which in some parts still had segregated hotels and restaurants. Except for a few hoots and hollers at the black players in Columbia, which Harold noticed made Clevon sad and the other three angry, things were fine until they went down to Cape Girardeau. Harold was excited to be so close to the Mississippi, and asked Clevon if he'd like to walk over to the "cape" overlooking the mighty river, once they got there.

"It's a misspelling of *Giradot*, a French soldier who established a trading post there in the early 1700s at a prominent bend in the river." Harold had read a book about French exploration of the Mississippi river valley, and it had one paragraph about Jean Baptiste Giradot. "They called it a cape because there was a massive rock that jutted out over the river, but it was blasted off when they built the railroad a hundred years later."

"I'm not too keen on being outside anywhere down here by ourselves. We should stick with the whole team."

Clevon's instincts were right. When the team bus pulled up to the Capeview Motel a few miles outside of town, there was a big sign out front that said "No Coloreds." A smaller sign below said, "Sorry, no air conditioning." Todd must have saved a bundle on this joint. Wally had to deal with this segregation bullshit a little in the Texas League. He was younger then, and was ashamed at how he'd crumpled. He was in no mood now.

"So I guess none of us can stay here, is that right?" Wally asked the desk clerk.

"What do you mean?" He was a thin man with hair that was a little too long and a little too greasy for Wally's taste.

"I mean we're all colored."

"You're not."

"Sure. I'm white. That's my color. We got several white boys and a few black boys and none of us can stay here 'cause we're colored? You serve only invisible folks with no color in them at all?"

The clerk switched instantly from confused to bureaucratic. "Look mister, I only work here. These are the rules. There's a colored motel a few miles up that road into the hills."

"Get the owner on the phone, and tell him he's gonna let us all stay here or we will cancel the rest of our trip in this shithole state and I'll make sure every paper from St. Louis to Kansas City has headlines tomorrow about how much revenue he's cost the great citizens of Missouri." The clerk smiled nervously, went back into a rear office for a few minutes, and came back beaming.

"Good news, sir. The owner says your black boys are welcome. There are a few rooms for them at that far end, near the dumpster."

"My black boys will stay wherever the fuck they want, though I will encourage two of them, the biggest and meanest, to stay right here in Unit 2, next to you."

Greg was the only one who overheard this conversation, and he went back to the bus to repeat the gist of it to everyone, while Wally was settling the bill (prepayments were required at most of the dives Todd found). "Don't tell Wally I told you," Greg said to the team, "he'd be too embarrassed."

Every one of them played the best baseball of their lives that night, even the rednecks, and they didn't lose a real game the rest of the road trip. Wally adhered to the trickling strategy. He had Harold pinch hit in every game, but had him ground out in meaningless situations in the real games, to keep his average down. Even so, Harold got five RBIs and they went 13-0 in the real games, and split the two exhibitions.

They had one more incident before going home, in the last game in Springfield. There was a group of men sitting in the first base seats right behind the home dugout. They got drunker and drunker as the night went on and as their home team fell further and further behind, and their racial epithets got louder and crueler. But Wally drew the line at messing with fans. They paid their money and they could say anything they wanted during the game. His players were well instructed that fans were off limits, even just to yell back at. Well, all the players were well instructed about this except Harold, who was too new to have heard Wally's Don't-Mess-With-Fans speech.

Wally put him in in the seventh inning, with a man at third and two outs. Harold wasn't smiling, and stepped up to the plate as a right hander. *What's going on?* Harold could hit perfectly from either side, but always hit as a left hander to save him a few steps to first. *What's he doing?* Wally didn't get it for a moment. Then Harold smashed the first pitch right into the center of the mouthy bumpkins. The first foul ball anyone had ever seen him hit. It broke one of the dopes' arms, and he left for the hospital with two of his buddies. But the other three stayed behind.

Harold took a few pitches, waiting for the ushers to help the injured man out, then crushed another foul ball into the remaining idiots. It didn't do any damage, but they were spooked. They started moving to other seats, further down the line. Harold fouled off three more pitches, waiting for them to relocate. Wally called time. The team knew what Harold was doing, and loved it, but they figured Wally would call him off.

"What the fuck, Harold?"

"They are saying terrible things about Clevon and the others."

"So? It's a free country. Besides, you could kill someone. That ain't right. They are civilians." He paused, then glanced at them over Harold's shoulder. "Don't look at them now. They moved down the line and there are lots of empties around them. Can you keep hitting balls near them, but promise me not to hit any of them direct?"

Harold walked around a bit to steal a glance at where they'd gone. "Absolutely."

"Do it."

He did it. It took ten foul balls raining down around them, a few lucky ones bouncing off the seats and into a leg here and a stomach there, before they left. Wally was sure they didn't have a clue about what was going on, especially in their drunken state. Harold's legend had not made it to these parts. No one could intentionally hit foul balls so accurately. It must just not be their night. That seemed an unsatisfactory conclusion to Wally. So, after they started to pack up and Harold hit his single as instructed, Wally called another time out. Instead of signaling for the pinch runner, as usual, Wally turned and trotted down the third base line toward them.

All the fans thought Wally was checking on their health, and the health of their friend taken to the hospital. "Well, ain't that nice," the announcer announced, "that's real class. Give a hand to Wally Berens, folks, the visiting manager and a real gentleman." The fans applauded. The last of the dumbbells was gathering up his stuff to leave. Wally ran up to him, smiling, reached his hand out, grabbed him, and pulled him close.

"Just wanted to let you and your asshole friends know my player did that on purpose, and if I ever see any of you fuckers at another game, spewing your shit, we'll send all of you to the hospital. Pass the word. Now get your ass out of here or we'll break your arm too."

After a couple games in St. Joseph, the team headed home. Once again, the road hugged the Missouri. It seemed even wider than when they saw it coming in. The silent rocking of the bus, the snap of shuffled playing cards, the unfilled time, all made Harold think a lot about Ma.

Katherine cried when she wrote down parts of this installment and cried again when she read them to Joe. "Are you feeling these emotions when these words come out?"

"I've told you a million times, ever since the sneezing stopped I don't hear the words, I don't know I'm saying them, and I hear them the first time when you read them to me."

"But you're not even crying now, after you hear them. I think that means the feelings that poured into these words must have bubbled out already. You've heard this story before, even if just subconsciously."

"I don't know."

"Were there any Negroes at Greeley Central when you were there?

"No."

"In the Navy?"

"Just a few."

"What did they do?"

"Most were cooks and stewards, but there was one guy who worked on the torpedoes in the machine shop. He knew everything about torpedoes. Not sure how he learned."

"Were you friends with any of them?"

"No, they stayed to themselves."

"Your brain is sure well-rounded."

"How do you know?"

"No, I mean it sure has had lots of experiences that you haven't had."

In baseball, as in life, just about anything one can imagine happening has happened, and because of that the chances of anything in particular happening are roughly zero. Pop-up hits bird, Fleming discovers penicillin, Harold Fungo takes on pitching machine, family of four killed by drunk driver. We live at this charged saddle point of surprise, where everything is unlikely precisely because everything is possible. Baseball constantly jolts us alive with that surprise.

I began in earnest to follow this Hephaestus, this hammerer of baseballs and baseball records, after Sonny started sending me clippings from the local paper. In New York, and really in all the big-league cities to which I traveled, we were deaf to the broad rumblings in the minor leagues, attuned only to the single frequency of the top prospects in a team's triple-A affiliate. So I learned about Hephaestus exclusively from Sonny's clippings, to which he invariably appended notes like "He will change everything" and "If only he could play a position." From these notes and addenda, I began to hear the hammer.

CHAPTER 23
DRS. BRAINBERG AND CUTSTEIN

Hot Bats Headed Home. Fueled by rising sensation Harold Fungo, our local team went 13-0 on its 15-day road trip into Missouri, the longest of the year. Its season record stands at 27-16, putting it in first place in the Midwest League, two-and-a-half games ahead of Garden City. Fungo's stratospheric average has leveled off a little, as expected, but he is still hitting .378. The team will begin a seven-game homestand against three different teams tonight, starting with the Sioux City Sioux. It will be Old Cap Night. Fans wearing either the red or blue cap from the old Cooper Trucking or Cooper Equipment recreational teams will be admitted free.

After giving Joe another physical, taking more blood, asking a lot of questions about headaches ("Yes, I've had a little bit of one ever since I stopped sneezing"), and sending him over to the hospital for head x-rays, the neurologist, Dr. Stevens, said he would like to see Joe again day after tomorrow, when the blood work and x-rays should be ready.

"Day after tomorrow!" Joe growled to Katherine before they even got back to the car. "We drive all the way down to Denver, wait forty minutes in that waiting room, the actual appointment takes all of 15 minutes, we traipse over to the hospital where we wait another 30 minutes for the x-ray, and now we need to come back day after tomorrow?"

"I'm surprised they could fit us in so soon. Did you see that waiting room?"

"Well, I didn't hear anybody sneezing. And I'm not sneezing now anyway. Why do we have to do this? That waiting room was full of people in wheelchairs. I'm not having trouble walking."

"Joe, you heard what Dr. Stevens said. They need to look again at your blood and the x-ray of your brain."

"But I gave blood to Kasten and to Dr. Gold—Dr. Wilson. How much do they need?"

Katherine didn't answer. In fact, she said almost nothing else on the way home. Joe had to prod her, which was unusual. "Something wrong?" he asked as they passed through the dormant sugar beet farms near Brighton.

"I'm mad at you," Katherine announced, in a tone that Joe knew was more worried than mad.

"Why?"

"Because you never told me you were having headaches."

"They're not bad."

"But you should have told me, Joe."

When they passed Brighton, Joe thought about the one time he saw Lester in a real concert. It was early autumn, a few days before Halloween. They were 15 years old, and Lester was doing his first one man, or one teenager, show at a Christian Science church in Brighton. Mrs. Buckley had called Joe's mom a few days before and told her Lester thought it would be fun if Joe could join them, and asked if he could.

"Sure!" he told his mom as she held the telephone away from her mouth and asked Joe if he'd like to go.

"Mrs. Buckley said she thought it would be nice for you to give Lester some moral support at this concert. It's his first one by himself."

Joe thought it a little odd that if Lester needed "moral support," whatever that was, he wouldn't just ask Joe directly. But the idea of a Sunday afternoon drive in the Buckley's spanking new Mercury 8 was irresistible. Plus, he'd get to hear Lester play, and see if other people felt about it the same way he did.

Joe had been mesmerized for several weeks by a billboard on 9th Street at 14th Avenue advertising the Mercury 8. He was almost 16, and every cell in his body was getting ready to drive. The billboard had a picture of a sleek car, liquid blue. At the bottom, in bold red letters outlined in black, it said, "The car that truly dares to ask, 'Why?'"

When he heard about the Buckleys' new Mercury 8—not from Lester because he didn't really care about cars, but rather from his own father, who said, "How'd they possibly afford that?"—Joe decided he'd ask Lester about the mysterious slogan. Surely now that Lester's family actually owned a Mercury 8 Lester would know not just what the marketing question was asking but also the answer to the question. Lester didn't have the foggiest. And now Joe was cruising down the highway toward Brighton actually *inside* a Mercury 8!

It was bottle green and had a finish like a mirror. The ride was a lot smoother and quieter than his dad's old Ford Model A. And faster. The dashboard looked like Joe imagined an aeroplane's would, or a rocket ship's. Round green dials everywhere, split by thin red needles. There was soft and luxurious light gray cloth all around the inside of the car, even on the interior of the roof! He imagined the car stayed cool in the summer and toasty in the winter, not like the frying pan and freezer that was the Model A.

"Thanks again for inviting me along, Mrs. Buckley."

"It is our pleasure, Yosef."

"This is a really nice car. It's a Mercury 8, isn't it?"

"I think so."

"Have you seen that billboard on 9th that advertises it, and that says *The car that truly dares to ask, 'Why?'*?

"I don't believe I have." Lester had been sleeping, but when Joe starting talking he opened his eyes. When he heard the conversation, he rolled his eyes at Joe and went back to sleep.

"What do you think that means? What exactly is the question the car is asking, and by the way how can a car ask questions, and why it is so daring even to ask the question, and what's the answer to the daring question?"

Margaret Buckley laughed and said, "Yosef, these are all interesting questions, but I am afraid I know nothing about cars or advertising. You should ask Carl."

Yeah, sure, thought Joe. Mr. Buckley had said maybe three words to him his whole life. He was always downstairs building model ships, whistling or singing to himself. He was a walking advertisement, a giant 6'3" advertisement, that said *Don't dare interrupt me.* Joe looked over at Lester, hoping he would have heard this preposterous suggestion by his own mother, but Lester was still sleeping.

The Brighton church "auditorium"—it was really just the church sanctuary with the pulpit pushed off to one side—was surprisingly full. Almost to capacity. There had been flyers announcing the "Boy Genius from Greeley" and "Weld County's Own Piano Prodigy." The church's young music director hopped up onto the chancel and made her introduction.

"We are delighted to have with us this afternoon a very special guest. Lester Buckley is a deeply gifted pianist from a gifted musical family. Some of you may recognize his mother Margaret Buckley nee Rothstein, who was a star in her own right with the Berlin Philharmonic, which at the time was led by none other than Antonia Brico."

No one recognized Margaret Rothstein's name but almost everyone recognized Antonia Brico's. She was the barrier-breaking pianist and conductor who was the first woman ever to conduct the New York Philharmonic, among many other orchestras. Sibelius himself once invited her to conduct the Helsinki Symphony Orchestra. She settled in Denver, and in fact she was the reason Margaret found herself in Colorado. She was also instrumental in getting Lester admitted to the Curtis Institute.

"You will discover this afternoon that Margaret's stunning musical gifts have not fallen far from the tree, although she'll have to explain to us how in the world she allowed her son to be corrupted by the keyboard instead of becoming a singer [audience laughter]. Lester will dazzle us this afternoon with Mendelssohn's Third Piano Sonata. Oh, and did I mention Lester has achieved the ripe old age of 15 [audience laughter]? Without further ado, we at the Brighton Church of Christ, Scientist, are delighted to present Mr. Lester Buckley [applause]."

But Lester was nowhere to be seen. One of the strangest things about him, and there were plenty to choose from, was that he would get very sleepy right before performances, often falling fast asleep. Because this was his first formal concert by himself, there were no other performers backstage to wake him and tell him he was on.

When his mother realized what happened she told Joe to run as unobtrusively as he could down a side aisle to the small cubicle behind the altar and wake Lester up. She stood and announced, "Sorry, he gets fery sleepy before performing. It's not boredom, it's the way his body handles nerves." The audience loved it. Lester came out, blinking at the brightness of the lights, and ripped off his Mendelssohn without a hitch, earning two standing ovations. He played a Chopin nocturne for the encore.

After that experience, Margaret always stayed with Lester backstage to wake him when it was time. Although she forgot all about it for Lester's biggest performance of all—his audition at Curtis. Antonia was a surprise guest. Margaret was so happy to see her, so nervous about the audition, and so honored that the faculty had made an exception to their usual rule that parents were not allowed to attend auditions, that she left Lester in the side warm-up room all by himself. When the faculty member in charge went to retrieve him, he was sound asleep. Snoring. Everyone heard her say, "I hate so much to disturb you, Master Buckley, but would it be convenient now for you to wake and honor us with your Beethoven?"

When Joe's mind wandered into Philadelphia, he shook himself into the present, noticing the Christmas decorations in Platteville. Most Christmas decorations looked junky and tinny in the daylight, but even the junkiest and tinniest shone like the star of Bethlehem when darkness came. In fact, the junkier by daylight the better at night. These were some of the junkiest and tinniest he'd ever seen, so he had faith they'd be spectacular at night. "We should drive here to Platteville some night to see the Christmas decorations," he suggested to Katherine.

Two days later he and Katherine were back in Dr. Stevens' office. A second doctor was standing in the corner as Joe and Katherine were ushered in by a nurse. He was holding up x-rays, which he quickly put down as he turned back around.

"Joe and Katherine, this is Dr. Reynolds and I've asked him to join us today to be part of our team. Dr. Reynolds is a neurosurgeon. Dr. Reynolds, this is Joe Skelton and his wife Katherine."

After everyone exchanged handshakes, Katherine asked, "Are those Joe's x-rays?"

"Yes," replied Dr. Reynolds, "and they are normal, except for these spots, which are calcium deposits."

As he was speaking Reynolds flipped on a light box hanging on the wall, slipped one of the x-ray films under the clips at the top, and the long and delicate fingers of his right hand, scrubbed an unnatural pale pink, hovered over the white spots that were sprinkled on a corner of the image like powdered sugar.

"These are the calcium deposits. They can be byproducts of some brain tumors, and thank goodness, because they show us where the tumors are when they are too small and dispersed to show up themselves."

He said the words "brain tumors" like he was saying "tan slippers" or "big snowstorm," but to Katherine they were tremorous. The room started to vibrate then wobble, and she even looked over at the pitcher of water on Dr. Stevens' desk, puzzled that it was not sloshing.

The doctors explained that Joe probably had some kind of growth in his brain, and that they wanted to do some exploratory surgery soon. Very soon, as in this week. Katherine caught most of the words. She remembered some nice words like "benign" and "nothing at all," but they were whispers compared to the shouted words about the red monster. It had a name now. Glioblastoma M-something. GBM. Joe thought the acronym sounded like some agricultural product.

He had the exploratory surgery later that week. They'd asked him whether he wanted his whole head shaved or just half, since they'd be going in through his left temple.

"Wouldn't just half look stupid?" he asked Katherine during the Report the night before the surgery.

"For a while. You could have them shave just half and then go over to Tommy's and have him crew cut the other half. Then you wouldn't be completely bald, and the bald half wouldn't have as much to catch up with."

So that's what Joe did. A few days after the surgery he went over to Tommy's and got a crew cut on the other half. From the right side, Joe looked like an aging athlete, maybe a football coach, a little like Mr. Weisen. From the left side he looked like he'd just escaped from a mental hospital, a little like Mr. Weisen.

"Shavin' it wud look bedder, match the udder half," the Swedish-born Tommy announced in his sing-song English to the entire crowded barber shop.

"I could have had them do that in the hospital."

"Shud have."

Dr. Reynolds did the surgery. He and Dr. Stevens explained that if they were able to snag a piece of the tumor, they would suck it out and test it. They could tell by the test if it was benign or cancerous, and if it was cancer they might even be able to tell what kind. GBM was the worst. No way to treat it, three months life expectancy. That wouldn't even get us to firefly season, Joe thought. Katherine's mind had gone blank. She was still looking over at the miraculously stable pitcher of water.

After the surgery, Dr. Reynolds came out and told Katherine that Joe tolerated it fine, and that they got a piece big enough to test. They agreed that Dr. Stevens would call Dr. Kasten with the test results, and that Dr. Kasten would pass them on to Joe and Katherine. It would take three or four days.

The day after Joe's half crewcut they decided to have pizza for dinner. It was Katherine's idea. She was so worried about getting the phone call from Doc Kasten that she couldn't eat at all the first few days. She suggested pizza because she loved it, and thought she might actually have an appetite for it.

Pizza was still a fairly new thing in Greeley, and of course home delivery was unheard of. There was just one pizza parlor—Paisan's, on 10th Street. Katherine called and ordered a medium pepperoni. Soot got very animated when he heard them discussing pizza and especially after he heard Katherine say "pepperoni" on the telephone. He knew a couple pieces of pepperoni and a pizza crust were coming his way. Katherine made a salad and put a glass for beer in the freezer while Joe drove over to Paisan's.

Outside, to the right of the entrance, was Paisan's famous caricatured statue of a fat Italian chef, swaddled all in white but for his red-checkered scarf. One of his chubby white arms was under a big disc of pizza dough held out in front of him. The other arm was raised in the air, flared out behind him, for balance, stubby fingers apart like a gymnast's finishing salute. A black mustache was stuck on his white face, threatening to fall into the dough. Depending on one's direction of travel, the light, and the time of day, the floppy white chef's hat sometimes looked like a second pizza, which had fallen on the overambitious juggling chef's head.

Everyone called the sculpture Johnny Two, or just Two, to distinguish it from Paisan's proprietor, Johnny One. Johnny One was Johnny Carbone, who was a nephew of the late Father Carbone. The Carbone family was part of a large Italian contingent of agricultural workers that had settled in the area at the turn of the century to work the farms. Many eventually bought their own farms. Beans, potatoes, peppers, and lots of cantaloupes and other melons.

Local teenagers regularly vandalized Johnny Two. "Vandalize" is too strong. They would have vandalized it except Johnny One chained it to the door, kept vigil over it during working hours, and moved it inside at closing. Johnny One had himself been a ravenous vandal when he was young, so he knew the enemy. Despite these precautions, every once in a while the moustache might get painted out, a game of tic-tac-toe played on the checkered scarf, or suggestive things done to the groin area.

"Hi, Two." Joe always greeted the sculpture, and every time thought about the perils of trying to spin two pizza doughs at the same time. Once, someone put a big floppy white hat on top of Two's free hand, and he looked like he was juggling *three* pizza doughs, though Joe never actually saw that, only heard about it.

"Hi, Johnny," Joe said, opening the door and walking inside. Frank Sinatra's "Fly Me to the Moon" was playing on the jukebox. "You know someone's put a rubber on one of Two's fingers?"

"Goddamn teenagers," Johnny spit out angrily, as if he'd never put rubbers on dozens of public displays.

Johnny pulled Joe's pizza out of the oven with the big wooden peel, slid it onto the wide counter, keeping the peel nearby, and rocked his big knife over the pie four times, leaving eight perfectly matched steaming pieces. "Those rolling pizza cutters are for amateurs," Johnny once told Joe when he asked him why he never used them.

Then he grabbed a flat cardboard cut-out off the top of a deck of them, moved his hands over it like a magician doing a card trick, so fast that Joe could never really make out what was happening—he thought of Lester's hands over the keyboard—and Johnny conjured a pizza box. "Hot Delicious Pizza" was blazoned across the top in strange red and green cursive writing, supported by the image of a small fat chef in the center who looked like he might be Two's nephew. Johnny grabbed the peel, slipped it deftly under the slices, slid them into the box, and threw the top closed, all in what seemed like, but couldn't possible have been, a single movement consuming a half second. Then he ran out front to remove the offending contraceptive, armed with tongs.

"What's with the hair, Joe?" he asked as he dropped the condom into the bin and the tongs into the sink.

"I had a little surgery, and they had to shave half my head."

"Shoulda had 'em shave the whole thing."

Katherine set the light green kitchen table with her special red placemats. Pizza was always a treat, plus the red placemats made it look like Christmas, which was only 18 days away. She poured her beer into the chilled glass when she heard Joe drive up. Soot was getting increasingly excited. They usually ate dinner silently, probably because they knew the Report would be coming soon. But tonight, after they toasted—they always toasted at every dinner, no matter what they were drinking, tonight Katherine clinking her beer glass against Joe's Coke can—Joe couldn't help himself. "Teenagers put a rubber on Two's finger."

Katherine spit out a small wedge of pepperoni, which looked like its own miniature slice of dark red pizza sliding and spinning across the table and onto the floor, an unexpected appetizer for Soot. It took her a minute to stop laughing. She hadn't laughed since the surgery. She was struggling not to start giggling again when the phone rang. It was Doc Kasten. It was GBM.

It was a cold Report that night, snow blowing in off the mountains, obscuring the winter moon, its diffused glow spread wide by the low clouds. Bundled up on their big chairs, they both thought about GBM, about how long three months was, and about the spring.

Katherine hadn't stopped crying since Doc's call. Joe tried to comfort her with hugs, which were nice, but she needed talking and that was not Joe's forte. She knew she could get some talking out of him during the Report, so she mustered every ounce of strength, fought every nerve that told her to curl up inside on their bed, and pulled on her coat.

They sat on the chairs, Soot as usual between them. His black coat turned salt and pepper and then sheet white as the snow accumulated. Every few minutes he would stand and shake, shooting snow onto Joe and Katherine, return to black, and lay back down. For years Joe had been saying to himself, and occasionally to Katherine, that one of these days he would put up an overhang so the back porch would be covered. He never got around to it, and Katherine never insisted; they both wanted to feel the weather.

The snow was really coming down now. High up, above the roof lines, the giant flakes glowed green and red, reflecting the Christmas lights that were up on so many eaves, and on the Foxleys' tall pine tree across the street in the front. As if on stage under the spotlight of the Tanner's streetlight, the tumbling flakes danced precociously until they fell offstage, into Tiny's shadow. Right at the shadow's edge, the flakes were still dressed in green and red, though darker now, until the stage lights went out. The snow made everything so quiet.

CHAPTER 24
SOUTH DAKOTA, IOWA, AND KANSAS

Fungo Watch. Our Joltin' Janitor continues to flirt with baseball history, as his average now sits at a gigantic .381. Opposing pitchers are starting to walk him intentionally in some situations, but even then they are having trouble with our humble hero. Last night, the hapless relief pitcher for the Sterling Strikers tried to walk Fungo, but he reached far out over the plate and knocked in an RBI single smack down the left field line. The team begins a long road trip tomorrow, including an exhibition in Des Moines against the triple-A Iowa Cubs. When they get back, will Fungo still be flirting with .400, and, more importantly, will he still be with us, or will he have been called up by the hapless Reds, who could sorely use him?

Harold promised to send postcards to everyone back home, and he always bought a bunch in every town where they stopped. Iowa towns had the best. "Dubuque: The Iowa Riviera," had a picture of a hog farm with girls in swimsuits walking around and sipping drinks. "Davenport: Come Sit Down with Us for a While," had a couch in front of a stack of hay bales. "Rome: Come Discover Us," had hogs standing around a red and white checkered tablecloth, placed on the ground and set with plates of spaghetti and a bottle of wine.

On the second road trip, they played in one town in northeast Nebraska, Norfolk, and one in southeast South Dakota, Yankton, on their way to the outermost stop on this trip: a non-league game in Mitchell, South Dakota, home of the Corn Palace. They finished up with a bunch of games in Iowa, and one in Kansas on the way home.

When they got to Mitchell, South Dakota, Harold and Clevon took a tour of The Corn Palace. The two-story Moorish Revival mansion, rising in the middle of a flat downtown, had an exterior built entirely of corn cobs.

"Who shucked all this corn?" Clevon asked suspiciously of the tour guide.

"Farmers from all around here," the young and eager college-aged guide answered. Clevon wasn't buying it, but he didn't let his skepticism interfere with Harold's enjoyment.

Most of the interior of The Corn Palace was consumed by a gift shop and a large auditorium with stadium seating, where, according to the tour guide, local high school teams still played basketball. After stocking up on post cards and souvenirs, Harold and Clevon walked all the way up to the last row of the auditorium.

"We need to get you to run faster," Clevon said, sporting his new corn cob sunglasses. They had bright green frames, and big yellow and green smiling corn cob cartoon characters at each corner, facing sideways. "How we gonna do that?"

"I don't know. Wally mentioned they may send me to a doctor."

Each man knew they were actually talking about their friendship, and about the threat to it that Harold's slowness posed. If he couldn't get faster, he might go down to Shithole, Texas on August 1. But they also knew there was an opposite, and more likely, threat—that Harold would be called up to triple-A or even to the big leagues and leave Clevon behind, where he had toiled for four years without ever making it out of double-A.

"And you need to learn how to hit a curve," responded Harold, addressing the second threat.

"I know."

"How are you going to do that?

"I dunno."

"I know. You and I are going to practice so long and so hard on the pitching machine, and Greg will help, that you'll be able to hit a curveball blindfolded. It just takes lots of practice. That's all it takes. Why do you think I hit so well?"

Clevon, like the whole team, was busting with curiosity about that very subject. Harold was so much better than any of them—better than any hitter ever—they figured it was just a gift from God. But they weren't sure.

"I don't know. Lots of us was wondering."

"I practiced for 30 years. At least four hours every day."

"Well, I ain't got 30 years, or four extra hours every day."

"But you don't need to hit 1,000. You just need to hit the curve ball better. How much do you think you need to increase your average with the curve to have a realistic chance at the majors?"

"I don't know. I hit the fastball at about a 300 clip, but the curve at 210. If I could get the curve up to past 250 that should be good enough, if I don't lose too much power."

They agreed that every morning, home and away, if a field or even a town park were available, and a pitching machine or a willing pitcher, Clevon would take extra batting practice with the curve, until his average was above 250. They called this The Corn Palace Pact. Every morning when Clevon wanted to stay in bed, all Harold had to say was "Corn Palace," and Clevon dragged himself up.

Harold starting catching Corn Palace practices, whether they had a pitcher (usually Greg) or were using the machine. He wasn't too bad. He caught almost every ball, whether Clevon swung or not, which was unusual for beginning catchers, especially because he was so tall and insisted on standing up. The only balls that occasionally got past him were ones in the dirt. But he could barely throw the ball back to Greg, and had no accuracy.

When the rest of team heard Harold was helping Clevon with his hitting, they asked Clevon about it.

"Dammit, there's no secret. Harold says he's good because he's been practicing four hours every day for 30 years, and I'll get a little better (never as good as him) but I'll have to practice my ass off."

This news depressed some of the players, for whom hard work was just as far from being a realistic strategy as hoping for a gift from God.

At night, Harold tried his best to write something on all the postcards. But his shaky hands made it almost impossible. Nick volunteered to write them for him, which he did for a while. Then he got the idea of a typewriter.

Harold was skeptical that punching letters with his fingers would be any easier for him than writing letters with a pencil, but Nick persisted. They found a small Smith-Corona in a pawnshop in Iowa City, small enough to fit in Harold's suitcase. It turned out to be much easier for Harold to punch the letters on the typewriter than it was to move a pencil up and down and across and over paper.

He had 30 years of words piled up inside him. He had so much to say he'd send multiple postcards with the typed message continuing from one to the other. The postcards became a kind of poetry, the ones to Sammy a kind of children's literature.

> Dear Sammy,
>
> Today we are playing a game in Des Moines, Iowa, a much bigger city than we are used to. Des Moines is a funny-looking name because it is French. It looks like Dez Moins, doesn't it? But it is actually pronounced Duh Moin. Ask your mommy or daddy to help you find Des Moines on a map. Then find where you live. Then draw a line between the two spots and that will be the line we've been traveling in our bus. Make sure mommy or daddy say it's OK to draw on the map—if you use a pencil, you can erase it later. (Continued on Card #2.)

Pirates like Long John Silver used maps to find hidden treasure. Have you ever read that book about Long John Silver, or other ones about pirates? I have a pirate game for you to play, to help us find a kind of hidden treasure. Find our hometown on the map. Then find a squiggly line already on the map that goes down from our hometown. It will probably be red or yellow, and it will be marked with a number 77 in a little shield. (Continued on Card #3.)

Follow that line down and down, to the dot for Manhattan. We played there a couple nights ago. They called the game Zoo Night, and everyone who dressed up like a zoo animal got in free. Their players wore zebra striped uniforms. And instead of umpires at the bases they had monkeys, for one inning, the third inning. (Continued on Card #4.)

I am not kidding you. If the monkey jumped up and down then you were out. If he was still then you were safe. Wally said he thought the monkeys were getting signals from the other team, but I'm not sure. Wally put me in to bat in the third inning. I got a hit, and Wally let me stay on first. Not only that, he told me to steal second. Me! Remember, I don't run very fast. (Continued on Card #5.)

I was out by a mile, but the monkey must have liked me because he called me safe (he didn't jump up and down). Then Wally signaled to me to steal third! Again, I was out by a mile, but that monkey liked me too. The home plate umpire was a regular person, not a monkey, so I didn't get to steal home. (Continued on Card #6.)

But guess what? My friend Clevon knocked out a homer so I got to run to home plate, step on it, and score a run. My first one ever. And I'm guessing my last, unless more teams use monkey umpires. Tomorrow, I will send you the picture from the newspaper showing the monkey umpire calling me safe at third. You can't see my face, but you can see my number 15, and the monkey. (Continued on Card #7.)

Traveling is hard because I miss my friends, like you and your mommy and daddy, and Sparky. But traveling is also hard because we meet so many nice people who could become new friends, but we don't have time to get to know them because we must leave after a day or two. (Continued on Card #8.)

We played in Des Moines for one special game against the triple-A team—they are better players than we are, so it was an important game for us. Have you ever played a game with bigger, stronger boys? You really want to show them you are just as good as they are, but you wonder inside of you whether you really are. They want to show they are better than you are, but they wonder inside too. So, there was a lot of wondering in this game. (Continued on Card# 9.)

I did very well, but most of my teammates did not. We got clobbered, 10-3. My teammates were sad. But then we played the next day, and won against boys our own size. We should be home soon after you get this last postcard. I will be happy to see you and Sparky.

Love, Harold

In addition to the postcards, Harold started to type on typing paper, addressed to no one. He wrote about everything. The more he wrote the more he realized this must be poetry, so the more poetry he read. Ma's library had a few collections, mostly 19th century English poets but also all of Shakespeare's sonnets.

At first, the perfection of the sonnets, burned permanently into his memory, warned Harold off doing his own serious poetry. But he became more and more courageous as he read three and a half centuries of others trying to dodge the master's shadow. Harold bought collections of poetry every chance he got. He was especially enamored of Wallace Stevens, among the new bunch. He even wrote a poem he never published, in honor of and with apologies to Stevens' Anecdote of the Jar:

> I swung a bat in Iowa
> And round it was, and tapered up
> It made the careless infielders all
> Surround that bat.
>
> The fielders rose up to it
> And lay down, no longer deployed
> The bat was round and tapered
> And tall, a lightning rod in air
>
> It took dominion everywhere
> The bat was white and smooth
> It did not give of strikes or outs
> Like nothing else in Iowa.

He wrote about bus rides in the Midwest, groupies, his teammates, Clevon, Wally, Greg, Sammy, Jack, Sparky, Ma, everything. He felt like an archeologist, the words digging deeper and deeper into the past.

Tales of Harold was getting good, but Joe was fading fast, faster than he would ever let on to Katherine. They'd talked so much about his death that he didn't really think much about it anymore. He didn't even worry that much about Katherine. She'd done such a good job of comforting him, not about his own death, which he could see still worried her greatly, but about how she would cope with it.

What Joe worried about most, and what seemed to light the fire of what little was left of his own dimming survival instincts, was Harold. He had to finish. But Katherine was ready to stop.

"Joe, I don't think I can keep writing your words down every night. I can't stand it."

"I'm gonna die whether you write the words down or not, Kath."

"It's not that. It's that I have to *hear* you say them. You get to hear me read them but I have to hear you say them. I'm starting to not know who you are anymore. I'm losing you while you're still here."

Joe didn't fully understand, because to him Tales of Harold had nothing to do with Joe Skelton. Katherine read him the story every morning, and might as well have been reading a regular book by a real author. But he desperately wanted to find out how Tales of Harold was going to end. He got an idea.

"How about we borrow Paul's and Mary's tape-recording machine? Then instead of writing the words down we could listen to them together. It would even save you sleep."

"I would still hear you say the words, but it might be a little better if I didn't have to write them down all night long. I'll ask Mary for it today. But what should we say we need it for? I don't really want to tell anyone about Tales of Harold yet, do you?"

"No."

"I know. I'll tell her you are giving us an oral history of your growing up, your family, your friendship with Lester, your time in the Navy and at the store."

"OK."

It worked out better than Katherine imagined. Every night before bed she'd make sure the big reel-to-reel machine was all set up and ready to go. She'd stay up reading as usual, but right before her big breath, she'd turn the recorder on and go to sleep. She'd turn it off in the morning, and at breakfast they'd discover whether Joe said any words. She stopped writing any of the words down, which, as she hoped, helped a little with her feelings of disconnectedness.

But for Joe it was a disturbing change. Katherine was no longer reading him a story; he was hearing his own gravelly voice telling one.

Where the heck was all of this coming from? He began thinking more and more about the tumor, and more and more about his death. Not big things, but little ones. What day of the week would he die? What time? What would be the last thing he saw? What would be Katherine's last words to him and his to her? All his guesses were wrong. Turns out death is just as unpredictable as life.

In my mind, Harold's famous Hillerich & Bradsby bat, now on display at Cooperstown, is forever bound to Pee Wee Reese, who worked for the Louisville bat maker after his playing and broadcasting days. And Reese, in everyone's mind, is forever bound to Jackie Robinson.

In 1947, rumors were flying that the Brooklyn Dodgers were going to call Robinson up. Several Dodgers players were circulating a petition declaring they would not play with Robinson. They assumed Reese would sign the petition because he was from Kentucky. But Reese, who had just returned from serving three years in the Navy during World War II, refused.

After Robinson's call-up, the team was in Cincinnati and Robinson was enduring the usual pre-game vile from the crowd. It stopped suddenly and completely when Reese walked up to Robinson and put his arm around him. Years later, at Reese's funeral, Joe Black, a Negro League star and later a Dodger teammate of both, said that "when Pee Wee touched Jackie, he touched us all."

There is a statue in Brooklyn, at the minor league park just north of Coney Island, that I visit every mid-April, after dropping my tax returns off at the Mermaid Avenue post office. It depicts that moment in Cincinnati when Reese put his arm around Robinson. If you stand in just the right place, Coney Island's decommissioned Parachute Jump tower looks like a fountain of red fireworks celebrating the moment, its shower spraying out and down to envelope and protect the two infielders.

Some baseball historians have questioned whether this event happened in Cincinnati on the date reported, or on a different date or in a different city. Some have even questioned whether it happened at all. I'm not sure it matters. Some truths are too big for proof.

I have often wondered whether it was the God of Fate or the God of Chance who put Pee Wee and Jackie on the same team. Today, I am also wondering whether Pee Wee touched Harold's bat on its way out of the Louisville factory, whether he put the same hand on it that he placed on Jackie's shoulder.

CHAPTER 25
FIDELITY MUTUAL

Fungo Watch. Readers have asked why manager Wally Berens doesn't start phenom Harold Fungo as a position player. It seems Fungo's leg injury is still giving him problems, as anyone watching him run to first base can plainly see. Until those injuries resolve, Fungo will just have to bide his time pinch hitting at a .388 clip! That's right, his average went *up* over this last long road trip. So did the team's first-place lead, which stands at a full five games over the Garden City Bluebells. The team hosts the Bluebells tonight, the first of an important four-game series before it heads back out on the road. Get well, soon, Harold, so we can see your bat four or five times each game instead of just once!

After their mother died in a car accident in Denver, driving proudly in her white chariot, Mary joined the Army. She and Joe had a special bond based entirely on their oddly patriotic responses to tragedy. But for that bond, they probably would never have gotten along.

"Why don't you like Mary?" Katherine asked him the day of their mother's funeral.

"She's mean."

"Not exactly mean," Katherine laughed sadly, "but maybe a little strident."

"Strident?"

"It means she's sure of herself, a bit of a know-it-all."

"She is."

"Try to learn to like her, Joe. She's had a hard time being at home, taking care of Mother and Father while I was at college and teaching. She means the world to me, even more now that Mother's gone, so cut her some slack."

But the rope just didn't have any slack in it, not until Mary joined the Army two days later. Then it drooped like a dead snake. When she was on leave visiting, Mary and Joe spent hours exchanging glances, talking about the military without using any words.

When she got out of the Army, Mary went to business school in Denver. Katherine was sure that had their mother still been alive she would have cajoled Mary into going to a regular four-year college. But Mary was always interested in business. Even when she was young, she was fascinated by the business end of farming. She couldn't care less about the work that went into planting, caring for, and then harvesting crops, except what it cost to do all those things, but she was spellbound by their market prices, how the prices went up and down, and how fortunes were made and farms lost on the vagaries of that mysterious tide.

When she graduated from business school she started working in Denver as a secretary to the vice president of sales for the western division of Fidelity Mutual Insurance Company of Minnesota. After just a few months she bullied her way into sales, taking over a tiny region in northeast Colorado that nobody wanted. She was the best insurance salesman Fidelity Mutual had west of Chicago, and its only female salesman in the whole country.

She made her bones in life insurance. Mary knew that in most families it was the wife, not the husband, who made the actual decision to buy life insurance. Men cared about yesterdays, and a bit about todays. Women cared about tomorrows. Mary pretended to talk to the men while she talked to the women.

But her real interest was in the actuarial tables the company used to set its premiums. She knew millions could be squeezed out of a fiercely competitive insurance market just by making better actuarial judgments, way more than by trying to find new customers. She developed systems for improving the company's life and casualty tables by doing empirical customer studies and surveys, though she had to present the plan to management through a male supervisor, who took all the credit. He rocketed up the corporate ladder, and, out of a blend of guilt and debt, he made sure Mary could do pretty much anything she wanted at Fidelity Mutual after that. What she wanted was to go back up to Greeley and continue her actuarial work unencumbered by corporate politics. So they hired her as an actuarial consultant and paid her gobs of money.

If they were honest, Mary and Katherine would have to admit that Mary's wealth became a bit of a sticking point between them. Katherine wasn't deeply jealous of Mary's financial success, but she couldn't help feeling an irritated tinge every time she and Joe had to put off buying something because they couldn't afford it. Mary felt a corresponding tinge of guilt whenever she and Paul bought something she knew Joe and Katherine couldn't afford. But these feelings stayed small and offstage, because neither Mary nor Katherine was terribly material, and, more importantly, because they shared one big thing that outshined those small material differences. They were both students, no, Nobel laureates, of human nature.

Katherine had spent her whole life reading what the world's most articulate observers had to say about love and hate, loyalty and treachery, kindness and cruelty, punishment and forgiveness, and Mary measured how all these quirks of the human condition actually made us behave. This shared obsession with human nature and its effects helped Katherine and Mary weather Mary's success. It also helped Katherine and Joe weather, with Mary's help, their biggest failure. Katherine's infidelity.

They'd been married a little less than four years. He was a visiting professor of French literature named Montgomery Royce. Katherine took a summer night course from him down in Denver. Mondays and Thursdays, 7 to 9.

He was tall, blond, handsome, and spoke in long flowery sentences oozing with emotion. When he said "Next week we will discuss Flaubert's Temptation of Saint Anthony," it sounded to almost every woman in the class like foreplay, including Katherine. He was sophisticated. He'd studied at the Sorbonne and was an assistant professor at UCLA. Everyone wondered why he'd come to the middle of nowhere to teach for the summer.

Katherine loved day dreaming about having an affair with Monty—he insisted all his students call him Monty—precisely because she had no intention of doing so. After all, she was no impressionable undergraduate. She was in her mid-thirties and happily married. But feelings have a funny way of knocking intentions off course. It started when she invited Monty to have dinner with them. Joe didn't like the idea from the beginning.

"But he's out here all by himself. He doesn't know a soul. It's the Christian thing to do, Joe."

"He should have brought his family out here with him." Katherine had made a point of telling Joe that Monty was married and had two children.

"I told you, they couldn't afford it. He doesn't make much as an assistant professor, and the University here paid only for a small one-bedroom apartment."

After meeting Professor Royce—which Joe insisted on calling him throughout the evening despite, and to be honest maybe even because of, the professor's repeated protestations—Joe's initial negative impression turned to something more like revulsion. The professor had long hair which made him look girly, long eyelashes which made him look girly, a delicate face which made him look girly, and hunter's eyes that Joe remembered from a few guys in the Navy, which made him look very very male.

The worst thing was his incessant talking. He had something to say about everything, and Katherine was drinking it in like she was at an oasis in the desert. Joe knew he was the desert.

"So, Joe, what do you do to keep busy when you are not working at the grocery store and entertaining your lovely wife," Professor Royce asked, giving Katherine a not-too-subtle vertical once over when he said the word "entertaining."

"Woodwork."

"Ah, a craftsman! How interesting. These arts are being lost. What do you make?

"Dovetail joints."

"Excellent! For furniture?"

"No just the joints."

This conversation-killing answer did its trick. Katherine and the professor stopped even going through the motions of including Joe in the conversation.

When Professor Royce left, he shook Joe's hand like a girl, said "Good luck with those dovetails!" laughing, then turned to Katherine, took her hand, and kissed it, saying "Thank you so much. Joe is a lucky man. See you in class Monday."

Cleaning up together, Katherine said, "See, Joe, wasn't he nice?"

"No. He was a phony, a phony on the hunt, on the hunt for you."

"Why, Joe, you are jealous. How sweet."

"It's not sweet, my guts are aching."

"You have nothing to worry about."

"I'm telling you, Katherine, you'd better worry about this or it will get out of hand."

It did get out of hand. There was lots of hand and shoulder touching when they talked after Monday's class. Then the very next Thursday, after class, he said, "Come dine with me." Katherine heard a voice that sounded like Mary's saying *Don't do it*, then heard herself saying "I'd love to." Joe was always on his own for dinner anyway on her class nights, then off to work at the store all night.

Monty ordered French champagne at the only French restaurant in Denver, in French. The bubbles floated Katherine away from her life in Greeley, away from the restaurant, and into Professor Montgomery Royce's comically small bed in his comically small apartment. They laughed all night about the challenges the small bed posed, and devised several clever positional solutions, fueled by two more bottles of champagne the professor had stashed in his comically small refrigerator.

Katherine was still floating on a thinning layer of champagne bubbles, and still giggling about how her right foot was touching the floor, when suddenly she said, "But you can't leave your wife and children."

"No," he said, a little too quickly. "And you can't leave Joe."

"Then what was all this?" she asked, sitting up, now with both feet on the ground.

"A shaft of sunshine in a dreary damp Rocky Mountain coal mine. We can keep the summer bright, my delightful Esmeralda, for five more weeks!"

She wanted to slap him, but would rather he slap her. She grabbed her clothes, ran to the tiny doorless bathroom and dressed.

"Don't ruin this with stupid bourgeois sensibilities," he said, leaning naked against the bathroom's useless doorjamb. He pronounced "bourgeois" perfectly. "We just had an extraordinary experience, you and I, magical I might even say, and there is no reason we cannot continue the magic, explore new magic. None of this has to have anything to do with Heloise or Joe."

Katherine burst out a laugh, popping the few remaining bubbles. "Heloise? Your wife's name is Heloise? Are you joking?"

"No," he said, no longer leaning against the door jamb but standing with feet apart and petulant hands on hips, his Abelard dangling lonely.

"Give her my condolences." Then Katherine left. She dropped out of the class, and never saw, or heard from, the professor again.

She spent two hours driving around Denver trying to figure out what to say to Joe. He would get off work at 6:00 a.m. At 5:30 she called the store from a pay phone across the street from a homeless shelter that had a big red neon sign, "Jesus Saves," above its entrance, with

Jesus horizontal and Saves vertical, the two words sharing the middle S in Jesus, as in a crossword puzzle. One of her prayers was answered when someone at the store actually picked up the phone and agreed to get Joe, who finally answered after a few minutes.

She told him she was still in Denver, that she'd spent the night with Royce (using his last name now, but Joe didn't notice), and that she was on her way back home to ask for Joe's forgiveness. She didn't give him a chance to say anything. She hung up, got back into The Turd, and pointed it north for home. When she got there the dogs were locked outside, but Joe was inside sitting at the kitchen table.

It was early but he had to talk to someone. He didn't know what else to do. He left work as soon as Katherine hung up, went home to let the dogs out, put on two sweaters and a coat, grabbed another coat just to be safe, and knocked on the big house's thick back door, then knocked again two more times. Mary finally opened it, with squinty sleepy eyes. Thank God it was Mary. He had no idea what he'd say if the old man answered.

"Katherine's left me. For that professor." He heard the deep distant voice of the old man, but couldn't hear what he said.

"No, everything's alright, Father. It's just Joe." More quietly, "Go back to Tiny. I'll get dressed and be over in two shakes."

After getting the bare bones of the story, and realizing bare bones was all she was ever going to get from Joe, they sat in Tiny in silence, Joe balloon-like, still wearing his sweaters and coats. They both regularly checked the ticking mantel clock to see how much time they had before Katherine would arrive. Mary correctly guessed that Katherine would take a lot longer than the regular 90 minutes to drive up from Denver, but then she realized she was just assuming Katherine had called from Denver. Heck, she could be here any minute.

"Look, Joe," Mary finally spoke up when she realized time might be short, "Katherine is not leaving you. I know her. I know how she feels about you. She will never leave you."

"Except to go fuck her fuckin' professor all night long."

"OK, let's just assume that's what went on."

"It was. She said so."

"OK, but I'm telling you that doesn't mean she's leaving you."

"I've already told you. She said she is coming up to ask for forgiveness."

"Forgiveness for what's already done, not for what she's going to do. She wants you to take her back."

Joe had never considered this possibility. He turned from anguished to joyful to angry to hopelessly worried he could never forgive her, all in the span of a second. Whiplashed, he said, "Well maybe I don't want her back."

"Maybe not. But please, Joe, will you promise me one thing? That if she wants back, you won't make any decision until you talk to me again?"

"OK." It was an easy promise to make, since Joe now had no idea what Katherine was going to say, or whether he'd even have any decision to make.

She did want back. After what seemed like hours of name-calling, once they were all name-called out they began having a more useful though even more hurtful conversation. She told him everything, every sordid detail that she could remember, not to hurt him but to cleanse herself. From her daydreaming about an affair to all the things they did on the tiny bed. She even went out of her way not to blame it on the champagne. She told him she had succumbed to temptation, but that she now realized it was a silly school girl kind of temptation that had nothing to do with Joe, except, honestly, his maddening silence, and everything to do with Royce's predation and her naiveté.

"So, if this just came out of the blue for no reason, why won't it come out of the blue again?"

"I didn't say there no were no reasons. I mentioned two. Your gift of gab and my immaturity."

"Well, are those suddenly going away?"

"This is not your fault, Joe. You are who you are. But since you asked maybe you could try to talk to me a little more. And I would promise you, if I had not already cheapened my word to worthlessness, that this terrible mistake has made me realize how young and silly I still am, and has itself matured me."

"That's a weaselly kind of promise."

"Yes."

"I need to think about it."

CHAPTER 26
SOUTH PACIFIC

Fungo 400! Our Joltin' Janitor is still just pinch hitting, but who can complain when his average stands at .401? That's right, folks, a whopping .401! The minor league record for batting average in a single season is held by Bill Krieg, who slugged .452 for Rockford way back in 1895. Baseball gurus tell this reporter that Harold's current average would not be an official record if his season ended tonight, because players must have at least 100 at-bats to qualify for season-long batting records. Come on, manager Wally Berens, get Harold into the starting lineup so he can get more at-bats and smash this record! After winning three of four against arch rival Garden City here at home, the team heads out for a road trip to Grand Island and Sterling.

Joe went to talk to Paul, taking a bit of an accusatory tone based on Paul's claimed power to predict eternal love.

"But you two do love each other. I wasn't wrong about that."

"I'm not sure I can still love her, Paul."

"Love's not a choice. You can't decide whether to love her. You do love her. You can decide whether to take her back, whether this pain she has inflicted on you is too much. But you can't just decide whether to love someone or not."

"So what do I do?"

"Let's listen to South Pacific together. I have the screenplay here somewhere. We'll read it together out loud and I'll play the music. It's all about how love is so weirdly delicate and robust all at the same time, about jealousy and what jealousy can do to love, and about forgiveness."

So that's what they did. Paul expertly played the correct songs at the correct times. When they were done, he said, "Now go home, think about this, and let's talk tomorrow."

The next day they had a long talk. "So what did you think?"

"Nellie and Emile really loved each other, but it wasn't enough to overcome Nellie's jealousy of Emile's first wife, and the whole race thing. But then it was."

Paul did a belly laugh.

"Only because Broadway wanted a sappy ending. What really happens is forgiveness comes too late for the Nellies of this world. They think they can never forgive the Emiles, decide not to marry them, and change their minds after it's too late. Most Emiles never come back, and most Nellies die regretful and alone. That's what happens in real life, Joe. You wonder whether you can forgive Katherine, but you also need to wonder, if you tell her you can't forgive her and won't take her back, whether she will ever be able to forgive you if you change your mind."

It was a lot to think about.

Katherine stayed over at the big house for two nights. On Saturday Joe had another talk with Mary, who told him she'd had several long talks with Katherine and was sure this was all just a delayed school-girl crush fueled by champagne, had nothing to with their marriage, and would not happen again.

Katherine spent all of Friday and Saturday in the big house in her old bedroom. She needed to steel herself before she talked to her father. After her talk with Mary Friday night, during which she purged herself again by recounting all the same dirty details she told Joe, the two of them agreed that Mary wouldn't tell Father anything, and in fact didn't even tell him Katherine was there. Mary snuck food to her, though she ate almost nothing. They agreed they would talk with Father after church. Katherine didn't go with them. As agreed, Mary told Father that Katherine was not feeling well, and that Joe was staying home to take care of her.

When they got back from church, Katherine had made a pot of coffee and was waiting for them at the big kitchen table. Father knew something was wrong. She told him about her tryst with the professor, minus the details she'd shared with Joe and Mary. Mary was relieved they'd all talked about it, and assumed, as always, that the talking would make it go away.

Father knew better. He told her that all he wanted for her was to be happy, and maybe she wasn't that happy with Joe if this happened. She said no, it had nothing to do with Joe and everything to do with her being stupid and drunk.

Once he knew she wanted to stay with Joe he got very quiet. Then he told her that men had delicate egos that could be collapsed by winds that felt like gentle breezes to women. He told her what she already knew—that there was nothing for her do now but wait for Joe's decision. That the hard part would come after that, either way. He hugged her and rocked her in his strong old arms, and she felt like she did when Dutch died, when Father told her she would be alright but she couldn't imagine she ever would.

When they talked again on Sunday night, Joe raised all these South Pacific questions with Katherine, and he could tell she was relieved that he'd at least been thinking about them and was willing to talk about them. In the end, though, she had to answer all his questions honestly, with an "I don't know," which drove the same answers from him to all of her questions.

After eons of silence, she said, "If we get back together, we have to come up with a way of keeping track of how we're doing, to keep it all in our consciousness so it doesn't sneak away, get bigger, then come back and kill us."

"Keeping score," is how Joe interpreted this suggestion.

"Yes, a pain score. And a guilt score. How much did I hurt you, Joe?"

He said a million, but she said such a big number would be meaningless. They agreed on 10,000. 10,000 JMRUs, as Joe dubbed it, for Joe's Montgomery Royce Units.

Katherine immediately agonized over whether her guilt number, KMRUs, should be the same as Joe's pain number. She realized that the two numbers, like their two lives, were impossibly entangled. If she said she did not feel sufficiently guilty, that would hurt Joe even more, which would make her feel more guilty. If she said she felt more guilty than Joe felt cheated, she again would be increasing his pain and her guilt. If her number just went up and down with Joe's, what was the point?

So with great trepidation she suggested to Joe that her guilt would be best measured by her behavior—by her renewed fidelity—rather than by a number that was really apples to Joe's oranges, even though in reality they were the very same orange. He agreed. JMRU became shortened to MRU. She also promised to tell him if she was day dreaming about having an affair with anybody. And he agreed to talk to her every night after dinner. No matter what. Thus were born the Reports.

Joe's pain stayed at 10,000 MRUs for almost a year, during which they were civil to one another but never intimate. The knot in Katherine's stomach grew, but part of her was glad of the penance. Then during one late May Report, after declaring as usual that his MRU was still at 10,000, Joe asked her how the professor was in bed. She started to laugh until she saw he was serious.

"As far as I can remember, he was fine. I mean, everything worked. But for women, Joe, sex is not a physical sport judged like in the Olympics. What matters to us is what we think the man is thinking about us before, during, and after sex. I thought all night, from dinner through bed, that Royce was admiring my mind. But he was just out for some easy sex, and I hate him for it, and for him ruining sex for you and me."

"Was he bigger than me?"

She started to protest, but then said "As far as I can remember he was longer but not as thick."

"Did you come?"

"No." Then, pursuant to her new scrupulosity, she added, "But I only came with you about half the time." They both noticed her use of the past tense. "Orgasm is a weirdly unpredictable thing with women."

After that conversation, Joe's reported MRUs began to inch down. Katherine had to try hard not to laugh when he proudly announced the first decrease down to 9,991, shortly after their uncomfortable sex performance talk.

When it dipped into the 8,000s in late September Joe asked Katherine if she'd like to go to bed early. That was their euphemism.

"No, but I'd like to fuck your brains out." She said it because she felt it, but then immediately regretted it. She didn't want to put any pressure on Joe. But he was fine.

"I'm sure glad you said what you said earlier tonight. I was afraid I wouldn't be able to get it up." They agreed to use the new non-euphemistic euphemism from now on.

Over the next several years the MRU score meandered down to 1,750, but then stuck there. Katherine was a little surprised that it didn't evaporate entirely, especially after Joe's diagnosis, that his fear of dying didn't crowd out his lingering decades-old hurt. But it didn't, and she understood. They even talked about it during one of the Reports right after the diagnosis. Joe announced the MRU at 1,750, as usual, and Katherine said, "Joe, I have got to ask you, after all these years together, and especially with this diagnosis, why are your MRUs still at 1,750?"

"I don't know. Don't you still feel guilty about what you did?"

"Yes, but I hardly ever think about it. Only when you announce your MRU every night. Then I think about it."

"Wasn't that the whole idea?"

"Yes. But maybe after 20 years we should retire the stupid thing. The scab is long gone."

"I'd be afraid. It's helped get us through, hasn't it?"

"I suppose."

"Then why change it?"

Katherine had no answer. What she really wanted to say was that she was tired of having her nose rubbed in this 20-year-old mistake every single night, but she didn't say that. Instead, she suggested was that they cut the MRU report to once a month instead of nightly. Joe agreed. Now, he reported only monthly that his MRU was still at 1,750, where it stayed until he died.

Hitting .400 in a single major league season has a curious history that reflects baseball's deep romance with randomness.

In the very first year of the National League, 1876, Chicago Whitestockings infielder Ross Barnes hit .429. The accomplishment went unnoticed, both because no one was paying attention to baseball let alone to any baseball statistics, and also because, even if they had been, they would have been writing on a butt-bare blank slate, so there was nothing to tell them that this might be a difficult task or an easy one. And in fact, in those early years the fates couldn't make up their minds.

No one repeated Barnes' accomplishment for eight years, until one player did it in 1884, but then two separate players hit the mark in 1887. When five players made it in 1894, it stopped being worth the trouble to mention, and indeed it was repeated by at least one player, and often more than one, every year through the rest of the century and into the next.

Then there was a ten-year drought, until the 20-year deluge brought on by Ty Cobb and Rogers Hornsby. Each reached the mark three separate times, the only two players to do so, and during these pre- and post- Great War years, five different players managed the feat once.

Just when it seemed to be common again, the record retreated for another decade, until Ted Williams hit it in 1941. Since then, not a single member of this exclusive 29-member club has been added. This is the longest drought in the history of the 400 club.

I often wondered through these dry years whether this was the year that somewhere, probably in the unlikeliest of places, a minor leaguer was emerging, or a high schooler being coached up, or at the very least a baby being born, destined to end the drought.

CHAPTER 27
FREE

Fungo Watch. Folks, this is getting downright crazy. Our homegrown pinch-hitting hero is now batting .412, having gone three for four against Sterling and Grand Island. Our first-place team will be back at Municipal Field Sunday against Cedar Rapids. It will be WWII Veterans Night. All WWII veterans will be admitted free and given a team cap, while supplies last.

Pursuant to the Corn Palace Pact, every morning when at home, and even on the road if they had access to a field and a pitching machine or pitcher, Harold made sure Clevon took at least a hundred curve balls, mixed in with a few fastballs. Greg joined them when he could, to provide some live pitching. All the extra Corn Palace practice dramatically improved Harold's catching, but Clevon hardly improved at all.

He still couldn't hit the curve even when he knew it was coming. After about two weeks his average facing the curveball climbed only from 210 to 215. He was discouraged. "Harold, this ain't getting me anywhere. 215 ain't enough."

"You've added five points to your curveball average in two weeks, Clevon. At this rate you'll be hitting curves at a 250 clip by next spring."

"We ain't got 'til next spring, Harold. And even 250 might not be good enough to get me to where you're goin'."

"What wound did ever heal but by degrees?"

"What the hell does that mean?"

"It means be patient. I've been training hard for 30 years, and you can damn well put in some hard work for a couple months to save our friendship."

Clevon had never heard Harold cuss. He bore down, but with caterpillar results. By the time Wally told Harold he'd heard rumors about Harold's call-up, Clevon was still only hitting curves in practice at about 225. And that was when he knew they were coming. In games, and in practice when pitchers mixed speed with off-speed, Clevon was still hitting curves miserably, in the low 200s. He might have even gotten worse.

But Harold was knocking the cover off the ball. Though Wally had not come right out and told the big shots that he was trashing the trickling strategy, they saw all the stats and they knew. From the moment Wally let him loose, Harold batted 1,000.

That moment came in a road game in Grand Island. Wally called Harold out to pinch hit in a blowout in the seventh inning, to bat for Buzzy, who had pitched a fine game. As usual, Harold's atomic smile appeared the moment he heard Wally call his name. He took his teeth out and grabbed his bat to warm up. When Wally told him to ground out the smile disappeared, and at that exact moment the baseball gods hit Wally with bolts out of the blue.

"This is wrong, dammit. It's not fair to Harold, it's not fair to the team, it's not fair to that pitcher out there or his team, it's not fair to these fans, and it's not fair to the game," the Gods said through Wally.

"You're right Wally," the big smile back on.

"Knock the hell out of it, Harold."

Opposing teams now started trying to walk him regularly. After he reached out and hit a few intentional balls, they started throwing so far outside that the catcher often missed it. Then a few even started rolling the balls along the ground. But that was dicey with the poorly groomed fields on which they often played, and plenty of rolled balls bounced unpredictably for wild pitches. Even when they managed to roll in near the plate, Harold was able to smack them, golf like, for solid hits. His teammates started calling him Benny, for Ben Hogan.

Then came the behind the back intentional walks. It was time for Wally to unleash Ping Pong, which would become known in the newspapers as the Fungo Faceoff.

It was at home, in a tight game in late innings. They were behind by two. Wally had pulled the pitcher the inning before and told Harold he would be up in the pitcher's spot, to lead off. Harold took his teeth out and grabbed his bat.

The opposing team's manager called time and went out to the mound to talk to the pitcher. After the mound conference, the catcher signaled for an intentional walk, but instead of putting his gloved left hand out, to indicate that the pitcher would intentionally throw outside to the left-handed hitting Harold, the catcher stuck out his ungloved right hand, indicating the throw was to be behind Harold.

A few pitchers had tried this on their own, and Harold had some difficulty spinning around in time, especially because he had to avoid the plate. But this really steamed Wally. These guys were now formally *announcing* they were going to throw behind Harold. This was a sin against baseball. Time to fight sin with sin. Wally called time and went out to talk to Harold.

"OK, Harold let's do it. It's Ping Pong Time."

When Harold stepped over and put his left foot into the left side of the batter's box, the home plate umpire called time, both managers ran out and the other umpire—the crew chief—ran in. After a big pow wow in which the crew chief actually pulled out and read the rule book, the chief determined, as Wally knew he would, that this insanely suicidal stance was permitted, as long as Harold did not step on the plate or out of either box during his swing.

It all had to do with the fact that there was a definition of a singular "batter's box" in Rule 3.1, requirements that the batter's feet be entirely within "it," and no express prohibition of putting one foot on one side and one on the other side of "it." Harold later wrote a poem about it called Here nor There, which critics said was about schizophrenia.

"But how will I be able to see?" both the plate umpire and catcher blurted out in duet as soon as the crew chief determined the stance was legal.

"You won't have to see 'cause Harold won't ever let that ball get past him, if that chickenshit on the mound doesn't try to walk him," said Wally. The chickenshit on the mound heard this comment and started to run to the plate, but the crew chief pointed a finger on an aggressively extended arm and the pitcher stopped like a well-trained police dog.

"Cal, why don't you come out from behind the plate and stand behind the mound, a little off to one side," the crew chief suggested. It worked great. Why didn't all umpires call balls and strikes from there?

"And what am I supposed to do?" asked the catcher.

"Make sure your mask's buckled on, son," said the crew chief.

The pitcher threw right at Harold's head, and Harold knocked a seeing eye single right over second base. Lee Williams pinch ran for Harold, Charlie Swanson tied it with a homer, and Clevon knocked in what would be the winning run in the eighth with a sacrifice fly.

A newspaper photographer captured Harold's ping-pong swat, and the photo was published everywhere. The press went crazy, but it was a PR nightmare for the Cincinnati Reds. Thousands of letters and telegrams flooded in from angry fans demanding that Harold be called up. A story in the New York Dailey News—front page of the sports section—asked, "Sixth Place Reds Too Good for Fungo?"

The big shots were all traditional baseball men, and they didn't like the idea of some guy who never even played high school baseball being catapulted from double-A to the big club, let alone a guy who couldn't run, couldn't play a position, and batted like a girl. These complaints would all have been entirely reasonable in the baseball world they knew. In that world, people did not bat 1,000.

There was a boy in a wheel chair. He was sitting with a man, his father I assumed, who had wheeled him right up against the last row of the first base seats. The man was patiently solicitous toward the boy—his head frequently turning toward the boy's trying to engage the disengaged child, who looked nine or ten. When Harold stepped to the plate, I waited for the boy to energize. Surely he was here to watch the lame janitor, surely his father brought him to be inspired. But the boy paid no more attention to the Hammerer's runs scoring single than he had to anything else all night. I left wondering whether it was cruel of the father to bring the boy to this game.

I arrived back in New York wondering whether it was cruel of me to wonder about the father's cruelty. The Fates were at it again. Of course, they were always at it. A Brooks Robinson mid-air snag here, a murdered woman twelve blocks from Memorial Stadium there. Hephaestus hammering out an unachievable hitting streak here, a paralyzed boy being compared to him there.

I began to think it was all a matter of gage. Harold Fungo was important because he was small. Because he couldn't cure illness or hate, but he could hit the damn ball anytime he damn wanted anywhere he damn wanted. A small act of free will in a universe of determined failure. Harold was our hero because he unfailingly did the small things we could do once in a while. He was immune to the Fates, a golden thread in baseball's tapestry of disappointment.

I was at a barber shop in Boston when the mailman brought in the new Life magazine, hot off the presses. I was thumbing through it, thinking about last month's electric bill, of all things—did we pay it before we schlepped the children here to Martha's Vineyard for the summer? If not, all our indoor plants will die from the heat no matter how religiously Joey waters them—when I came upon the stunning photograph of the Fungo Faceoff. Here was our Hephaestus, toothless mouth agape, turning and facing the pitcher, facing the Fates without fear.

CHAPTER 28
SPACE

Fungo Watch. Folks, our hometown hero Harold Fungo is stretching this game of baseball in all sorts of ways. Last night at Municipal Field he rewrote the baseball rule book in a thoroughly strange way when he came to bat and put one foot on each side of the plate, facing the mound head-on. The Oaks protested, heaven knows why, but the umpires agreed the suicidal stance was legal. Of course, Harold smacked a single. He is now batting .423, after going 4 for 4 on the road against Grand Island and Sterling, and one-for-one tonight. That's five straight pinch hits, folks! If you are asking whether that's ever been done, the answer is yes, many times and for many more than four straight. Although the major league record is a paltry seven, held by dozens of different big leaguers, our Joltin' Janitor has quite a way to go to match the minor league record of 22 consecutive pinch hits, held by Hap Gumler of the 1922 Grand Rapids Gears. Sioux City visits tonight. Tickets are going fast.

Harold and Nick were both used to Spartan living. Nick had just come from a year at college, where he shared a dorm room with a 6'2" 270-pound football player. His small apartment near Municipal Field felt like the Taj Mahal, as did all the hotel and motel rooms they stayed in on the road, even though Todd booked them.

Harold loved all the space, too. Ma's house couldn't have been more than 700 square feet once you deducted the library. There was one tiny bathroom—toilet, sink, and shower, no bathtub. The toilet was crammed behind the door, preventing it from opening inward all the way. The kitchen had just enough room for a hot plate and a small square refrigerator, which Ma had to put up on the counter, cutting the total counter space to about two lineal feet. There was no oven. Harold attributed his inability to cook to Ma's meager kitchen. He knew she was least happy when she was jammed into it cooking, so far from the books.

When Harold was seven, Ma divided the small bedroom they shared into two even smaller bedrooms, with a wall of books separating them. She used the sturdy volumes from two different sets of the Encyclopedia Britannica to form adjacent doorways into each half.

They had identical twin beds of worn maple, which looked more substantial when they were together but seemed out of place and lonely after their separation. Each bed had confusingly exotic red minarets on top of their small posts. Harold accidentally discovered these could be unscrewed when he was helping Ma move them to their separate rooms and one of the appley orbs turned ever so slightly in his hand. He said nothing to Ma because he thought he'd broken it.

Once he was safely alone in his new room, he discovered that all four orbs were screwed into the tops of the posts. He was sure they contained secret messages from his father Hillerich, but when he took them off, wood screws squeaking, there were no hollowed chambers in any of them, just the flat unfinished surface of the orb, with a wood screw sticking out, and its reciprocal unfinished flat top of the post, with a screw hole in the center. It took him a full year to gather up the courage to inspect the orbs on Ma's bed, one afternoon when she was at the store. No secret messages.

When he was 10, and now running to the store himself, he dared to use one of Ma's small kitchen knives to dig a tiny hollow into one of the posts on his bed. It took a long time to dig it big enough to hold even the smallest scrap of folded paper. It took an even longer time to think up his secret message, which, given the dimensions of the clandestine cubby and Harold's difficulty with writing, was severely limited in word length. He was never really satisfied with his final composition, his first written poem: *Harold Bradsby, age 10.*

At about the same time they moved into adjacent half-bedrooms Ma explained about her teeth, which were missing, and her plan to save Harold's. She said her hands were just too shaky to do a very good job of brushing, and because of that she lost all of her teeth before she was 20. She said she was not about to let that happen to Harold, and that she was worried because she noticed Harold's hands were getting shaky too. He'd already lost one permanent tooth.

So she showed him Captain Fuzzy Wuzzy. It was a block of wood she painted like a pirate, whose moustache was made from the head of a toothbrush. She even painted a small parrot on his shoulder. She fastened Captain Fuzzy Wuzzy to the teeny bathroom vanity with a small c-clamp, put some toothpaste on his moustache, and told Harold to brush his teeth by leaning down and moving them back and forth against the Captain, rather than trying to move the toothbrush with his shaky hands. She was right that this was much better.

Harold used Captain Fuzzy Wuzzy to brush his teeth until he just had four left. By that time the wooden pirate's paint, and parrot, had long disappeared, and Ma had replaced his mustache a dozen times. This strange tooth-brushing method delayed Harold's tooth loss, but didn't prevent it because he could never figure out how to brush the backs of his teeth. They rotted from the back, even though Ma showed him how to swish around there with mouthwash and even rub tooth paste on the back sides after he was done brushing.

He thanked Captain Fuzzy Wuzzy regularly for his four remaining teeth, which were four more than Ma had. The Captain died in the house fire—Harold imagined him swinging on ropes, with a glittering knife in his teeth crowned by his brush—after which Harold started using the regular toothbrush Jack gave him at the firehouse. With just four teeth, his shaky toothbrushing was even more hit or miss than he remembered it as a boy.

Harold felt like he was living in a palace when he moved in with Nick. The small kitchen was twice as big as Ma's, and it had an oven, just like at the firehouse. The living room he shared with Sparky felt like all of Municipal Field compared to his tiny half-bedroom at home. It was even bigger than the storage room at the firehouse. And Nick's place had a bathtub, with a shower right in it! Harold had never taken a bath before, or even seen one, and watched in amazement when Nick first bathed.

"You are creeping me out, a little, Harold. Can I help you?"

"No, sorry, I just have never seen anyone taking a bath. I've read about it of course."

"Well, when I'm done, and after we give the hot water heater time to recover, you can take one."

Harold took a bath every night. And Sparky joined him occasionally. At the beginning Harold let Sparky join him every time, but then Nick told him that lots of baths probably weren't good for a dog, even one who looked like a dolphin. Harold had to close the bathroom door otherwise Sparky would jump in. Sparky spent the whole time clicking and whistling at the door.

When Nick and Harold were on the road and Sparky stayed over at Jack's, every night at around 9:00 Sparky would get up and walk over to the bathroom, sit by the tub if the door was open or just by the door if it wasn't, and click and whistle until Jack retrieved him with a, "It's OK, Spark, Harold will be home soon."

There is a joyous egalitarianism in baseball, celebrating all the failure by spreading it around democratically. Every player, no matter his station, is thrust to the plate and required to hit. The least skilled fielder, ex-communicated to right, as well as the invaluable pitcher, must each eventually take his turn at the plate. This was the abomination of the designated hitter rule adopted in the American League. It coronated the pitcher into a royalty immune to the everyday drudgery of failure.

There is also an exhilarating freedom in the game, made more exhilarating by its relentless and grinding compulsions. The pitcher is compelled to throw, the batter compelled to go to the plate when his name comes up in the lineup, and to run to first if he hits the ball in play, the runner at first to run to second. And yet within all these compulsions there is considerable freedom. Pitchers are free to throw a curve or a fastball, batters free to swing or bunt or take, runners to advance or return after tagging up, fielders to try to get the lead runner or the sure out. It is a perfect dance between rules and liberty.

Once in a while, someone discovers a gap in the rules, usually a coach or manager. Then they speed through that gap to their advantage, and eventually everyone does, until the players have run the poor game off the dance floor. Then off-season rule changes restore the order. This is how it's always been, and we thought how it would always be. But then along came our Hephaestus.

He not only took chance out of the game, he made damn sure everybody knew it. That's what the Fungo Faceoff was. The most dissonant aspect of the Faceoff was that here was a discovered loophole in the rules that put Harold at a disadvantage, put his batting average, not to mention his face, in more peril, not less. Here was a man making this impossible job more impossible, and in the bargain putting his noggin smack in the middle of the fastball rifle range.

But of course it was all part of the act, the taunting of the fates. The magician not only wrapping himself in padlocked chains inside a padlocked trunk, but then having the trunk hurled into the icy river.

CHAPTER 29
FLEAS

Fungo Watch. A record Municipal Field crowd of 2,400 saw our Joltin' Janitor get yet another pinch hit last night, bringing his streak of consecutive pinch hits to eight, and his average to an unworldly .452. On the bad news front, I am sorry to report that there was a scout from Cincinnati at last night's game. Our homegrown hero probably won't be with us for long. Come see him while you still can.

Major leaguers these days stay in five-star hotels, board private jets from special gates, and are generally treated like royalty, creating a yawning gap between life in the majors and minors. But in Harold's era the everyday lives of ballplayers were not very different across most professional levels. Other than the spending money, the differences were almost all attributable to the different sizes of the towns and cities in which they played.

By the time Harold was playing, most of the major hotel/motel chains had expanded into the small towns of single- and double-A. Heck, some of them even started there. And the TV riches hadn't yet started flowing to the majors. So most minor leaguers stayed in Holiday Inns and Howard Johnsons and Best Westerns just like major leaguers usually did, just smaller versions.

Minor leaguers stayed in fleabags only when they played in exceptionally small towns or when they had a cheapskate traveling secretary like Todd. So, in the lowest levels of professional ball, played in the smallest of towns, fleabags were still a regular part of those poor players' routines. Wally used to tell the guys that when he was managing in Amarillo, in the Texas League, lice epidemics sometimes disrupted whole seasons. Wally's team, like most, had its own blue lights for detecting lice, and all the players had to go under them every night after showering.

Wally's favorite fleabag story was about how fleas catapulted one of his young pitchers, Bobby Sandolfsky, to the majors. They called Sandolfsky "Itchy," because he was always twitching and jumping and touching his face and his arms and legs while he was on the mound. Itchy came to Amarillo right out of high school in New York City, so Wally assumed he had bed bugs or some other urban blight. But the doctors said no, he just had a "high metabolism."

Itchy had a serviceable fastball but a great, almost unhittable, curve. His problem was control. Wally tried to help.

"Stop jumpin' and twitchin' out there so much, Itch. If you calm down maybe your control will get better. Hell, no one could throw where they wanted if they were yippin' and jerkin' like you do."

Itchy tried, but he couldn't help himself. Then he got fleas, they think from a motel in Lubbock. It took everyone a while to notice them, because he was always scratching and itching on the mound. But when one of the coaches saw Itchy's mottled back side in the locker room, he knew right away.

The team doctor gave Itchy the standard flea treatment, which was some pills and some cream. Itchy pitched that very night—a one-hit complete game. His best game ever. He kept taking those pills and putting on that cream for the rest of his career, long after the fleas were gone. Within a year he was pitching for the Detroit Tigers.

"Sometimes the mind's itch is worse than the body's scratch," is how Wally summed it up. To Itchy, it seemed like destiny that he finally got the fleas that he acted like he always had.

Harold loved the motel and hotel rooms, especially when they had bathtubs. The players had to double up to share a room, which was often a delicate problem when a new guy joined a team. But because Harold came with Nick, and because the two of them already lived together at home, they naturally became road roommates, though, because of Nick's carousing, they actually saw less of each other now than they did when Harold was sweeping up and Nick was on the grounds crew.

Nick went out almost every night because some of the night-owling players were kind enough to invite him to join them, and allowed him to bask in the reflected light of their semi-fame. Nick was flabbergasted at how the label of "professional athlete," which they allowed him to don as an honorific, changed everything about the dance of the sexes. There were girls looking for them in every town. Hell, they rode up and down in the hotel elevators, for cryin' out loud. It was a good thing Wally had a midnight curfew, which most of the night-owlers tried hard to honor. Nick and half the others would probably be dead today but for that curfew, killed by jealous husbands, dead from the clap, or just worn out beyond recovery. Nick made sure, if he was physically able, to be back in the room by midnight.

One night-owler who just couldn't abide by the curfew, the Hercules of the Night, as Wally called him, was Sam Fresne, one of their relief pitchers. Sam was the only player on the team who had been up to the big show. It was a sad and sadly common story. Sam caught lightning in high school, lurched into the major leagues long before he was ready, couldn't believe how easy baseball was, then spent the rest of his career not believing how hard it had become. At this point, at age 32 and down in double-A for God's sake, Sam knew he would never get back to the majors, and that he might as well enjoy the minors. Wally called these players "sinkers," because they could sink a whole team with their attitudes. Luckily, he had just one now, Sam.

Sam never made a curfew during the descending two-thirds of his career, not one. That's what got him sent down from triple-A. In the beginning, Wally threatened him daily with being sent even further down, but Sam didn't care. And the big boys in Cincinnati didn't want Sam screwing up their youngest players, so they refused every time

Wally demanded Sam's demotion. Double-A was perfect for everyone—far enough from the bigs so that Sam wouldn't get his hopes up again, and far enough from the really young kids not to poison them. Plus, they figured that if anyone could contain the disease of the Hercules of the Night it was Wally.

He did a pretty good job. He was upfront with the kids.

"Look, Sam is the exception that proves the rule." This phrase usually caused puzzled looks on the faces of the brighter players, so Wally clarified.

"If anyone of you behaves the way he does, if you miss one goddamned curfew, I'll send your ass down to Fleaville so fast it will start itching before you're on the bus."

Some young player would always ask about fairness.

"Not my call. I've begged the office dickheads to send Sam down, but they just won't. They don't want him fuckin' up all the kids. But you are men. You know the world ain't fair. You play hard and follow the rules, you'll have a shot at the show. You act like Sam, you'll be picking lice out of your head near the Mexican border until you retire."

The players' favorite story about Sam was the time in southern Kansas when he told Wally he had to buy 15 tickets for that night's game. "I didn't know you were from Kansas, Herc."

"I'm not, but I guess I have tons of kids here."

Sam was tall, blue-eyed, and blond, but he had a distinctive dark stripe of hair on the left side of his head. That night, in a section of stands right behind the visitors' dugout, there must have been 10 kids, from toddlers to teenagers, all with blue eyes and a dark stripe down the left side of their blond hair. All the guys thought it was hilarious, but Wally thought it was disgusting.

For Harold, the most delightful aspects of road games, before the Corn Palace Pact, were the late mornings and early afternoons off, when he and Clevon, sometimes accompanied by Nick, became tourists. They must have visited every "World's Largest" roadside attraction across the Midwest. The world's largest haystack, world's largest frying pan, world's largest troll, world's largest egg, world's largest ball of string, and world's largest (and only) liberty bell made from wheat. They also visited real places, monuments to local war dead, history museums, art museums, zoos. Harold dragged them to every bookstore he could find.

The biggest day-to-day difference between life in the majors and the minors at that time was the travel. Big leaguers only occasionally had to take buses, between nearby cities like Washington and Philadelphia. The rest of their travel was by airplane. In the minors, even in triple-A, everything was by bus. Except, again, for those poor creatures in the lowest rungs, who sometimes didn't even have the luxury of buses. Some of them had to drive their own cars between stops, in snaking caravans that one pundit called Podunk Parades.

Distances and travel time determined virtually everything in the minors, including how numerous and far-flung the individual leagues could be. Harold played at a time when there were so many teams at all levels that even with the challenges of bus travel it was still easy to construct full schedules between teams that were reasonably close to one another.

Still, Harold and his teammates spent more time on buses than on playing fields. It was an easy adjustment for Harold, because he loved watching America pass by out of the bus window. And the firehouse had gotten him used to "killing time" with cards and games. But it was harder on the other players.

Gifted athletes cooped up, whether on a bus or at a theater, do the same thing the world over. They get *physically* bored. They have to move, they have to compete. Pitchers were almost never on the bus without a baseball in their hands, fingering it, rolling it, tossing it, often unconsciously. A few position players even brought bats on board, constantly hefting them, feeling the knob at the bottom edge of their hand and the weight the fat part exerted on the handle as it rocked first against thumb then forefinger.

Wally regularly warned them, just like their moms did, not to play ball inside. He told them what he later admitted to Harold was an apocryphal story of a bus full of dead players in South Carolina, killed when their driver was knocked out by an accidental line drive. So instead they threw and hit and caught wadded up balls of paper.

At one point Harold bought a dozen ping-pong paddles and balls, and they played various games, including trying to keep the ball from hitting the ground, until Wally put an end to it, claiming it was getting too close to that South Carolina situation, even though Stick complained that no one could be knocked out by a ping-pong ball. Someone brought a whiffle ball, of which Wally was more tolerant until Clevon belted a rope right into his face. Left a Swiss cheese red mark on his cheek that stayed for two days.

There was a definite rhythm to the players' pent-up energy on long bus rides. It waxed and waned like a toddler's. One moment they were knocking the paper ball around to cheers and moans, and the next moment they were all swaddled in silence, waiting for the time to pass.

The team driver, Willie Franks, always got a little maudlin when the toddlers went quiet. It reminded him of his own family, lost so long ago because of his drinking.

When Big Bob took over, he fired Willie because Willie was also a certified mechanic and was getting paid almost as much as some of the coaches. He replaced Willie with a nephew who knew nothing about internal combustion engines. After a half-dozen breakdowns and lost road trips, Big Bob had to go back to Willie hat in hand to ask him to come back. Willie agreed, for a big pay raise. Now he was making more than all the coaches except Wally. And had stopped drinking. Life was all about timing, Willie often thought when the boys went silent.

Willie was the best driver not only because he was a wizard with engines but also because he understood the players. He himself had played on a Negro team back in the late 1940s in Florida, and traveled lots of miles on a bus exactly like this—it might even have been this very bus—all across the Southeast.

It was a two-toned 1947 GM model that seated 37, just big enough for the 22 players, the six coaches, and the bags and bags of equipment. The bottom half of the bus was a dirty red and the top half, framing the windows, a dirty cream that extended from the roof down into a widow's peak at the front. At just the right time, and if the light was right, travelers along some tiny Midwest road might see the strange sight of a white paper ball flying around inside an ugly red and cream bus.

They are a sad lot, those who tasted the major leagues when they were too young or too stupid, realized their shortcomings only after it was too late, and never got back again. But do not pity them, for they have done what most of us only dreamed. Many were prized prospects, coddled through several big-league seasons, everyone holding their breath at the photo finish between potential and playing. They made the promised land and then were banished for their own breach of promise. A little sad in the Disneyland of baseball, but not a bone-rattling injustice in the game of life.

CHAPTER 30
CHRISTMAS

Fungo Watch. The Streak now stands at 15, and the average at .485. I am afraid, folks, it is only a matter of time before our hometown phenom gets called up. Lucky for us, his leg is still giving him problems, which might delay his call-up. The team has pulled nine games ahead of the Garden City Bluebells, who they face in a three-game home series beginning tonight. First pitch, as usual, is at 7:00 p.m. Tickets for all home games may be purchased at the Municipal Field ticket office, at Cooper Farm Equipment on Elm, and at Cooper Realty on Adams.

Joe loved the big fireplace at Paul's and Mary's because the mantle carving was bigger and clearer than the one at home. But Joe had a special feeling for all fireplaces.

When he and Sue were very young, they confronted their dad a few days before Christmas about how Santa would be able to get inside their fireplace-less Mediterranean house. Stan thought for a moment and then pointed up at a small grill covering a recessed exhaust fan in the kitchen ceiling.

"See that grill? I take it off Christmas Eve, and that allows Santa to drop down." The children looked up in wonder.

"Let's take it off now, Daddy, tomorrow's Christmas Eve," Sue pleaded. Stan was a little worried. Removing the grill would emphasize the completely inadequate size of the hole, and would also expose the Santa-chopping blades not far up the sheet metal tube.

Joe joined in, "Yeah, let's take it off, Dad. I'll help."

Of course, neither Joe nor Sue ever even imagined that the hole was too small for Santa, or that the blades, which were easily seen once their father removed the grill, would give the great man any trouble at all. This was the power, and danger, of faith, Joe thought when he was older. But there was something else—a comforting feeling that as long as you made some small effort—removing a grill—enough magic could seep in, even around dangerous blades, to do its work.

At Lester's, the suspension of disbelief by the faithful seemed entirely different. Predicting that their young but precocious son might notice that their Mediterranean home's "fireplace" was just a small flueless cove in the drywall—a cove which housed some shelves on which Ms. Buckley displayed her collection of German knickknacks— and that their "chimney" was just a couple extra layers of exterior brick, Mr. and Mrs. Buckley decided something must be done. Actually, Mrs. Buckley decided something must be done. Christmas was especially important to her, as it seemed to be to so many Germans. She always made dozens and dozens of Christmas cookies in an endless stream that started right after Thanksgiving, though she never baked anything other than bread any other time of year.

She baked bread two or three times every week. Lester and Joe could smell it was a bread day when they got halfway up the front sidewalk after school. There was no smell like it. A warm and gentle welcoming, but proud not toadying. *Come on in, boys, but only if you wish. You don't have to.* It smelled healthy and basic, yet with dangerous hints of fermentation. *This is safe and good now, but only after some occult brew made it so.*

On bread days the snack they each got before Lester's practice, naturally, was a thick slice of hot bread foamy with butter. The bread was always hot; Mrs. Buckley must have timed it that way on school days. On bread days at Christmastime, they each got a slice of bread and one Christmas cookie, Lester sneaking his cookie to Joe. Mrs.

Buckley made so many Christmas cookies that Lester got sick of them by early December, though Joe never tired of them. On non-bread Christmastime days, they got two cookies each, which made it twice as hard for Lester to sneak them to Joe.

Once, Mrs. Buckley caught Lester red-handed passing his two cookies to Joe under the table. "What do you have there, Yosef?" she asked in that way teachers ask when they know the answer, as she reached under the table and intercepted the contraband. "Well, I'll be darn, it's Lester's cookies!" she operatically feigned surprise as she opened up the paper napkin.

"I'm so sorry mama," Lester blurted. Joe had never seen him so flustered. His face was red and his eyes panicked.

"Sorry? Why? I am around these cookies so much I can't stand the sight of them, neither can your father," she said laughing. "Not surprised one bit you can't either." She hugged him. "You are sick of these too, Yosef?" she asked as she held out the two unmasked cookies.

"Oh no, Mrs. Buckley, I could eat a million."

She laughed and handed them back to him, "That's a good thing because we've got to shovel these off to someone!"

"But why do you bake so many if no one around here wants them?" Joe asked as he munched down his first extra.

"To remember my mama, and hers. And to give you two something to remember." Then she made Lester half a peanut butter and jelly sandwich.

When Mrs. Buckley decided something had to be done about the problem of Santa access, she decided on a fireplace insert. She'd seen one the year before at Sears & Roebuck down in Denver.

It was a small plastic grate on which an axle turned, driven by a miniature electric motor. The whole insert was only twelve inches deep—just perfect for the "fireplace" cove. The axle was wrapped with tiny white lights, and the whole assembly was surrounded by plastic "flames"—strips of soft plastic of different lengths, some red some yellow, hanging from the frame above the turning axle. When the switch was turned on, the plastic strips reflected the rotating light, and were gently blown by a small fan mounted next to the motor. If you turned out all the room lights, stood far away, and squinted severely, it almost looked like a burning fire.

When the two young boys saw the contraption in action, they were awed that a house with no fireplace could so quickly and completely be turned into a house with a fireplace. To them the fireplace was perfect in every way. All others—with their noisy crackling wood, irritating smoke, and dangerous hot flames—were cheap imitations.

The boys and Mrs. Buckley sat around it for quite a long time, the boys even mimicking Mrs. Buckley as she rubbed her hands together and held them up to the turning plastic spit. This was before the Hamburg Concert Grand took over the front room, so when Mr. Buckley walked up the front sidewalk, returning from the VFW, he saw the three of them huddled around the indentation, and the red and yellow lights dancing around them. When he got in, he played along.

"Brrr, it's cold out there," and he joined them holding his hands out toward the plastic fire.

After everyone warmed up it was time for Joe to go home. As he was heading out the door, he turned back and told Mr. Buckley, "Remember to take the grill off the fan in the kitchen. That's how Santa gets into these houses with fake chimneys."

***

Paul handed Joe an elf hat as soon as Joe and Katherine walked through the front door. Joe knew it was to cover his still strangely schizophrenic hairdo. "Merry Not Christmas," Paul bellowed in his very best bowl full of jelly laugh.

In years past Paul had wanted to play Santa at his Not Christmas Dinners, but he could never find a Santa suit big enough. Mary once offered to make him one, but Paul demurred, saying, "Now that I think of it, this is a Not Christmas Dinner, so I should be the Not Santa." From then on, Paul played Not Santa. He wore shorts, the loudest loosest fitting short-sleeve shirt he could find, and flip-flops. That was actually what he always wore at home, at least in the summer. The only additions for his Not Santa get-up were Viking horns (Not Reindeer Horns) and a large empty canvas bag, which all guests had to fill up with contributions to the dinner.

Katherine put in a small wicker picnic basket containing all the fixings for the salad: three heads of lettuce; small bottles of oil and vinegar; and several bunches of scallions and celery. Joe, the teetotaler, put in three bottles of wine. They never knew how much to bring because Paul never knew exactly who would be coming. A lot of your down-and-outers weren't so good at the RSVP. Paul and Mary contributed the turkey each year, which was already beginning to fill the big house with its unmistakably happy smell. Doc brought his eternal potato casserole. The Millikins always brought desserts.

Joe and Katherine were the first to arrive, and after handing Joe the elf hat Paul gave him a big hug, and whispered to him, on the escaped mental patient side of Joe's hairdo, "Tell me what I can do."

"Thanks, Paul, I will."

Eyes were averted and expressions glum. Mary announced before the door was even shut, "The others are not coming for a bit. And Joey and Lizzie are at a friend's house for a while longer. Paul and I thought the four of us should talk about the situation, get it all out in the open, so we can have a happy Not Christmas Dinner."

Mary had been like this since she was a little girl. She believed bad news was largely the product of failing to confront it, and that it evaporated upon confrontation. When their mother died in a traffic accident in Denver, Mary insisted that Katherine visit the scene with her and discuss exactly what had happened, though the police had already told them. Katherine took no comfort from Mary's grisly re-enactment, and Mary seemed almost surprised that their mother stayed dead after it.

Paul and Katherine knew Joe would hate this, but that he wouldn't say he hated it. They deferred to Mary. They all sat around the fireplace. Paul began, with a small shaking voice none of them had ever heard before.

"First of all, well, as far as anything financial, for medical or for after, you know Mary and I are happy to help, and lucky to be able to. And so anything that you need . . . ."

Joe started to respond, but Katherine saved him.

"We are actually OK there, Paul. Ironically, because there's really no treatment, the medical bills have been manageable. And after . . . ." She faltered but composed herself. "Joe has a good life insurance policy from his days at King Soopers, which we've kept up. Between that and my school check, we'll be fine." The plural pronoun was still fiercely manning the crumbling castle walls.

"Let me look at that policy, Kath. And you should think about selling Tiny and moving into this house with us."

Joe was staring at the lions, pineapples, and giraffe on the mantle, feeling like the giraffe.

"No, I've lived over there so long, even before Joe, remember. It's my home. And we are only a half block away."

Paul couldn't take it, and flipped-flopped into the kitchen, where they could all hear the world's loudest nose-blow. When he came back, with red nose and eyes, he a took a big breath, and machine-gunned out, "What about wills and all that stuff?" It was clear Mary had assigned Paul specific topics of inquiry.

"We don't have one, but we have an appointment with a lawyer downtown, recommended by David Seeley, you know, the son of the writer who used to live next to Lester." A sharp silence took over. When it had matured into awkwardness, the meeting was over. The smell of the turkey returned to everyone's consciousness, and lifted spirits.

The doorbell rang as if on cue. It was the Millikins. Barb was carrying small wrapped gifts in each hand, one for Joey and one for Lizzy, her purse dangling from an elbow. She was wiry and short, a full ten inches shorter than Davey, and she walked with a perennial stoop, which probably brought her down to less than five feet. When she and Davey walked together, Davey always politely behind her, they looked from the side like the letters "l" and "r," if you ignored Davey's mushroom cloud of hair on top of the "l." Davey, straight as a board, was carrying a tower of cakes—a Bundt cake at the foundation, two pound-cakes for walls and a roof of cupcakes for the children.

"Merry Not Christmas," Paul hollered, hugging them both and almost toppling the tower of desserts.

"I know we are to dump these in the Not Santa Bag, but I take them into the kitchen," Davey said after managing to save the teetering tower. Barb placed the two gifts for the children under the Not Christmas Tree.

The Not Christmas Tree was a canary island date palm that started out just 18 inches tall, but had grown over the years and now was almost seven feet. Paul decorated it each year by building a mound of different fruits around the trunk, the lip of the pot preventing the first layer from spilling out. Each year he tried to build the mound higher and higher up the trunk. He learned over the years that grapefruit worked best for the first few layers, and that increasingly smaller fruit as you went up— oranges, tangerines, lemons, limes—gave it a stabilizing and pleasing taper. The children loved to help.

In the early years, of course, one or two rows was enough to cover the whole trunk up to where the tree flared into its fronds. But as it grew taller the task became harder, then impossible. Paul still imagined each year that this would finally be the year of the return to the Full Canary, as he called it when the fruit covered the trunk entirely, but after the palm got to be about four feet tall he was never able to achieve it.

Once, when Mr. and Mrs. Lee were able to attend and the palm had just passed the four-foot mark, Mrs. Lee suggested that Paul just lean three big long watermelons up against the tree trunk. Then on top of them some long zucchini squash. That would get him three or four feet right there. Mrs. Lee was a lifelong rule bender.

"First of all," Paul explained, "watermelons and zucchini squash are not in season. Second, that would be cheating. The fruit has to be round."

"But I see some lemons in there," Mrs. Lee pointed near the top of that year's not-quite-tall-enough tower of fruit. Rule-benders delight in applying rules rigidly to others.

"Mostly round," Paul retorted.

The guest-list this somber year was smaller than usual. The Millikins, Doc Kasten, Joe, Katherine, a thin bum named Dwayne, Paul, Mary, and the two children. No relatives on Paul's side, all of whom spent that Christmas at different nodes in the extensive Taavalaa family tree.

As usual, Paul sat at the head of the old kitchen farm table, moved into the living room to accommodate one of its two seldom-used leaves, and Doc sat at the other end. The children usually sat at a card table off to the side, but this year's small entourage allowed them to join the grownups. Joey was old enough to sit on a regular chair, with a Denver phone book for a boost, and Lizzy was in the unnecessarily dovetailed wooden highchair Joe made, pushed right up to the table. Dwayne sat between the Millikins.

Paul had found Dwayne three days before, scavenging in the giant dumpster at the back of the store.

"Come have Christmas dinner with my family Thursday," Paul said from the seat of the forklift without even seeing who was in the dumpster.

"Are you joking, man?" asked a strong sounding gravelly voice, its owner still unseen.

"No."

"What's the catch?"

"No catch, we always like to invite some down-and-outers every year to share our good luck."

Dwayne appreciated Paul's choice of words. "Bum" was the conventional term, and Dwayne actually didn't mind that. But "down-and-outer" seemed a tad less judgmental. And the reference to luck was nice, though Dwayne knew it was mostly a lie. He'd intentionally screwed up his life in more ways than he could remember. Maybe that was some kind of bad luck. "Wino" hurt the most because it hit home.

"Oh, there is one catch," Paul remembered.

"I knew it."

"You need to take a shower right before and wear clean clothes." It was Mary's only rule. "Do you have a place to shower?"

"Sure, I'll sleep over at the Salvation Army tonight and tomorrow, and if I put in for it today I can reserve a shower for Thursday morning."

"Perfect. What about clean clothes?" Paul asked as he peeped over the edge of the dumpster and saw a rail thin man, maybe 30, but it was hard to tell. "Because I can lend you some if you need them."

"Yeah, that would be good. These are all I have. Will there be wine?"

"Tons. I'll meet you here tomorrow at noon with the clothes."

Paul had invited three others but Dwayne was the only one who showed. He was wearing the clothes Paul delivered, work clothes Paul intended to let him keep because he had two other sets.

The dark green pants were a foot too short and a half-foot too wide, scrunched up around the waist with one of Mary's mauve dress belts. They looked like beachcomber shorts on Dwayne. A lighter green long sleeve shirt looked like a mini-kimono. It had a King Soopers logo on the breast pocket, which on Dwayne was closer to his collar bone. At Paul's suggestion, Dwayne tucked the shirt in, though there was so much of it in circumference that he had to bunch it up and it formed a bit of a tire below the waist. The fake extra weight looked good on Dwayne.

Paul had given him a pair of his old work boots, and four pairs of socks to fill up them up. One of Mary's wraps—the mauve one to match the belt—completed the outfit. Doc Kasten thought the ensemble looked like a King Soopers' eighteen-wheeler had crashed into a car being driven by a woman on her way to the country club, and that the wreckage had entangled a bum crossing the street, but he was far too kind to say so.

"Wear as many of those socks as you need to, these boots are awful big," Paul instructed him when he dropped off the clothes and gave Dwayne directions to the big house, guessing it was 50-50 whether he'd ever see him again. Dwayne heard Paul singing "I'm Gonna Wash that

Man Right Outta My Hair" as he drove off, which he figured was a not-so-subtle reminder about the shower.

Next only to Joe, Davey Millikin was the second quietest guest at Not Christmas Dinners, other than that time Paul invited two itinerant deaf mutes. So everyone but Dwayne was surprised to hear Davey clear his throat and begin to speak, right after Paul said the blessing, which was his usual strange yet moving mishmash of religion, references to fruits and vegetables, and phrases from Broadway show tunes.

"I want to say something to you, Joseph. And to all of you about Joseph." Joe thought of Mrs. Buckley, whose "Yosef" was not nearly as thickly accented as Davey's, but which stood out so much more against the rest of her more delicate accent. "This life we have been given, it is not ours. We rent it. Like a tux we rent it. Sure, it is precious because it can go just like that [snapping his fingers]. So what? Ice cream melts on a hot day just like that [again snapping his fingers]. We are not ice cream.

"Do you know who we rent it from, this life? You are going to say God. I'm not so sure about that, to tell the truth." He had been looking right at Joe, whose head was bowed. But now Davey bowed his own head and rubbed his left forearm. Barb put her arm around him.

"This life we rent from each other. It's theirs, not ours," and he swung his left arm across the table indicating to all present, now looking up at everyone. "*They* are what make us people, and not ice cream, or animals.

"But that's just half the story, the easy half. When we are in this tux, it is ours. We have a responsibility to take care of it. It is our responsibility, not theirs." Another wave of the arm. "Bad luck, good luck, what's the difference? Little puffs of wind against the battleship inside us. And this is how we should live until we die. I will miss you, Joseph, because you are a good person. Because you know this confusing secret that we are responsible for them but they not for us."

CHAPTER 31
AULD LANG SYNE

Harold Watch. The eyes of the nation will be on our small town tonight, where our own Harold Fungo is on the verge of making baseball history. He has batted 1,000—that's right, folks, 1,000—for the last 22 straight games, tying a 1922 minor league record for consecutive pinch hits. He can break the record tonight. National reporters have been beating a path to manager Wally Berens' door asking him why Fungo is not playing full time. Although reports are not confirmed, it seems that Fungo's leg problems are chronic and not the result of any recent injury. That's all that's keeping him from being called up. To that we say, "Good news for us and bad news for the Garden City Bluebells and the Cincinnati Reds." Having won the first two games against the last place Manhattan Muskrats, the team looks for a sweep tonight before they head back out on the road. Tonight's contest begins as usual at 7:00. The game is sold out, the first Municipal Field sellout in its history.

As almost always in northeastern Colorado, Christmas Day was sunny and unseasonably warm. Even though almost every Christmas was warm and dry, people were surprised by it. "Awful warm and dry for Christmas" they would say, though what they actually should have said was, "We never get a White Christmas." On the rare occasions Christmas was white, people would never say, "What unusual weather." From which Joe concluded that people and weather are strange bedfellows.

The night sky was clear and the almost full moon already up, bathing the big house and the Collins shed in a mysterious luster. Soot shifted from bottom to side, and Joe leaned over to caress him. They talked exclusively about the Not Christmas Dinner.

"Doc seemed especially quiet tonight, didn't he?" Katherine began.

"It's because of me."

"I suppose. He feels helpless. He *is* helpless, and I'm sure that sticks in his craw. But he is also our friend, and he's sad."

"Why is everybody sadder than we are, Kath?"

She smiled. "You know, I never thought about that, but I think you may be right. Though I don't know why." She looked over at the big house. "Maybe it's because we live with this all the time. Doc, even Paul and Mary, get stung new every time they see us."

"But it will be worse for you than for them when it actually happens," Joe said, still petting Soot.

"Yes."

The gibbous moon, slightly dented at one edge like a soap ball dropped in the shower, was now high above the Collins house. It washed the whole landscape in light. The garden of the big house was aflame in a cold fire that spread through the Collins yard, over their house and shed, through the chain link into Tiny's garden, and all the way up through the opposite side right of the house and out onto the front street, where it met its match in the Tanner's streetlight.

"The other thing is that you don't seem sick. You gained a little weight, which Doc Kasten said you might, and you still have the headaches, but they haven't gotten worse. *Have they*, Joe? Tell me the truth."

"No, really, they haven't."

"And all the other terrible things he said you might get—paralyzed, lose your memory, get mean—none of those happened."

"I feel like I've been told a piano is going to drop on me sometime in the next few months. It might be better to have at least some signs I'm getting close."

"Doc said you might have trouble sleeping. Are you?"

"No. But I am dreaming a little more."

"And writing! Tales of Harold has never been going faster."

"I wonder if I'll finish. God, Kath, I'm afraid for you."

"Me? You are the one dying, not me. I'll keep my battleship going."

Joe had a memorable dream on New Year's Eve. He was back on the Utah, but it wasn't the old Utah. It was more like a cruise ship. The decks were party-colored geometric jigsaws, all fitted with dovetail joints. Joe's old gun was painted pink. It looked like a wad of bubble gum stuck on the deck, with a short pink straw sticking out. He was giving Lester a tour.

"Here's my old gun."

"You actually got up inside there and shot at Japanese planes?" Lester asked as he jumped behind the thick pink metal shields and into the pink metal gunner's seat, four holes at the bottom for monsoon drainage.

"Well, we shot blanks at our planes and real shells at balloons pretending to be Japanese planes."

"It's a complicated problem," Lester mumbled as he put his shoulders in the rests and gazed through the sight. "There is the speed and direction of the plane, but of course the plane is not ballistic and could change at any moment."

"They did. That was a problem."

"Your shells of course are ballistic, but at their speed I'm guessing we can largely ignore gravity. What's their muzzle velocity? And how far away was the average plane when . . . ."

"Let's go over to the slide. We have time for one more before we have to go."

In the middle of the aft deck, where there used to be a large smoke funnel, there was now a tall canary yellow slide. It corkscrewed down into a swimming pool. The bottom of the pool was striped black and amethyst, the stripes running port to starboard and getting wider the closer they got aft, to the far deep end. The yellow mouth of the slide deposited crew members in the shallow end, but it was safe because the angle was nearly horizontal.

Joe and Lester started climbing the bright blue ladder for a final run. A bosun's whistle signaled an incoming message.

"D, A, and F sharp," Lester reported as he continued his climb, ahead of Joe.

"Yosef, take those shoes off," Mrs. Buckley's voice came over the loud speaker. Joe looked down and saw he had loafers on, and kicked them off. There wasn't a soul behind him on the ladder, and the loafers clattered to the deck, bounced and flipped through the air but then landed right next to one another and smack in the middle of a lime green puzzle piece which was itself in the shape of a very large shoe.

As Joe was climbing up, he could see some of his shipmates sliding down when they came into sight on the outer curve of the coil. There was Slim Cohen. "Hi, Slim!" Joe yelled and waved, not sure if Slim could hear him. Then there was that chief with the devil tattoo. Now the devils were paddling their shovels along with the small current cascading down the slide, trying to pick up speed.

After Lester got to the top and plunged down Joe lost sight of him. But he could see the whole pool now, a black and purple striped postage stamp. At its top, the curve of the slide obscured all of its occupants, though Joe could hear their screams. He hesitated for a moment. "Go ahead, Joe, you're clogging up the whole line," Katherine said, suddenly behind him, with a hundred others behind her. She was beautiful as ever, wearing an orange swimsuit. Katherine smiled then gave him a little push. Down and around he went.

As he approached the slide's mouth, he felt it push up against his rear as his trajectory flattened. Once under the water, he realized that the pool bottom was not striped but was laddered with purple slats. The black "stripes" were openings between the slats, openings right into the dark sea under the ship. He saw six crew members walking on the purple slats underwater toward Jacobs ladders at the sides of the pool, several holding tropical drinks. Holding drinks underwater? This might be a dream. All of them were waving to him as he shot between the slats and into the Pacific Ocean. The black water turned cobalt as he rose toward the surface and escaped the ship's shadow.

When he bobbed to the top a roiling ocean greeted him in every direction. He couldn't even see the Utah. There must be a helluva storm brewing to cause these waves, yet the lapis sky was utterly cloudless. Sun and moon were both up, at opposite edges of the horizon, like gunslingers.

The waves nearest him were so big he couldn't see more than a few feet in any direction when he was surrounded by them, but could see forever when his wave crested. He once saw the Empire State Building off to the east and the Eiffel Tower to the west. These were really tall waves.

Then, while on the crest of the biggest one yet, he noticed something in a valley a few ranges away. Then it disappeared. Just as it was appearing again Joe went into a deep valley. He thought shallowly of whether the frequency of the waves would *ever* give him another glimpse of that object. Lester could have figured out the math, but all Joe knew was that it might be a while before he could see it again.

And then suddenly, or maybe it was after years—who knew with dreams—Joe and the object began to rise and fall in tandem. They also began to draw closer. It was Lester, and he was playing a floating Hamburg Concert Grand, undulating now just a few waves away. Despite the ocean's roar Joe could hear Liszt's Consolation No. 4 clear as a bell. Lester and the piano disappeared as the waves between them swelled, then reappeared when their own waves swelled. Each time Lester reappeared he sneezed three times.

CHAPTER 32
KANSAS AGAIN

Harold Watch. Our own Joltin' Janitor broke a decades-old minor league record last night before a capacity crowd of 3,079 at Municipal Field, extending his pinch hit streak to 23. His batting average is just as unbelievable, standing at a whopping .468. He returned to the pages of Life magazine this week with a half-page photo of his suicidal Fungo Faceoff, a stance he developed to ward off intentional walks. The photo first appeared in the pages of this newspaper several weeks ago. After sweeping last place Manhattan, the team is now nine games ahead of second place Garden City. It heads out on the road tomorrow to Garden City, Sterling, and Grand Island, before returning next Wednesday for a single game against the Sioux City Sioux. Better buy those tickets now!

Harold met Rose McClaren at the restaurant of the team's hotel in Garden City, the first leg of a trip out to southern Colorado.

He noticed as soon as the bus crossed the state line that the signs in Colorado listed each town's altitude instead of its population. Even pancake flat Burlington, Colorado, claimed to be over 4,000 feet above sea level (that's what Nick said—Harold just caught the town's name). If true, Harold calculated that in the 700 miles from St. Louis, say, to Burlington the land rose at a rate of less than six feet every mile.

He wondered whether the first explorers realized they were walking ever so slightly uphill all the way from the Mississippi to the foot of the Rockies, or whether they thought they were still at sea level when they first laid eyes on the saw-toothed wall ominously blocking their way. Harold wrote a poem about it years later, called Thrust, which the critics thought was about Rose.

Rose was a 19-year-old Wichita native who dropped out of high school at 16 when she got pregnant. Her parents sent her to Denver, to the Salvation Army's Booth Memorial Hospital, where, inexplicably, she took classes in mothering to prepare her for giving up the baby for adoption. She suspected the classes were all part of a plan to get her to change her mind and keep the baby. She didn't change her mind, and she never went back to Wichita.

She got a waitressing job in Denver, then a job answering the phone at a body shop in Fort Collins, then a really good job as a receptionist at a doctor's office in Hays. She told herself that each move was geographically coincidental, that she was just going where the money was better, but part of her worried she was being pulled back to Wichita by an invisible moral force to face some kind of shaming ritual, or worse.

She met Rita Jansen when Rita came into the doctor's office for a pregnancy test. They struck up a conversation, and eventually Rose joined Rita and a couple of other girls going out to bars together in and around Hays to try to meet men. It wasn't hard. As Rita put it, trying to meet men is like trying to find air to breathe. Each girl was comforted by their safety in numbers, though each also knew the safety was a mirage once they went off with their dates.

In the summer, one of their favorite places to meet men was at the Holiday Inn in Garden City, where visiting baseball teams stayed. At least these men were going somewhere, the girls figured, not grease monkeys stuck in a Kansas filling station. But if you asked any of the girls whether they were trying to find a husband, they would honestly have told you no. They didn't know what they wanted, except to escape for a few weekend hours from their dull and aching lives. Different aches for different girls, but the analgesic was addictive for them all.

It was there, in the bar/restaurant of the Garden City Holiday Inn, that Rose first laid her heavily made-up eyes on Harold. She recognized him from Life magazine. None of the other girls did. They weren't as well read.

Harold, as usual, was eating dinner with Clevon and Nick. He and Nick were having pork chops, Clevon a salad, back on the diet. They loved playing in Garden City because, for some reason they never understood, Todd always booked them into the Holiday Inn there, a big upgrade from their usual fare.

Rose came right up to them, looking only at Harold, and said, "Buy me a drink." It wasn't a question. She sat right down in the empty fourth chair and never took her eyes off Harold until she excused herself to go to the restroom.

"She's trouble, Benny, don't mess with her," Clevon warned.

Even Nick, who still was not as experienced as Clevon, raised warning bells. But Harold was besotted. Rose was gorgeous. She was short, but very curvy. Her tight yellow dress was a promise that hid just enough. Her blue eyes were framed with coal black hair. Her mouth was always a little frowny, even when she laughed, the frown outlined in a red lipstick that bordered on brown, and looked like it would taste like strawberry honey. 'Sultry" was the word Harold kept rolling around on the tongue in his mind.

He knew all about animal reproduction. He'd read about it in some of Ma's science books, including Darwin's The Origin of Species and, less known but more pertinent, his The Descent of Man and Selection in Relation to Sex. Harold was able to put two-and-two together, or to be more precise, to put this science together with Anna Karenina and The Scarlet Letter.

He'd read endlessly about being in love. Love was, in the end, what all great literature was about. He loved Ma more than he could express, and he'd come to love Jack, Sammy, Sparky, Nick, Wally, Greg, and Clevon, but not until souls and bodies met in Garden City did Harold know what this kind of love was, what it felt like. And the feeling took over everything, though, strangely, it had no effect on his hitting.

Harold spent every night, every meal, and every free moment with Rose, for the entire three-game series in Garden City. Then he invited her to meet him in Colorado Springs, which she never actually agreed to do, though he assumed she did because he just couldn't imagine her not agreeing. Clevon tried to talk to him, but they seldom saw each other anymore. And when they did Harold wouldn't listen.

"But I love her," Harold explained.

"Does she love you?"

"Of course."

"How do you know?"

"She told me, and we've become one soul."

Clevon was getting nowhere, and decided he had to tell Wally. Wally was in the visiting manager's "office," a cubicle with half walls right next to the showers, working on his line-up card for that night's game, the final one in Garden City.

"Benny got bit by a groupie bad. He wants to bring her to Colorado."

"Goddammit, Clevon, you are supposed to protect him from this shit."

"Sorry, SG, but you know he's got a mind of his own, and he's really got it bad." Some of the older players called Wally "SG," short for Speedy Gonzales, a gentle ribbing for him getting thrown out stealing as a pinch runner in his only appearance in the World Series. "I think this is his first girl ever. He's talking about marrying her when we get to the Springs."

"Goddammit. OK, I'll talk to him."

Wally spent more time talking to his players about life—about washing clothes, saving money, eating fruits and vegetables, making beds, cooking meals, and of course girls—than he did about baseball. He didn't mind. They were so young and so stupid.

He once had to order Stick Downey, who was old enough to know better, to drop a Three Musketeers Supplement Plan that Stick had heard, from God knows where, would be a good way to gain weight. Stick ate two of the candy bars with breakfast, three with lunch, four with dinner, and two right before bed. After a few days he passed out running in the outfield, and was hospitalized while the doctors tried to keep him out of insulin shock (they did) and determine whether he'd given himself an ulcer (he hadn't). After all that he still wanted to stick with the diet.

"I lost a few pounds in the hospital, and now I really need to gain weight."

Wally ordered him, on pain of being sent down, to drop it.

The worst ever was Reggie Williston, a promising young shortstop from Detroit who Wally had down in Amarillo. They called him Wrinkles, because he was an albino and his delicate skin got damaged terribly by the hot Texas summer sun.

Wrinkles suffered from the twin misfortunes of insatiable greed and profound stupidity. He was always trying to make a quick buck using the mind of a born sucker. Once, he bought ten $15 dollar bills for $50 from a guy who said he was desperate for smaller bills. Wrinkles would have landed in federal prison for passing the phony bills had he not crowed to Wally about his good fortune. Wally grabbed the bills and tore them up on the spot.

Wrinkles' end came when he had the bad luck of roping an equally dumb mobster into a telephone pyramid scheme. Wrinkles himself invested $500, and then had to get ten friends to invest $500 each before his $10,000 return would be guaranteed. He'd gotten commitments from nine. It was the off season, and he called Wally to be his last investor.

Wally not only declined but did everything he could to get Wrinkles to drop the whole thing. But Wally was always more persuasive in person than on the telephone, and especially more persuasive during the season. Wrinkles said he'd try to find someone else.

He called Wally the very next day to tell him not to worry about screwing up his $10,000 return because he was able to get an old high school friend from Detroit to take his place, Bobby Feinberg.

A few weeks later Wrinkles disappeared. Forever. Wally reported the missing Wrinkles to the Detroit police and mentioned Feinberg's name. They knew it well. Feinberg was a legendarily stupid enforcer for Detroit's Purple Gang, but police were never able to charge anyone with Wrinkles' disappearance because they never found a body or any witnesses. In fact, Feinberg himself disappeared a few months after Wrinkles did. Wally figured mobsters were just as embarrassed by idiots as the rest of us were.

Harold knew why Wally wanted to see him. He seldom called Harold into the office. Most of their baseball discussions took place during batting practice or in the dugout during games.

"Harold, you are the oldest rookie I've ever coached, but you should know better than anyone that age is not the same as experience. And that books are not the same as experience. And that feelings cloud judgment."

"This is about Rose, isn't it?"

"Goddamn right it's about Rose. Let me tell you a little story about me. Just between us, agreed?" Wally didn't wait to get Harold's agreement.

"I was playing in double-A in Kansas City, right out of high school. In those days they didn't have all this instructional bullshit, just single-A, double-A, and the bigs. I was pretty good. The Yankees' top infield prospect, so they said, and they started me in double-A. just like you. Anyway, I never dated at all in high school because I spent all my time and energy on baseball. The first woman I fell in love with, the first woman I ever screwed, was the first woman who I ever noticed said hello to me.

"It was a road game in Toledo. Her name was Marie. I was walking up to hit, she was in the first row on the third base side, right behind the visitors' on-deck circle, and she said, smiling, 'Knock it outta here, handsome.' I knew it was love because she noticed me, she talked to me, she smiled at me, and she called me handsome. We had a torrid time. She even met me back in Kansas City. Then she told me she might be pregnant."

"I know about contraceptives."

"Shut up, Harold, I'm not done. This story isn't about babies. She was not pregnant, but to this day I think she thought she was, or so hoped she was that the hope and the belief got all mixed up. Anyway, regardless of the baby that wasn't, I was sure she loved me and sure I loved her, and even after she told me she wasn't pregnant I told her I'd marry her right after the season, which was almost over. We even picked out an engagement ring in the window of a Kansas City jewelry store.

"But then I got sent down because I couldn't hit the goddamn curve. Down to single-A, to Binghamton, New York, in the middle of goddamn nowhere. I called her. I wrote her. I even went AWOL to take a red eye one night from where we were playing in Reading, PA, all the way to Toledo. That goddamn train took a whole day out and a whole day back. I was lucky they didn't can me. She was gone. People said she'd moved to St. Louis. Never heard from her again.

"I met a few more girls after that. But I realized immediately that my feelings for them were just the same as my feelings for Marie, different only because they weren't the first.

"A few years later real love hit me over the head when I met my Lois. It was completely different from all the others. The difference between a breeze and a tornado. You will just have to take my word for it. Love, real love, is too important to confuse with accidents.

"Does real love at first sight happen? Sure. It happened with my Lois. Do men fall in real love with the first woman they ever meet? Sure. I have a good friend, Jimmy Catarelli, coaching now in Cleveland, who married his junior high school sweetheart. But I'm telling you, Harold, the fake kind of love happens right out of the box way more often than the Jimmy C kind. So you have to play the percentages. Wait this out for a month or two, hell, even for just a couple weeks. If this is the real deal, it will survive a couple weeks. Lois says the best stews have to come off the boil and marinate."

"But I am sure she loves me too."

"This fake new love happens to women just like it happens to men. Maybe I was the first man who ever paid attention to Marie. Maybe she was tricked by the newness every bit as much as I was."

This suggestion made a big impression on Harold, who said nothing for the longest time, bouncing his knees up and down and playing with his false teeth, taking them in and out.

"Do this for me, Harold. We have four games in Colorado Springs, then we go down to Pueblo for four and Trinidad for three. Then we head back home and stop for one game against triple-A Wichita. Have her, what's her name again?"

"Rose."

"Tell Rose to meet you in Wichita," he paused to look at his calendar, "two weeks from today. See if you feel the same about her, if she feels the same way about you." Harold agreed, just because he trusted and respected Wally, but he knew as sure as he knew anything that this cooling-off period was unnecessary and wouldn't change a thing.

He talked to Clevon about Wally's view of fake love and real love. Clevon was considerably less romantic.

"Nah, it's all just having that feeling that somebody else likes you, goosed up with sex. There ain't no fake love or real love. Just like plus sex."

"But how do you know who you want to spend the rest of your life with?"

"You don't. It's all just a crap shoot, Benny. We trick ourselves into believing we've found true love because the alternative is just too scary."

Harold preferred Wally's universe, where his eternal love for Rose made sense. Clevon's world was the scary one. Harold also just didn't believe, from the admittedly thin slice of the world he'd seen so far, that feelings could be so misleading.

He thought of Plato's allegorical description of true love, which seemed strange when he first read it so long ago but which now seemed deeply true. Humans once had two heads, four arms, four legs, and two sets of genitalia, one male and one female. When we became too powerful Zeus cut us all in half. So now we spend our lives looking for our missing half.

Harold of course could still recall the exact words Plato put into Aristophanes' mouth:

> Love is born into every human being; it calls back the halves of our original nature together; it tries to make one out of two and heal the wound of human nature. Each of us, then, is a 'matching half' of a human whole, because each was sliced like a flatfish, two out of one, and each of us is always seeking the half that matches him.

Harold was sure Rose and he came from the same flatfish, and that he was feeling the wound of human nature without her.

Nowhere does life intrude more joyfully into baseball than when women intrude, though the joyful intrusions don't get much ink. For every crazed Ruth Ann Steinhagen shooting an Eddie Waitkus, for every empty groupie, for every marriage blown asunder by the distance and by the jealous mistress that is baseball, there are a hundred, no, a thousand women who have bound their lives to the men they love despite the game, and made rich successes of their marriages and their own lives.

Eleanor Gehrig watched her husband ascend to heights no one in the game had occupied, then watched him die just eight years after they married. In between, they made quite a life, though it was harder on Eleanor than on most baseball wives.

Lou was pathologically shy, even with her, and she was pathologically outspoken, with Lou and everyone else. He couldn't even get the words out to ask her to marry him, so she helped him along. He hardly spoke to anyone other than Eleanor, and even with her his words were dear. A sentence or two was for him a soliloquy. So he wrote letters to her. Wonderful, long soaring letters.

He was profoundly competitive and painfully sensitive. If he had a bad day at the plate or in the field, or even if the Yankees lost despite his best efforts, he was so devastated he could not talk to her for hours. He wasn't pouting. He was just so distraught about what could have been that he didn't think he could be proper company.

His shyness, competitiveness, and sensitivity conspired to produce in him an irrational and all-encompassing insecurity. Even at the height of his playing prowess, Gehrig was positive that he was playing so poorly that the Yankees were about to trade him. Once, when Eleanor redecorated their Manhattan apartment, his first reaction was, "My God, don't you know I might be traded at any moment?"

Baseball was not Gehrig's life, Eleanor was. In 1934, after their first anniversary, Gehrig melted down every scrap of his baseball hardware—rings, pins, and trophies, including those he won for World Series championships and All-Star appearances—and made Eleanor a bracelet. They made a pact in 1939 that Lou would retire after that season, no matter how well he was playing, so that they could start a family.

When he removed himself from the lineup on May 2, 1939, ending his unimaginable streak of 2,130 straight games, he wrote this in a letter to Eleanor:

> It was inevitable, although I dreaded the day, and my thoughts were with you constantly—how the thing would affect you and I—that was the big question and the most important thought underlying everything. I broke before the game because I thought so much of you. Not because I didn't know you are the bravest kind of partner but because my inferiority grabbed me and made me wonder and ponder if I could possibly prove myself worthy of you.

CHAPTER 33
COLORADO

Harold Watch. The streak grows, and so does the team's lead over second place Garden City. Our Joltin' Janitor got pinch hits in every road game last week, all wins, and another pinch hit in the home loss to Sioux City. The streak stands at 28, the average at .498, and the team's lead over Garden City at 11 games. Our heroes head out today to southern Colorado for games in Colorado Springs, Pueblo, and Trinidad.

"I knew it! A girl has just got to be in this story. It's in the constitution."

"Don't be a smart aleck, Joe. Anyway, it's your story, you put the girl in."

"So you say."

"Do you think you and I were meant for each other, Joe, or was it all just dumb luck?

"I'm not sure."

"I mean, after all, there are billions of people in the world, and we can't meet everyone. So a big chunk of it must be dumb luck. The chunk that put our grandparents in Europe instead of China, for instance."

"Sounds right, at least for the chunk."

"OK, but then, within the chunk, is it still dumb luck all the way down?"

"It don't feel like it."

"I suppose that's what matters most—whether it feels like dumb luck or not."

They went on their swing through southern Colorado. Harold, as usual, was unstoppable. He even hit a ground rule double in Pueblo when a hard-hit ball down the left field line bounced off a weird jutting projection and landed in the stands. It would be the only double of his career. They won every game, and were hunting for triple-A bear in Wichita after their earlier embarrassment in Des Moines.

They stopped overnight in Garden City, something Wally had forgotten. Harold couldn't resist trying to see Rose. He felt terrible about breaking his promise to Wally, but it was the madness. Besides, it had been 11 days, which is almost two weeks. He called her at home and work, but she didn't answer. So he went down to the restaurant/bar to ask the other girls if they'd seen her.

And there she was. Sitting at a table with the Garden City pitcher who tried to take Harold's legs out just last week. A knife stabbed him, big and serrated, not like the little knives he felt when they had to part because he had to go to the ballpark. Or even the knife when he had to leave for Colorado. He thought that would be a big knife, a hard and sharp conversation, now that his promise to Wally meant he'd have to take back his Colorado invitation to Rose. But she seemed fine with it. Now, here she was cavorting with a pitcher. A pitcher! And he was the very guy who tried to cripple Harold.

Still, the madness made him think there must be a good explanation. They were talking, with perfect innocence, all about Harold. Or, he was her cousin and she just didn't mention it when Harold told her about the guy who'd tried to knock his legs out. Or, he was asking for directions. Or, he was flirting with her but she was resisting. Heck, there were a hundred perfectly plausible explanations, and, because of their real love, one impossible one.

"Rose, are you getting ready for Wichita?"

"Wichita? I ain't going back there, honey." And she grabbed one of the pitcher's hands in both of hers. "I'm having a fine time right here," though she didn't really sound fine. "We had a good thing, Harry, but I ain't never going back to Wichita."

"But we agreed."

"Beat it, retard," the pitcher said, standing. Harold snapped, just like he did with the O'Malley brothers, but this pitcher was no rubbery fatso. He blocked Harold's swing, then took a swing of his own. This time it was Harold who was knocked out cold.

Neither the local paper back home nor the Garden City News covered the story in any depth, but two big city papers had a field day. "Famous Fungo Felled over Femme Fatale" read the sports headline in the Cincinnati Enquirer. "Spastic Cincy Sub Snared in Sexy Scandal" was the headline in the St. Louis Post-Dispatch. No one knew how they learned about the row.

Harold apologized separately to Wally, Greg, Clevon, and Nick, and then to the whole team. Groupies were never again an issue for him. He tried to stay away from all women, and when he couldn't he'd revert to his old way of talking and they couldn't understand him. If they persisted, he'd tell them, in his clearest slowest voice, "Sorry, ma'am, but I have crabs." That was Clevon's suggestion.

Harold missed Rose terribly. It was a smothered shriek between his stomach and throat, especially at nights. He had no idea this poetry about hearts breaking was literal. It took the whole summer for the shriek to shrink to a moan and another year for it to become an ache. The ache never left until he saw Rose again.

As his heart healed, he started worrying about the scar tissue. Had he become too deadened to see the real thing if the real thing ever came along?

Wally counseled him to forget about it. That when the right girl came along she would strike him like lightning and she'd be impossible to miss. Harold worried that Miss Lightning couldn't get within striking distance of his deeply grounded heart even if she wanted to, and that his Clevon clap excuse would insure she wouldn't want to.

Clevon and Nick both suggested that Harold worry about baseball, which would help him get over Rose. But hitting was so easy for Harold that he never worried about baseball. Then it struck him—*there are all kinds of things in baseball at which I am abysmal. In fact, everything except hitting singles. Hitting for power, running, catching, throwing. Concentrating on getting better at those things might help me heal, help my deadened feelings return.*

He knew his power was probably not going to get any better. They'd already worked on that for ages. He probably would not get faster without medical intervention, which no one had had the time to seek. But he'd never really tried to get better at throwing and catching.

So he and Clevon made a new pact, The Garden City Pact, in which Harold agreed to work his ass off with Clevon, who was a fine fielding first baseman, and with their infield coach, Dickie Brannan, to try to teach Harold to catch and throw.

Harold quickly developed an accurate arm, once Dickie explained to him that throwing and hitting were really just two versions of the same thing. Harold imagined the ball he was holding had just been pitched to him and he was hitting it back without a bat. It recalled his years hitting that tennis ball up against his bedroom wall with just his hand. All he had to do was slow all of that down, chop it into pieces, then reassemble. Catch the ball with his gloved hand instead of hitting it with his palm. Grab the ball out of the glove. Reach his arm back like it was the bat. Shift his weight to his front leg while swiveling his hips.

He was incredibly accurate, but didn't have the arm strength for the outfield, the middle infield, or third. That left catcher and first base. They focused on first base because Harold was so tall, and could throw left-handed.

Along with Dickie, Clevon spent hours trying to teach Harold to field grounders, catch line drives and pop-ups, stretch out on close plays, and throw to other bases. After a few weeks Harold got reasonably good at all aspects of fielding, except the grounders. He could never get the hang, literally, of fielding grounders. Despite his lankiness, he simply could not reach down far enough to snare grounders when they hugged the ground. This, too, might be a solvable medical issue, but in the meantime The Garden City Pact moved on to see if Harold could become a catcher.

He had, after all, been catching Clevon during Corn Palace practices. He was awfully tall for a catcher, but Wally remembered a few string beans behind the plate. There was Gary McCracken, who played for him in the Texas Leagues. And going way back, Wally remembered hearing about a guy named, believe it or not, Larry McLean, who played for the Giants. At 6'5", both of these catchers were a full inch taller than Harold.

The team's two catchers, Buddy Johnson, the starter, and his backup, a kid just up from single-A named Kevin Reynaldo, spent hours and hours they did not have trying to teach Harold to catch, to take their jobs.

Harold soon realized that almost everything about his 30 years of training aligned completely with the job of catching. His single, maniacal focus on the ball cured him of most amateurs' biggest problem with going behind the plate: that damn bat swinging right in front of them and obscuring the path of the incoming ball, both literally and attentionally. Harold was not distracted at all.

The hardest part for him was learning to squat and then to catch and throw from that squat. Kevin and especially Buddy gave him lots of tips, including how to sit more comfortably with one knee down and the other leg outstretched, when no one was on base.

Everyone was worried that he'd have the same trouble with balls in the dirt that he had with grounders in the infield, but he didn't. Bending over while standing up was the problem in the infield. He had no trouble at all reaching balls in the dirt when he was already squatting.

By the time they were finished with the Garden City Pact, Harold was an above average fielding catcher with a below average arm, who could hit 1,000, and whose heartache was slowly healing.

I had visited Trinidad, Colorado's Central Park several years before the conflagration that was Harold Fungo. It was part of a piece on minor league baseball fields across the country, and I must confess that I made it my first stop simply because of its name. Alas, this Central Park is nothing like the one I grew up bounding around. Like all of Trinidad, Colorado, it is nestled up against teetering outcroppings of menacing rock. I found myself glancing at them between every pitch, helping them stay put, when normally I would glance at benches, bullpens, the crowd around me or, if I was desperate, the sportswriters next to me.

Glancing is among the many worthwhile things fostered by the unique pace of baseball, along with thinking, talking, arguing, daydreaming, sleeping, and, for a special breed, scoring. Scoring a baseball game requires wellsprings of concentration, detail, and a dedication to irrelevance matched by only a few activities—stamp collecting and putting all the detritus on your desk at right angles to one another are two that come to mind. Don't confuse fan scoring with official scoring. Official scorers are the authors of baseball's Book of Heaven—the record of what every batter does with every pitch and, if he manages to hit it, what every fielder and baserunner does with the hit ball. The fan scorer is a kind of monk in an obscure sect, copying religious texts no one will read, re-recording for no one what the Book of Heaven is simultaneously recording for all time.

A fan scoring a baseball game cannot enjoy any of the worthwhile activities other fans take for granted. A fan scoring a game cannot for the briefest moment talk, yea even glance, for fear of missing a pitch. I gather that asking a fellow observer what happened on that last pitch is, for baseball scorers, a mortal sin. How they manage to record every pitch of a two-and-half-hour game without once visiting the little scorer's room remains to me one of baseball's deep mysteries, especially at my age.

Central Park—the threatening boulders version—is built next to what looks like the face of a grass-covered earthen dam, forming what would have been the right field stands, except there aren't any right field stands, or left field stands, or center field bleachers. Just a grandstand behind the plate, and that bulging dam. I had to alternate my glances between the falling mountain behind me and the about-to-burst deluge to my right.

The grandstand is a covered corrugated pavilion, far too high for its narrow width. The whole set up, cradled by a Quonset-hut home dugout overbalancing the barely below ground-level visitors' dugout, leaves the impression of a dog track. Between worrying about landslide and flood, I watched a reasonably well-played double-A game.

Now, a few years later, I am back at Central Park, this time to see Hephaestus. The fact that in the intervening years the dam has not burst nor the mountain collapsed does nothing to soothe me. I am deeply distracted, until he swings his bat, and the ball leaves the bat, destined for a hole. At that moment I forget completely about the dangers of my surroundings. He Frankensteins to first, a dead man brought to second life by baseball's jolt. I'm not sure what I'm seeing, but I'm sure it's important.

CHAPTER 34
DETACHED

Harold Watch. Our hometown hero was part of some altercation at a Garden City hotel last week, apparently involving a Bluebell pitcher. No wonder. What pitcher wouldn't want to try his luck at fisticuffs off the field if he had to face Fungo on the field? He has 34 consecutive pinch hits, and is batting a torrid .513. The team returns Saturday for "Dunk an Opponent Night," a tradition at Municipal Field. Some lucky fan will get to pick someone off the opposing team—player or coach—and get a chance to dunk him. Tickets are available but going fast.

Tiny itself was pretty much in the same condition as the day Joe and Katherine got married and first moved into it. Joe re-tiled the kitchen floor once, and re-painted innumerable interior walls. They both liked to paint, and Katherine liked to change up the colors every few years. Joe fixed many a roof leak and many a broken gingerbread trim, and occasional problems with plumbing or wiring. And he replaced all the drawers. But there were no big improvements, except the detached one-car garage, which Joe and Katherine built themselves shortly after they married.

Joe couldn't have done it without Katherine's expertise. The summer before, Katherine had signed up for a class on "framing" down at a vocational school in Denver, hoping to learn how to re-frame some of their paintings and family photographs, especially the ones in the big house. She knew something was wrong at the beginning of the very first class, when she noticed she was the only female, and the only person not wearing a tool belt. But she stuck it out, and all the guys, including the instructor, were really quite nice to her.

She learned how to frame walls, and became the invaluable job boss on the detached garage project, especially during the middle phases of building the walls, raising them, and setting the trusses. In fact, although they'd been talking about building a garage for a while, it was Katherine, armed with her new expertise, who first suggested that they could actually build it themselves.

They had a Garage Raising Barbeque and several family members, friends, and neighbors pitched in to raise the four walls. All were surprised, and a few a little annoyed, that Katherine was not only calling all the shots but also clearly knew what she was doing. In fact, she seemed to be the only one who knew what she was doing. Everyone else was unskilled labor, now that Katherine had forbidden Joe from cutting all the boards in half and putting them back together with dovetail joints.

Instead, Joe did all the "ironwork," as he jokingly put it—climbing up high on the trusses and ceiling joists to hammer in nails. Katherine was a little afraid of heights and the lumber was afraid of Paul's weight. So it was Joe who temporarily tied the raised walls in place with two-by-fours. Everyone cheered when the fourth wall went up and Joe tied it in place. He climbed down and fired up the barbeque, and of course Paul sang "How Do You Raise a Barn?," from Plain and Fancy.

There was only one scary ironwork moment during the whole project. It was the day after the wall raising barbeque. Joe was on an extension ladder, attaching the ridge board to the trusses, when Colonel, their very large German Shepherd, raced out for some defensive maneuvers against the mailman and knocked the ladder right out from under Joe. Somehow, Joe managed to hook one arm around a truss. Nobody else seemed to be around. After some considerable amount of time hanging (and eventually yelling), the next thing Joe remembered was sitting on the ground near the knocked over ladder, with Paul cradling him and singing "Try to Remember," from The Fantasticks. Paul could really be a pain in the ass.

***

Mr. and Mrs. Buckley got a divorce a year after Lester's murder. They sold their Mediterranean house to some real Italians—Father Carbone's brother and sister-in-law, Johnny One's parents—who probably didn't think it was all that Mediterranean. Mrs. Buckley moved to a hotel in downtown Philadelphia so she could nag the Philadelphia police in person, who had still not solved Lester's murder.

This was a white boy murdered in West Philly, so the police took it more seriously than the usual black-on-black killings that decimated that neighborhood. But Mrs. Buckley didn't think they were taking it seriously enough. She distributed flyers all over the City, wrote letters to the newspapers, chief of police, mayor, and every city councilman, and even issued press releases and held press conferences with the anonymous help of the PR people at the Curtis Institute.

The police didn't take kindly to her interference, but she had so many artsy fartsy friends down at Curtis that the higher ups told the division chief not to torpedo the investigation like they normally would if any other bitch had stuck her nose into police business.

They eventually found a witness who admitted seeing, and hearing, the whole thing from her fire escape, and who surely could have identified each of the three murdering muggers, but who was willing only to identify the juvenile—15-year-old Germaine "Half-Dead" Davis. Half-Dead succumbed to threats he would be charged as an adult, and eventually named his two accomplices: 19-year-old Orlando "Big O" Smith and 20-year-old Lionel "Choo Choo" Moore. Big O was a well-known member of the notorious Tops and Bottoms gang, but the other two seemed just to be hangers on.

Half-Dead's statement to police matched up in most important details with the statement given by the witness on the fire escape. They came upon some lost white boy, Big O asked him what the fuck he was doing on their turf and coldcocked him before he could answer. Laughing, all three searched him for anything valuable. Choo-Choo took a crappy watch. Half-Dead grabbed his wallet, which had a lousy three dollars in it.

The white boy came to, and just to scare the shit out of him Big O told him they usually kill mother-fuckers like him. But the boy didn't scare. Instead, he sat up and asked O whether his use of the phrase mother-fuckers meant one guy fucking a lot of other guys' mothers, or a bunch of guys fucking one of the guy's mother. O lost it and began stomping on the boy, and the other two laughed until O kept stomping and stomping. They tried to pull him off but O was in some kind of trance. He didn't stop until the boy was a grisly flat pancake.

As agreed, Half-Dead was charged as a juvenile, pleaded guilty to robbery and accessory to murder, and was sentenced to five years juvenile detention. Half-Dead became all dead just three months after his release, shot in the eye. Police suspected Big O's friends in the Tops and Bottoms, but that case was never solved.

Big O and Choo-Choo were tried together. Margaret attended every minute of every pre-trial hearing and every minute of the trial. Both young men were convicted of first-degree murder and sentenced to death, even though Choo-Choo never laid a hand on Lester, except when he took the watch. Something called the felony murder rule. Margaret would have thought it was unfair to punish Choo-Choo the same as Big O had she had the capacity to slice justice so finely. But she lost that capacity the moment humanity divided into just two pieces: those whose child had been murdered and those whose child had not been murdered. She often reflected that the two young black boys' mothers would soon be joining her in this terrible club.

Both boys were executed one week before Christmas, the second Christmas after the murder. Lester's father Carl attended the executions, but Margaret didn't. She had moved back to Vienna.

Because failure is everywhere in baseball, forgiveness is everywhere too. I was in Cleveland covering an Indians game when I had the chance to interview Harvey Haddix, he of the infamous 12-inning perfect game loss. On May 26, 1959, Haddix pitched nine innings of perfect baseball, facing 27 Milwaukee Braves batters and getting all 27 out. No hits, no walks, no errors, no baserunners. But his Pirates team couldn't push a run over the plate either, so the scoreless game went into extra innings. Haddix pitched three more perfect innings, for a total of 36 Braves faced and 36 Braves retired. In the bottom of the 13th, Haddix's third baseman Don Hoak bobbled a grounder hit by Braves leadoff hitter Felix Mantilla, ending Haddix's bid for an extra-innings perfect game. Mantilla eventually scored and Haddix lost the game, 2-0.

Forty years later (the Fates are patient), and just three years before Haddix's death (and they are cruel), Major League Baseball changed the definition of a perfect game to mean that if the game went into extra innings, the pitcher had to remain perfect to be credited with a perfect game. Haddix's 12-inning perfection was removed retroactively from the Book of Heaven.

He was living in a nursing home in Springfield, Ohio. We met in the cafeteria, which smelled surprisingly appetizing, the one spot in the facility forgiven from the astringent odors of alcohol and vinegar battling decay. Haddix, who was only 5'9" and a thin 160 when he played— which, even then, was small for a pitcher—was a blanched white elf when I interviewed him. He was 66 years old, but looked 96. Small people age fast, is what my mother always told me, threateningly. Haddix was stooped to 5'4", a pixie looking for some dropped dust.

Shining through everything, through his labored breathing, occasionally assisted by an oxygen mask that he was supposed to wear all the time but which he complained "cramped my style," there was the Cheshire cat grin for which he was famous during his playing days, which I could see once he sat down. A grin so big and bright that they called him The Kitten, which was apropos of his whole demeanor. The grin was even brighter now, with perfect looking false teeth that only occasionally clicked. I struggled to imagine, here in the nursing home cafeteria, that this Kitten once clawed down 36 straight Milwaukee Braves batters, with names like Joe Adcock and Henry Aaron.

When I asked the kitten-elf about baseball's decision to take his perfect game away from him, Haddix was dismissive, his smile bright as ever.

"I know what I did, and everyone who was there that day knows what I did. Hank and Joe know. I don't care what the bean counters say." There wasn't an iota of irritation in these words. He really didn't care about the bureaucratic theft of his record.

But when I asked Haddix if he'd forgiven Hoak for that error that cost him the perfect game, he became indignant.

"Forgive him? Hell, if I had struck out that sumbitch Mantilla instead of letting him get his bat on the ball, Donnie would never have had to field that grounder, never had to take all this crap for all these years. He needed to forgive me, and I think he has."

This thing we call baseball isn't just about the God of Fate battling the God of Chance. They fight through us, we are their imperfect weapons, with all our defects and divinity, our capacities to hate and to forgive, our glorious free will. Harvey Haddix's profound act of forgiveness, his kind turning of forgiveness on its head, his attempt to ease the pain of his suffering friend, was perfect.

CHAPTER 35
RISING BOATS

Harold Watch. The Streak stays alive. With his hits on the road this week Fungo's consecutive pinch hits now stand at 39, and his average at an equally impossible .545. This reporter received an interesting question from a reader about whether the streak is legitimate, considering that Fungo has had several walks in between his hits. So, I asked baseball guru Bill Conlin, the legendary sports columnist from the Philadelphia Daily News. He says that since the streak is a pinch hitting streak and not a regular hitting streak, we should probably mention the intermingled walks. Fair enough.

Despite the reluctance of the Reds' baseball executives, owner Powel Crosley knew a hot seller when he saw one. He ordered Harold to be called up. When Wally got the telephone call, the only thing that surprised him was that it hadn't come weeks before. He called Harold in to give him the news.

"I won't go."

"What?"

"I won't go to Cincinnati without Clevon, Greg, and you."

"Clevon? He's headed down, not up. And Greg is not ready to coach in the majors. And I'm not going anywhere."

"It's in my contract, Wally, I get to stay here until August 1. That's still seven weeks away."

"But that was to keep you from having to go to Shithole, Texas, not to keep you out of the big leagues."

"The contract provisions are quite unambiguous. I can stay here until August 1."

"Think about what you are saying, Harold. Players give their whole lives to this game to get a chance to play in the big show."

"But I'm an accidental baseball player, Wally, not a real one. I'm an idiot savant."

"You'll be thumbing your nose at everyone else if you don't go. And you're no idiot."

"I just need a few more weeks with Clevon. I think he'll turn it around. Just a few more weeks. Can you put them off for just a few weeks and keep all this from the other players?"

Wally didn't say anything for a long time.

"OK, let's do this. I'll tell the big boys that you don't want to go, and that you and your lawyer say your contract gives you the right to stay here until August 1."

"It does."

"That will put a scare into Crosley, who won't want to pay a jillion dollars to lawyers. He's an award-winning cheapskate. But I'll also mention that you pulled a hamstring catching and are back to pinch hitting until it heals. That will get their baseball attention. And it ain't really a lie because last week you really did pull it."

Yes, he pulled his hamstring last week but now it was fine. Harold thought that St. Augustine would probably not agree with Wally's notion of what was and was not a lie, but didn't want to get into a theological discussion with him.

Wally's disingenuousness worked. The Reds backed off temporarily, and Harold and Clevon enjoyed some precious additional workout time, enough that Clevon's curve average, after lollygagging near .200 for a month, suddenly took off one day while they were back home, after a road trip to the Quad-Cities.

"Hey, that one felt good," Clevon said after hitting a line drive off one of Greg's curves during Corn Palace practice. "And so did that one."

Clevon stayed in a groove the rest of the month, and his curve average shot up over 230, his combined batting average to a little under 260. He was over the hump and on his way.

"Is this how it worked for you, Benny? Nothin', nothin', nothin', then all of a sudden somethin', for no damn reason?" Clevon asked one night at dinner. They were at a Mexican restaurant Mrs. Tejada told them some of her relatives ran called Por Casualidad. It became one of their favorites.

"I actually don't know, because I was so young," Harold answered, straining to remember. "Funny, I have this photographic, audial, really, memory for words but not for my own non-verbal experiences."

"I'll say. Remember that time in Council Bluffs when you left your wallet at the diner? It was right after that first article about you in Life magazine, so everyone recognized you, and the owner brought your wallet to the next the stop."

"That was really nice of him. But back to your question of whether my hitting exploded like yours has. Maybe. Although I remember only one time when I hit a seam in the shingles and the ball went out of the yard, it must have happened often because I remember Ma telling me over and over not to hit the ball out of the yard. I don't think she ever understood that they were bouncing off the seams and edges of the shingles, otherwise she'd have probably put up a big piece of smooth plywood and I probably wouldn't be here today. Anyway, I remember that one day she stopped telling me not to hit the ball out of the yard, and never said it again. So I surmise that one day, quite abruptly, I stopped hitting those edges.

"I think this is how some kinds of learning, especially physical learning, must work. The learning comes in small packages, like this quantum energy you may have been reading about, so small you don't notice them." Clevon's face said he hadn't been reading about quantum energy. "Or like those locks on rivers we saw back in Illinois. Training is like those locks. You work and work, and nothing happens. The water is building up in the locks, but the boat is not moving forward at all. Then suddenly, the lock is filled, the gate lifts, and your boat goes on, higher than before."

Harold wasn't entirely comfortable with the analogy, but he knew that what Clevon was asking about was whether this sudden improvement could just as suddenly disappear. This was the fear that gripped all ballplayers, and made them so superstitious.

"As long as you keep filling your locks with hard work, the boat can't go back. It might not go on forever, but it can't go back."

But Harold was worried they'd run out of time, that they'd be on different rivers when Clevon's boat finally got high enough to move.

"And we need to enlist Fred to help us."

"No, I hate that chickenshit."

"He knows a lot about hitting, Clevon, much more than I do."

"But you hit better than that chickenshit ever did."

"That's not fair to Fred. I hit better than everyone." Atomic smile. "Look, Clevon, doing is not the same as teaching. I'm positive Fred will help you get better faster."

"God, Benny, I not only gotta get up at dark thirty every morning with you, now I gotta see Fred's goddamn arrogant face?"

"Yes."

It wasn't easy for Harold to convince Fred to sacrifice his mornings. In fact, he didn't. Hell, Fred didn't even like to coach during the times he was supposed to be coaching. Harold tried to sweet talk him into it. He didn't want to pull rank with Wally, and risk a completely ineffective, sulking Fred. But when Fred told Harold to "blow," Harold was forced to pull rank. Wally told Fred he had to do it or Wally would fire his woeful ass, so Fred was in full sulk when he met up with them, late, that first morning.

The night before, Harold, Clevon, and Greg decided to approach the Fred problem the way Tom Sawyer approached the fence-painting problem. It was Clevon's idea. They didn't say a word to Fred, and Fred was happy to sit in the morning sun, disengaged. But he wasn't disengaged. Fred Christianson could no more ignore a swinging bat than a cat could ignore a sprinting mouse. He was an above average hitter, not a great hitter, but he was a genius at analyzing other people's' hitting, a genius that propelled him into coaching despite his lousy personality. So he watched, and pretended not to.

"Maybe if you open your stance a little it will give you a better look at the ball," Greg erroneously suggested, as the three agreed he would the night before.

"No, no, no. He has to get further back in the box," Fred blurted out. He couldn't help but correct stupid advice of any kind, especially stupid hitting advice. "Opening your stance won't help a lefty see the ball coming from a righty. It actually makes it a little worse."

Slowly, slowly, Fred Christianson became a full if not enthusiastic member of The Corn Palace Pact. And Clevon's average really started to take off. It took off so fast that Clevon was called up to triple-A Syracuse in mid-June.

"Corn, Corn, Corn," the team chanted for Clevon at his going away dinner, at Steak World. They started calling him Corn because he seldom took off his Corn Palace sunglasses. To the fans' delight he wore them out at first base even in regular night games. Wally asked him if they made it harder for him to field, but he claimed they helped, because the lights on the pole behind the third base seats cast a terrible glare. Wally believed him, but went ahead and checked that his fielding percentage hadn't gone down after donning the shades. It hadn't.

"Dammit, Harold, this worked but it didn't work," Clevon said during his after-dinner speech. "You and Greg, and Fred, helped me so fast I got called up before you. But it's not soon enough for me to see you in Cincinnati this year. You're going there August 1, no doubt."

"Benny, Benny, Benny," everyone cheered. Well, not everyone. The rednecks didn't come to the party, and neither did Lee Williams, who had not only been ostracizing Clevon over his friendship with Harold, but who was especially angry that Clevon's call-up was attributable to Harold's tutoring.

Harold helped Clevon clean out his locker after the going away dinner. Then they rode the bus together to the Omaha airport. They talked about everything except baseball.

Clevon told Harold about his momma and daddy, and about how his momma died in the fields when he was only 6, and how his daddy tried to explain her death by telling him, "Your momma was just too big for this world," and how this puzzling explanation made Clevon think he was dying every time his daddy's measurements of him against the shed door showed he was growing.

Harold told Clevon about his Ma, about her deafness and her burning books. About how she never let him go away from the house and yard, except to run to the store. About how he never went to school or had any friends or knew his last name.

"But I thought it was Fungo," Clevon responded.

"Wally made that name up. Ma never told me what our last name was. I'm not sure she knew. I thought it was Bradsby because of my bat. I thought my dad's name was Hillerich Bradsby. That's why I use B for my middle initial." He smiled sadly.

"Well, I suppose Sumford is made up, too. Don't sound African to me, and my daddy says his grandpa was African. Harold, we are two outsiders with made up names headed to play some big ball!"

Clevon was indeed headed to play some big ball. He finished out the year in Syracuse, made the Reds roster the next spring, their second black player ever, after Chuck Harmon, and was a fixture for Cincinnati at first base for almost a decade.

There is a paradox of pacing in the minor leagues. The game is slower because the players are slower, the pitches slower, the infield and outfield throws slower. But the slowness cannot be perceived, and it isn't just because no one looks slow when everyone is. It's also because the pace of life in these small towns is slower than in big cities, and so by comparison the baseball seems faster.

We aren't clocking Joe Blow against Luis Aparicio, we are clocking Joe Blow against the rhythms of the farm, against two-hour morning coffees at the local diner. And we clock Luis Aparicio against the frenetic run-walking of commuters late for their trains. Then, in that blissful balance that seems unique to baseball, Joe Blow, speeded up by Slow Town, and Luis Aparicio, slowed down by Chi Town, end up playing at exactly the same perceived pace.

CHAPTER 36
NATURE ABHORS VACUUMS

Harold Watch. At last, our Joltin' Janitor has found a place in the starting lineup! Last night he debuted behind the plate, subbing for starting catcher Kevin Reynaldo, who had the flu. Fungo did a workmanlike job, calling a good game and allowing no passed balls, though he was unable to throw out a Cedar Rapids runner stealing second. He went four for four at the plate, raising his average to an eye-watering .582. Ironically, starting behind the plate puts his record streak of 41 consecutive *pinch* hits on hold, but now we should start talking about regular consecutive hits, whether pinch hits or not, which now stand at 45. In sad news, fan favorite Clevon Sumpter was called up to triple-A Syracuse this week. We'll miss the hard-hitting first baseman. Good luck, Clevon! Remember fans, Saturday is Dunk an Opponent Night at Municipal Field, the final game of a three-game homestand against Iowa City. Get those tickets now while you still can.

With Clevon gone, the three remaining black players stopped talking to everyone else, and started sitting by themselves in the dugout. Lee Williams had taken over as their leader. Greg tried to intervene. He went to talk to them in the right field corner where they began gathering by themselves before every batting practice.

"I guess you guys forgot how Wally stood up for you back in Cape Girardeau."

"We don't need anybody to stand up for us," Williams responded.

"Well, you did that night or you would have been freezing your asses off in some shed in the mountains."

"We can take care of ourselves."

Greg was surprised at Wally's reaction when he told him about the conversation. "Lee's right. They can take care of themselves."

"No, they can't. Not with people like those assholes in Missouri."

"Greg, give 'em some room. These poor people have been told their whole lives they are pieces of shit. No one would suddenly start acting normal just because the shit storm lightened up a little."

"Clevon did."

"Clevon was one of a kind. And don't let him fool you. This hatred hurt him bad. You saw him crying. And it screwed him up. He'd be in jail if it weren't for baseball. 'Course, that's true of most of us."

The bigshots didn't like pushy Negroes. They somehow found out about the situation (probably from one of the rednecks), because in a few days all three of the black players were gone. Two traded and Lee sent down. Wally felt bad for them, but had to admit things were a lot less complicated now.

Jack, Dee, and Sammy brought Sparky to the Saturday night game right after Clevon's call-up, to cheer Harold up. They didn't tell him because they wanted it to be a surprise. The folks at the gate wouldn't let them bring Sparky in at first.

"Sorry, son, no dogs allowed."

"But this is not our dog," Sammy tried to explain, "he belongs to Harold Fungo, our friend."

"Has Mr. Fungo asked you to bring the dog?"

Jack took over. "No, we want it to be a surprise. But we cleared it with Bob Cooper."

The mere mention of Big Bob's name, especially in the formal way Jack did it—Bob Cooper—opened the gates like the Red Sea.

Last summer Jack's crew put out a brush fire that was threatening the Cooper real estate building on Adams Street, and Big Bob called Jack directly to thank him and tell him to let him know if there was ever anything he could do for Jack or any of his firemen. When Harold came along and Big Bob discovered Jack was Harold's "agent," the Big Bob IOU was gold. He was more than happy to give the green light to Sparky, and even paid for all their tickets. It was he who had the idea that they should sit a little off to the third base side so Harold might see them when he went up to bat.

"Should I get something in writing from your office?" Jack asked.

"Hell no, just tell them Big Bob says the dog's OK and that I'll fire their asses if they don't let him in."

Wally was in on the surprise, and he agreed to put Harold into the game much earlier than usual because it was a school night for Sammy. Harold was back to just pinch hitting, to rest his fully healed hamstring.

They were all hoping Harold would notice them when he walked up to the plate. Plan B was to yell to get his attention. Neither plan was necessary. As soon as Harold stepped out of the dugout Sparky saw him and started whistling. Harold immediately heard the whistling cutting through the crowd noise, and looked up to see Sparky on Sammy's lap. Jack and Sammy waved, and Jack had to restrain Sparky from running onto the field. Harold broke into an atomic smile and gave Jack and Sammy an animated wave with both hands, bat still in one of them.

When Harold got his hit, Sparky added some clicking to the whistling. Once Harold was out of the game, Sparky stayed silent and motionless, until the seventh inning stretch.

It was "Dunk an Opponent Night," one of the most popular promotions at Municipal Field. During the seventh inning stretch one lucky fan, picked by ticket-stub lottery, was allowed to designate an opposing player or coach, who would then be placed atop a water-filled hog trough on a hinged platform, held in place and released by a wooden arm attached to a small target. The fan, standing on the third-base line twenty feet away, had three chances to hit the target with a baseball and dunk the opponent.

The bigshots eventually banned these dunking promotions, which were common across the minors, when a fan in Spokane, Washington, hit a promising pitcher right in the head with a hard-thrown ball, delaying but fortunately not ending his career.

When Sparky saw the contraption being rolled out, water sloshing in the trough, he lost all control. He wriggled out of Jack's grip, ran down the aisle and jumped on top of the visitors' dugout, then onto the field. He ran directly to the trough, jumped in, and began swimming. The crowd cheered.

Security guards were about to grab him, probably with some attendant injury to them, when Big Bob got on the public address system and boomed, "Leave him alone. That's Sparky, Harold Fungo's dog." More cheers. "I guess he's given a reprieve to you boys from Iowa tonight." Big Bob didn't attend many games, but he couldn't resist Dunk an Opponent Night.

"How do you know about these crazy kinds of minor league promotions?"

"I'm not sure."

"Did they have many of them down in Denver when you saw games there?"

"Not really. The Bears were triple-A, closest to the major leagues, and triple-A teams don't do as many of these goofy kinds of promotions. They don't have to."

"Did the lower-level teams really have Dunk an Opponent Night?"

"I don't know."

"Father took Mary and me down to Denver for a Bears game one time, when Mary was in sixth grade, so I would have been in high school. It was the only time I ever saw a baseball game in person. Mary had gotten straight-As, and every sixth grader in Greeley with straight-As got in free that night. Father was so proud of her. I was livid. I'd gotten straight-As every year since kindergarten, and no one ever took me to a baseball game to celebrate."

"But Mary had to try harder."

"I know. That's what Mother told me when I complained to her, and of course I knew she was right. But it didn't make it seem any less unfair."

"I couldn't have gotten in free on straight-A night or on Fools Night," Joe volunteered. "I was waiting for Straight C Night, but it never came."

I had been working, half-heartedly, on a biography of Henry Chadwick, the inventor of baseball statistics. He was born in England, but his family moved to Brooklyn in 1837, when he was just 12. Young Henry fell in love with the piano and dreamed of composing and performing, but eventually followed his father's footsteps and became a journalist. He was a rabid cricketeer, and discovered a new-fangled sport called baseball just about at the same time he landed the job as The New York Times cricket reporter. Chadwick turned his personal and journalistic attentions to the new sport, and became its principal booster. In his newspaper columns relentlessly touting the new game, Chadwick coined many of the slangs still used in baseball to this day, including "fungo."

He invented the box score in one of his columns—the device to report on hits, runs, and errors in each inning by each team—and the box score led to a ravenous demand for more and more detailed statistics. He got the idea to number the players on the field by their positions, and invented a short-hand coupled with those numbers that allowed games to be scored for every pitch and its result to be documented.

It was Chadwick's love affair with detail that gave birth to baseball's Book of Heaven. Every act of every major league baseball player is recorded for all to see, forever. How many Dodgers did Cubs starting pitcher Hippo Vaughn strike out in his eight-inning 4-3 loss on July 14, 1920? Four. The day before, did Rogers Hornsby knock in any runs in the game against the Giants? Uncharacteristically, no.

The actions of the heroic and irrelevant alike are recorded. Of the almost 15,000 men who have been blessed to play this game in the major leagues, several hundred were blessed only for one day. One day in the big-leagues then never again. These mayflies of the majors are common enough to have earned a nickname: cups of coffee. But they are, all of them, still in the Book of Heaven.

Most cups of coffee, of course, had no hits, no runs batted in, nothing. Their box scores look like the EKG of a corpse. But there were a few spectacular torrents of success, lighting up the scoreboard so bright that their immediate departure hints of some tragedy. There were a few tragedies, but mostly the Fates were just screwing around.

Aubrey Epps, a catcher, played in one game for the Pittsburgh Pirates on September 29, 1935. He went three for four, hitting two singles, one triple, and knocking in four runs. He never played another major league game. But his departure was no mystery. In eight innings behind the plate, he made two errors and allowed three stolen bases.

Baseball's cruel transparency is unknown in any other walk of life. We all have people watching our work, judging it in a myriad of ways, but not in such painful detail. No one can look me up in any book and find out how many spelling and grammar errors my editors caught in the essay I turned in last Tuesday.

But bound to the pain in the Book of Heaven is an equally unique dignity. Every player, whether Babe Ruth or Aubrey Epps, is recognized for the extraordinary achievement of being part of this brotherhood of knights. Not for us, my Lord, not for us, but to Baseball give the glory. Though Chadwick was interesting and important, my attention was becoming indentured to the unlikeliest of knights. And he got me thinking an awful lot about Aubrey Epps, the great hitting cup of coffee catcher with the rag arm.

CHAPTER 37
THE CEMETERY

Harold Watch. The hitting streak now stands at 49, and the pinch hitting streak at 43. Fungo is batting .628. Fans in Cincinnati are clamoring for his call-up, but Reds officials remain mum. Our Joltin' Janitor is struggling with a hamstring injury, which is keeping him out of the starting lineup, and maybe also keeping him out of Cincinnati. Just when you thought the Fungo story couldn't get any better, his dog Sparky made a guest appearance Saturday on Dunk an Opponent Night, jumping onto the field and then into the water tank. His antics saved Iowa City Oaks manager Buddy Sanders from a soaking. Is there anything Fungo and his dog can't do? Just pray the Reds let us keep Harold and Sparky for the rest of this season. Outfielder Lee Williams was sent down to single-A Tulsa. Here's hoping the winner of this year's Rebel Plaque will be back soon.

Joe worked as a night stocker at the Greeley King Soopers No. 51 uninterrupted for 28 years, a job he took right after the Navy. His various bosses periodically offered him promotions. One time Lloyd King himself asked Joe to manage a new store. But Joe always politely declined. In the early years they tried to move him to days, but the commotion was too much for him. He enjoyed the solitude of a motionless horizontal space teeming with things that people needed and wanted, but with no people needing and wanting them at the moment.

They kept giving him raises until he hit the company cap for non-salaried workers. But he and Katherine got by fine on their two small incomes from King Soopers and St. Thomas Catholic High School. Her father left them Tiny when he died, though Katherine and Joe had been living there ever since they married. Mary inherited the big house. She offered to trade, since she was single, but Katherine insisted she keep it. That's what Father and Mother had wanted. Tiny was plenty big enough for Katherine and Joe, with no children.

Three years before he started sneezing and writing Joe quit his night stocking job. Like many supermarkets, King Soopers changed to twenty-four hours, and although the nights were not as busy as the days, they were no longer Joe's refuge. He just didn't see the point of being away from Katherine all night, of being so tired all weekend, if he still had to deal with people. He might as well work a quiet day job.

When he told her he wanted to quit, Katherine said, "But then I can't tell my students I'm married to a night stalker," reprising her old joke. "Seriously, Joe, what job has fewer people around than a grocery store in the middle of the night?"

"A cemetery." Katherine started to laugh but stopped when she realized Joe was serious. "Mountain View is looking for a groundskeeper. You know how I love to mow the lawn and take care of the garden. It'd be perfect."

It was perfect. Joe didn't have to talk to anyone. In the summers he spent the mornings mowing different sections. No worries about waking anybody up since the cemetery was half a mile from the furthest outcroppings of the town. Burials were never scheduled before 10:30 a.m., but it took five full mornings to mow the whole cemetery, so Joe had to juggle the burials with the morning mowing. The rest of the day was taken up with trimming, weeding, planting, all the myriad of things summer landscaping requires for keeping the jungle at bay.

In the winters, Joe worked just two days a week. When he took the job he hadn't even thought about winters, about how his work might be cut back. But after he discussed finances with Katherine, she agreed the two of them could scrape by between November and March. His main job during those months was to gather up the cut flowers people left at gravesites, though toward winter's end there was also prep work to do in the flowerbeds.

Every week, no matter the season, there was the columbarium's marble walls to clean and polish. Joe didn't know the word "columbarium" until he took the job at Mountain View. Tom Hilton, the cemetery's marketing director, made a joke about it. "Hi, I'm Tom Hilton, director of marketing. They call me The Columbarium. Know why? 'Cause I call 'em, and they bury 'em." Joe liked the sound of the word, even after hearing Hilton's dreadful joke. Katherine of course knew it—she knew way more words than Joe did.

A few weeks after starting, Joe decided he'd mow in stripes like they did on baseball fields. He knew those stripes didn't come just by mowing in different directions, but that the groundskeepers dragged a wide chain link mesh behind the mower to bend the mowed grass in one direction. Joe had always wanted to try this at home, but didn't have a riding mower. He gave some fleeting thought to dragging a piece of chain link behind him, tied by a rope around his waist, but decided he would look so stupid that people would stop and want to talk to him about it. But now he'd be using a big riding mower just like the baseball grounds crews, with no nosy neighbors making inquiries.

He bought some six-foot chain link fencing and attached it to the mower with some cables. The striping was spectacular. His boss complimented him several times and said he'd gotten rave reviews from customers. He must have meant live customers.

When there were interments, Joe would work as far away from them as possible, not just to be respectful but also because he didn't want to talk to anybody, let alone strangers in mourning. The only people Joe ever saw was the occasional teenager learning how to drive, the nervous father sitting shotgun ready to grab the wheel. Joe never had to talk to them either. If they passed, Joe would simply wave his hand. This often caused the father's face to blanch in contemplation of whether his teenager was about to take a hand off the steering wheel to return Joe's greeting. There was an occasional swerve.

Before he took this job Joe had no idea how popular cemeteries were with parents teaching their children how to drive. Joe never learned that way. He and his father Stan got in the car and Stan said, "OK, let's go." Joe protested, "But what do I do?" And his father said, "Start the car." Joe deduced that "starting" must have something to do with the black button his father was pointing to, so he pushed it. His father, incredulous that he'd tried to start it before pulling out the choke, quickly did so. The engine engaged and the car leapt forward and died. "You've got to put the clutch in." "What's a clutch?"

After working there for a full year, and getting the lay of the land, Joe started bringing Soot with him. In the summer Soot loved to ride in the riding mower, though Joe couldn't imagine how the dog could stand the noise. Katherine fitted Soot with a small pair of children's earmuffs, and she and Joe were both surprised that he tolerated them as well as he did, especially since he didn't seem to mind the noise without them.

Next to mowing with earmuffs on, Soot's second favorite summer cemetery job was helping Joe trim the grass around the headstones. He sniffed and sneezed and wagged around every marker. Joe wondered whether Soot could smell any decaying bodies, especially on fresh graves.

Soot also learned three more words, "mow-time," "urns," and "dome," which he quickly added to his already impressive vocabulary. Right before Joe started the mower, he'd tell Soot, "Mow-time," and Soot would jump up on the mower's seat, just like he would in the car at home. His tail, trying hard to wag, was usually pinned back against the seat, so his body wagged instead.

Joe would retrieve the earmuffs he hung on the handles, and place them on Soot. This was Soot's signal to make room for Joe to sit down, after which Soot would plop down on Joe's lap, paws on the mower's steering wheel. This freed his tail, which was a big problem on the first couple mows, slapping at Joe's face and blocking his vision, a fuzzy windshield wiper. They figured out a diagonal adjustment, and Soot got comfortable enough to lie down, so the half-liberated tail hit Joe's left shoulder on the back side of each wag, instead of his head on both sides of each wag. And Soot wagged the whole time, from start to finish.

When it was time to work around the columbarium, Joe would announce, "To the urns!" Hearing these words Soot would race off to the columbarium, which was a good 300 yards from the tool shed, and lie down in front of it, lion-like, waiting for Joe to join him. Once Joe arrived Soot would wander a little nearby, after which he mostly just slept.

Soot loved the cemetery winters best. He flew through the snow unconstrained by any obligation to attend to Joe, who usually just sat in a chair near the shed after finishing his truncated winter chores, watching Soot run.

Joe learned a lot about the tracks that dogs make, as Soot painted his signatures across the cemetery's snow. Joe got to the point of being able to distinguish the tracks from Soot's walk from those of his trot from those of his run, and even a regular run from an "I am chasing a rabbit or squirrel" run. Joe especially enjoyed the tracks Soot made when he would run a little sideways, left feet akimbo. It made Soot's modest tracks multiply into what looked like the tracks from a 20-mule team. Well, maybe a two-mule team.

There was a special place in the cemetery where Joe liked to take Soot after their work was done. About halfway between the tool shed and the columbarium there was a dense swath of tall elms that separated two large sections of headstones. Rumor was that the smaller of the two areas was originally designated for Catholics, Jews, and other non-Protestants, and that the elm grove was planted for separation. Hidden inside the dense elm forest was a small round clearing, maybe 40 feet across.

They'd both lay down, and Joe would gaze up at the small dome of the sky, which in the winter looked like it was being held up from the brown grass disk of the forest floor by a ring of spidery wooden girders. In the summer the blue dome was supported by a thick leafy gasket of dark green.

Joe called this spot "the Church of the Dome," and as soon as Soot heard "dome" he'd run there, and wait for Joe to join him. It was a secret place—he never told Katherine about it, until the end.

Joe quickly realized he'd be fired from the cemetery job unless he implemented two rules for Soot's behavior: no digging and no running off to other human voices.

The first rule came into play that day in the late summer when Joe first brought Soot with him. The moment Soot jumped out of the car he immediately began digging, right at the biggest and most famous memorial in the cemetery. It was the final resting place of Anthony Inverness VorHorst, one of Greeley's most prominent turn-of-the-century business and civic leaders. Before Joe even knew what happened, Soot had excavated a hole that must have been a foot deep. The tailings from the excavation formed a conical pile leaning up against the VorHorst obelisk, and several flecks of dirt stuck to the plaque.

Here Lies A.I. VorHorst
Beloved Father, Husband, Civic Leader
May He Fest in Peace

The right side of the R in Rest had been flecked out with a small dirt clod, courtesy of Soot.

"No!" screamed Joe as soon as he saw the dig, and Soot immediately stopped, confused. Joe never objected to his escape tunnels at home. Watching Joe replace the dirt and shredded pieces of sod while cussing and glancing over at him seemed to reinforce the command, and Soot never again dug at the cemetery, though he was regularly and deeply tempted.

The second rule had more perilous origins. It was the first time Katherine tagged along, later in that first summer. There was an interment scheduled for 10:30. Joe and Soot were finishing up their mowing on the other side, far from the mourners. Katherine stayed back at the tool shed, reading on a chair in the sun.

Everything was fine until Joe finished the mowing, pulled the riding mower into the shed, and turned it off. Soot jumped down and immediately ran full stop toward the voices he could now hear with the mower off, despite still wearing his earmuffs. When she saw Soot rocket off in the direction of the interment, Katherine ran after him as fast as she could, knowing that Joe's legs weren't so good for running.

When she arrived at the gravesite, she saw Soot darting around madly, dashing like Whizzer White between black trousers and black skirts, deftly avoiding every black draped arm reaching out to stop him. Funereal tears and gloom had universally turned to anger. Men were shouting, cursing. Women were shaking their heads and glaring.

"How dare you bring a dog here! Look what he's done," a large man in a tight dark suit yelled as he got within feet of Katherine.

"There you are," Katherine quickly extemporized. "I'm so sorry folks. This little guy, his name's Soot, belonged to dear Mrs. Phelps, rest in peace, who's urn is over in the columbarium. Every year on the anniversary of her death Soot jumps the fence at the old Phelps place, runs three miles, and sits by her vault the whole day. Every year I drive him back home to the widower Phelps. Soot must have been so lonely today that he just couldn't resist running here when he heard your voices. I thought the earmuffs would prevent this. I'm so sorry."

There was a group sigh, and everyone started calling "Here, Soot, come boy," in very different voices than before. Soot's tail began to wag, he slowed down to a trot, and was collared by a mourning sister, who cuddled him until Katherine prised him away.

"Goodbye, Soot," everyone said, starting at slightly different times so the greeting sounded like a cheer and lasted several seconds. The gloom had left the mourners, replaced by a rising heat of guilt. Now they were sorry they had been so rude to Katherine, and sorry again at no longer being as sad as they were before Soot's invasion.

All of this resulted in the rule that Soot was leashed whenever there was a scheduled burial.

The next year Joe got the idea of transporting some of his fireflies to the cemetery. One night he trapped a dozen or so in a mason jar, and let them out down on the west side of the cemetery, in a grove of trees where the ground sloped down to a small, usually dry, stream. He'd prepared the area by soaking it earlier that day.

He felt bad at first about splitting the fireflies up. Was he separating families, ripping parents from children? He thought of Davey Millikin. Then he remembered that fireflies live for only one season. So the worst he was doing was separating siblings, and that's not so bad, as he thought of his sister Sue.

When he got back Katherine had already called the Report to order. Good thing Soot was there, lying as usual between the red wooden chairs, or there wouldn't have been a quorum.

"How did the fireflies seem to like it?" Katherine asked.

"I think they'll make it. It's pretty warm at night, and damp in the day, like our garden here."

"It would be really something to be there some early summer evening and look out at those groves of trees sparkling. It would comfort people, don't you think?"

"I suppose."

"Of course, if the fireflies don't make it, we can always bring Soot to lift mourners' spirits."

CHAPTER 38
THE GARDEN

Harold Watch. Harold Fungo's consecutive hitting streak now stands at 53. Fifty-three times, beginning way back in May, our Joltin' Janitor has stepped up to the plate and gotten a hit (intervening walks not counted). Fifty-three times. He's also batting .689 and approaching the 100 at-bats required for that record-setting average to count. Even if everything ended tonight, these are records that will never be broken. But there's no reason to think they will end tonight. Could he get to 100 straight hits and bat .950? Probably not before the dreaded call-up. Meanwhile, the team remains in first place, 15 games ahead of the Garden City Bluebells, who they face for a four-game series beginning tonight. Only a few tickets remain.

Joe and Katherine got married at St. Thomas, Father Carbone officiating. It was the old-fashioned wedding mass, with the wedding rites integrated into a full Latin mass. Father Carbone didn't allow the nonsense of any best men or bridesmaids or maids of honor, which actually suited Joe and Katherine just fine. Joe was relieved because the fewer people the better; besides, he only had a few friends and one was dead. Katherine was glad they didn't have to pay for all those ridiculous bridesmaid dresses.

The traditional Catholic wedding also didn't allow Wagner's Bridal Chorus, or even the usual procession. Father Carbone and Deacon McNair walked down the aisle first, after the altar boys lit the candles. Purcell's Trumpet Tune—a forgettable processional fit more for Elizabeth and Phillip in London than for Katherine and Joe in Greeley—announced the wedding party, and the congregation rose. Katherine and Joe came in together, holding hands, followed by their families. The couple walked up to the altar and kneeled, where they remained for almost the entire ceremony. Joe's legs began to ache after fifteen minutes, and when the tortuous service was finally over Katherine had to help him up. Gary Herndon, the music director, played Beethoven's Ode to Joy for the recessional, but on the big burping organ it didn't sound joyful at all. More like Ode to Duty.

They had the reception at Tiny. Other couples had caved into Father Carbone's demands to hold their receptions in the church basement. But those basement receptions were always disappointing and musty, and occasionally disastrous.

When the Andersons got married—the first basement reception under Father Carbone's regime—everyone was so used to sprinting out to the parking lot after Father Carbone's regular services that less than half the guests remembered the reception. Even Father Carbone forgot about it. Since that experience, he announced at the end of every wedding mass that the basement reception would follow. But he steadfastly refused to announce any receptions that were not being held in the church basement. Why advertise the competition?

The Tomkins' basement reception was almost tragic. Tilly Tompkins' wedding dress caught on fire when part of it got too close to the electric warmer under the lasagna. A well-meaning deacon tried to put the fire out by dumping a carafe of wine on the flaming dress, but of course that just made it explode into a big boozy ball of fire. Tragedy was averted (well, any tragedy beyond the loss of the bottom two-thirds of Tilly's wedding dress) when an alert guest poured lemonade on the blaze, then smothered it with the rest of Tilly's train.

The groom, John Tomkins, couldn't stop laughing, which some took as a bad omen for the marriage. But the Tomkinses have been married for almost 40 years now. At every anniversary Tilly takes out what is left of her wedding dress—a smoky, winey, lemony white-laced miniskirt—and hangs it up in the doorway to their bedroom. John laughs as soon as he sees it.

Even when they are fire-free and fully attended, church basement receptions still have that church basement feel. Not just the metal folding chairs sliding over the asbestos tile into shaky card tables, or the Cheez Whiz in the celery, or the bad wine, or the musty moldy smell. It is the feeling that we are down here, the world is up there, and we are probably missing out on a much better reception somewhere on the surface.

Then there are the poor bride and groom. Who wants to start their lives together already under the earth, on church grounds no less? People also just don't know how to act around the priest at a church basement reception. On the one hand it feels safely secular—it's a *party*, after all. And yet we are in church, or under church. It didn't help that Father Carbone insisted on wearing his full vestments to the basement receptions. So, Joe and Katherine held their reception in Tiny's garden.

Weddings are always exercises in abject faith, but some are less abject than others. Paul wasn't the only one who knew this day was the beginning of an important and permanent new set of lives for Joe and Katherine. Even Father Carbone sensed that this was a wedding unlike many others he'd performed. Not the beginning of an uncharted trip but the sanctification of a fated one.

The reception was perfect. Paul brought over his hi-fi, and the house and backyard filled with music. The July stars joined the celebration as soon as the sun set. Joe had put up tiny white lights in the garden. He switched them on at sunset, to oohs and aahs. They became the inspiration for his fireflies.

When the champagne had sufficiently circulated, Joe's father, Stan, made the first toast. He had to be prodded. He had written it down and read it like it was an order for sides of beef. He got along famously with

Katherine's father—they had known each other for years—and so when Stan's painful toast elicited only a smattering of uncomfortably polite applause, Katherine's whole clan, prodded by the old man, started whooping and hollering, putting a wan smile on Stan's face.

Then it was Joe's sister Sue's turn, but she just kept shaking her head no, one hand holding a handkerchief up to her nose and the other waving the invitation off, signaling she was too emotional to say anything. Katherine's family then made their toasts, all of which included references to Katherine's late mother and her sister Mary, who was in the army and unable to attend. Then it was Paul's turn.

"Before I make my wedding toast, which some of you won't be surprised will be musically based [crowd's laughter completely drowned out by Paul's own], I want to toast someone who's not here, who I never met, but who I know Joe and Katherine are thinking of tonight. To Lester Buckley. His music, one way or another, brought us all here."

"To Lester," everyone shouted with raised glasses, even though most of them had no idea who Lester was. Then, in honor of Lester, Paul sang "Some Other Time," from On the Town. There wasn't a dry eye in the backyard, except for Joe's. They must have been thinking of other lost people. Then Paul toasted the couple.

"Joe and Katherine were meant for each other. I knew it long before any of you did. [Shouts of feigned protest from the audience.] Grandma used to tell us a love story about flying fish. She said Tagaloa, the god of all things, was angry one day because his daughters presented him with some bad tasting fish. So, he made all fish too stupid even to realize they are in the ocean. But then Elo, the god of the underworld, gave fish the gift of love. When fish fall in love they jump out of the ocean and see the world for the first time. Only in love can we see the world for what it really is. Until we are in love, we are fish swimming stupidly in the sea. Grandpa sometimes added a coda: upon seeing the world, the love-struck fish still drop back into the ocean where they belong.

"This story, from all I have been able to learn about Samoan religion, was completely made up by Grandma to try to teach us about love, and edited by Grandpa to try to teach us about life. Looking back, I think that was because the real Samoan story of love was too racy and too sad for young children. You be the judges, here it is.

"Two lovers began a long journey between islands, avoiding marriages their parents had arranged for them. The gods were angry at the lovers' disobedience to their parents, not to mention their acts of love outside the ceremonial sanction of village and heaven [here, a few whoops from drunken guests]. So the gods blew gales that churned the seas. After paddling their canoe for days, it finally capsized, and the lovers began swimming. But they swam with only one arm each, because they could not bear to release their hands from embrace. They drowned just a short distance from the beach of their island destination. The gods were so moved by their devotion to each other that they turned their bodies into two tall flowering rocks, which watched over the island, and each other, for eternity.

"If there were ever two people who could watch over us and over each other for eternity, it is Joe and Katherine. They are flying fish who will never get back into the water. May both of you remember the sight your flight has given you, forever." Then, without dropping a beat, Paul went right into "Some Enchanted Evening." The original version, not his "Someone Stole My Wallet."

***

Winter came and stayed in waves of furious snow. Joe and Katherine usually listened to just 20 or 30 minutes of music every night on their hi-fi as they cleaned up from dinner, before the Report. But this winter, on what turned out be almost every single snowy weekend, after shoveling they would often spend the better part of both days listening to the hi-fi. It was a guilty pleasure, for which they thanked the season's snow gods, and Davey Millikin.

Davey had generously bought the hi-fi for them several years ago, ostensibly for their anniversary, after overhearing Joe marveling at Paul's. It was terribly expensive and extravagant. They protested a little, but knew that if they refused, it would hurt Davey's feelings, and anyway he would just give it to them for Christmas, or a birthday, or Arbor Day.

Joe was speechless when Davey dropped the record on the little rotating table, lowered a metal arm onto it, and the music blew out of the speakers. It was Toscanini conducting the NBC Orchestra playing two Tchaikovsky symphonies. Davey didn't know much about music, so he asked Barb for a recommendation, and she picked out the Tchaikovsky. It sounded like the orchestra was in the living room.

Davey said, "That's too soft, here's the volume control," and he turned it way up. After a few quiet passages came the roar of the full orchestra. Joe thought Tiny's windows might shatter. He'd never heard anything like it, even at the few concerts they'd attended, where they were always up in the nosebleed seats.

Katherine suggested that for financial reasons they buy just one new record every month, and Joe agreed. They both knew that having any music you want being played in your own living room would be a big temptation. In fact, their first purchase was Arthur Rubenstein playing Liszt, which of course included Consolation No. 4, but Katherine also bought a recording of Aida she couldn't resist, violating the one-record-rule on its first application.

When they got home, they reached a new, more realistic, accord: two records per month, not counting birthdays, Christmas, and other special occasions. Katherine discovered a record shop in downtown Denver that specialized in classical music. They drove down once a month, usually on the last Saturday.

The spring made as colorful a splash as either could remember. The crocuses all seemed to poke out of the snow on the same day, green bishop's miters first, followed by reluctant acolytes of spindly striped leaves. Joe always thought crocuses were a little sad, ridiculously optimistic and unrealistic trumpets of spring that always blared too early then died after just a few days of color. "That's why they call them crocuses," his dad always joked. Then their hibernating leaves perked up and remained for weeks, green headstones.

The hyacinths were hardier. They had those thick pineapple-like leaves that started out almost vertical, forming a green yurt protecting the alien-looking pods in the center. When the pods bloomed, snow still dusting the ground, the pinks, whites, yellows, and purples looked like spilled paints. Joe smelled the first blooms before he saw them—a couple early pink varieties near the sunniest back part of the garden. Hyacinths had that distinct, almost sickly sweet smell, as if a winter's worth of fragrance had been building up inside them for months, perhaps even rotting a little, until it finally burst.

The daffodils, tulips, Icelandic poppies, and irises all followed, more orderly and longer-lived additions to the palette. Katherine was especially pleased with her Harmony irises, which she had planted a decade ago. She'd started with just four bulbs, split them every year, and now they covered a large section of the spring garden. Each of the deep blue flowers was set off with a bright yellow tongue, which Joe thought looked mocking.

He had planted a row of cherry trees on the south side of the garden to provide some summer protection for the shade plants. The cherry trees were eight feet tall now, ten inches around at the trunk, and although they had bloomed sporadically in the past, this year there were hundreds of buds getting ready to open. It would be a spectacular pink splash.

The Millikins began to spend lots of time with Joe and Katherine. Davey had lunch with Joe two or three times a week, first at the cemetery and later at Tiny after Joe stopped working. They alternated who would bring the sandwiches and who would bring the drinks.

At the cemetery, Davey would play catch with Soot after lunch. Joe could no longer throw the tennis ball as far as Soot demanded. He used to be able to launch it all the way from the tool shed to the first parts of grass surrounding the nearest section of headstones. Soot loved to retrieve the ball off the grass and simply refused to pick it up off the gravel. Davey couldn't throw as far as Joe used to, but he could still get it to the grass.

At Tiny, after lunch, they'd throw the ball from the porch into the backyard and right up against the garden. It was a short enough throw for Joe to make, so they alternated. Soot got a little anxious if either of them threw out of turn, looking back and forth between them as if to say *No, it's not your turn, it's yours.*

Barb and Katherine fell into knitting. Barb was an accomplished knitter, and Katherine a beginner. The joint activity gave them something to do with their hands when they talked, almost always about Joe's impending death, while Joe and Davey were outside throwing balls somewhere. Barb was always "dressed to the nines" as Katherine's mother would have put it, the benefit of being a tailor's wife. She usually wore dark skirts and colorful blouses, favoring reds and oranges. Bracelets regularly jangled on both wrists. Sparkling bejeweled reading glasses hung from a gold chain, glasses she needed for knitting.

She had delicate features, except for her arms, which reminded Katherine a little of Doc's. The overall effect, dominated by Barb's severe stoop, suggested to Katherine an impressionist painting of a peasant woman working in the fields, a very well-dressed peasant woman.

Like most people, Barb started out expressing concerns for Katherine and for what her life would soon be like without Joe. But Katherine couldn't quite understand this whole perspective. She was worried about Joe. He was the one dying, not she. He was the one who soon would be gone, unable to pet Soot, or hear music, or see his fireflies. She was unwilling to express this view to the string of casual and even intimate comforters she saw daily, but now that she and Barb seemed to be exploring the topic more deeply, she felt free.

"Remember, Joe's dying, not me. He's the one we should feel sorry for, more than me. I will get to go on, to enjoy this life somehow even without him. But he won't. It seems everybody has this backwards." Expecting Barb to argue, Katherine was taken aback when she laughed.

"Well, isn't that a refreshing point of view! And you are so right. I've lived a lifetime with Davey, and not a day goes by that I don't see the death camp in his eyes. But he is almost always thinking of his loved ones, the lives lost for no reason, *their* loss, not his. When I catch him feeling sorry for himself—I can always tell because he stoops a little, which I'll tell you doesn't happen often—I yell and even sometimes whack him with a little slap, and say, 'You've had a nice life Davey Millikin, the kind of life they were cheated out of. These memories you carry are about them, not about you.' Davey's a good man, and that always does the trick.

"This strange obsession with the survivors instead of the dead is even worse when it's the man who is dying, don't you think? Our men must take care of us, and what will we poor women do when they are gone? Ha! Chivalry has always been a mirror of men's own weakness. They think we are as weak as they." Barb announced this without a hint of misandry.

For Katherine, hearing these words from Barb was a jolt of freedom. Freedom to focus on Joe and not on herself. It led Katherine and Barb to a series of discussions, spread over many weeks, about the mysteries of life and its end. Both women were childless, which deepened their connections. And of course they were both married to damaged men, with different kinds of damage and different responses to it.

"Joe's silence is maddening to me sometimes," Katherine confessed one afternoon, "I wish he was more like Davey."

"Yes, I suppose my Davey is a little more talkative."

"The sphinx is more talkative."

"But Davey's not talkative about the camp. He talked about it non-stop when we first met, as if he were a used car salesman disclosing a bad transmission. When he realized I loved him, both despite and because of what the camp made him, we never spoke of it again. The only time it is even mentioned is by me, on those rare occasions when I have to slap him out of his self-pity."

Katherine smiled, and told Barb that Joe was the same way, thinking back to that night at Paul's when Joe machine-gunned a hundred composers' names, and later talked non-stop about Lester and Pearl

Harbor. It was the first time Katherine had talked to anyone other than her sister Mary about what Joe had told her that night.

Although Katherine believed she'd see Joe again in the afterlife, it would be different than regular life. Ever since she was a little girl Katherine imagined heaven as a talking place, not a doing place, where long-lost relatives and friends sat around catching up about what they had done since the other died. She'd get to talk with Joe, but not do anything with him. She hoped he would be a little more talkative dead than he was alive. Boy, it was a good thing he was going first. Otherwise, she'd have to spend an eternity in heaven trying to wheedle out of him what he'd been doing since she died.

"Don't you find it interesting that our two men were hurt when they were vulnerable adolescents?" Barb asked. "They were both teenagers when death grabbed them and made them look."

They didn't say another word that day until it was time for Barb and Davey to leave. It was one of the things Katherine liked best about Barb. They shared the rare ability not to feel compelled to talk just because they were in the same room. She wondered whether Barb was born with that knack or whether it was forced on her like it was on Katherine—living with a man who hardly spoke at all.

One of the pleasures that poured from Tales of Harold was that it got Joe talking a little more, though it was still like pulling teeth. Katherine felt like she was back in college, discussing a novel's meaning and trajectory with those reluctant classmates, and there were always one or two, who acted like they would rather have their eyes poked out than speculate about authors' intentions lurking behind words. Even she occasionally forgot that this particular reluctant classmate was also the novel's author. Wasn't he?

There are huge speed differentials built into baseball, and they appear suddenly, jarringly. This enormous variation in velocity, abruptly juxtaposed, is one of the most charming aspects of the game. It's a little like watching fleeing bank robbers pause to pick up litter. The pitched ball comes at close to 100 miles per hour and is often hit back even faster; yet when they are not batting or fielding, players lounge around in the dugout as in an opium den. Runners dash between bases like soldiers under fire seeking the nearest tree for cover, but with a walk or a home run they stroll carefree, allowed to gain ground under the flag of a strange truce.

In the dugouts and in the stands, old men teach teenagers. Slow old men on their way out who have seen almost everything, and fast young men on their way in who have seen almost nothing. Harold was a startling exception. An old man by baseball standards, a god at the plate, and a babe in the field and in life. What was this god-man-child going to do to this fragile game?

CHAPTER 39
WYOMING

Harold Watch. For the last two home games the tiny press box at Municipal Field has filled not just with national reporters but international ones as well. Reporters from Canada, Mexico, and Cuba were on hand to watch our hero's hitting streak climb to 55 as he pinch hit for singles in both games. The pinch hitting streak extends to 45. He's batting .701, and that's no typo, folks. He was held out of the starting lineup for the last three games because of a mild hamstring injury, but is set to return in tomorrow's sold-out game against the Bluebells. The team then heads out for a road trip to Wyoming before returning to host the Sterling Strikers next Thursday.

Joe's fireflies typically emerged in mid-June. Now it was mid-April and he was still alive, so his thoughts turned to whether he'd see them again.

"Doc Kasten called today and asked how you were doing," Katherine began that night's Report. "I told him your headaches are still the same as always, but that the last prescription seemed to improve your strength a bit."

"I still can't hit the grass."

"What?"

"I still can't throw Soot's tennis ball from where we sit by the shed to the grass in front of those first headstones. Davey has to do it."

"Why don't you move your chairs closer?"

Joe laughed a laugh that Katherine knew meant that neither he nor Davey had ever considered such an obvious solution, but would do so tomorrow.

They listened for the first crickets, but were a little early. The sky was potted black crystal, stars everywhere. No moon. The smell of spring enveloped the patio, despite the cold.

"I'm probably gonna have to quit working soon. I get so tired. I don't understand it. I haven't even started mowing yet."

"But it's all the other things you do. That's a lot of headstones to keep clean. A lot of walking, and polishing the columbarium."

"I suppose." After several minutes of silence Joe said, "Been a wet spring already and warm, except tonight," shivering in his winter coat, under which there was a sweater. "Maybe we'll get early fireflies."

"Oh, Joe, wouldn't that be wonderful?"

Doc Kasten came over for dinner the next night. He'd brought Katherine a fresh chicken a farmer had given him that morning for services rendered, so she invited him to share it for dinner. She roasted it in a bed of apples, onions, and sage. Doc brought his potato casserole and a bottle of white wine.

"You should think about retiring, Joe," Doc said after the coffee cake. "You are doing so well, better than any of us imagined, but if it is making you tired you should probably stop. The x-rays we've taken don't show it spreading at all, but the additional strain of working could accelerate the disease. It not only makes you tired, but getting tired can make it spread."

Doc had explained early on how the tumor grows like a cracked windshield, reaching further and further into the healthy tissue of the brain. That's why the symptoms can be so different. It all depends which parts of the healthy brain the tumor starts to crack.

"I must have a huge brain, since nothing is happening other than the same old headaches," Joe joked. But now he felt himself getting very tired. He didn't realize how tired until he saw that tennis ball drop yards in front of the beginning of the grass, its six weak bounces mocking him in cadence: "Lost it, Joe. Lost it, Joe."

"Have the two of you ever talked about going on a trip?"

They had, back in February. Katherine's dream vacation was to spend a week in New York City. Joe's was to watch a major league baseball game, anywhere. New York was too far, so they compromised on Chicago.

"We have. We were thinking of a trip to Chicago, weren't we Joe?"

"That's a wonderful idea. I'd be happy to watch Soot for you," offered Doc.

"No, we'd take him," said Joe.

"But we can't go until my summer break."

Doc Kasten couldn't help but think of the statistics, and how Joe had already outrun them. He guessed the chances of Joe lasting until June were about 10%. He thought of those nails and marbles.

"Couldn't you take some time off before then?" he asked Katherine.

"You don't think we'll make it to summer, do you Doc?" Katherine asked, smiling sadly.

After about a week, Wally felt obliged to announce that Harold's phantom hamstring was on the mend. He started to let Harold stay in at catcher after he pinch hit. It was still typically in the late-innings, but eventually Wally had to start him at catcher, just to give Buddy a breather. Harold felt bad for Buddy and Kevin, but it all worked out. Buddy soon went up to Syracuse. Kevin became their everyday catcher, and he appreciated getting a day off regularly because he wasn't used to all the work. Kevin never did make it to the big leagues. He became a plumber and lives in Redding, Pennsylvania. Buddy became a fixture for the White Sox. Both still keep in touch with Harold.

They were at home, playing the Garden City team for the first time since Rose left him, and Harold was a little worried about what he would do if he saw the pitcher who knocked him out at the Holiday Inn.

He was also worried about what this guy would do to him if he was pitching and Harold was hitting. Everyone was worried about that.

Sure enough, in the second game of the series, the pitcher/puncher was scheduled to start for Garden City. His name was Ray Johnston. And sure enough, Wally was planning to start Harold behind the plate.

Wally called him into the office in the early afternoon and told him he was thinking of keeping him out of the game entirely, but had come around to the idea that this problem between the two players was like a blister that was better popped than allowed to fester.

"I'd rather pop the blister, too."

"But don't do anything stupid, Harold. This guy probably isn't even seeing Rose anymore."

"He's not. I reconnoitered."

"Don't do anything stupid. If you can't promise that, I'll keep you on the bench."

"I promise."

What Harold intended to do was to kill Ray Johnston with the hardest line drive ever hit in a baseball game. He didn't consider that stupid. But it was. He struck out, with two outs and two on. Harold Fungo's only strikeout in his professional career.

Wally was livid. He ran out of the third base coach's box and confronted Harold as he was walking back to the dugout.

"You promised me you'd not do anything stupid."

"I did not consider trying to kill that guy with a line drive stupid, though I now see that the consequence of that decision was that I struck out, which was stupid," Harold said as he sat down and started strapping on his catcher's gear.

"Give me one reason I shouldn't yank you out of this game right now."

"By striking me out—the only pitcher ever to do so—I surmise that Mr. Johnston's anger at me has subsided. He's reached the pinnacle of his minor league career. His blister's popped."

"What about your blister?"

"It feels much better. Not popped by a needle, but humiliated into a general loss of pressure."

Wally smiled and kept Harold in. He shouldn't have. In the top of the fifth inning the visiting team's bats got hot. Even Ray Johnston got a hit, and he moved over to second on a sacrifice. Wally called time out and walked out to the mound.

"I can get this guy, SG," said Stick.

"I know, Stick. This mound conference ain't for you, it's for Don Juan here," Wally said, glaring and pointing a thumb at Harold. "I figure you may still be itching to do something to Don Juan II, like try to pick him off second, but don't. With your arm, he'd be home before your throw even got there."

The Baseball Detectives didn't yet have a book on Harold's arm strength. Most everybody figured it had to be good, just looking at his accuracy when the pitchers were warming up on the mound. Harold threw every single warm-up-finishing strike to second base exactly to the same place, right on the first base side of the bag for an easy hypothetical tag. He looped it there in a high arch, but they didn't yet know that his easy-going velocity was actually the hardest he could will himself to throw.

What no one figured was that Don Juan II would be fast enough, or stupid enough, to try to score on a soft single to left field, especially with two outs. But here he came, huffing and puffing, red-faced, around third. Apparently, his blister wasn't completely popped.

He would have been out by a mile, but it became a close play when Tommy Konig bobbled the ball in left. Harold caught the late throw, looked up and saw Don Juan II's red face, and snapped again. He felled Don with a forearm shiver that broke two ribs and punctured a lung. Don was out for a month.

His teammates slapped Harold on his back and shook his hand in the dugout. He felt a coital surge of glory, followed by deep guilt when he heard Ray Johnston was taken to the hospital. After the game he asked Nick to drive him to the hospital, but Wally called him into the office.

"What the fuck was that?"

"I guess my blister wasn't fully deflated."

"Neither was his, the dumb shit. It's a good thing you managed to hold on to the ball while you were assaulting him, otherwise you might have been thrown out and fined."

"I know. I feel terrible. I'm going to visit him in the hospital."

"You do that."

Ray Johnston appreciated the visit. Harold appreciated that Ray told him his fling with Rose lasted only a few days, and that she seemed distracted. Harold and Ray stayed in touch regularly by letter, and Ray sent him a nice note years later when Harold's cover story in Life came out. The note ended with, "I've known all along that the real reason you retired is that you knew I would strike your ass out every time."

After that home game they left for a short road trip to Wyoming, whose contrasts to home were even sharper than Colorado's. Flat dry moonscapes in the east suddenly jutted into jagged blue mountains so high and cold that their tops were still covered with snow in June. Harold had read a lot about Yellowstone in Ma's library, and was terribly disappointed to learn their trip would not take them near it. But he spent lots of time—in the evenings before sleep and, he was embarrassed to admit, even in the dugout at one particular Wyoming ballpark—day dreaming about Yellowstone and writing poems about it.

The visitors' dugout in Riverton, their last stop, offered a great view of a blue and white mountain range swaddled below in spring green. They were playing the first game of a day/night double header, and out across the field to the northwest, beyond the rickety wooden fence, whose peeling army green was rescued by a few cheesy advertisements for insurance agents, motor oil, and gun stores, Harold could see the blue, white, and green stripes. He was sure they were the mountains of Yellowstone.

He imagined geysers and bears and silver lakes rimmed with dark blue-green pines, patrolled by rangers dressed like drill sergeants. He was in the middle of writing a poem—he usually wrote and edited them in his head and typed them up later—when he heard Wally say, "Get your head out of your ass, Harold, we are here to play ball," but even as Wally was saying this he was staring over at the snowy range. "But they sure are beautiful, ain't they?"

"Have you ever been to Yellowstone, Wally?"

"Fished there in the off season a couple times, but those mountains there ain't in Yellowstone, its 400 miles further north," then over at the home plate umpire, "Jesus, Timmy, that was a mile outside. Get your partner in here and go have your eyes checked. I saw they are giving free exams at the Safeway in town." Then back to Harold and shifting his gaze from home plate back to the mountains, "It was beautiful."

"Tell me about it."

"Not now, Harold, we have a game to play." Wally looked over once more at the mountains before trotting out to the mound to yank Buzzy.

Some of the boys got into a fight the night before in a cowboy bar. Nick knew it was a cowboy bar because it was called The Poke, and because its neon sign had a cowboy throwing a rope over a steer, the rope lights alternating in three spots to simulate the rope going from behind the cowboy's head to out in front of his horse to around the steer's neck. Wally was not pleased about the fight.

"The next dick-wad who wants to fight cowboys can stay here when we leave tomorrow and fight them for the rest of his goddamned life," he said at the team meeting the next day. He was staring at Hercules the whole time, who had shiners on both eyes.

Of course, Harold was not part of the fight. He stayed behind at the motel, writing. After a while he went down to the lobby to see if he could find Greg, who wasn't in his room. He found him on the pay phone.

"Greg, do you have a few minutes to chat?" Harold asked once Greg hung up and came out of the booth.

"Sorry, Harold, I've never been to Yellowstone."

"No, not about Yellowstone, about baseball."

They went back to Greg's room—the coaches didn't have to share—and talked for an hour. Harold wanted to know about Greg's drive to succeed as a pitcher. He was a high school star, like almost all professional players, but struggled when he started out in the lower professional levels, as many players do, especially pitchers.

"I was going to go to college to be a doctor like my dad, and had even been accepted at Berkeley when the Phillies came in late and made their offer. It seemed like so much money then! I told myself, and my dad, that I'd play just a few years and then go to college, but I never got around to it.

"Baseball kidnapped me, like it never had in high school. I couldn't get enough. I couldn't stop trying to learn to pitch a little better every day. Before I knew it ten years had passed and I was nearing the end of baseball and was already too old for doctoring."

"Did you ever go to college?"

"No. I met Janet, and then we married and had the kids. I told her that the money was just too good to stop quite yet, but it wasn't that. It was the game. I just couldn't give it up. I still can't.

"Janet is special. Ask a lot of older guys around here and they'll tell you their marriages failed. Their kids hate them. They are back to one-night stands like they were 18. They'll die alone. But they wouldn't change a thing. Baseball's a crazy drug."

After the nightcap game in Riverton, Wally called Harold into the visitor's manager's office. Greg was there. Harold knew they were going to tell him he'd been called up to Cincinnati. But that wasn't it.

"Look, Harold," Greg started, "Wally and I have been staring at those mountains, too. We figure we could drive up to Yellowstone real early tomorrow morning, spend a few hours fishing, and then drive directly back home in time to make Tuesday's game. Want to join us?"

"Of course! But how will you get up there? Do you have a car?"

"Billy Jackson—" Wally began.

"The other team's manager?"

"Yeah, we go way back. He wants to come with us. He'll drive us up, then all the way back home. They have a game in Grand Island on Tuesday."

They rode in Billy Jackson's ochre Rambler station wagon, packed with food and fishing equipment. Billy and Wally must have brought all that equipment knowing they'd be going fishing somewhere. The two of them talked the whole time about the good old days in the Texas leagues. You would have thought they were best friends, though just last night they were cat calling each other over a controversial call at first base. Greg was considerably younger than they, but he occasionally joined in when the discussions turned to players he knew.

The Rambler took them from Riverton to Dubois to Jackson, then through the Great Tetons National Park, which would have been a fine destination all by itself. There was still snow on the north sides and tops of the mountains, and it was cold. They pressed on, through West Yellowstone and up to West Thumb. They picnicked at Old Faithful, shivering. Stayed two hours and managed to catch two eruptions.

The rest of the afternoon they fly fished on Grey's River, well, Greg, Billy, and Wally fished. Harold just soaked it all in and tried to stay warm. He didn't even write any poetry. He just sat and looked, and occasionally thought about Rose.

Grey's is a tributary of the Snake, and they picked a gorgeous flat spot a few miles upstream from the confluence, where the mountains opened on two sides into a verdant meadow, still March by temperature.

Harold noticed right away that the surrounding slopes were not the thick and bright green pine blanket of his imagination, not the Land of Sky Blue Waters from the Hamm's commercials he'd seen in magazines. The trees were crippled, each strangled from the cold and lack of oxygen. Fewer needles attached than dead on the ground, and even those were brown and blueish-gray. Trunks twisted. Not a forest at all but a snapshot of accidental trees, sickly strangers in the waiting room of a remote high-altitude hospital.

Then he thought of Wordsworth's cloud floating over daffodils. What would that wandering cloud see here, flying far above this waiting room? No daffodils yet, not this time of year this far up. But certainly a forest. Maybe a Hamm's-worthy green blanket of forest magically emerging from this scraggle. And who's to say at which altitude the real Yellowstone lies?

They left sooner than they planned, when a grizzly bear came screaming down the mountain at them. Well, Billy was sure it was a grizzly bear. "Grizzly!" he yelled at the top of his lungs as soon as they heard the screaming. They grabbed as much gear as they could, slogged back across the meadow, and ran to the car. Harold was 30 yards upstream, where the intersection of the mountains began choking out the meadow. He was standing up facing the screams, calm as could be.

Greg got out of the car. "Harold, get over here. It's a bear. Run!" Greg yelled.

But Harold just stood there. The screams were not on the run, they were still, in a tree. It was a mountain lion, not a bear. Greg started to run toward Harold, but then the screams stopped, and Harold walked back to the car.

"Why the hell didn't you get out of there?" Greg asked.

"I was trying to understand his screams."

"Mountain lions don't talk, son," said Billy, "they just growl. And bite and claw."

"I suppose so," said Harold. He was thinking of a neighborhood cat he sometimes saw on his runs to the store for Ma. It was striped, tan and orange. Except for the stripes, and the size, this cat was exactly the same. Same languid posture, same diffidence. Same sudden screams, one a piccolo and one an 18-wheeler breaking, but the same animal angst.

On the drive back, Billy found a real good cowboy station out of Cheyenne. They played Marty Robbins gunslinger and trail songs for a whole hour. Listening to "El Paso" and "They're Hanging Me Tonight," Harold thought about the path his life had taken since the fire. Sometimes he felt like he was a fleck of Texas sand being blown across a continent. Sometimes he was one of those maple helicopter seeds spinning and spinning to make sure he didn't fall too close to the tree and the body hanging from it. Other times he was the tree, stuck forever. And always there was Ma, Madam Jingle Heimer Smith, propelling him across horizons, even when he was a tree.

When I learned about Harold's mother, the deaf women who so lovingly protected and prepared him, I realized Harold was no Hephaestus, no cripple thrown to the rocks by a vain goddess. Harold was Icarus, and though I wasn't yet sure whether baseball was his wings or his sun, I was sure he was flying awfully high.

CHAPTER 40
CHICAGO

Streak ends! Our Joltin' Janitor struck out in the seventh inning of last night's game against the Garden City Bluebells, ending his record-setting streak of 55 consecutive hits in dramatic fashion. And who struck him out? You can't make this stuff up, folks. It was Bluebell pitcher Ray Johnston, the same fellow with whom Fungo had that beef a few weeks ago in Garden City. But what an achievement. 55 straight pinch hits. This is a record that will almost certainly never be broken. In better news, Fungo is now staying in the lineup after pitch hitting, as a replacement catcher. Manager Wally Berens said Fungo may even spot start. The Bluebells organization put on an impressive fireworks show after the game, but Fungo supplied the real fireworks. He held onto the ball in a bone-rattling collision in the eighth inning, preserving a 4-3 victory. And who did he tag out? That's right, Ray Johnston!

April finished, and still no fireflies. Except for the very early bulbs, whose dead leaves marked their spots with yellowed Xs, the spring flowers were not even beginning to fade, probably because of the warm afternoons and unusual amounts of rain.

But then there was an unexpected early May freeze. The tulips that edged Tiny's garden drooped, heads still full of colorful petals but bent down almost touching the ground, like sniffing dogs in bright Elizabethan collars. The bent stems looked like a croquet course laid out by a crazy person. The purple and white alliums sprinkled across the garden were now just big brown balls. The only color other than green, and the sadly prostrate tulips, was supplied by the purple Jacob's Ladders, hardy bridges between spring and summer, still going strong.

But buds on the early summer bloomers survived the freeze and promised an imminent reinvasion of color. The clematis that climbed around a downspout and spread on the east wall of their bedroom was heavy with onion-shaped buds. Columns of penstemon were dotted with tiny spots of red that soon would turn to shards of bright pink. The day lilies sprouted dozens of giraffe-like stalks topped with dabs of pistachio destined to become bright orange flowers.

The wall of late blooming peonies that Katherine planted just west of where the wind break used to be was bright green, splashes of blood red at the base of every artery, heart-sized balls of nascent flowers everywhere. When those peonies bloomed big as grapefruit the sweet smell was almost too much to take, a little like hyacinths. On some early summer nights, they could get a whiff through their bedroom window if the wind was right.

Like its wind break ancestors, the wall of peonies also served a function. When the smell from the packing plants invaded from the northeast, the perfume of the peonies stood firm to meet it. The battle usually ended in a draw.

Lawns were greening. First at the edges and around trees in mid-March, then spreading like a lime rash from edge to center, then, by the first of May, shooting skyward in clumps of splotchy riotous inconsistency. Those early disobedient May lawns reminded Joe of Davey's hair. They also reminded Joe that in a few weeks he would have to start mowing. That would be too much for him. He decided to give the cemetery his notice.

His last day was May 16. He and Katherine took Soot there for a final trip. He knew he could keep bringing Soot, his boss even said so. But Joe never liked the idea of doing recreational activities at cemeteries. Even the teenage drivers were there for a purpose other than recreation. Cemeteries were for the dead, and for the living visiting the dead. The small exception for teenage drivers was one thing. But taking strolls there, or running dogs (Soot excepted during work hours), was as sacrilegious as playing touch football. So, Joe knew this was the last time for Soot at the cemetery.

The three of them left in the early evening with the hope they'd see a firefly or two after sunset. Katherine brought a picnic dinner. Soot seemed to know this was his final visit. He must have sniffed every headstone. He didn't even seem too disappointed when some of Joe's throws fell short of the grass, despite his relocation. Soot picked them all up, even though they were on the gravel, with a pitying look.

Katherine brought a camera and posed Soot on one side of the columbarium and Joe on the other. They were supposed to act regal. Joe was supposed to play a Pharaoh. He crossed his arms and puffed out his chest a little, but it's hard to take the manual labor out of the dying manual laborer. By contrast, Soot was a terrific lion in repose. His feet were perfectly laid out in front of him, head straight ahead, gazing down the centuries. Was he really bulging out his neck to mimic a mane?

After she said "cheese" and snapped the picture, Katherine began to chant.

> I met a traveler from an antique land
> Who said "Two vast and trunkless legs of stone
> Stand in the desert. Near them, on the sand . . .

"What?" Joe interrupted her theatrical reverie.

"It's a famous poem about a Pharaoh's statue dissolving in the sand."

"Hey, I'm the poet, remember?"

"Ha! How are your headaches?"

"Same."

Their shadows began to lengthen, resembling Mr. and Mrs. Praying Mantis, Soot's a little like Tiny's giraffe carving. They walked down the hill toward the stream, which now had a trickle in it. Joe spread the blanket on the incline and Katherine set out the picnic things. Soot smelled around the food a little, then laid down, still the royal lion, smack in the middle of the blanket. Joe and Katherine ate laying on their sides, almost perpendicular to one another, watching the grove for any signs of fireflies. Nothing.

"Well, since you are officially a bum as of tomorrow maybe we should take that Chicago vacation now."

"But what about your school?"

"I think Doc and Father Stokely might be behind this, but this morning Sister Sophia told me I should use some of my vacation time and take you on a trip."

So she did.

They had planned to drive, and take Soot with them, but one day Doc Kasten knocked on the front door with other plans. He handed Joe an envelope. Joe looked at Katherine for some signs of worry; surely this was a bad medical report. But Katherine just smiled. She and Joe had arrived at a strangely peaceful state about his impending death, but this seemed beyond the pale to Joe.

"Paul, Davey, and I all went in on these," Doc said. Joe opened the envelope. They were two round-trip plane tickets to Chicago. "We figured why waste two days of Katherine's one-week vacation on the road when you can fly there in just a couple hours? We asked Katherine ahead of time if it was OK, and she said yes. I'll keep Soot for the week."

So they flew. It was Katherine's first time in an airplane, and Joe's first since his days in the Navy, when he flew on a couple creaky transports between bases. These new planes were something else. Jets. They were so quiet and comfortable. And so fast.

Katherine couldn't take her eyes off the green and brown checkerboard 30,000 feet below. Squares of spring farmland curved and swelled over hills and up against the hairline cracks her brain knew were formidable rivers, but her eyes would not believe. Then they crossed the Mississippi, and the skirmish between eyes and brain broke into war. That brown ribbon couldn't possibly be Twain's mighty river, where to the right, unseen over the horizon, it fanned into the famous gulf.

Joe mostly slept, but he'd occasionally look across Katherine's window seat to share some of her observations. He thought about the clouds as they flew past the window at different speeds, wondering how big they were and how far away. They looked like amusement park targets traveling across the range in different slots moving at different speeds. Joe wondered whether Lester could figure out how big they were and how far away.

They had a wonderful time in Chicago. The concerts and the ballgames melded in Joe's increasingly imperfect memory, so that when he thought back on the trip, he heard Beethoven's Seventh Symphony being played at the beginning of the games instead of the national anthem. And he smiled as he misremembered Going Home, from the Dvorak's New World Symphony, playing over the loudspeakers when that first Cubs player rounded third and scored.

Katherine dragged him to the Art Institute of Chicago and the Field Museum on their last day, but gave him a reprieve from the Chicago Public Library. There was a White Sox game that afternoon, and Joe jumped on the El to take him right to Comiskey Park. Katherine spent the afternoon at the library, and they met up for dinner at their hotel restaurant. It was on the top floor, and commanded a spectacular view of downtown, including one slice of the meandering river cutting through the tall buildings. The bridges across looked like a ladder laid down carefully between the skyscrapers.

Katherine had read how the river once emptied into Lake Michigan, and how at the turn of the century the city shrugged its flow in the other direction, connecting it with canals that eventually discharged into the Mississippi river basin. If we can reverse the course of rivers, and connect Great Lakes with the Mississippi, Katherine wondered, was there anything we could not do with sufficient will? Cure GBM, was the answer that infected her rhetorical question, uninvited.

"I can't believe we are here," Katherine started off in what seemed to be the beginning of that night's Report, eastern edition, while they waited for their after-dinner drinks, just coffee for Joe.

"I can't believe we are already going home tomorrow."

"Do you wish we were staying longer, Joe?"

"Not really. I miss Soot, and Paul, and Davey, and everyone else."

"Oh Joe, it never occurred to me that I'm taking away that time by dragging you here."

"No, no. I wanted to come. The time that matters most is our time. But their time matters too, and it's time to get back to them."

When they first left, they wondered whether Joe would continue with the Tales of Harold in Chicago, or whether the author would also take a short vacation. Katherine packed the Big Chiefs just in case— Paul's clumsy tape recorder was far too big for their luggage—and it was a good thing, because Tales of Harold didn't miss a beat.

"I'm not sure where this story is going, Joe. I like all the characters but I'm losing them a little in all the baseball stuff."

"Don't blame me. It's the tumor. Besides, I like the baseball stuff. But I just don't see how Harold is going to make it in the majors."

What Joe was actually thinking was that he just couldn't see how he was going to live long enough to find out whether Harold was going to make it in the majors. He was more tired than ever, and now he'd started to lose weight. At the beginning of the weight loss, he was glad to be headed back to his pre-tumor shape, after the initial weight gain. But now that he was headed for the other extreme, he figured he'd just keep losing weight until he died.

Katherine didn't notice right away, probably because Joe's appetite was the same as always. But Doc Kasten mentioned the weight loss at one of Joe's checkups, which he had every other week.

"You're down two pounds since right before the trip. Feeling more tired?"

"A little."

"Any trouble sleeping, nausea, forgetfulness, hallucinations?"

"I'm hallucinating that I'm dying."

Baseball has a churning, bubbling language all its own, powered by the hormone-filled imaginations of churning and bubbling twenty-year-old boys. It is a boiling pot of gumbo whose bits sometimes come to the top, cool, and become a permanent part of the game's vocabulary. We've heard them all. Can of corn, Baltimore chop, good cheese. Twenty-year-old boys are always hungry.

One spring training down in Florida a few years ago, I decided to keep my ears open for prospects, for phrases that might one day be called up to the language big leagues. I quickly re-discovered what I already knew: that most of them had no chance because they were obscene. No way even a triple-A announcer or beat writer is going to compare a very private part of a women's anatomy with a runner's exaggeratingly curved path around first on his way to second, or a towering pop-up to John Dillinger's legendary member.

Others that would never make it were the ones so intensely local as to be meaningless ten miles from their birthplace. I once heard Wayne Cage, the Cleveland Indian first base prospect, call an umpire what sounded like a "sorry show." Cage was born in Lafayette, Louisiana, and was difficult to understand. When I asked him about it, I eventually figured out he was saying souris chaude, which means "hot mouse" in French but in Cajun apparently means bat, as in blind as a.

After throwing out these hopeless candidates, I gathered a half-dozen or so of those I deemed to be most likely to succeed. No need to bother you with them now, not a single one caught on. The obstinate unpredictability of baseball infects its very language.

But I can't resist disclosing my top prospect, which I heard during a single-A game in Portland, Oregon: A "Milland" is one of those home run fly balls that starts out fair but bends foul. The reference is to Ray Milland, who went on bender after bender as the star in the movie Lost Weekend. Maybe appearing in these pages will assist the ascension of this marvelous descriptor, though I doubt it. Baseball is so stubbornly democratic.

I'd heard his teammates call Harold "Benny," short for Ben Hogan, and understood this had to do with his uncanny ability to hit balls rolled to him along the ground by desperate pitchers. But I also heard fans, home and away, call him "killer."

CHAPTER 41
THE RED-EYED GOOSE

Harold Watch. Fungo the Phenom began another consecutive at-bat hitting streak the very day after being struck out for the first time in his career, ending his streak at 55. We wrote in this column last time that no one would ever break that record. But we forgot about the one man capable of breaking it: our own record-killer himself. He has hit in every one of his plate appearances since that record-ending strike-out, and his current run stands at 5. Now that he can stay in the lineup by catching, and maybe even mix in some catching starts, Fungo's at-bats will skyrocket, so will his average, already at .751, and so will the chances that he breaks his own record.

About a month after they returned from Chicago the fireflies also returned. Joe and Katherine were in the middle of a Report, discussing the puzzling results from the last x-ray, when Katherine noticed the first one. There was a high three-quarters moon, and it was overcast. The clouds broadcast the moonlight like a bulb inside in bass drum, which is probably why neither of them had noticed the firefly sooner.

"Joe, a firefly!"

"But just one?" He got up and went to the garden. "No, there are a bunch, it's just hard to see." In fact, it looked like a full complement this year. He was dying to see if the ones in the cemetery had returned. "I'll call over there tomorrow and ask the nightwatchman."

"No, let's just drive over there tomorrow night." Katherine said that since Joe planted the fireflies in the cemetery it was within his rights to visit it just this once to see if they stuck, and Joe agreed.

They returned to the Adirondacks and the subject at hand. The new x-rays, unlike the ones before, showed significant spreading of the calcium deposits. The small corner of powdered sugar had become a milky spray of stardust inside Joe's brain. This was bad news, but the good news was that his symptoms were fairly stable. The mild headaches hadn't changed at all. He was still tired, and slowly losing weight. But there were no other symptoms.

The Denver doctors were puzzled, but when Katherine suggested the calcium deposits might be from something else, they both firmly dashed that hope. They reminded her they had tested the tumor and it was GBM. All they could say was that Joe could die tomorrow, and probably should have died months ago. That he didn't was, for them, a kind of academic disappointment, which they did their best to hide.

For Katherine it was a complicated blessing, and for Joe a complicated curse. "Well, we just have to look at these days as gifts," Katherine heard herself saying tritely, as they were rolling around this unsatisfying paradox of dying but not getting sick. "Be glad you don't have worse symptoms."

"I can't stand it, Kath. It's a piano I'm standing under that won't drop and we're both waiting. Waiting and waiting and waiting with no signs at all. If I am going to die soon, it might as well be now. The only thing keeping me going is Harold."

Katherine had never heard this kind of despair from him. She was also more than a little jealous that Harold had become Joe's reason for living. What she wanted to say to him was:

Don't say that, Joe. If you died tonight, we couldn't see Paul and Mary for dinner tomorrow. If you died tomorrow, we couldn't go down to Denver and watch the Bears Monday night. These are real things, Joe, not a story.

Then he would probably respond by saying:

Well, it will always be some real thing.

Then she would say:

That's exactly right, and that's what I need it to be. I need every moment I can get with you. Even if you start to fail. I'll need you if you can't walk, or talk, or go to the bathroom yourself. I need you. I can't imagine how hard this is for you, but it is hard for me too, you know?

She knew this would get him, and that he would say:

I know.

Then she would say:

Then help me do one last thing for me before you leave me.

To which he would say:

Anything.

Then she would say:

Stay as long as you can.

But Katherine didn't say any of these things because this whole dying business was about Joe dying, not her. Sure, she understood that through the miracle of love his death would kill part of her, and that he was terribly worried about that. But it would kill all of him.

The next night they drove into the cemetery to see if the fireflies had made it. They had, although just a handful. "Are there enough to make babies for next year?" Katherine asked.

"I have no idea. I don't know much about their life cycle. I should learn more."

A week later, after Katherine brought home a book on fireflies from the high school library, which lay unopened on the kitchen counter, Joe began to hallucinate. It took him a while to realize it. He was sitting on the porch listening to Chopin nocturnes playing from the hi-fi inside. Katherine was at church for the morning. She hesitated to leave him alone, but he insisted, and she agreed it would probably be best for both of them if she got out of the house once in a while. But she limited her church work now to one hour, two at the most, and just a day or two each week.

Joe opened his eyes when he heard the honking of Canadian geese, a large gaggle flying southwest. He should have realized right away. Canadian geese flying south in late June, isn't that a little early, or a lot late? But he didn't think these things, he just watched the pulsating triangle cross the sky, then looked down to see the front point of its dotted shadow bisecting the line between Tiny and the big house.

Then, like a dive bomber, a single goose halfway down the left flank broke formation and corkscrewed down toward the house, pulling up right before touchdown, landing gracefully in the middle of the backyard lawn, not ten feet away. A goose landing gracefully? Another sign.

Soot was asleep in his usual place between the chairs, and the perfect landing did not wake him. Joe figured he'd smell the bird soon, and when he didn't Joe softly announced, "Bird!" This word was at the reactive top of Soot's lengthy vocabulary, and he immediately snapped up into a sit, machine-gunning his head around in short jerky ratchets, nose twitching for scent and eyes scouting for movement. After an unsuccessful reconnaissance he returned to his nap, flashing a definite glare of disapproval at Joe for the false alarm.

All the while the goose stood motionless. It was large—how did these things manage to fly?—with a fat teardrop-shaped body echoed by similarly shaped but inverted wings. The wings were striated with dozens of gradations of brownish gray. Where the wings stopped and the body began the striping continued to spill out a short distance onto the body, but then dispersed into an uninterrupted dull white. This short amount of body striping made the wings look larger at rest than they actually were, their true, smaller, size revealed only when they fluttered away from the body. This only deepened the aeronautical mystery.

The white body supported a long curving and delicate black neck that emerged from it suddenly, both in shape and color. Black continued up the curves of the neck and head, even to the tip of the beak, interrupted only by a girdle of white that ran under the chin and up around the face, behind the eyes, terminating in rounded bulbs halfway around the head. The white bulbs looked a little like Soot's earmuffs, but hanging from behind the head instead of from the top. The goose's knobby black legs looked far too spindly to support its fat body.

Its monocular eyes were red, which should have been another clue. Beady dots of fire Joe could somehow see even as the goose's head remained fixed and pointed straight at him. After just a couple minutes it turned, ran away awkwardly, Lester-like, until liftoff, and then soared over the Collins tool shed and behind the big house.

Joe didn't mention the visit to Katherine. He wasn't entirely sure he was hallucinating, and if he was, he wasn't about to worry Katherine with it.

Any doubts that he was hallucinating disappeared when the goose returned the next day, and started talking. Katherine was at the store.

"Do you know your whole house looks like a dot when I'm up there?" the goose said in an aristocratic kind of Mid-Atlantic accent.

"Pardon?" was all Joe could think of saying to a talking goose.

"Is the tumor making you deaf?"

"No, I heard what you said." Joe noticed Soot stirred but only when he talked, not when the goose talked.

"Since your whole house is just a dot, you aren't visible at all, and we geese have quite remarkable vision."

"So?"

"Is the tumor making you grouchy?"

"No, I just wonder why you are telling me this. I know I am hallucinating you, and that the tumor is making me see and hear you."

"You've got it quite backwards, old stick. You are the hallucination."

And with that the red-eyed devil scrambled down the lawn's runway again and took off over the Collins tool shed. Joe was now sure he would not tell Katherine about the goose.

The goose returned on the third day, with some disturbing news.

"If you weren't a figment of my own imagination," the goose began, "I'd tell you that you only have a few more weeks to live. Three, four at the very most. And if Katherine weren't also fiction, I'd tell you that you owe it to her to tell her. And if Lester were also not all part of the invention, I'd tell you he is looking forward to seeing you again."

The goose again took off in an awkward manner, but this time circled back and headed west, back over Tiny. Joe ran through the house and out the front door to see where it went. The goose tipped its wings like a fighter pilot saluting, right before disappearing behind the tops of the trees in the cemetery that formed the Church of the Dome, trees that, other than in hallucination, were much too far away to be seen from Tiny.

During that night's Report, Joe didn't tell Katherine about the devil goose, but he did tell her he felt the end was near.

"I'm getting a lot more tired, and I'm still losing weight. I don't think we have much time." Katherine already knew, from Joe's weight loss and from the way he was acting. So they talked about Joe's things and what Katherine should do with them. It was easier to talk about things, things that would still be there when Joe was gone. Things that would leave a vapor trail of his life.

He really didn't have much that was not shared with Katherine, or in fact brought into the marriage by her. They racked their brains about things that belonged just to Joe, besides his clothes, which they agreed Katherine would give to Paul so he could outfit his Christmas down-and-outers.

"Haven't these people suffered enough?" Paul joked with a short laugh when Katherine told him about the clothes. As soon as he said it, he imagined Katherine, at the next Not Christmas Dinner, sitting across from a bum wearing Joe's clothes. "I'm so sorry, Katherine, that was a bad joke. Maybe this isn't such a good idea."

"No, it's OK. Joe made the same joke. I don't think I'll mind seeing his clothes put to good use. And of course it's entirely up to you to decide whether to dribble them out at Not Christmas Dinners or just to give them away in bulk wherever you think they'll do the most good.

"But it turns out that except for coats and sweaters, Joe doesn't have much in the way of clothes. I never realized that in all these years. He always bought his own clothes, and I just assumed he had lots of duplicates. I do all the washing but he folds his own laundry and puts it away.

"I was shocked to discover, as we did an inventory," and here she pulled out a piece of paper from her purse and began to read it, "that Joe has exactly one suit, two pairs of jeans, one pair of dress slacks, one dress shirt, two King Soopers work shirts, two King Soopers work pants, two sports shirts (one with the King Soopers name and logo and one with the Mountain View Cemetery name and logo), two white tee shirts, seven pairs of underwear, seven pairs of white sox, two pairs of dress socks, one pair of sneakers, one pair of loafers, one pair of snow boots, and one pair of wingtips." She looked up from the list and put it back in her purse. "This load won't exactly supply a homeless shelter."

"And the sweaters and coats?" Paul asked.

"Those will supply a small department store. We only have rough estimates, because he has them squirreled all over and can't remember where he put them, but we think there are around 15 coats and 30 sweaters."

Joe told Katherine to give all his tools—mostly for dovetail joints—to Doc, who at his ripe old age was taking up woodworking, and all his sports stuff—bowling ball, football, mitt, several baseballs, bat, and glove—to Frankie Hurtado.

CHAPTER 42
THE PRESS CONFERENCE

Rumblings. our Joltin' Janitor went 3 for 3 to help the team to a victory over the Cedar Rapids Raiders, extending his new consecutive hitting streak to 17. The team heads out on the road tomorrow, and will be in Sioux City on Independence Day. In troubling news, this reporter has heard rumblings that the Reds may call Harold up any day now. All-star Reds catcher Hank Foiles is out with a knee injury, and is expected to be out for a couple of weeks. Reds officials are happy about Harold's progress behind the plate, and this injury to Foiles may be just the excuse they need to yank Harold up to Cincinnati directly, bypassing triple-A.

As August approached, Wally asked Harold if he would now agree to go to Cincinnati. They were demanding it, and Wally was running out of excuses, especially after some of the bigshots watched Harold catch a few games. Harold argued with Wally for a while about Wally joining him, but eventually relented after Wally promised that he'd try to move up into some coaching position in Cincinnati next year.

Harold dreaded the call-up. A malignant worry was growing in his gut that maybe the big leagues just weren't right for him, a feeling that began with his hospital visits with Ray Johnston and continued through their correspondence.

Ray talked to Harold, in a way that even Harold's own teammates never did, about the relentless ambition that consumed all real baseball players, pressure cooked with the fear of failure. Harold was feeling more and more like a baseball imposter. But he went up to Cincinnati anyway, on August 4.

Jack, Dee, and Sammy threw a going away party at the firehouse, right before the team left for Sioux City. All the coaches came, even Fred Christianson. So did most of the players, and Clevon flew in from the east coast. Nick and the whole grounds crew were there, as was Mrs. Tejada and Demetria. Sparky clicked the whole time, no whistling. Harold decided he would not take Sparky with him, at least for a while. Sparky knew he would not be seeing Harold for a long time, and was sad.

But the tenor of the party, at least surrounding the non-Harold humans, was celebratory. This was a going to party, not a going away party. It was the final leg of Harold's baseball journey, something every player dreamed about. Each of them imagined that someday soon they would get to have their own going to party. That's probably why there were no speeches, no parting gifts. Those should be at the other end, the retirement end. Everyone was happy for Harold except Harold, who's mood was more like hopeful pessimism, and Sparky, who was inconsolable.

Harold and Nick took a bus to Omaha and from there flew to Cincinnati. Although the Reds were on the road in Chicago then headed to New York, the Cincinnati big shots had scheduled a press conference at Crosley Field to introduce Harold to the hometown press.

It was Harold's first plane ride. He wished he could keep his mind on the experience, but all he could think of was how small everything looked from up here, how Wally, Greg, Rose, and Sparky had all shrunk to invisibility. He didn't even begin to notice the city of Cincinnati until the taxi from the airport was halfway to Crosley Field. The stadium was as big as the Roman Coliseum.

The press conference took place inside, near the lion's den, in a large room jammed with cameras, lights, and reporters. There was a podium at the front of the room on an elevated stage. Harold, Nick, and a few bigshots sat on metal folding chairs behind the podium. The Reds' owner, Powel Crosely, a gentle-looking pale man with a high forehead, thick nose and lips fallen to the bottom of his face, arrived last and walked right up to the podium.

"Gentlemen, it is my pleasure, as the proud owner of the Cincinnati Reds baseball club, to introduce our newest player, Harold Fungo. I've got to know Harold a little bit in the last 24 hours, and let me tell Reds fans around the world that we are in for a real treat. He may have Earl Webb's personality but he's also got Lou Gehrig's bat."

"And Webb's legs?" the reporter from the St. Louis Post-Dispatch interrupted.

Earl Webb, nicknamed The Earl of Doublin', was the pathologically shy and painfully slow outfielder for the Boston Red Sox who hit a record 67 doubles in 1931. That record has never been broken. When reporters asked his manager after that record-breaking season how in the world Earl had hit so many doubles, he said, "He hits a long hard ball and he's too damned slow to make it to third."

"I'm not taking questions, this is Harold's press conference," Crosley said, glaring at the reporter from St. Louis.

"As most of you already know, Harold's smart as a whip but he has a little trouble talking. We have his good friend Nick Farrell here to help if any of you members of the press have trouble understanding any of his answers.

"There are also a few ground rules that I know you will respect. Harold's mother died in a fire less than two years ago, as all of you know. He is still grieving that terrible loss, so please don't ask any questions about the fire, about his mother, or about his childhood. Baseball is why we are all here, and baseball is what Harold wants to talk about. Harold has a short statement to read and then he will take questions. But before that, we have a treat for you, Harold, your new Cincinnati Reds jersey. Number 15. Go ahead, try it on."

Harold took off his suit coat and slipped on the jersey. It was tight over his dress shirt.

"Button it up, son, so we don't have to look at that God-awful tie [audience laughter]. And Harold, you'll need to thank Ray Jablonski for giving up that number. We all thought you'd like to keep your old number, the one you wore when you set all those minor league hitting records, and Ray was kind enough to oblige. All you have to do in return is start setting those records up here. OK, folks, now I'm going to turn these festivities over to our PR director Mort Heller. Morty?"

"Thank you, Mr. Crosley. Before we start, I have a few words for you, sir, and I know I speak for all Reds fans in this regard. Thank you, thank you, thank you [audience laughter]. Thank you for finding then signing this remarkable player down in double-A, and then for bringing him directly up to Cincinnati just a few months after that signing. Thank you. This is the beginning of a new era for the Cincinnati Reds.

"Now, gentlemen of the press, I understand Harold has a few remarks to read before he takes your questions."

Harold stepped up to the podium. From his pants pocket he pulled out some sheets of typing paper, folded in half. He unfolded them and began to read very slowly, at the speed and cadence he used when he told girls he had the clap.

"First, I want to thank Mr. Crosley and the entire Cincinnati Reds organization for their faith in me, and for their generosity, courtesy, and kindness, both to me and to my good friend and sporadic interpreter, Nick Farrell. Please let me know if you have trouble understanding me. That's why Nick is here. I can read loud and slow, but when I get to the part of answering your questions, I might get a little excited and it might be hard for you to understand me.

"My deepest thanks are for my firehouse family, who rescued me in more ways than one." And then he pulled out his God-awful tie so it hung on the outside of his jersey. "Jack, Dee, Sammy, Mattie, Teddy, Barry, Mick, Tony, Jerry F., Jerry T., Randy, John, Terry, and Jimmy. And of course my dear little Sparky. I miss being part of that family every day."

Heller approached Harold, covered the colorful array of microphones with his hand, and whispered, "Sorry, Harold, but we need you to move this along so you can catch your plane to Chicago."

"Sorry, sir, but I have just a few more people I must thank," Harold said, also whispering.

Voice back up to normal, he continued, "I would not be here today if it were not for the courage, patience, friendship, and guidance of Wally Berens, Greg D'Antoni, Dickie Brannan, and Fred Christianson. These are giants toiling in remote fields across America, and it's heartbreaking that more people can't see them perform their magic on lumps like me. I assure you, any magic you might see from me now that I'm up here in Cincinnati comes directly from them.

"Many other coaches and players deserve my thanks, but I do not want to abuse your time, or miss my plane. Forgive me, my teammates and coaches, for not singling out each of you. But I think of each and every one of you every single day. There is one I must mention. Clevon Sumpter is my friend and brother, and he will be my friend and brother long after we hit our last baseballs. That's it. Thank you for your patience, Mr. Heller."

Every reporter stood and applauded, except the guy from St. Louis. No one had ever seen sports hacks applaud anyone, let alone at a press conference and let alone stand and applaud. They were experiencing what most people experienced when they met Harold for the first time—a soaring, uncontrollable joy at his overachievement. The joy of watching not just an underdog succeed, but a damaged man excel.

"OK, thank you Harold. I know all of you have lots of questions, but please limit it to one each. I'll try to get to all of you," here he looked at his watch, "in the next 20 minutes but I make no promises. We have a hard stop at 2:15. And remember the ground rules. OK? Billy."

"Billy Samuels, Cincinnati Inquirer. We all want to know, Harold, how exactly you are able to hit the ball so perfectly despite your physical problems, and what exactly those physical problems are."

"That was two questions, Billy, but we will forgive you seeing as you are the local beat writer."

"There's no secret to my hitting, nothing other-worldly. I practiced every day for four or five hours hitting a tennis ball against the back wall of our house, for almost thirty years. I'm not entirely sure why I can't run like most everyone else can. I've always run this way. They are going to send me to some doctors to try to find out if anything can be done. I think I speak this way because my mother was deaf."

"Tracy Gilford, WABC radio. Harold, do you mind everyone calling you Harold instead of Mr. Fungo?

"Not at all. Harold is my real name. Wally just made Fungo up."

"Why did he make it up?" "What's your real last name?" "Couldn't they teach you to talk at school?"

"Gentlemen, gentlemen. One at a time, please, and no questions about Harold's childhood. Micky."

"Wait, I didn't get to ask my question."

"That was your question, about his name. Sorry, we've really got to move this along."

"Micky Spellman, Cleveland Plain Dealer. What's your real last name?"

"I don't know. My mother never told me. That's why Wally had to make it up. And I never learned to talk correctly at school because I never went to school."

"Never went to school, that's impossible." "Why didn't your mother send you to school?" "How did you learn to speak at all if you never went to school and your mother was deaf?"

"One at a time. We will not answer these questions shouted out. Over there in the bow tie."

"Phil Anders, New York Times. How did you acquire your impressive vocabulary?"

"Reading books."

"There in the back. I'm so sorry, ma'am, I've been addressing everybody as gentlemen, I didn't see you back there earlier. It's not every day we get the fairer sex at a Reds press conference."

"No apologies needed, Monsieur Heller. Genevieve Tourot, Paris Match. Monsieur Harold, my editors want to know a thousand things, but since we are limited here, let me just ask whether you will be moving to Cincinnati, and if so where you will live, and whether you have ever been to Paris."

"Why does she get to ask three questions, Morty?"

"Pipe down, Richie."

"I probably won't move Sparky until after the season is over, and I've never been to Paris, but would like to go. I've read a lot about it."

"Eduardo Gonzales, Havana's La Nationalista."

"I would also like to go to Cuba, or really anywhere there is an ocean. I've never seen one, in person."

"My question for you, señor, is whether there is anything you plan to do to improve your arm strength when catching. You never threw out a baserunner in the minor leagues, even just one, in fourteen attempts."

"Maybe the doctors can with help that too."

"Freddie Burnstein, Time Magazine. Do you have a girlfriend, Harold, someone special?"

"Yes. Rose McClaren. She lives in Hays, Kansas."

"Is she, you know, deaf or crippled?"

"One question only."

"No, Rose is perfect."

"Hugh Warren, Los Angeles Times. What do you like to do when you are not playing baseball?"

"Read and write."

"Now, come on, Morty, that was a three-word answer. Can't I have one follow-up? Just one?"

"OK."

"What do you like to read, Harold?"

"Everything." [Audience erupts into laughter, even Hugh Warren.]

"Tom Powell, Chicago Tribune. Do you plan to crack the starting lineup here at catcher? After all, Hank Foiles is an all-star."

"I'm not sure where or when I will play."

"Monty Perl, St. Louis Post Dispatch. How old exactly are you, Mr. Fungo?"

"I'm not sure. I think I'm around 35."

"Well, why don't you just tell us when your birthday is, and then we can do the math, how about that?"

"One question, please."

"April 29." [Audience laughs, except for Mr. Perl]."

"Sorry folks, one last question. Harold needs to get on the plane to Chicago. Morey."

"Morey Charles, Pittsburgh Post-Gazette. Where do you see yourself in 10 years, Harold?"

"In school somewhere. I never got to go."

Our hero had slain the God of Chance on a small field, but not just any field. This was where we catalogued with relentless precision the results of the ten thousand causes, where at every turn the God of Chance made a mockery of Fate. Until now. Now, Fate was in charge. Its three witches had spun the wool of Harold's threads and measured the tapestry of his life. They built him to kill baseball, and given him the shears to do it.

CHAPTER 43
MINNESOTA

Say it ain't so. We knew it couldn't last. The Cincinnati Reds have called up our beloved Joltin' Janitor. He is scheduled to appear at a press conference in Cincinnati tomorrow afternoon. The Reds are on the road in Chicago, and Fungo is expected to join them there Tuesday. Farewell, sweet Harold. We hope you never forget us down here at Municipal Field. We know we will never forget you. Recognizing how important Harold has been to the fabric of this community, I am delighted to announce that this newspaper has agreed to assign this reporter to follow Harold's journey in the big leagues. So we are not losing a minor leaguer, we are gaining a major leaguer. Watch here in the next few days for my first column, from Cincinnati.

The folks in Cincinnati were nice enough. But they weren't like Wally, Greg, or Clevon. They were not learning a game, or even playing a game. They were trying to win games, and not get sent down. That made everybody edgy. The fear of failure after success is so much more desperate, and sadder, than the fear of never achieving success. Harold wrote a poem about it called Sent Down.

No one in the Reds front office really told him what their plans were. He pinch-hit in the late innings of the first two games, going 1 for 1, with one intentional walk and one RBI. In the third and final game in

Chicago he got to stay in and catch after pinch hitting. He went 2 for 2 in that game, but a guy stole third on him in the late innings. Baseball World noticed.

They mothballed the Fungo Faceoff. Every numbskull in the minors was trying it. Even kids in little league. Noses were being broken. Teeth were flying out of mouths, landing on both sides of the batter's box. Rules were changed. Everyone knew the big-league rules would change over the winter.

After that last game in Chicago, before going home to Cincinnati, the coaches told Harold they'd made an appointment for him to see a doctor the next day in Minnesota, at the Mayo Clinic. He'd read about the Mayo Clinic. He and Nick took the short flight to Minneapolis that night.

When they checked in with the Mayo receptionist, who seemed atwitter at the idea of meeting a real professional baseball player, she smiled at Nick. When Nick told her Harold was the player and he just a friend, she was confused but recovered nicely. She was apparently not a reader of Life magazine, because almost everyone else in the large complex recognized Harold immediately, a few even asked him for autographs. A second story about him had appeared in Life shortly after his call-up, this one titled "About Time," a two-page story featuring a half-page photograph of his toothless Fungo Faceoff.

Autographs were becoming a difficult part of Harold's and Nick's lives. It would take Harold a good 20 seconds to scrawl one, even with the best of writing instruments and on the smoothest of surfaces, and when he was done it looked like a child's illegible petulant scribble. And they were never the same.

Nick volunteered to sign Harold's name on a bunch of index cards as he had on balls (Harold's baseball card was still in the works), but when Harold handed out the cards they were received with almost universal disappointment, and occasional ridicule. A man in Chicago said, "Too big now to sign autographs in person?" They had better luck with the signed baseballs, but they couldn't carry dozens of those around with them all the time. They decided to add to the bottom of

Nick's signature cards this line: "Mr. Fungo apologizes for the impersonal autograph, but he's injured his hand and cannot write." St. Augustine be damned.

The amended index cards worked like a charm at the Mayo Clinic, where everyone assumed Harold was there because of his hand injury. The doctor who saw him, of course, knew that the Cincinnati Reds were asking him to examine Harold's gait with recommendations for how to improve his speed. When the young orthopedic surgeon first saw Harold walk for him in the examination room, he knew at once he'd most likely be dashing everyone's hopes.

Harold had cerebral palsy, likely responsible for all his motor problems, his walking, his talking, his inability to sign autographs. It was a relatively rare mild form. Still, the young doctor was astonished that Harold could swing a bat let alone hit a baseball let alone hit it with unprecedented skill. He was fascinated to hear about Harold's 30 years of practice, and was sure this was the stuff of a clinical article, maybe even some important treatment directions.

Without much medical history, it was impossible to tell what had caused the incurable neurological condition. It could have been a traumatic injury to Harold's brain, an infection like meningitis, loss of oxygen during birth, or even a few infectious maternal conditions, like German measles or herpes. The doctor was very interested in Harold's mother, including her deafness, her shaky hands, the loss of her teeth, and her report that Harold had "trouble being born," and opined that in all likelihood his cerebral palsy was a combination of oxygen deprivation at birth and his own genetic predisposition.

"You mean my mother had this?"

"We can't be sure, but her deafness, some of her other behaviors you've described, and the fact that we know CP can have some genetic component, sure suggest it."

The doctor explained that some limited orthopedic interventions were being developed, but that these surgeries were aimed at releasing tightened muscles and, in some cases, repairing bone abnormalities, in order to get wheelchair-bound CP patients to walk.

The doctor was skeptical that any of these would help Harold *run*. But he wanted to discuss matters further with his orthopedic colleagues and some CP specialists, take some additional x-rays and other tests, and talk again with Harold tomorrow afternoon.

They'd taken a bus from Minneapolis to Rochester, a trip of about 100 miles. The plane and bus rides, jammed together, reinforced for Harold how much he preferred the bus. Likewise, Minneapolis and Rochester, separated by swelling farmland nestled with idyllic dairies, reminded Harold how much he preferred towns to cities, well, at least to the cities he'd seen up to that point. Rochester looked just like the dozens of other towns in which they'd played ball in the minors—in fact it had its own developmental team—except for one towering nouveau medieval spire exploding out of its uniformly one- and two-story flat town center. It was the tower of the Plummer Building, the latest addition to the Mayo Clinic.

At dinner in the hotel's restaurant, Harold and Nick talked about their first impressions of the big leagues. They agreed on easy things, like the money was better, but disagreed about a bunch of others, like the food and travel. Nick said the food was better, but Harold said he missed those delicious greasy things they had for lunch at the sides of two-lane highways. Nick said planes were better than riding for hours on a bus, but Harold said planes were "travel's lobotomies," that they just transported you from one place to another, cutting out all out senses in between. They agreed that the major leagues just weren't as much fun, though Harold tried to push back a little, thinking of Wally's speech about first loves.

"Of course, we are comparing three months in the minors—our very first experience with professional baseball—with one week in the big leagues."

Nick at once loved and loathed that Harold always thought of his baseball adventure as *their* baseball adventure. But they were actually having very different experiences, which Nick would eventually have to raise with Harold. All Nick did was sit around, and occasionally interpret. He never got to put on a uniform (not that he could play baseball at all, even on sand lots), and he never got to feel the game, though he was frustratingly close enough to feel that others could feel it. And he didn't get any exercise at all. He was fattening out quite a bit. Soon, he'd have to go on the Clevon Sumpter diet. And he wanted to go back to college in the fall, in just a few months. Maybe now was the time to talk about it.

"That's true, Harold. And Cincinnati is a big opportunity for you. But for me, it's just the same old thing, and I probably don't want to do this after this season. I want to go back to college."

"Of course, I completely understand. To tell you the truth, with these false teeth I really don't need an interpreter. I've been embellishing a lot just to keep you around [atomic smile], but now it's time for you to make your life and be done with helping me make mine. Besides, after almost killing poor Ray Johnston, and especially after today's examination, I'm not sure how long I will do this anyway. But I know I couldn't have done it without you, Nick." A gloomy silence persisted, interrupted by the waiter delivering the check.

"What will you study in college?"

"I was majoring in history, so I think I will stick with that, maybe focus on ancient history. Maybe be an ancient history teacher. But I also love Spanish. Maybe I'll teach that."

"That's fantastic, Nick. You'd be an exemplary teacher. I always wished I went to college, or really any school at all. Who's your favorite Roman Emperor?"

Nick thought for just a bit. "Probably Marcus Aurelius, because he was so intellectual. Or maybe Augustus."

"Do you know that every time I go up to bat, I incant a saying attributed to Augustus? I say to myself, 'Festina lente,' Latin for 'make haste slowly.'" They both laughed. "When I run to first, I should be chanting 'tunc inibus proelium,' roughly 'hurry up,' but I can't chant anything when I'm concentrating on running." More laughter. "And one of my favorite books is Don Quixote."

"You should read it in Spanish!"

Ever since the call-up, Harold had been having vivid dreams. He dreamed he was a tadpole in a small fetid pool that was evaporating. He dreamed about when he started losing his teeth, but in the dream when they fell out, dark and rotten, they remained connected by tiny red capillaries to Ma's mouth. He dreamed about the time Ma took him to the church to test his hearing, but in the dream he could also *see* the music, streaming in bright colors through the crack in the front door and through the thin stained glass.

The night after the first visit to Mayo Harold started weaving these dreams into the poem that would become Poison, which, when published many years later, would help vault him to literary fame.

The next afternoon Harold and Nick returned to the Mayo receptionist in the plinth of the Plummer Tower, who was less atwitter than yesterday and who immediately called orthopedics.

The young doctor they saw the day before came into reception and took them through a maze and into a large conference room where four other doctors were seated at a very fancy big table that reminded Harold of the one at the hotel back home, where they negotiated his contract. But no books. Just a blackboard and a wall of light boxes already showing ten of what Harold assumed were his x-rays. An oversized telephone, with a bunch of small lightbulbs protruding from its base, sat smack in the center of the table. Two Kleenex sized boxes, perforated with tony holes and connected by wires to the big telephone, sat on the centerline of the table, toward each edge. Harold assumed they were speakers.

After introducing the other doctors, the young doctor explained that Cincinnati Reds executives were on a speaker phone, including the team doctor, and that they very much wanted to be a part of the meeting, but that it was entirely up to Harold whether to allow it. He was the patient, and he could keep things private. Harold said they were paying the bill so he figured they had the right to be part of it all, which seemed to put the older Mayo doctor especially at ease.

What followed was a series of mini-presentations by four of the five doctors (all but the older one), interrupted by several questions from the team doctor, a few questions from the other team reps, and one question from Harold. Harold's question was, "Did my mother have cerebral palsy?" which the team of Mayo doctors agreed was "most likely." The doctors said they probably couldn't help Harold run any faster.

It is a bit foggy, especially by the standards of Harold's otherwise photographic audial memory, but what he recalls happened next was a long and heated conversation between the baseball people on the speaker phone, mostly about running and pinch hitting and catching and money. Then they asked the doctors to excuse themselves and for Harold to stay on the line, because they were moving to the "business" part of the conversation, which to Harold seemed to have started long before.

This second part was even more cacophonous than the first, disagreeing and disagreeable voices raised to new heights now that they were unrestrained by the doctors' professional presence. Harold can't remember the words. He remembers the sounds, a grating, expanding discord of interruptions. He remembers thinking how lucky Ma was never to have had to hear such sounds. He remembers how they talked about him like he wasn't even on the phone.

He remembers hearing Ray Johnston's ribs snapping and the air leaving his lungs, like stepping on a bag of potato chips. He remembers seeing the musical colors he saw in his dream streaming out of the church, now streaming out of the phone but this time all grays and blacks. He remembers hearing Mrs. Tejada, clear as bell, saying "stick to your ribs." He remembers the clashes from the speakerphone dropping to nothing after he said "I quit."

"That was awfully abrupt, don't you think?"

"Why are you asking me?"

"I mean, even if you weren't writing this book, just reading it . . ."

"I am just reading it."

". . . wouldn't you think Harold quitting came on awfully sudden?"

"I suppose."

When Harold Fungo quit baseball, his rocket boosted into a higher orbit. And he didn't kill baseball after all. He saw, sooner than most, that his perfection would starve this game that feasts on imperfection. Even the Fates could not force him to wield the shears. He resisted them to the end. He abandoned baseball for the sake of baseball, and of course also for the sake of his Rose and his poetry. If ever there were a player who shattered the sophomoric bromide that baseball is life, it was Harold Fungo. He was part of it for a short and magic time, his name still recorded in the Book of Heaven that marks the transitory, the dead. And it was part of him forever. But it was not all of him, not by a long shot.

CHAPTER 44
THE SACRAMENT OF
RECONCILIATION

Farewell. There were tears aplenty on Harold Fungo Night at Municipal Field, as we bid adieu to our hometown hero. In back-to-back stunners, Harold was called up to Cincinnati on August 4, only to retire one week later. Despite playing professional baseball for only two months, Fungo holds several minor league records which are likely never to be broken, including consecutive pinch hits (47), consecutive hits (59), and highest single season batting average (.712). He appeared on the field for the ceremonies along with his beloved dog Sparky and several friends and well-wishers. In his distinctive hard-to-understand voice, made even harder to understand because it was cracking with emotion, Fungo thanked manager Wally Berens, coaches Greg D'Antoni, Dickie Brannan, and Fred Christianson, former teammate Clevon Sumpter (who flew in for the ceremony from Syracuse), and all the friends, by name, who joined him on the field. Then he thanked the crowd for supporting what he called his "charmed and magical journey." No, sir. We thank you for your charm and magic. God's speed, Harold Fungo.

Joe got really worried when he started to lose his vision. If speech came next, he wouldn't be able to finish Tales of Harold, though it seemed to him the story was almost done. The day after his vision started to fail, he got another visit from the red-eyed goose. He and Katherine were sitting out on the patio in the morning cool. Tales of Harold had gone silent for a few days. Katherine was reading but her mind was wandering. Joe was dozing next to her when he heard the honking. As before, he looked up and saw the same undulating triangle cruising overhead. He noticed his hallucinatory vision was much better than his failing real vision. The aristocratic goose got right to the point.

"Look, Joseph, the time is nigh. I know you wanted to finish Tales of Harold, so I took the liberty of finishing it for you."

Harold called Wally from Minnesota that very night, and told him he'd decided to retire. Harold could immediately feel Wally's struggle, born of a life in the game. Wally grabbed Greg, who got on an extension. Greg wasn't surprised, given their talk in Wyoming. Eventually, they both said they knew it was the right thing for Harold, but even just saying those words was not easy for either of them. They had sacrificed so much for baseball, and Harold had sacrificed nothing.

"You both know I would have ruined baseball. It is so beautifully balanced. A breeze here, a glob of Vaseline there. Then here I come, killing the balance."

It was true. Part of what Greg and Wally were really mourning, especially Wally, was something they would never admit: it would have been so much fun to be part of the killing. Heck, that's what was really so much fun these past few months. Parts of them hated this game that took almost everything from them. They were also both a little jealous that Harold seemed immune to baseball's virus. He never loved it, and now he's quitting before he starts to hate it.

No one was sad, exactly. Wally and Greg had already said tearful goodbyes at the time of the call-up, and they never really expected to have Harold in their lives again. Neither asked him what he would do now because both knew he would write. They didn't know how that translated into a vocation, let alone a paying one. But they figured he'd made enough money to be OK for a while.

The Reds had a few internal discussions about demanding that Harold return some of his bonus and salary, which Harold would have been happy to do had they just asked. But the big shots decided that would be an even bigger PR disaster than the retirement itself. And they also didn't want to burn any bridges with Harold, imagining that one day his public glow might brighten their dugout as a hitting coach or, heck, maybe even as the manager. He was, after all, the most famous Cincinnati Red, no, the most famous big-league player anywhere, with less than 10 major league at-bats.

Nick went back to college and became a stockbroker, not a professor. He and Harold corresponded regularly at the beginning, but it dropped to Christmas cards once Nick got married and had a family.

Jack, Dee, and their children, two more after Sammy, had dinner with Harold the first Saturday of every month, Harold's travel schedule permitting. Sammy became a local high school physics teacher. He kept a signed poster of the Life photo of him on Harold's shoulders on the wall in the front of his classroom. He printed a label that he stuck to the bottom of the poster that said, "Sometimes things go up and never come down."

Wally made it to the majors as a hitting coach then a bench coach, but never as a manager. Being Harold Fungo's minor league manager branded him forever as a hitting guru, and he couldn't complain. He'd probably still be in double-A if it weren't for Harold. But he did chuckle at how a lifetime .223 batter could ever be considered a hitting guru. Baseball was funny.

Greg worked his way up the coaching ladder, and became the manager of the Pittsburgh Pirates, where he installed Wally as his bench coach. In the off season, Greg and Wally both kept in touch with Harold, by phone and occasional letter. Once, when Wally was still managing in the minors, the three of them got together for a weekend at Yellowstone. They saw a real bear this time.

Clevon and Harold remained best friends. After Clevon's call-up to Syracuse the two of them began a tradition of talking on the telephone every Sunday.

"These calls are costing me a fortune," Clevon joked at the beginning, and Harold volunteered to alternate who called whom. "I'm just pulling your leg, Benny. God, do you have any idea how much they are paying me up here?"

"Almost as much as they are paying me down here," Harold retorted.

After Harold's call-up they talked for hours about Harold retiring, then hours more after he did. They continued their Sunday phone calls for over 20 years. They also visited one another in person at least once a year, usually at Thanksgiving, alternating between residences.

Harold got his GED and then went to college. He was relieved to discover that none of his fellow students, and only one of his professors, recognized his name. John Jacob Jingle Heimer Smith was just John Smith, for now.

Soot was irritated that he had not been invited to take this drive. He knew they were driving to Denver for more music, and they often took him along. He heard Katherine say "Let's go." Heard her, instead of Joe, grab the car keys off the counter. Heard Joe say "OK."

Soot waited and waited for his name, but it never came. Oh, well. He didn't always get to go. He saw Katherine walk over to Joe and grab his hand like they sometimes did when holding hands to music, and lead him out to the garage, the callous excluding door slamming in Soot's face. He heard the car doors open and close, and a punctuating "Are you in?" from Katherine. "Yes," was the last word Soot heard Joe say.

Katherine always imagined it would come during a Report, lying in their angled red chairs. But it happened right at 10th Street and 23rd, in Turd 3. They were stopped at the red light when Doc Kasten blew right through it coming from the opposite direction. Good thing it was early on a Saturday morning and there was no other traffic.

"What are we going to do about Doc and these traffic lights? He's going to kill someone one of these days. Joe?"

The red-eyed goose was flying right alongside Turd 3, matching its speed exactly, four feet above the ground, hovering outside Joe's window.

"Time to go, Joseph." Or did it say Yosef? *Geeze, am I going blind and deaf?* "Just follow me."

Joe turned his head to look over at Katherine one last time, but his vision was so blurred he couldn't see her at all. "Here, let me help with that," the goose said, and suddenly Katherine was layers and layers of Katherines, all crystal clear. From the young woman at Paul's all the way up to the determined defender of his health. Then Joe flew out of the passenger window and joined the goose. They made a lazy circle above the intersection and saw Doc Kasten run the red light.

During the Report the night before Joe finally told Katherine about the Church of the Dome. "I'd like to be buried there."

"That may take some doing, with us being Catholic."

"No. I've already got permission. Some kinda perk because I worked there. Soot will show you where it is. Just say 'Dome,' and he will run there and wait. I'm not sure I could find it to show it to you, with the way my eyes are going."

It was a warm and bright late July day. The Church of the Dome was decked out. Below the green gasket holding up the blue sky, a ring of well-dressed mourners stood rigid on the soft lawn, which was gashed with a single rectangular ditch, its reciprocal but gravity-rounded fresh pile of earth nearby. The headstone, which the cemetery had so kindly rushed, also as an homage to Joe, stood at one end of the ditch, covered with a silky purple cloth. On the side of the ditch opposite the dirt pile was a strange jig-sawed casket. Frankie Hurtado and Doc had built it out of the hundreds of pieces of Joe's dovetailed boards.

"Are you sure this will hold him?" a worried Frankie asked Doc the night before.

"No idea. But I can tell you one thing, it won't break at any of Joe's dovetail joints."

No dogs were allowed at St. Thomas, so Katherine had to leave Soot at Tiny. Father Stokely gave a heartfelt but controversial funeral homily. It was so much easier to give a really meaningful funeral homily when he actually knew the deceased, and didn't have to waste words proving he'd absorbed the important points of a person's whole life in the twenty minutes of prep time he spent with the bereaved non-church-going family.

His first "stranger funeral," as they called it in the business, was a disaster. To show how well he knew the dead man he made a point of calling him by his nickname, Buster, whenever he could, but he had confused that nickname with one of the deceased's grandson's. The dead man was known as Billy, even though his real first name was Robert not William. No wonder Stokely got confused.

It was quite uncomfortable for the stranger family to hear over and over what a wonderful husband and father 10-year-old Buster was, how he had gone to a greater reward, and how he'd made us all better for having known him. The very much still alive Buster kept crinkling up his nose, rolling his eyes, shrugging his shoulders, and raising his palms into the air, and he finally started to complain out loud, to a wave of shooshes that were louder than his complaints. If all that weren't enough, Father Stokely erroneously reported that Buster was a proud member of the Knights of Columbus, when in fact Billy had been an Elk.

Today, at Joe's funeral, Father Stokely decided to base his homily on Joel 2:25. He talked about the passage of time, about how time is a mirage, about how the years that the swarming locusts eat are really the same as the years of milk and honey, the earth revolving inattentively around the sun, and about how the only interruption to this meaninglessness is us. It was a bit too much humanism for most folks, too *Jewish* sounding really. The Book of Joel? Is that really even a book of the bible? It was way too much for Bishop McDaniel, who spoke rather harshly to Father Stokely afterwards. The homily had Katherine and the Millikins in tears, but they were the only ones.

Davey then read from Judges and Mary from Ecclesiastes, only adding to the Old Testament feel. Music rescued the service. Sybil D'Luca, St. Thomas's fine pianist, played Liszt's Consolation No. 4. Then Paul sang a straight version of Ol' Man River, and everybody cried.

At the Church of the Dome, Soot sat lion-like guarding the casket. Frankie was worried that the dog might get hurt if the casket collapsed, but it didn't. Paul proudly pulled the purple coverlet off the headstone, a museum unveiling. With no energy to resist, Katherine had agreed on an epitaph suggested by Paul:

Joseph W. Skelton
Some Day Soon We All Will Be Together If The Fates Allow

"Isn't that from a Christmas song?" a perplexed Barb Millikin asked her husband quietly.

"Yes, Rosemary Clooney," Davey thought he had whispered. "But what's it doing on Joe's headstone?"

"It was Judy Garland in Meet Me in St. Louis, and I think those words from Hugh Martin's and Ralph Blaine's 'Have Yourself a Merry Little Christmas' are beautiful," insisted Paul.

"They are," admitted Davey.

Four cemetery workers grabbed the red straps and lowered the creaking dovetail casket into the grave. Davey walked over to the pile of dirt, grabbed a handful, and tossed it in. Barb did the same, then Katherine, then everyone, including Father Stokely.

After the last person, Doc Kasten, threw his dirt in, a gaggle of honking Canadian geese flew overhead. Soot looked up at them, and then climbed to the top of the dirt pile and started digging. The cemetery workers moved to intervene but Katherine told them to leave him be.

Soot didn't stop until the pile was gone and the grave half covered. It was only half covered because Soot's digging was not terribly accurate. The shoes of the mourners standing closest to the grave were covered in dirt, up above their ankles. They startled a little at the beginning, but couldn't bring themselves to move once they realized what was happening.

> Saints of God, come to Joseph's aid.
> Hasten to meet him, angels of the Lord.
>
> Receive his soul and present him to God the Most High.
>
> May Christ, who called you, take you to Himself
> May angels lead you to the bosom of Abraham.
>
> Receive his soul and present him to God the Most High.
>
> Eternal rest grant unto him, O Lord, and let perpetual light shine on him
>
> Receive his soul and present him to God the Most High.

And then Father Stokely added, "And protect him from the three foul frog spirits."

Paul, feet still covered in dirt, cleared his throat and announced that last week Joe had personally selected the closing song, admittedly from a list that contained only Broadway show tunes. "But it was a long list." The song Joe picked was "I Could Write a Book," from Rogers and Hart's 1940 Pal Joey:

> If they asked me, I could write a book
> About the way you walk and whisper and look.
> I could write a preface on how we met
> So the world would never forget.

EPILOGUE

Lincoln, Nebraska. Harold B. Fungo died today in his Lincoln home from end stage brain cancer, surrounded by family and friends, including his biographer, noted New Yorker essayist Roger Angell. Fungo was believed to be 57. He served as the Nebraska State Poet Laureate, and taught poetry at the University of Nebraska at Lincoln, where he also served stints as Chairman of the English Department and Associate Dean of Humanities. He published several volumes of poetry, including Running to the Store, which was short-listed for the Pulitzer Prize. Fungo was best known in non-literary circles for his record-setting though short-lived career in professional baseball with the Lincoln Chiefs. He still holds the minor league records for consecutive pinch-hits, consecutive hits, single season runs batted in, and batting average. His extraordinary skill at the plate landed him in the pages of Life magazine twice. His final appearance in Life, five years ago, was in a cover story chronicling his unlikely journey from crippled child of a single deaf mother to minor league baseball phenom to acclaimed poet. His three appearances in Life magazine have been eclipsed by only one other Nebraskan, actor Henry Fonda. Fungo's final work, published last year under the pseudonym Morris Hoffman, was a clever autobiography called "Pinch Hitting," in which he presented his minor league baseball story as a novel written by the fictional protagonist, who was himself suffering from brain cancer. Fungo is survived by his wife Rose, sons Clevon, Jack, and Wally, daughter Nikki, seven grandchildren, and his beloved miniature Doberman mix Sparky 3. The family requests that donations be made to the American Academy for Cerebral Palsy and Developmental Medicine.

ABOUT THE AUTHOR

Morris Hoffman was a trial judge for 30 years, during which time he learned much about Fate, Chance, and Will. He played lots of baseball when he was younger, all glove and no stick. He is a member of the MacArthur Foundation's Research Network on Law and Neuroscience, the author of a non-fiction book, *The Punisher's Brain* (Cambridge 2014), and a co-author, with four MacArthur colleagues, of a second non-fiction book, *Brain Basics for Lawyers, Judges, and Policymakers* (Oxford 2024). He lives with his wife Kate in Denver. They have two grown sons, two growing granddaughters, and two black dogs. This is his debut novel.

NOTE FROM MORRIS HOFFMAN

I want to thank my editor, Katharine Sands, whose thoughtful suggestions made *Pinch Hitting* immeasurably better, and all the folks at Black Rose Writing for turning it into a book.

Morris Hoffman

We hope you enjoyed reading this title from:

www.blackrosewriting.com

Subscribe to our mailing list – *The Rosevine* – and receive **FREE** books, daily deals, and stay current with news about upcoming releases and our hottest authors.
Scan the QR code below to sign up.

Already a subscriber? Please accept a sincere thank you for being a fan of Black Rose Writing authors.

View other Black Rose Writing titles at www.blackrosewriting.com/books and use promo code **PRINT** to receive a **20% discount** when purchasing.